Marrying My
COWBOY

Center Point
Large Print

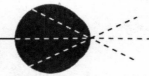

**This Large Print Book carries the
Seal of Approval of N.A.V.H.**

Marrying My COWBOY

Diana Palmer
Lindsay McKenna
Kate Pearce

CENTER POINT LARGE PRINT
THORNDIKE, MAINE

This Center Point Large Print edition
is published in the year 2019 by arrangement with
Kensington Publishing Corp.

The text of this Large Print edition is unabridged.
In other aspects, this book may vary
from the original edition.
Printed in the United States of America
on permanent paper.
Set in 16-point Times New Roman type.

ISBN: 978-1-64358-179-8

Library of Congress Cataloging-in-Publication Data

The Library of Congress has cataloged record
under LCCN 2019008901

CONTENTS

The Rancher's Wedding

Diana Palmer

To my friend Tara Gavin,
who has been with me through many adventures.
And to her lovely daughters,
Emma Grace and Mary Margaret,
who seem like part of my family, too.

CHAPTER ONE

Cassie Reed wondered why none of the other protesters had shown up at this ranch, where they were supposed to be picketing. At the restaurant where she was a waitress, one of the customers who flirted with her had told her horror stories about this place.

This rancher had three big chicken houses, the cowboy said, and he kept lights on all night so that the poor chickens would be forced to lay over and over again, without rest. It was just sad, he said. So he and some of the other men who worked on ranches near Benton, Colorado, were going to form a picket line and show Big Jack Denton that he couldn't get away with animal cruelty in this small community.

Cassie, who'd recently moved to Benton from a house north of Atlanta, on a huge lake, was shocked that such a thing would be tolerated. Couldn't the cowboy just call the local animal control people? He'd replied that they didn't have one. There was a county shelter, but it was hard to get people to go against Big Jack, who had a reputation locally for his hot temper. So if they picketed, maybe some newspaper or television station would come and do a story and put him out of business. The thought of

11

newspaper coverage gave her pause, but after all, this was Colorado. Neither Cassie nor her father were known here. That was a blessing, after the tragedy they'd sustained.

Her customer, whose name was Cary, said that she could join them, if she liked; they were protesting on Saturday morning. She'd agreed that she'd love to help. Her father had been skeptical, but she'd convinced him to drop her off at the entrance to the ranch. There would be lots of people, she assured him, and she'd phone him when he needed to come and get her. He was off on Saturday from his job at the local farm supply store, where he sold heavy equipment like harvesters and irrigation equipment. He'd gotten the job through an acquaintance. He couldn't go on living in New York City after the scandal. He wanted a change. He'd lost his wife, Cassie's mother, as well as a fabulous, well-paying job. The scandal had cost him. The stigma was so great that he and his daughter had moved across the country in the hope that they wouldn't be hounded by reporters anymore.

His full name was Lanier Roger Reed, but a lot of people would recognize that first name, with the story so fresh. So he used his middle name instead, hoping that in a small town like Benton, he would go unnoticed.

Colorado seemed like a nice place, and her father got along well with Bill Clay, the man who owned the agricultural equipment business. Cassie and her father had found a house and she'd lucked out finding an open job at the town's only restaurant, the Gray Dove, waitressing. It wasn't her true profession, but she had to take what she could get for the time being.

So here she was, several weeks after starting her new job, and she wondered if she'd left her mind back in Georgia. It was insane to be standing out here all alone in the driving rain. Because it was raining. Not only raining, sleeting. Her father had left her reluctantly. She had a coat, but it was better suited for Georgia's warmer climate, not freezing Colorado weather. Winter here was harsher than she'd expected, and her light coat wasn't doing much good. Her fingers were freezing as she carried the homemade sign that read CHICKENS SHOULDN'T BE MISTREATED! Her feet were freezing, too. What had seemed like a good idea in the warm restaurant was looking like foolhardiness in the face of icy winter.

She shivered. Surely the other picketers would eventually show up! Nobody was anywhere around. There wasn't even any traffic on this back road. There was a sign that read DENTON BAR D RANCH, and an odd-looking symbol that was probably his registered cattle brand. No cowboys were in sight, either. Maybe they were gathering eggs in those warm chicken houses.

She paced and marched some more, unaware

of a security camera that was recording her every move.

Minutes later, a big burgundy luxury SUV pulled up at the gate and the engine died. The door opened.

A big man in denim and a shepherd's coat with a black Stetson slanted over one eye and big boots peering out from under thick denim jeans stood looking at her incredulously.

"Do you . . . work here?" she asked, her teeth chattering as she shivered.

"Sort of. What are you doing?" he asked in a deep, amused voice.

"Picketing! The man . . . who owns this place . . . oppresses poor chickens!"

He blinked. "Chickens?"

"In his chicken houses," she explained. She pulled her useless coat closer. She didn't even have a cap on her long reddish-gold hair. Her blue eyes met his shaded ones. She wondered idly what color his eyes were, because they weren't visible under the brim of his hat. "He tortures chickens," she continued. "He keeps the lights on all the time so the poor creatures will lay eggs! It's an abomination!"

He pursed sensuous lips and cocked his head at her. "Chicken houses," he said, nodding.

"That's right."

"Who sent you?"

She blinked. "Nobody sent me. This cowboy in

14

the restaurant where I work said a whole group was coming to picket and he invited me, too. He's nice. His name is Cary."

"Cary." Now he looked very amused. "Tall guy, black hair, scar on his lip . . . ?"

"Well, yes," she said.

He chuckled. "He's my cousin. I gave him the scar on his lip."

Her eyebrows raised. "Your cousin?"

"Yes. And he's known for practical jokes. Although this one is low, even for him," he added, studying her. "Come with me. You'll freeze to death in this weather." He looked around. "You didn't drive here?"

"My dad brought me. Can I see the chicken houses, if I go with you?" she asked, trying to sound belligerent.

He smiled. "Sure. Come on."

She put her sign in the back seat—the letters on it were faded because it was cardboard. She got in beside the man and automatically fastened her seat belt. It was a nice vehicle. Big and fancy, with heated seats and powered windows and a CD player built into the dash.

"This is great," she remarked.

"It's functional," he replied. He wheeled the vehicle around and headed it down the ranch road. "You got a name?" he asked.

"Oh. I'm Cassie," she said. "Cassie Reed." She studied him. He had a handsome face, if a little

15

rugged. Sensuous mouth. Long nose. Square jaw. "Who are you?"

"You can call me JL," he offered.

"This is a big place," she remarked as he sped down the road.

"Thousands of acres," he agreed. "Plus a lot of leased government land for grazing. It takes a lot of cowboys to keep it going."

"Does Cary work for you?"

He laughed. "He does his best not to work at all," he said. "Mostly he goofs off and lies to people."

"Lies to people?"

He slowed as they approached a sprawling brick house sitting in the middle of other widely spaced buildings, including a barn, a stable, a silo, and a metal equipment shed far bigger than the house Cassie and her father lived in.

She looked around, frowning. "Where are the chicken houses?" she asked, surprised.

He chuckled as he pulled up the drive toward the house. "I don't keep chickens," he said. "I run purebred Black Angus cattle."

"But Cary said—" she began.

"Cary was pulling your leg," he assured her.

"How do you know that?"

"Because this is my ranch," he replied. "I'm JL Denton."

She ground her teeth together. She was embarrassed. "Why?" she asked miserably, pushing back a scrap of drenched red hair. "Why would he do that to me?"

"Cary likes a practical joke," he said. He was recalling another of his cousin's jokes, even less funny than this one was. Cary would spill his guts for enough drinks, and an unscrupulous woman had plied him with alcohol to find out enough about JL to come on to him in a big way.

JL had thought he'd found the perfect woman. She seemed to be exactly like him in attitude and politics, likes and dislikes, everything. She had taken him almost to the brink of marriage, in fact, until he heard what she'd said to someone on her cell phone when she hadn't known his cousin Cary was listening.

Cary was heartbroken to tell him about it. He said she was telling a friend that she'd found this reclusive rich rancher, and he was dumb enough to accept her pretense as fact. She'd learned enough about him to mirror his thoughts, and now he was going to marry her and she'd have everything she wanted. She wouldn't stay on this dumpy ranch for long, she added; once the ceremony was over she'd go out to Beverly Hills and get a nice apartment in some fancy building and shop, shop, shop.

It had seemed to surprise her, Cary added, when she turned around and found him standing right behind her. She'd stammered an excuse, and begged him not to tell JL. He'd refused. It

17

was a rotten, low-down, dirty thing to do, he'd said indignantly. And he'd marched right back to JL's ranch to tell him all about it.

JL had been livid. She'd come home that night and he'd met her at the door with her things neatly packed by his housekeeper into two suitcases. He'd asked for the engagement ring back and told her that he wanted nothing else to do with her.

She'd stared at him blankly, as if she feared for his sanity. Why was he doing this, she asked.

Because he knew what sort of woman she was, and Cary had told him what he'd overheard her saying on her cell phone.

She'd countered that she knew what he thought of her family, and she should have broken the engagement when he made that remark about her father.

He couldn't remember saying anything about her father, whom he'd met and instantly disliked, but he'd passed over it. He never wanted to see her again, he added. Cary had also mentioned her opinion of him as a lover, which put his pride in the dirt. He didn't tell her about that. It still hurt too much.

She wanted to talk it out, but he knew he'd cave in and take her back, and she'd stab him in the back. He'd closed the door in her face and she'd left. He hadn't heard anything else from her. Cary had mentioned that he heard she'd gone to Europe to take a job at some winery as a receptionist. JL hadn't paid that remark much attention. It didn't occur to him to wonder how Cary knew it.

The whole experience had warped him. He'd have staked his life on her honesty, but she'd sold him out. He'd never trust another woman. He'd had three months of absolute bliss until Cary told him the truth about his perfect fiancée. Now he was distraught. He drank too much, brooded too much. He'd let the ranch slide, endangering his livelihood. He didn't blame Cary, exactly, but he associated the man with his misfortune, and it was painful to have him around.

And here sat a victim of his cousin's warped sense of humor. She looked absolutely crushed.

"Don't take it so hard," he said. "Cary can fool most people when he tries." He glanced at her as they approached the huge, one-story brick ranch house. "Why did you think I kept chickens on a ranch?"

"I'm from Atlanta," she said, and then flushed because she hadn't wanted to admit that. "Well, north of us a lot of people have chicken houses. I'd heard stories about how they were kept, but Cary said . . ." She stopped, swallowed. "I guess Cary knew about them somehow. I'm sorry I picketed you," she added miserably.

He was surprised at how much he liked her. She was vulnerable in a way that most women today weren't, especially in his circle of acquaintances. She had a sensitivity that was rare. "What do you do?"

"I'm a waitress at the Gray Dove restaurant in Benton. Cary comes in there a lot," she added reluctantly.

A waitress. Well, he hadn't expected a debutante, he thought sarcastically. "Cary runs his mouth too much," he murmured.

"Yes, he does," she agreed.

"That coat is too thin for a Colorado winter," he remarked.

She winced. "I guess so. We don't get a lot of really cold temperatures in Atlanta," she added.

He chuckled. "I wouldn't expect it to be that cold in the Deep South," he agreed. He liked her accent. It was a soft, sweet drawl.

"Yes, well, we don't get much snow, either, only very rarely. And then the whole city shuts down," she added with a soft laugh.

He grinned. "I can imagine. We get used to snow because we have so much of it."

He pulled up in front of the ranch house. "Come on in," he said as he swung down out of the SUV.

She hesitated. She'd never gone to a man's house or apartment in her life. Her father and mother had sheltered her. She was an only child and she'd had a lot of health problems through her youth. She'd dated very rarely, and mostly double dates with her best friend, Ellen. She grimaced. She missed Ellen.

"It's all right," he assured her as he opened the door for her. "I don't bite."

She flushed. "Sorry. I'm not . . . well, I'm not used to men. Not much."

Both thick eyebrows went up over silvery eyes.

She cleared her throat. She unbuckled her seat belt and held on to the handle above the door so that she didn't fall out. It was a very tall vehicle.

"Shrimp," he mused.

She laughed self-consciously. "I'm five foot seven inches," she protested. But she had to look up, way up, to see his amused smile.

"I'm six foot two. To me, you're a shrimp," he added.

He went ahead of her to open the door. She hesitated, but just for a minute. She was really cold and her clothes were drenched.

"Bathroom's that way," he said, indicating the hallway. The floors were wood with throw rugs in Native American patterns. The furniture in the living room was cushy and comfortable. There was a huge television on one wall and a fireplace on the other. It was very modern.

"Thanks," she said belatedly when she realized she was staring around her.

"I'll see what I can scare up in the way of dry clothes."

"We're not the same size," she protested, measuring him.

He chuckled. "No, we're not. But my housekeeper's daughter left some things behind when she came to visit her mom. You're just about her size."

He walked off toward the other end of the house.

She darted into the huge bathroom and took off her coat. She looked like a drenched chicken, she thought miserably. At least the bathroom was warm.

She heard heavy footsteps coming back, and a quick rap on the door. She opened it.

"Here." He handed her some jeans and a shirt.

"Thanks," she said.

He shrugged. "Come out when you're ready. We'll throw your wet things into the dryer."

"Okay."

She had to put the jeans and shirt over her underwear, which was damp, but she wasn't about to take it off and put it in a dryer in front of a man she didn't know. She was painfully shy.

She came out of the bathroom. He called to her from a distant room. She followed the sound of his voice to a sprawling kitchen.

"Drink coffee?" he asked.

"Oh, yes!" she agreed.

"Give me those." He held out his hand for her clothes. "I'll stick them in the dryer."

"Thanks."

He gave them a cursory look, pursed his lips amusedly at the lack of underthings, and took them to the dryer in still another room. She heard it kick off.

He came back in and poured coffee into two thick white mugs. "Cream, sugar?"

"No," she replied, seating herself at the small table against the window. Outside, cattle were milling around a feed trough. "I always drink it black and strong. It helps keep me awake when I'm working. . . ." She stopped suddenly. Waitresses didn't work at night in Benton.

He raised an eyebrow, but he didn't question the odd comment.

She sipped coffee and sighed. "This is very good."

"It's Colombian," he replied. "I'm partial to it."

"So am I."

He sipped his coffee and stared at his odd houseguest. He wondered how old she was. She had that radiant, perfect complexion that was common in young women, but she didn't look like a teenager, despite her slender figure.

She lifted both eyebrows at his obvious appraisal.

"I was wondering how old you were," he said, smiling.

"Oh. I'm twenty-four."

He cocked his head. "You look younger."

She smiled. Her blue eyes almost radiated warmth. "Everybody says that."

She wondered how old he was. His hair was black and thick, conventionally cut. His face was strong, with an imposing nose and chiseled mouth and high cheekbones. His skin had a faint olive tone.

He chuckled. "Sizing me up, too? I have Comanche ancestors."

"I thought Comanches lived in Texas and Oklahoma," she began.

"They do. I was born south of Fort Worth, Texas. That's where my mother was from. My folks moved back here when I was ten. The ranch was started by my great-grandfather. My grandfather and my father had some sort of blowup and Dad and Mom left when I was on the way. I never knew what happened. Dad lived on the ranch, but he didn't own it. My grandfather held the purse strings until he died, and even then, he left the ranch to me instead of my dad."

"That must have been hard on your father."

"It was. They never got along." He smiled. "I missed Texas when we came here. It's very different."

"I love Texas," she confessed. "Especially up around Dallas. There's a place called Dinosaur Valley. . . ."

"With thousands of bones," he added with a glimmer in his eyes. "Yes. I've been there. My father was trained as a paleontologist. He taught at a college in Dallas."

She caught her breath. "I'd love to study that," she said. She laughed self-consciously. "I only had two years of college," she confessed. "I minored in Spanish. We have a large Hispanic population in Georgia. I thought of teaching. But I couldn't decide, so I just took core courses."

"I majored in business," he said. "You need to know economics to run a ranch profitably." He didn't add that the ranch wasn't his main source of income. His fortune was the result of an inheritance from his grandfather that included several million dollars plus thousands of acres here near Benton, Colorado, and a thriving Black Angus purebred ranch. He'd parlayed that fortune into a much larger fortune by investing in oil stocks and buying up failing exploration companies and refineries. His inheritance plus his business sense had made him a multimillion-aire.

It didn't show that he was rich. Right now, he was glad. This little violet was good company. He had a feeling that she'd have run right out the door if he'd shown up in a stretch limo wearing designer clothes and a Rolex—all of which he had.

"I've never been around ranches," she con-

25

fessed, staring out the window. "We have big farms in Georgia, but not so many ranches, especially not in the Atlanta suburbs. We're very metropolitan."

"But you know about chicken farms," he teased.

She laughed self-consciously. "Well, yes. I love animals."

"So do I," he added. "We use old-timey methods around here. The livestock are treated like part of the family. They're all purebred. We breed for certain traits that they'll pass down to their progeny. We don't run beef cattle," he added when she looked perplexed.

"You don't?" she asked, surprised.

He shrugged. "Hard to kill something you raised from a baby," he said. "I'm partial to fish and chicken. I don't eat a lot of beef."

She was fascinated. It showed.

He laughed. "Not that I mind a well-cooked steak," he added. "As long as it's not one of my prize Angus."

"There are always pictures in the local cattle journal of cattle sales."

"We have a production sale here in February," he told her. "It's a big deal. We entertain a lot of out-of-state buyers. We feed them great barbecue and hope they'll spend plenty of money."

"You sell off the little cows, then?" she asked.

He chuckled at her terminology. "Yearlings,

mostly," he said. "Some open heifers, some pregnant ones, a few bulls."

She was out of her depth. "It sounds very complicated."

"Only to an Eastern tenderfoot," he teased gently.

She smiled back, a little shyly, and sipped her coffee.

"I like your house," she said after a brief and vaguely uncomfortable silence. "It looks just like I'd expect a western ranch house to look."

He frowned slightly. "Never been out west?"

She shook her head. "No. Mom and Dad lived in New York and I went up to visit a lot, but I've only seen the states back in the East."

"Does your father still live there?"

"No." She sipped coffee, wincing at her blunt reply. "He came out here because he had a cousin who worked at the local equipment store," she added hurriedly. "His cousin had already moved on, but he gave him a good reference. Daddy's worked there for about a month. Like I have, at the restaurant."

"Big-city people," he mused, studying her. "The culture shock must be extreme."

She flushed and fumbled with her coffee cup. "It is, a little, I guess. I got used to traffic noises and sirens in Atlanta. The small house Dad and I rent is close to a railroad, so that's nice at night." She laughed. "It's like home." She didn't add that she'd moved into a luxurious house on the lake north of Atlanta, to get away from those traffic noises. She missed the lake.

"What did you do in Atlanta? Another waitressing job?"

She couldn't tell him that. It might lead to embarrassing questions about why she'd left such a lucrative position to get a minimum wage job out in Colorado. "I did feature stories for a newspaper," she said finally. It wasn't so far from the truth. She'd started out as a newspaper reporter after college, working her way up to news editor before her father introduced her to some people in New York. She'd ended up doing screenplays, a much more profitable career. Gone now. It was gone, like the life she'd had.

He wondered why she looked so stricken. "Newspaper jobs must be thin on the ground these days," he remarked. "Almost everything is digital now. I get my news fix on the Internet."

She smiled. "So do I. But the local paper is very nice. I like the features about old-fashioned ranch work, and the recipe page."

He smiled back. "Do you cook?"

"Oh, yes," she replied. "I'm partial to French cuisine, because of the sauces, but I like Tex-Mex, too. Anything spicy." She sighed. "I used to have a gourmet herb patch that I babied all year. I had raised beds, so I had herbs at Christmas to add to my recipes." Her face was sad as she recalled the past. Those had been good days, when her mother was still alive. Before the fame and then the tragedy that had taken her mother's life and sent Cassie and her father running far away from the notoriety.

"I have an herb patch of my own, but it's in a glassed greenhouse," he remarked. "Hard to keep little things alive out here in the winter. It can be brutal in the mountains."

"I've heard that," she replied. "They said one year you had a foot of snow."

He chuckled. "Most years we have a foot of snow," he mused. "Sometimes six feet."

She gasped. "But how do you drive in that?"

"You don't," he said. "Not until the snowplows come, at least. On the ranch, we have heavy equipment that we can use to clear a path to the road." He shook his head. "It's hard on the cattle. It's a lot of work to keep them alive. We have lean-tos in the pastures and a big barn and corrals where we can bring the pregnant cows and heifers up to get out of the worst of the weather."

She liked that. She smiled. "I never thought of ranchers being kind to cattle," she said. "I mean, we hear about slaughterhouses and—"

"We don't eat purebreds," he interrupted, and his eyes twinkled. "Too expensive."

She laughed. "I guess so." She searched his face. "Do you have pets?"

He sighed. "Too many," he replied. "We have

cattle dogs—border collies—that help with roundup. They're not really pets, but I keep a couple of Siberian huskies and we have cats in the barn. They keep the rodent population down."

"The cats, you mean?"

He grinned. "The huskies, mostly," he corrected. "Best mousers on the place. The cats, I'm told, are jealous of that ability."

"You talk to cats," she teased.

"All the time. I talk to myself, mostly," he added with a chuckle. "Bad habit."

"Only if you answer yourself," she replied.

He sighed and leaned back in the chair with his coffee cup. "I was engaged," he said after a minute. "Until someone overheard her bragging to her friends about how she'd marry me and then go live in a city and get away from this run-down wreck of a ranch."

She winced. "I'm so sorry," she said. "That must have hurt your pride."

He was surprised at her compassion. He was also suspicious. Marge had been very sympathetic at first, too, but it was all an act. A means to an end. He was warier now than he'd been before.

"It is a little run-down, I guess," he conceded after a minute. He grimaced. "I've spent a lot of time drinking. Too much." He didn't add why. He also didn't add that he'd let the ranch and the business slide while he got over the tragedies in his life that had dumped him in Marge's lap.

Marge had been a newer, worse tragedy, if that was even possible. He was usually a better judge of character, but he'd been lonely and Marge had played him. That was on Cary, whose sense of mischief was getting old. He'd introduced JL to Marge, and the mutual attraction had been immediate. He'd missed Marge. It took a lot of getting over, and not only because she'd left him.

"My dad drank for a while," she said unexpectedly, staring into her coffee cup. "It was hard to convince him to stop."

He frowned. "Why did he drink?" he asked bluntly.

She sighed. "My mother died," she said, wrapping up an anguished time into three quiet words.

"I see. Had they been married long?"

"Thirty years," she replied. "They'd given up hope that they'd have kids when I came along," she added with a sad smile. "I wasn't born until five years after they married."

"Marriage." He made a face. "Not a future I've ever seen for myself." And it hadn't been, until Marge caught him in a weak moment. As a rule, women came and went in his life. For years, they'd been permissible hors d'oeuvres. Now, after Marge, he'd lost interest. He never wanted another painful experience like the one he'd had with her.

"Don't you like children?" she asked innocently.

His face closed up. There was something dark and disturbing in his expression for a few seconds. He got up. "If you're ready, I'll run you into town."

"Oh, but, I can call my father," she began, flushing. "I've been too much trouble already."

"Not so much." He picked up her empty cup and put it, with his, into the sink. He picked up his keys. "Let's go."

She followed him out to the SUV. Only then did she notice that the ranch house needed a coat of paint and repairs on the front walk. The fences looked as if they'd once been white, but the paint was peeling off them now. The rain seemed to emphasize the neglect around her. She wondered why he hadn't made repairs, and decided that he probably didn't have the money. The SUV he drove was nice, but it wasn't the newest model and he was probably making payments on it. Certainly, his clothes—a shirt with a frayed collar and jeans that were torn where they draped over scuffed, worn cowboy boots—didn't reflect any great wealth.

"Your ranch is nice," she said as they drove away. She wondered once again how a poor rancher could afford to run purebred livestock. Perhaps he had a partner somewhere who contributed money.

"It keeps me running," he said with an absent smile.

They rode in a companionable silence. Cassie was surprised at the comfort she felt, sitting beside him. It was an odd thing to feel. He was handsome, in his way, and she liked his deep, velvety voice. But he wasn't the sort of man she was used to at all. Her male friends back east, and there had never been a serious one, were obsessed with the gym and proper diet and they preferred an evening at the theater or the symphony orchestra. None of them would have considered life on a cattle ranch.

"Where?" he asked when they reached Benton.

She caught her breath. "Sorry, I was lost in thought. It's on Third Street, just off Main, about a block from the Quick Stop."

He chuckled. "The old Barrett place," he replied. "Yes, I know it. Jed Barrett lived there all his life. When he died, there was no family, so the house went on the market to pay his funeral expenses. A local businessman owns it. He didn't want to sell it because of the property it sits on, so he rented it out while he decided what to put on the acreage."

"You mean, like a ranch?"

"I mean, like a subdivision," he mused. "Or apartment houses."

"Oh, dear," she said with a long sigh. "I loved it because it was so remote," she confessed.

"Lots of room to walk and think, and there's a little creek out back. . . ."

He grimaced. He liked lonely places to walk, too. "It will take him some time to work that out," he added comfortingly. "He's overseas right now, taking care of some business in Australia. He owns a huge cattle station there."

"He's Australian?" she asked, surprised.

He chuckled. "His father was. Rance was born here in Colorado, but his father had properties all over Australia and South America. Rance has managers for all of them, but he likes the hands-on approach. He says it keeps his employees on their toes if he walks in unexpectedly from time to time."

"I see," she replied.

"He's a nice enough guy," he said easily. "A little abrasive, but it's understandable. He's had some issues over the years." He glanced at her. "You didn't meet him, when you rented the house?"

"Dad did," she said. "I was at work. We'd been living in the local motel." She said that because there was only one motel in Benton. It was nice enough, but paying for two rooms indefinitely had threatened to wipe out their combined savings. Her father had heard about the place at work and called Rance Barkley at just the right time to obtain it as a rental.

"Expensive, living in motels," he remarked.

34

She nodded. "Very."

"Why Benton?" he asked curiously as he pulled onto her street.

"Because Dad's cousin lived here," she sighed. "It seemed as good a place as any to start over."

"I guess the city got too much for you," he teased.

She smiled back. "Yes. It did. For both of us. Honestly, we wanted to live someplace where we didn't have so many memories of my mother. Besides, Benton is nice."

"Nice, if you don't like nightlife," he chuckled. "They roll up the sidewalks every night at six sharp."

"That doesn't bother me," she replied. "I like the peace and quiet." She didn't add that she'd gotten used to it on the lake.

He laughed. "Good thing. We don't have much excitement around here."

"That suits me very well."

He pulled into the long driveway and pulled up next to an old pickup truck sitting in front of the little white frame house. The property was surrounded by pastureland that ran to the horizon in the shadow of the mountains.

"I always liked this place," he remarked.

"It's very pretty," she agreed. She grimaced. "Look, I'm sorry about the picket sign. . . ."

"I'll tear a strip off Cary and we'll be even. Don't worry about it."

"Thanks. And thanks for the coffee and the ride." She opened the door and jumped down, pausing to get her wet, faded sign off the floorboard in the back seat.

"Stay warm," he said.

She smiled. "Drive safely," she replied, and closed the passenger door before she saw his bemused expression.

He waved and drove off.

She propped her sign against the wall and opened the door.

Her father, tall and thin and graying, looked up from the sofa, where he was reading a book. "Back so soon?"

She grimaced. "He doesn't have a single chicken house," she said with a long sigh.

His eyebrows rose. "Then why were you picketing him?"

"It's a long story," she replied, shedding her wet coat. She hung it up and plopped down into the easy chair across from the sofa. "He owns this run-down ranch," she began.

CHAPTER TWO

"A run-down ranch, an owner who drinks, and purebred cattle?" he mused. "I think he was having you on, Cassie," he chuckled. "A poor man can't afford to run purebreds. They cost thousands of dollars. A good herd bull alone sometimes goes for half a million."

"Oh. I see. Well, he was nice about it, anyway. He gave me coffee and dried my jeans and . . . Oh, my gosh, my clothes are still there!" she exclaimed. "I forgot all about them!"

He was watching her with wide, stunned eyes.

"These clothes belonged to his housekeeper's daughter," she explained. "He handed them to me in the bathroom. I put them on and he put my things in the dryer. My outer things," she added. "I wasn't about to take off my underthings in a strange man's house."

He smiled gently. "You're so like your mother," he said with a sad smile. "She was straitlaced, too, very Victorian in her attitudes. I guess we didn't do you any favors, giving you such an old-fashioned upbringing when the rest of the world is so permissive."

"I like me just the way I am, thanks," she laughed. "I like being out of step with the world. I stay healthier, for one thing," she added, tongue-in-cheek.

He sighed. "Yes, but you don't date anybody."

"I dated Jackson Hill," she pointed out.

"Sweetheart, Jackson Hill was gay," he reminded her.

"He was great company, too," she replied, smiling reminiscently. "His parents were so conventional, and he loved them so much, that he didn't want them to know. We went out together so we could both hide. I didn't want a loose relationship with some career-minded man, and he didn't want notoriety. We suited each other." She sighed. "I miss him. He was so much fun!"

He nodded. "Well, I guess we settle for what we can get in life. I would have liked grandchildren, though," he added with a smile.

She had a sudden picture of the reclusive rancher with a baby in his arms and swatted it away. "Maybe someday," she said. "Right now, I'm busy learning how to balance a plateful of food on a tray without dropping it while I set up the tripod."

He laughed out loud. "And I'm busy learning how to persuade ranchers to buy equipment they may not know they need."

"I daresay we'll both do well, once we learn the ropes," she replied.

He sighed. "I keep hoping. I miss my crew."

She knew it was hard for him. To be such a

celebrity, with his own television show, loved by millions. And with one unfounded accusation by a vengeful woman, it was all gone and he was in hiding. The damage had been far-reaching. His attorneys had done their best, but social media had destroyed him. It was suggested that if he got away for a few months, things might calm down and they could reassess his position. The fact that he was innocent seemed to count for nothing. The woman who accused him, however, now had her own television show—his former one—and she was raking in cash and ratings, thanks to several special interest groups that had funded her. His attorneys knew this and they'd hired one of the best investigators in the business to do some discreet snooping. There was still hope.

"I miss my job, too, although it wasn't a patch on yours," she said with a wistful sigh. "The series is still on TV, and there were some terrific other writers on staff. But I liked to interject humor and they didn't."

"Maybe one day, we can both go back to what we love," he replied sadly. "But for the time being, we're in camouflage, pretending to be normal middle-class Americans. That's not a bad thing, either," he added. "You can get too addicted to five-star restaurants and expensive quarters. You can lose sight of the things that are really important."

"Yes, like no reporters trying to knock down

the doors, hiding in the trees, parachuting onto the roof . . ."

He chuckled. "It wasn't quite that bad, although I couldn't eat out or be seen in public. I was too recognizable." He shook his head. "Growing a beard and wearing glasses does seem to have put them off, for the time being."

"Yes. You look quite judicial," she teased.

He smiled. "At least you didn't have to modify your looks. Writers aren't quite as noticeable as television personalities with weekly shows."

"That was my good luck," she agreed. She stretched. "I'm using muscles I didn't even know I had. I got lazy. I spent my life at a keyboard, living in a fantasy world. I'm looking at the world in a totally new way."

"So am I," he said. He drew in a long breath. "And I hope we're far enough away that they won't come looking for us here."

"Who would?" she mused. "Honestly, working in equipment sales has to be the last place reporters would expect to find you!"

"We can hope," he said. He shook his head and his face tautened. "That woman," he bit off. "Stabbed in the back by my own executive producer, accused of sexual harassment and assault, the media flooded with lies and opinions and gossip. Journalism in this country has sunk to a whole new low."

"The major media outlets are owned by a

handful of people with agendas," she said simply.

"Well, there's nothing we can do about that," he told her. "Millionaires make policy, and corporations own everything of worth. It will take a disaster of some kind to provide a reset. And I hope I'm long gone when it happens."

"You're practically immortal," she teased. "And we don't need a reset. We just need people to demand objective reporting. If enough do, things will change."

"Optimist." Her father put down his book. "Speaking of news, which we never watched anyway until my sudden notoriety, I suppose we should buy a television set."

"What for?" she asked. "We hardly watched TV even when we had one."

"I was thinking about all the movies we had on the Cloud," he replied.

"Now, that, I wouldn't mind at all!" she agreed, laughing. "How about we buy one tomorrow? Something cheap."

"A used gaming system would be nice, too, so you can play those games you've also got on the Cloud," he teased. Her gaming habit amused him. She loved console games on XBox One and had several that were her hobby.

"I miss my games," she confessed. She frowned. "But I'd better play off the Internet for now. A few people knew my gamer tag," she added. "Best not to advertise that I'm still around."

He nodded solemnly. "I'll keep on my attorneys," he said. "If their investigator turns up something on Trudy Blaise, things may start to look up."

"They may. But meantime, I have a nice job and I'm happy to get a check every two weeks," she said. "We could have landed in a worse place."

"Yes, we could." He frowned as she sneezed. "You need to push your friend Cary into a thorny bush. You're sneezing. It was cold and wet, and you have bad lungs. . . ."

She shook her head. "I'm fine," she said firmly. "Nothing to worry about. I've been much better with the new inhaler."

He sighed. "If you say so."

She got up, smiling. "I'll start some rolls rising, so we can have them for supper," she said. "How about *coq au vin*?"

He gave her a droll look. "How about chicken and mashed potatoes?" he countered.

She sighed. "Ah, poverty," she laughed. "I guess it will be good for our characters."

"Everybody has hard times, sweetheart," he said softly. "Everybody gets through them."

She just smiled on her way to the kitchen.

JL pulled up in front of his house and studied it with a frown. He hadn't noticed how dilapidated

42

it was getting. Honestly, since he'd broken his engagement, things hadn't mattered much to him. Not even the ranch, which was his pride and joy.

But now it was falling apart. He'd been having a whiskey after dinner every night. Sometimes, it was two whiskeys. He hated what his life had become. He was alone and tired of his own company. His big romance had turned into a disaster. He was afraid to trust another woman, because of what his "fiancée" had done to him. The experience had turned him inside out. He was so depressed that he paid no attention to broken fences, to equipment that stopped working, to employees who pleaded for money to repair infrastructure. Now, it was all catching up with him.

He walked out to the big barn where his foreman, Isaiah Drummond, was staring under the hood of the truck they used to haul feed to the cattle in the near pastures. He had the physique of a range rider, much as JL himself did, but Drum, as most people called him, was a few years younger and had a temper that the cowboys tried to avoid. He looked up as the boss approached, his black eyes flashing in a lean, tanned face under a thick head of black hair.

"Damned thing's on the blink again," he muttered. "And the Bobcat has a flat tire."

"Horrors and wonders, the world's ending," JL drawled sarcastically.

Drum's chiseled mouth pulled down on one side. "It will, if you don't get on the ball, boss," he said curtly. "If things go downhill fast enough, you could end up with a wheat farm instead of a ranch."

JL shrugged. "Not likely. Beef's at a premium since all the flooding down in Texas last summer."

"Yes, well, growing cattle need food, and to have food, you need working equipment to plant things with."

JL sighed. "Okay, call that repairman from the equipment company and let him come out here and fix it."

Drum managed a smile. "Okay."

"Any other little headaches . . . ?"

Drum pushed back the beat-up old black Stetson he wore. "I hear you've taken up chicken farming."

JL's eyes widened. "Huh?"

Drum grinned. "You had a picketer out front, accusing you of abusing hens."

"Oh, that." He smiled reminiscently. "Cary told her I had chicken houses. She was soaking wet and sneezing. Funny little thing. Red-gold hair. Blue eyes. Thin as a rail. Repressed as all hell. Works as a waitress in town. I drove her home."

Drum waited, curious.

JL gave him a droll look. "I don't have any inclination to let a woman back in my life. Not in

44

the near future. Maybe never." His face darkened. "I've got enough trouble as it is."

"I can understand your viewpoint," came the reply. "But you have to understand that some women are as mercenary as some men. They have ways of hiding it. You have to look deeper than surface things, like beauty."

"You ever been married?"

"Never. I came close once." Drum shook his head. "She didn't want to live with a man who worked around cattle and smelled like fertilizer, she said." He shrugged. "Wasn't much of a sacrifice, at that. She couldn't cook and she wanted a life of leisure. I told her she'd have to look for a richer man than me. So she found one." He laughed. "I saw her once, when I took that trip to Denver to check out some cattle at auction for you. She said she wished she could go back in time and make a different choice. I guess she was paying a price for that wealth."

"People mostly do," JL sighed. "I don't understand greed."

"Me, neither," Drum replied. "Well, I'll go call that equipment repairman and see when he can get out here."

"The chicken picketer's father works there, she said."

"That must be the new fellow." He shook his head. "Owner says he sits and reads equipment manuals all the time so he can understand what he sells." He frowned. "Odd man. New York accent, and he doesn't have the hands of a man who does any sort of physical labor. I'd have pegged him as a businessman. He seems out of place."

"Curious."

"It is. But it's not my business."

"Nor mine," JL told him. "I've been taking a look around the place. We have lots of things that need to be repaired and painted. I've been living in a blue funk, whatever that is. Time I snapped out of it and got some things done. And don't agree with me," he said suddenly when Drum opened his mouth. "I'll call a contractor first thing in the morning and get the ball rolling. Another thing, the chicken picketer left her clothes here. I put them in the dryer, but she went home wearing Bessie's daughter's jeans and shirt. I guess I'll have to make time to take them to her."

"Is she pretty—the chicken picketer?" Drum teased.

JL chuckled. "She was pretty bedraggled while she was here. Not much to look at, but a tender heart and plenty of compassion. I used to think looks were the most important thing. Now I'm convinced that a good heart's better."

"I'll take pretty, thanks," came the amused reply.

"You're welcome to all the pretty women you

can find. I'm off women for life," he added. "I'm never being taken for a ride again."

"Where have I heard that before?"

"Never you mind. Get busy. I'm going to ride out to the line cabin and see how Parker's doing with the new horses."

"Why won't you let him work them here, close to the house?"

JL raised both eyebrows. "You ever heard him cuss?"

"Oh."

"I'm not having him around when visitors come to look at our new crop of cattle. He'll put everybody's back up and I'll have to sell my calves at a loss."

"We could rope him, tie him to a post, and gag him."

JL pursed his lips and chuckled. "What a thought. But, no, it's just as well to leave him where he is. If I have to call him down about his behavior, he'll quit, and he's the best man with horses I've ever had."

"I'll echo that. The man has a gift."

"It's that Crow in him," JL replied. "He said his people have a way with animals that runs all the way back through his lineage, all the way to his great-grandfather. He can gentle horses without any rough treatment. Horses love him. I mean they really love him. They follow him around the fence when he's outside."

"Imagine a guy with a talent like that," Drum said. He made a face. "And a mouth like that."

"He was in the military. He said he learned to cuss dodging bullets in Iraq." He shook his head. "I've dodged my share, but I'm not his equal in a cussing contest," he added, chuckling. "I guess we all have a few rough edges."

"His are sharper than knives. But he is good with the horses."

"Yes. Okay, you call the equipment people, I'll go talk to Parker."

"Sure thing, boss."

The line cabin was about a mile from the main ranch house, set back in the lodgepole pines, with majestic mountains making an exquisite backdrop for the long, open pasture, cross-fenced, that stretched to the horizon. The cabin was efficient, but small. With its rustic timbers, it looked like part of the landscape.

JL dismounted at the front porch and tied his horse to the rail. There was nobody around. He rapped on the door, but there was no answer. Odd, he thought. Parker was certainly here, somewhere. He wondered what was going on.

He opened the door and walked in. There was a fire in the fireplace. A hot, fresh pot of coffee sat on the counter with an empty cup by it. Wherever Parker was, he must not have expected to be gone long.

JL went back outside and looked around. "Hey, Parker!" he called.

No answer. He walked around the house and saw hoofprints headed down the road. He got back in the saddle and followed them.

He hadn't gone far when he heard a rifle shot. Heart racing, he turned his horse in the direction of the shot and urged him forward.

"Nothing to worry about, Hardy," he told the horse, patting him gently on the mane to calm him. The horse was nervous enough without loud noises. "Come on, fellow. Just a little way to go."

The horse moved forward, but not quickly. In the distance, JL caught sight of a red plaid shirt. Closer, he could tell that it was Parker by his tall, lean body and the white Stetson he wore. But he could tell better by the language that was audible even this far away. Parker was eloquent.

He rode down to the pasture. Parker had left his horse on this side of the fence. He was on the other side, standing over the carcass of a calf.

He looked up at JL with narrowed blue eyes in a face as hard as stone. "Wolf," he said angrily. He indicated the calf.

JL grimaced. The calf had been savaged, while it was still alive, from the look of it. Parker had obviously put it out of its misery.

"I wish all those damned bleeding-heart liberals living in apartments in cities could come out here and see what we have to deal with because of their blankety-blank legislation!" Parker said angrily. "In fact, I wish we could shove a few starving wolves into the apartments with them. My, my, what a change of heart the survivors would have!"

"Bad cowboy," JL said, shaking a finger at him.

Parker sighed. "Yeah, I know. I just get tired of seeing little things like this in such agony."

"Was it Two Toes?" JL asked, referring to an old and wily wolf who was known to the ranchers locally. The wolf was past his prime and couldn't find a pack that would let him join, so he went hunting for game he could catch. That meant helpless calves that wandered too far from the herd.

"I think so. Didn't really have time to count toes," Parker added, "or see his face to identify him. But he was snow white and limping and he looked like ten miles of rough road. That limp pretty much identifies him as Two Toes."

"We need to adopt him, lock him up, and feed him canned chicken," JL said whimsically. "He'd be a threat to nobody, then."

"Or find a wildlife rehabilitator who could be bribed or threatened to take him on and feed him canned chicken."

JL chuckled. "That's really not a bad idea," he said. "I'll talk to Butch Matthews and see if I can sell him on the idea. He's always talking about wolves. He loves them."

"I don't mind them in a pack. Mostly they avoid ranches. Two Toes is a separate and individual case. You can't scare him, you can't intimidate him, he just does what he wants to and lopes off when he gets a scent of you."

"We'll be old and toothless and hungry one day."

Parker gave him a dirty look. "Well, I won't be eating poor little calves who get lost," he returned.

"If you were starving, you just might."

That earned him another nasty look.

JL sighed. "Well, I'll go back home. I'll let you know when I talk to Butch. We may have to take a few men and hunt Two Toes, in that case."

"Don't mind hunting him if he'll be leaving here," Parker replied. He pursed his lips. "I have been wondering if wolf stew tasted any good."

"You'd have to parboil that old devil for a week to get him tender, and he's too stringy to do much for your taste buds," JL pointed out.

Parker chuckled. "Point taken."

Cassie was back at work at the Gray Dove two days later. At least, she thought, she'd learned to carry a tray without dumping half the drinks on it. Her boss, Mary Dodd, had been very kind and patient. It made Cassie work even harder. So few people these days were patient at all.

"You're doing very well," Mary told her.

"Except for the coffee," Cassie said, grimacing. "I'm so sorry."

"You've only dropped a cup one time this whole week," Mary said, trying to find a bright note. "And we allow for ceramic breakage in the budget, you know." She leaned forward. "When I used to work here, years before I bought the place, I turned three plates of spaghetti on a tray into the lap of a vacationing millionaire from DC."

Cassie's lips fell open. "What did you do?" she exclaimed.

"I bawled and apologized and bawled some more."

"What did he do?" she persisted.

Mary smiled. "He married me."

Cassie chuckled. "I begin to see the light."

"He gave me the money to buy the restaurant, with the idea that I might never improve enough to be able to hold down a job in it. So I hired people who were less clumsy than I am."

"Not so much," Cassie began.

Mary patted her on the back. "You're doing fine. Really you are. Don't worry. Life is an adventure. Every day is a gift. You have to live an hour at a time, kid. It's what keeps you going."

Cassie smiled. "Thanks. I really mean that."

"You're welcome. Back to work."

"Yes, ma'am!"

It had been several days since Cassie had gone haring off to JL Denton's ranch. The rancher had been very kind to her, despite her antagonism when they first met. She still hadn't called him about getting her clothing back. She was too shy. Besides, she had plenty of other clothes. She wouldn't have to go naked.

Secretly, she wished she had the nerve to call him. There was an odd vulnerability about him. He loved animals. He had a kind heart. That was far more important to Cassie than wealth. Not that JL was rich. The peeling paint on the house and fences testified to that. If he'd had money, he'd have kept the ranch up better than he did.

But he had told her that he ran purebred cattle, which her father said only a rich rancher could afford to do. Still, he might have inherited them from a wealthy relative. Cassie always tried to make allowances for people. Most people. It was hard to make allowances for the woman who'd ruined her father's life and driven her poor mother to a desperate act after the scandal broke.

She cleaned tables and filled orders. It was getting easier as she went along. Mary had known that Cassie had never waited tables in her life. But she was getting the hang of it, and she worked hard.

That Friday, she had a familiar customer at her table. She glared at him.

Cary held both hands up. "I'm sorry," he said before she could go on the attack. "I'm really sorry. Cousin JL read me the riot act. I swear, I'll never tell another lie. Well, not to anybody he knows, at least," he added with a charming smile.

"That was a really nasty thing to do," she pointed out.

He shrugged. "Life gets boring. I like to liven things up."

She sighed. He wasn't getting it at all. She pulled out her pad. "What would you like to eat?"

"What's good?"

"The beef stew and the lemon pie."

"Fine. I'll have that, with black coffee. You off tomorrow?"

She gave him a cold, hostile look.

"No more games," he promised. "I'm not planning any more nonexistent picketing parties." He pursed his lips. The scar on the lower one was blatant. She could picture a furious JL slugging him.

"Why did your cousin slug you?" she blurted out before she thought it through.

He grimaced. "Sorry. Best not to drag up painful memories."

"I shouldn't have asked," she said quickly. "Stew and lemon pie. Be right out."

She turned to go.

"There's a bowling alley in downtown Benton," he said before she walked off. "I wondered if you might like to try it out with me. It's brand-new."

She was disconcerted. She gnawed her lower lip. She didn't quite trust him after he'd played that practical joke on her. She didn't know him, either. JL had been disparaging about him. Those things added up to a distrust she was too polite to admit. She forced a smile. "Thanks, but I promised Dad I'd help him with a project this weekend."

He just smiled, seemingly not offended at all. "No problem. Maybe I'll ask you again sometime."

She didn't reply. She went to get his order. His narrow eyes watched her go and there was a calculating expression that she couldn't see.

Nobody told her, but Cary held grudges, especially when women gave him the cold shoulder. The woman who'd messed up JL's life had started out as Cary's girl. JL thought that when she'd seen the size of his ranch, and knew he was rich, she tossed Cary out of her life and wormed her way into JL's affections. It wasn't true, but Cary had told JL all about it when he succeeded in prying Marge out of his cousin's life.

Cary had been shattered when Marge walked right over him to get to his cousin. She'd been really in love, but Cary felt that she belonged to him. They'd dated for several weeks before he introduced her to JL. He'd wanted her for keeps, but she'd gone running to his cousin.

Well, it had turned out badly, especially when he told JL a few things that caused him to throw her out of his life. JL had started drinking shortly thereafter and he wanted nothing to do with Cary. His cousin had never admitted to being the serpent in paradise, but JL was suspicious these days. It had soured their relationship. Cary was sorry about it, from time to time, but she'd been his girl first. He'd been upset about losing her to a richer man, even if the man was his cousin.

He'd sent the red-haired waitress out to picket the ranch as a joke, but he'd found Cassie interesting and he wanted to take her out. She was cool with him, which made her a challenge. He liked a woman he had to chase. Now it was just a matter of finding a way to get close to her. And keep her out of his cousin's sight. He wasn't going to lose another woman to JL.

Cassie, blissfully ignorant of her customer's thoughts, brought out his meal and dessert, along with the strong black coffee he'd ordered.

"Bowling is fun," he remarked as she wrote out the ticket. "You really ought to put off your father's project and come with me."

She just smiled. "Sorry. No can do."

He shrugged. "Your loss." He tossed her a flirty smile. "I don't have any trouble getting women to go out with me."

"How nice for you," she said with a careless smile.

He glowered at her. "Look, I'm sorry I tricked you into picketing JL's ranch," he said reluctantly. He didn't like apologizing; it made him feel weak.

She laid the ticket beside his plate. "No problem."

He slid a hand around her waist and smiled. "You might give me a chance to make it up to you. . . ." he began, and his hand slipped lower, whether accidentally or not.

She turned her hand, bent his the wrong way, pulled him out of his seat, and put him on the floor.

He lay there, looking up at her with wide eyes and a bruised arm.

"You touch me like that again," she said very softly, "and I'll cripple you, before I sue you for sexual harassment."

Mary Dodd had seen what went on. She moved to the table and stood over Cary. "And that's called just deserts," she told him coldly.

"My hand slipped!" he said, wincing as he dragged himself to his feet. "I swear!" He turned to Cassie. "I'm really sorry. It truly was an accident! I'd never treat a decent woman that way on purpose!"

He looked so pitiful that Cassie believed him. "Never again," she cautioned him.

He put his hand over his heart. "I'll just sit here and eat my stew and pie, and not make another accidental move!"

"If you do," Mary said softly, "it will be the last time you eat here. Is that clear? Nobody harasses my waitresses," she added.

"I'm really sorry," he repeated. He grinned. "No more slippy hands. Honest!"

He was incorrigible. Mary rolled her eyes. She walked off, shaking her head.

Cassie laughed. He did look so miserable.

"Am I forgiven?" he persisted.

"This once," she replied.

He crossed his heart. "I'm turning over a new leaf right now, ma'am," he said, and grinned. "Honest."

He sat down and dug into his stew.

Several people had amused smiles on their faces as Cassie went on to the next table and the next order.

"You okay?" Mary asked Cassie a little later, after Cary had left and the customers had thinned out a little.

Cassie smiled. "I'm fine," she said. She was uneasy. Confrontations unsettled her, especially after what she and her father had suffered publicly only a short time ago. "I'm sorry I caused a scene."

"Nonsense," Mary said. "Just as well to let that man see his limits. He's not mean, but he can get overbearing. He won't again. Not with you," she chuckled.

Cassie smiled. "I almost felt sorry for him," she confessed.

"How did you do that, if you don't mind saying?" she asked.

"I'm a black belt in tae kwon do," she said simply. "I've taken lessons for five years. I used to compete," she added sadly. She smiled. "I can't do it anymore."

"That's a shame. It was a sight to see," Mary told her.

Cassie grinned. "I truly enjoyed the look on his face. And maybe his hand did slip."

"Maybe it didn't," came the amused reply. "But that's Cary. He's been no end of trouble to JL, his cousin," she added in a lowered voice as they walked back behind the counter. "In fact, he was responsible for his cousin's broken engagement."

"He was?"

"He carried tales to both of them. It was a shame what he did to JL. He really loved the woman," she said. "Gossip was that she fell hard for JL, too. Cary put a stop to that with a few whispers in her ear and JL's. There's no excuse for the way Cary treated her. He was jealous, you see, because she was his girl first and she threw him over for JL."

"He was trying to get me to go bowling with him. I don't like going out with men I don't know," she added softly.

"Wise woman," Mary said. "In Cary's case, very wise. He drinks to excess. JL just goes to bed when he's had too much liquor. Cary gets in fights. Or he used to." Her eyes twinkled. "Not so much since the last one. Anyway, JL can handle him when he's drunk, if he has to. When JL's sober, that is," she added.

"When he's sober . . . ?" Cassie probed.

"Best not to carry tales," Mary replied. "Sorry."

"No, it's my fault. I shouldn't have asked. It's just that Cary set me up picketing Mr. Denton's ranch because Cary said he was torturing chickens in his henhouses." She made a face. "I must be far more naïve than I thought I was. I went out there alone and stood in the freezing cold and rain until Mr. Denton drove up and found me. He took me to the ranch house and let me dry my stuff. He even made me coffee." She sighed. "He's very nice. I felt so bad about what I'd done."

Mary grinned. "Trust me, JL will dine out on that story in a few weeks. Chicken houses." She shook her head. "Eastern tenderfoot," she chided affectionately.

Cassie laughed. "That's what he called me. I guess I am. I'll get back to work. Thanks for standing up for me," she added softly.

"Nobody messes with my employees," Mary said simply. And she smiled.

CHAPTER THREE

Cassie didn't tell her father about the unpleasantness in the restaurant with Cary. He had enough on his mind without having to worry about her. She fixed supper for him and they watched a movie on the little television set he'd bought from a coworker. She didn't let on that she had a care in the world.

The next morning, she was surprised to find JL Denton occupying a booth in the restaurant where she worked. He'd dropped his white Stetson onto the seat beside him. He had thick black hair with a faint wave, and he was wearing a western-cut shirt with jeans and boots. Cassie's heart skipped when he looked up at her as she came to take his order. But he wasn't smiling.

"What did Cary do to you yesterday?" he asked quietly, and there was a look in his dark eyes that made her faintly nervous.

She hesitated. She didn't like carrying tales. Gossip was what had cost her father his job, and the ensuing notoriety put Cassie on the run as well.

"Come on," he said, his deep voice dropping softly. "Tell me what happened."

She took a breath and glanced around. The boss was in the kitchen and there was only old

Mr. Bailey in the restaurant this early and he couldn't hear a cannon go off.

"He wanted me to go out with him," she said, lowering her voice. "I didn't want to. He kept trying to coax me and then he slid his hand over my, well, my bottom"—she fought a blush—"and I put him on the floor."

"You . . . ?" he asked, spellbound.

"I put him on the floor," she said simply. "I'm a black belt in tae kwon do."

"Did Cary know that?"

She pursed her lips and her blue eyes twinkled. "I think he might suspect it, now. He was very apologetic. The boss saw what happened from the kitchen. She told him if he ever did that again, he'd never get back in here. He apologized for three minutes straight. He said his hand slipped," she added. She drew in a breath. "I'm so sorry for making a scene. . . ."

"Why?" he asked, searching her eyes. "That's what should have happened. No man has the right to harass a woman on the job. I've fired cowboys who got fresh with my housekeeper's daughter."

She was impressed. "I thought you might be mad," she said. "He's your cousin. . . ."

"By marriage, not by blood," he said shortly.

She didn't mention what she'd heard about Cary and JL's fiancée, but it ran through her mind.

"If he starts giving you any trouble, you call

Todd Blakely. He's the police chief here in town, and a friend of mine. Tell him I told you to call. He'll take care of Cary, and he'll enjoy it," he added. "It was Todd who put Cary in jail for assault. Cary's girlfriend slapped him. He called the law on her." He smothered a grin at Cassie's expression.

"He called the police because his girlfriend slapped him?" Cassie asked, wide-eyed. "But you said he went to jail for assault," she added, confused.

He pursed his chiseled lips. "Well, see, when Todd got there, Cary swung on him. Our chief's a martial artist, too. Cary had lots of bruises. But assault on a police officer is a felony and Cary couldn't talk Todd out of the charge. So he spent a couple of weeks behind bars before his attorney pulled a few strings and got him out." He shook his head. "Whatever he is, Cary's still part of one of the founding families of Benton. That reputation goes a long way around here. And Cary had been drinking, which he almost never used to do."

"I heard about him going to jail," she said. "I thought it was because he was dangerous."

"No, he's not dangerous and he doesn't want to go back," he assured her. "So he'll be more careful. But don't trust him. I don't mean that he's dangerous. He's mostly mischievous. He's like old Two Toes; he's a sneak."

"Two Toes?"

"Our resident bad boy. He's an old wolf. He preys on our calves because he can't get a pack to take him on, apparently, and he sneaks around my ranch looking for helpless little strays."

"Oh, how awful," she said softly.

He smiled. He liked her nurturing attitude. She reminded him of his mother, long ago, when he was small. She'd been like this, all heart.

"We're hoping we can talk the local wildlife rehabilitator to take him on. I don't want to kill him, but we have to stop him."

"Do they let people keep wolves as pets?" she asked.

He laughed. "Not so much. You have to have training for that sort of work. Most of the rehabilitators are overworked. All of them around here specialize. We have one for raptors, one for small mammals, one for large mammals, that sort of thing."

"What a wonderful job," she sighed.

"You wouldn't think so if your phone rang off the hook all hours with people needing help."

"I don't know," she replied. "It sounds like a worthwhile occupation." She glanced toward the kitchen. Her boss was just coming out of it. Cassie's worried expression told him a lot.

"Two eggs, scrambled, with bacon and toast and grape jelly," he said at once. "Strong black coffee to go with it."

She smiled and her eyes mirrored her gratitude as she jotted down the order. "I haven't spilled anybody's coffee so far today," she said.

"I spill mine half the time," he said easily. "I trip over my own feet. I catch pot holders on fire." He shrugged. "I won't mind if you spill the coffee."

She laughed. "Okay. Thanks."

"No problem."

She went at once to get his order. Mary gave her a secretive smile and a hidden thumbs-up. Cassie flushed. Mary laughed as her newest employee dashed to the counter and gave the order to the cook.

Cassie managed to get the coffee to JL in one piece, without dropping the cup. She let out a sigh of relief when she had it on the table before him, along with a napkin and silverware.

"Not bad," he remarked. "You know, your clothes are still at the house."

"Oh, gosh, I keep forgetting about them!" she exclaimed apologetically.

"It wasn't a complaint," he replied. "But I thought you might like to come over and get them Saturday. You can see the calves."

Her eyes lit up. "You have calves?"

"Lots of them. Even a pair of twins," he added. "We have our cows drop calves in the early spring, when the young grass is just coming up and most of the snow and sleet is done with." He sighed heavily. "Not that it's quite spring just yet," he added, shaking his head. "We've got our hands full with this latest snowfall."

"I love snow," she said softly. "It's so beautiful."

"Not when you're trying to shovel it out of cattle pens and feeders."

She laughed. "Yes, but I don't have to do those things."

"Don't they have snow where you come from?"

She made a face. "One or two days a year."

"Heaven," he retorted.

"It's a matter of perspective," she pointed out. "What we don't have often becomes a joy."

"I can think of several inappropriate replies to that," he said with a wicked smile. "The main one being raging indigestion."

"Oh, boy, can I sympathize with that!" she said. "I have heartburn so bad! I have to take medicine for it."

"Acid reflux?" he asked.

She laughed. "Yes."

"I have it, too." He shook his head. "The sad part is that I love spicy food, preferably Tex-Mex with lots of salsa and peppers. Can't eat it very often."

"I like spicy Asian food," she confessed. "Especially Chinese."

He laughed. "Kindred spirits. So," he added.

"Saturday morning, about ten? I'll come and get you."

Her face colored. She was shy and it was difficult for her to be herself with a man. But she was excited and happy, and that showed as well. "I would like that," she said, trying to rein in her enthusiasm.

"So would I. Cassie, isn't it?"

She nodded. "Cassie."

"Is it a nickname or your actual name?"

She sighed. "My actual name is Cassandra," she confessed. "My mother was reading a romance novel just before I was born, and she loved the heroine's name. So Cassandra I became. But everybody just calls me Cassie."

"I like it," he said softly.

She smiled. He smiled back. They exchanged a look that made her toes curl inside her shoes. "Oh! Your order . . . !" She laughed self-consciously and retreated to the counter to pick up his breakfast.

"Aren't you lucky that we're not crowded?" the cook, Agatha, asked with a wicked grin. "He's a dish, isn't he?"

Cassie went red from her forehead down. "Oh, Agatha . . . !"

"Never mind me. I always wanted a little bow and an arrow and a cherubic face. . . ."

Cassie wrinkled her nose at the older woman and carried the plate and the saucer containing the toast on a tray to the table where JL had cleared a path in between his coffee cup and his utensils for them.

She eased the plate down and almost lost the saucer, but she recovered it just in time. "Oops. Nearly a disaster. Sorry."

He chuckled. "Nice reflexes. I'll bet you're a terror on the tennis court."

"I don't play tennis," she said.

"I do. I'll teach you."

She laughed. "I'd trip over my feet and go headfirst into the net."

"Okay. How about horseback riding?"

"I've only ever been on a horse once or twice, but I really liked it," she replied.

"Fine. We'll forget tennis and go riding."

"I'd love that."

"Me too."

She picked up the empty tray and held it under her arm. "Ten o'clock Saturday."

He nodded. He smiled. "I'll look forward to it."

She hated her helpless blush. "Me too." She went back to the counter and put up the tray quickly, because a party of four just walked in the door. The morning rush had started.

JL paid the bill at the counter, because Cassie was in over her head trying to cover three tables at once.

"She's shaping up nicely here," Mary told him as she returned his change, indicating Cassie. "She'd never waited tables, but she's honest and quick to learn, and she works hard."

"Nice character traits," JL replied.

"She's pretty green. . . ." She said it hesitantly, not wanting to interfere.

"I noticed that, too," he said softly, and he smiled. "Another very rare trait, in these overly modern times."

She laughed. "It is."

"Tell Agatha the eggs were perfect. Nobody cooks them like she does."

"I'll tell her. She'll swoon," she teased. "She thinks you're the dishiest man since Sean Connery."

"My God, what an image to have to live up to," he returned with a grin. "I'll have to grow a beard and practice my Scots accent."

"Then she'll really swoon," Mary assured him.

He turned and caught Cassie's eye and waved. She tried to wave back, dropped her order pad, and then scrambled to pick it up again. She was as red as a beet.

He chuckled with pure pleasure and waved again as he walked out the door.

"You're very unsettled tonight," her father remarked when they were eating supper.

"It's been an odd couple of days," she replied.

71

"Cary hasn't been back, has he?" he asked with some irritation.

She just stared at him. "Cary?" she asked softly, fishing for how much he knew.

"Small towns run on gossip," he reminded her. He chuckled. "What I heard was that Cary got fresh with you and you put him down. One of my coworkers said he wished his wife had that kind of spunk."

She laughed. "I wasn't going to tell you," she confessed. "You've had so much worry lately. . . ."

"This doesn't worry me. Actually, it was nice to have something to laugh about. People say Cary's bad to drink with and he gets aggressive. I was afraid he might come back and say something to you."

"No," she told him. "That's not what happened at all. He swore that his hand slipped, and he apologized profusely. But JL Denton heard about what happened, too, and he came for breakfast to ask me about it."

"Protecting his cousin?"

"No. Protecting me, actually," she said. "He doesn't like his cousin."

"A lot of people don't like Cary, from what I've heard."

"Mr. Denton asked me if I'd like to go horseback riding with him on Saturday."

"Well!"

"He's got lots of calves," she added.

He chuckled. "Say no more. I can drive you over there and pick you up later."

"He's coming to get me," she returned.

"A gentleman."

"I hope so." She finished her meat loaf and mashed potatoes and put the plate to one side. "I don't really know him."

"Everybody in town knows him," he replied. "He's respected and well liked. People are still sorry for him about his fiancée walking out; something his cousin provoked, they say."

"That's what he says, too."

"You should be safe enough. You can always call me if you run out of defensive techniques."

She laughed. "I don't plan to throw Mr. Denton around, Dad."

"He was in the military," he said surprisingly. "And he was a master trainer in hand-to-hand combat, they say. I expect you'd have your work cut out to put him down the way you did his cousin."

"Well!" she said with a quick breath.

"He does drink, like his cousin," he told her. "So be careful."

"I will."

"Make sure you keep your cell phone charged, so you can call me if you get into a situation you can't handle. And make sure you don't leave without your meds," he added firmly.

"I will. Worrywart," she teased.

He grinned.

She didn't sleep that night, thinking about JL. She didn't know much about men, despite working around them for several years. Most of them were businessmen or entertainers, and they wore nice suits or expensive leisure wear, not denim and cowboy boots. JL Denton was completely out of her experience. He was very attractive. She hoped she could keep her head. She didn't want to become a notch on his bedpost.

On the other hand, he seemed like a gentleman. Her mother always said that a man treated a woman the way she signaled that she wanted to be treated. If she acted like a lady, that's how she'd be treated.

Her mother would have been taken aback if she'd seen Cary in the restaurant putting his hand on her daughter's bottom.

Accident or not, that had been offensive and it made Cassie angry. No man had the right to be that forward with any woman. It was condescending and crude.

She was glad that JL was angry about it, too. It made her feel better. In all the years since she'd graduated from high school and then college, she'd never had a man treat her that way. She'd never worked for the public, though, especially in a job like waitressing. And she'd been sheltered, mainly because she'd been sick so often. When she was a reporter, almost every man she knew treated her like one of the guys. Only one man had asked her out in all those years, but she'd turned him down. He worked for the same paper she did. She didn't want to risk a workplace romance. She smiled, remembering what her mother had said about the fellow reporter. Her mother had been very protective.

It hurt her to remember her mother, shamed and flooded with e-mails and nasty notes on social media. Neither Cassie nor her father had known about them until they checked her computer after she died and found them. Several had invited her to kill herself because she was married to a nasty and obscene lecher.

Cassie's father had never been a lecher. He was a perfect gentleman, and he was completely faithful to his wife, a rarity in the circles he moved in. Her mother had snapped under the unrelenting pressure of crusading newsmen and newswomen, ceaseless pointing fingers at her father for being one of those overbearing animals that preyed on women who were subordinate to him at work. The tragedy was something that Cassie and her father still couldn't talk about. The wound was too new, too fresh.

The only good that had come out of it, and it was small consolation, was that the media backed off after the tragedy. One newscaster was angry enough to castigate his colleagues on the air for being so aggressive and unfeeling that they cost a human life. But it was like closing the gate after the horse was gone. It didn't bring back Cassie's sweet mother.

She rolled over in bed and fluffed up her pillow. She had to stop looking back. Life was sweet again. It was a new start. She could live in Colorado for the rest of her life in total obscurity. No reporters would come here to harass her and her father. They'd left no trail that could be followed, even by an aggressive reporter. This little town was like shelter in a storm, and Cassie looked forward to making a new life here with her dad.

It might be a pipe dream, she thought as she closed her eyes. But dreams were sweet, when you had little else to cling to. She smiled, thinking of JL and Saturday, as she drifted off to sleep.

Saturday morning, she was up at seven o'clock. She made breakfast, cleared away the dishes, and then spent two hours trying on clothes to see what looked best on her. She didn't have a large wardrobe; she and her father had packed the bare minimum to come out here, putting everything they owned in storage for the time being. Back home in Atlanta, she had nice clothes, even a few designer ones, especially things for evening.

But she didn't want to wear anything fancy around JL. It would be stupid and cruel to wear designer clothes around a cowboy who lived in a house with peeling paint, on a ranch with broken fences. She wasn't going to do a number on his pride. So she wore simple off-the-rack jeans with a pullover yellow sweater and ankle boots. She left her hair long, curling around her face and shoulders, and she used a bare minimum of makeup and cologne.

"You look nice," her father remarked as she folded the clothes she'd borrowed, which she'd washed and dried, to give back to JL.

"Thanks," she told him. "I didn't want to look too dressy."

"Nice manners," he said softly. His face saddened. "Like your mother."

She bit her lower lip. "Oh, how I wish we could go back there and punch those reporters!"

"Life pays us out in our own coin," he reminded her. "God gets even with people who hurt us. They'll find that out one day, in this life or the next," he added. "You can't dwell on wrongdoing, even things that make you miserable. Hating only hurts you. It never hurts the person you hate."

"I guess not," she conceded.

"Got your rescue inhaler?"

"Yes," she said, smiling.

"Okay. EpiPen, too?"

"Right here." She patted the small purse where

she carried her necessary medicines. "But we're not too likely to run into stinging insects in the snow," she pointed out.

"There are still venomous spiders about."

"I hope they have overcoats, so they don't freeze," she said, tongue in cheek.

He laughed. "All right. I'll stop being overprotective. Where's your coat?"

"Oops. Forgot."

She went back to the closet and pulled out her swing corduroy coat. It was tan and matched her ankle boots. She drew it on.

He frowned. "Is that going to be warm enough?"

"Surely it will," she said. "I'm layered."

"I'm used to cold weather, but you aren't, sweetheart," he replied softly. "Colorado is very different, especially here in the mountains."

"I'll be fine," she assured him. She listened and heard the loud purr of a truck approaching. She dashed to the window and her heart raced.

"It's him!"

"Well, have fun," her father said.

"I will. See you later. Love you, Dad."

"Love you back."

She opened the door and ran outside just as JL was climbing down out of the cab of the big SUV.

He looked surprised to see her running toward him. He laughed with pure delight and went around to open the door for her.

"Handhold's just inside, above," he said.

"Thanks! It's a long way up," she laughed as she got inside.

"For a shrimp like you, it is," he teased, closing the door on her mock-indignant reply.

He climbed in beside her and put on his seat belt, glancing at her to make sure hers was in place as well before he started the big vehicle and turned it around, heading it down the driveway.

He was wearing a shepherd's coat over a red-and-black flannel shirt, with jeans and big boots and that creamy Stetson. He looked like a man who lived on the land.

There was patchy snow on the side of the road. She glanced over the rolling landscape to the snow-peaked mountains beyond. "It's so beautiful here," she murmured.

He smiled. "I think so."

"Were you born here?" she asked.

He smiled. "No. Near Dallas, remember?"

She ground her teeth together. "No, sorry."

"No problem. My father was born here. So was his father, and his grandfather, and so on."

"It must be lonely, with your parents gone," she said delicately.

He nodded. "It's hard to lose both parents within a few months. Dad was never the same after she died. They were married for a long time, and they loved each other desperately. I had an older brother. I lost him overseas, in the last Gulf

79

war." He sighed. "It's lonely when you don't have anybody. Well, except for Cary, and I'd give him away to anybody who wanted a bent and broken relative to keep. He's not even a blood relative, at that."

She grinned.

He laughed at her expression. "I told him to keep his hands to himself, but it wasn't necessary. He said he was getting into a tub of liniment and he hoped you'd understand if he went searching in another direction for company."

She laughed, too. "Oh, I understand perfectly. No problem."

He pulled up in front of the sprawling ranch house. There were men working everywhere, including on the front porch.

"This is why I said we'd go riding," he said under his breath. "They seem to multiply every time I leave home."

"What are they doing?"

"Upkeep and maintenance," he said as he got out of the SUV and went around to help her down. He held her just in front of him for a long moment, savoring the closeness. "Something I should have been doing all along. Now it's piled up and it takes a lot of manpower to set things right. Your eyes are the oddest shade of blue," he added, searching them in the long silence broken only by hammering nearby. "They're china blue."

"Like my mother's," she said with a sad smile. "But her hair was black. I inherited mine from her grandfather. I'm the only redhead in the family right now—well, what there is left of it. I have an uncle in Grand Rapids, Michigan, and a grandfather somewhere in Canada. He roams."

"I had a great-uncle who lived in a cabin up in Alberta with a black bear." He shook his head. "No accounting for taste, I guess."

"The bear didn't eat him?" she asked.

"Not that we know of. He died slumped over a poker hand at his weekly game. He'd won the pot, too."

"That's a shame," she said.

"Not so much. He was always happy, always smiling. We figured he went the way he would have wanted to go. Quick and easy, no long stay in a hospital or a nursing home. There's a lot to be said for that."

"I totally agree," she said.

She reached back into the SUV for the bag she'd put the clothes in. "I almost forgot to give these back. Thanks so much for the loan," she added, handing it to him.

"I'll put these," he indicated the bag, "in the house and bring yours out. Bessie washed and dried them for you."

"Bessie?"

"My housekeeper. The clothes I loaned you were her daughter's."

"Oh." She smiled. "Thank her for me."

"She wouldn't mind. Nita works for a bank down in Denver. She's sweet."

"I see."

He cocked his head and smiled at her. "No, you don't. I'm not carrying a torch for her. She's sweet, but she's outlived three husbands already. She's on number four now. And she's only thirty-one."

"My goodness!"

He sighed. "I guess some people have a hard time with marriage."

"I guess."

He led the way to the front door. "Want a cup of coffee before we go?" he asked.

"That would be nice."

"And warming," he added, noting her slight discomfort in the way she hugged her arms around herself. "You're not used to Colorado weather yet, I see."

She raised her eyebrows in a question.

"This is fur coat country. Or shearling coat country. Lightweight jackets won't cut it out here."

"I'm not really cold," she lied. "I just had a chill."

"Uh-huh," he murmured.

He led the way into the kitchen.

She remembered it from the last time she'd been here. It was roomy, spotless, with appliances like the ones she had in storage, that she'd cooked on when she lived in Atlanta.

"I love your kitchen," she said with a sigh. "You must have every gourmet tool they make."

"Bessie does," he said, smiling. "She can cook anything. Food's great, too."

"I'll bet."

"Do you cook?" he asked.

She nodded. "I can't do haute cuisine, but I can do most any food there's a recipe for. And I can make any kind of homemade bread and rolls. I do those for Dad. He loves fresh yeast rolls," she laughed.

"Bessie doesn't do breads. I'd love to try those rolls sometime," he added, pouring the brewed coffee into two cups.

"I'll make you a pan of them, if you like."

His dark eyes searched hers and he smiled. "Yes. I'd like that."

She flushed a little from the intent gaze she was getting.

He put her coffee in front of her and sat down next to her at the table. "Do I make you nervous?" he asked.

She drew in a breath. "A little."

"In a bad way?" he asked, without looking at her.

"N . . . No. Not . . . in a bad way." She was floundering like a child in school facing an oral book report for a book she hadn't read.

He turned and stared at her quietly, his dark eyes intense. "I speak pretty bluntly sometimes. But it's best to set boundaries, don't you think?"

She swallowed. "Yes."

He leaned back in the chair and sipped coffee. "Okay. It's like this. I'm still getting over a failed engagement. I'm pretty raw and I'm still not quite myself. So suppose we begin as good friends and let it go at that. For the time being."

She let out a sigh. "I'd like that."

His thick eyebrows arched. "You look relieved."

She bit her lower lip. "Look, my mother was overprotective. A lot. I wasn't allowed to date until I was in my late teens, and then only double dates. I don't know much about men, I've never had an affair, and I've tried to avoid men who were aggressive because I'm not . . . well, modern." She felt as if she'd rambled, but he only smiled.

"In other words, you don't sleep around."

"That's it."

"No problem. Even if I were over my ex-fiancée, you'd have nothing to fear from me," he said softly. "I don't amuse myself with innocents."

She laughed. "Thanks."

He drew in a long, heavy breath. "I'm glad we got that out of the way. I didn't want to give you the idea that I was in the market for a serious relationship."

"I'm not, either," she confessed. "Dad and I have had a traumatic time just lately. Neither of us is quite ourselves, either."

"Oh? What happened?"

"My mother killed herself."

CHAPTER FOUR

"I'm sorry," she said at once. "I didn't mean to blurt it out like that!"

He winced. "God, you poor kid!"

She linked her hands around her coffee cup. "It's hard, getting over it."

"Was she always depressed?"

"Never," she said softly. "She wasn't a selfish person. She always put all of us before herself, in everything. She would never have put such sorrow and guilt and heartache on us if she hadn't been half out of her mind . . . !" She stopped, fearful of saying too much.

He tugged one of her hands loose and linked it with his. It felt good, that big, calloused hand so tender as it curved around her own. "What happened to her?"

She hesitated, trying to find a way to put it that wouldn't make him suspicious. Even out here, they'd probably heard of the scandal. She looked at his clean, flat nails instead of his face. "She was harassed on social media, constantly," she said finally. "She had . . . enemies. She never hurt anybody in her life, but something happened to someone she loved, and she became a target." She closed her eyes and shuddered. "She walked out onto the balcony of her twentieth-floor apartment and . . . jumped."

"Dear God." His hand tightened.

"Dad had to identify her at the morgue," she said. She bit her lower lip. "We had a closed casket. Even morticians can't fix some things. She'd have hated having people stare at her. Not that there was a crowd at the memorial service. It was just me and Dad."

"Didn't you have family, friends?"

Their friends had deserted them and their family, sparse as it was, ran from them, fearful of being connected to the scandal.

"They were too far away to come," she said, forcing a smile. "It was very sudden."

"What about the culprits who harassed her?" he asked. "Did you file suit against them? Surely there are laws that apply in a case like that."

Of course there were laws, but if you were a public figure, as her father was, you had no right to privacy. Especially if you were the biggest story in the headlines. But she couldn't say that.

"Dad isn't the type to sue people," she said finally. "Neither was my mother. We used to say that she could find one nice thing to say about the devil."

He smiled. "My mother was like that, too. She never moved with the times. She was a founding member of our local Baptist church."

"I'm Methodist," she said softly. "Or I was."

His fingers closed around hers for a minute and then let go. She felt cold and empty and alone, all of a sudden, and smiled to hide it.

"I hope you have a horse who likes people for me to ride," she said. "The last one I was on tried to scrape me off against a tree. Maybe it was the soap I used," she confided.

He chuckled. "Not likely. If you're afraid, horses can sense it."

"I'm not afraid of most of them. Just the ones that try to scrape me off against trees," she said, grinning at him.

"I'll make sure we don't give you one of those," he promised. He finished his last swallow of lukewarm coffee and got up. "Ready to go?"

"You bet!"

He laughed. "Are you always so enthusiastic about things?"

"I've never been on a real ranch in my life," she said. "I'm looking forward to seeing the calves."

"We've got a nice crop of them this year. We've only lost two, and that's very few considering the size of the herd."

"What happened to them?" she wondered aloud.

"Two Toes," he said curtly. "But not for long. We're going to track him and trap him and give him to that wildlife rehabilitator I told you about. He can eat soft food and lay by the fire in his old age."

She laughed at the picture that popped into her mind. "Just make sure you don't dress him in a granny gown and put a frilly cap on him. And don't let little girls wearing red hoods into the house where he lives."

He stared at her pointedly.

"I don't have a red hood," she said quickly.

He chuckled. "Come on."

He had a cowboy saddle two horses. The one he gave her was called Buck, and it was a very gentle gelding.

"Why is he called Buck?" she wanted to know as they rode lazily down the trail that led around the stables toward sprawling pastures dotted with black-coated cattle.

"In his younger days, there wasn't a cowboy on the place who could stay on him."

She looked worried.

"He's twenty years old," he added when he saw her concern. "And Parker tamed him seven years ago. He's converted."

"Parker?"

"Man who works for me," he said. "He's part Crow. He has a way with horses. I've never seen one, however wild, that he couldn't calm just by talking softly to it. He's the best wrangler we've ever had."

"Was he the man who saddled the horses back there?"

"Oh, no," he said. "We keep Parker out at the line cabin."

"Should I ask why?" she teased.

He chuckled. "He was in the military. He's got a mouth that ten bars of soap wouldn't wash clean, so we keep him away from the house. Great with horses. With people, not so much."

"He sounds fascinating."

"A couple of single women felt that way, too, until they talked to him for five minutes. One developed a sudden headache, the other had a hair appointment she'd forgotten. Neither of them ever came back."

"Maybe he likes being alone," she pointed out.

"That's exactly my take on it," he agreed.

"Does he say why he cusses so much?"

"He said he learned how while dodging bullets in Iraq," he sighed. "I know how he feels. I learned a few bad words of my own, doing the same thing."

"It's rough for soldiers over there," she said, recalling a friend who'd helped her with research for a screenplay she was writing; one that later was made into a TV movie.

He glanced at her. "And you'd know this, how?"

"I had an acquaintance who was in spec ops over in the Middle East," she said. "He told me a lot of things that civilians don't usually get to hear."

"Civilians?"

She took a breath. "I started out as a newspaper reporter," she confessed. "Newbies get to do the police beat. Things you have to see, you don't share with people who don't have a connection to news or emergency services. I loved it," she laughed. "I got to know all the local law enforcement, the EMTs, the dispatchers, the politicians. It was hard to leave it."

"Where did you work?"

"A small town outside Atlanta," she replied. "I got a better job, but I missed reporting. I always knew where the bad guys were," she added with a grin.

He laughed. "It's like that here, too. We only read the paper to see who got caught. We already know everybody's business."

Not mine, she thought thankfully, *or my dad's.*

They came to a fence post that was leaning, with the wire attached to it bent down by a tree limb that had fallen. He swung out of the saddle, looped the reins over the horse's head, and let them drag, while he went to right it. She noted that he had thick gloves on those big hands. Muscles rippled in his powerful legs as he lifted the limb off the fence and then righted the fence post and straightened the wire. He pulled out his cell phone when he was finished and called out some numbers to someone and instructed them to get out and fix it before cattle poured out onto the road.

He came back and climbed into the saddle with the ease of long practice. "Can't afford to let cattle get out," he said as they rode forward. "Even on a spread this big, every head counts."

"Are they all Black Angus?" she asked.

"Every one. We sort them when we start branding. Those with good conformation go into one pen, the others are gelded and put into a separate pen. We feed out the yearlings for the sale lot, for breeding stock."

"And the others, the ones you don't breed?"

He glanced at her and pulled his wide-brimmed hat over one eye. "I think you can guess."

She made a face.

He laughed. "That's ranching," he said. "We can't keep them all. I sell the steers and keep the rest."

She frowned. "Why don't you keep them for beef?"

"I can't eat something I've raised," he said simply. "Some ranchers have gone into signature beef that they produce and slaughter and package and sell, right from their own ranches." He grimaced. "I'd never be able to do that. So I run purebreds."

She smiled. "I like that."

He glanced at her with warm brown eyes. "Tender heart."

"I can't help it. I take after my mother."

He drew in a long breath. "I guess I'm more

93

like my dad," he said. "He was a third-generation rancher, but he was so educated that he never really took to the chores. I hated the ranch when I was in high school. There was a girl I liked, and she said she didn't like boys who smelled like manure." He shook his head. "I told my grandad that, and he hit the ceiling. He was good for thirty minutes about snooty city girls with stuck-up noses. They'd never get down in the dirt and work with you, if you had to grub for a living, he said. They lasted only as long as the money did. Better to find a woman who wanted to make a home and have a family, even if she didn't wear silk dresses and look like a magazine cover."

"Smart man," she murmured.

"Sometimes money would get tight and my grandfather would work for a mechanic in town, just part-time, you know, to tide us over." He didn't add that his father didn't offer any such thing. Not that there was a college in Benton where he could have taught. "That was when my brother and I were in grammar school." He didn't add that it was also before their grandfather died and left them a fortune. The ranch had never fallen on bad times since. "Dad was bad to drink after we lost Mom."

"What happened to him? If you don't mind telling me," she added quickly.

He shook his head. They rode down the long, wooded path toward the mountains. "We found

94

him sitting up in a line cabin, stone dead." He grimaced. "It was one of the coldest nights of the year, snow piled up six feet deep. It looked to us like the fire went out in the fireplace after he dozed off. He just never woke up." He glanced at her. "Not a bad way to go, I guess, but Mom had died a few months earlier of a heart attack. We didn't even know she had a heart problem." He smiled sadly. "She wouldn't go to the doctor for what she thought was simple indigestion. It wasn't." He pushed his hat down over one eye. "My dad was never the same, after. He blamed himself because he didn't make her see a doctor."

"Sometimes things happen because they're meant to," she said simply. "It doesn't make sense to some people, but it does to me. I think we die when we're supposed to."

"Maybe we do."

"Was it a long time ago?"

"Six years," he said. "My older brother's unit had been called up three years before all that and he died over in the Middle East."

"I'm truly sorry. At least I still have my father."

"I miss my grandfather," he confessed. He'd missed his mother, but he and his father weren't close. They had very little in common until after JL went to college and then his father found him interesting. His dad missed teaching. It was the only thing he ever talked about.

They rode along in a peaceful silence for a few

minutes, with only the creaking of saddle leather and the pleasant rhythm of the horses' hooves on hard ground making a noise.

Snow was just starting to fall. She lifted her face to it and smiled. The wind picked up and she shivered slightly.

"Cold?" he asked, reining in.

"Just a little chill," she lied. "I love snow."

"Nobody who ranches out here loves it, I can promise you," he chuckled. He glanced out over the landscape. The mountains were topped with snow. The ground was getting lightly covered with white.

"I hope we get enough to make a snowman," she said, laughing.

He glanced at her, fascinated with the way she looked when she laughed. She was pretty, in her way. He liked her all too well.

"We'd better get moving before we turn into snowmen," he teased.

"I guess so."

They rode on down the trail when a sudden blur of movement stopped them in their tracks. Wolves!

There were several of them. Cassie's heart almost stopped as one of them halted just a few yards away and growled. Her horse neighed and reared.

"Don't jerk on the reins," JL said suddenly. "Just sit still. They aren't after us."

She shivered, and not from the cold. She'd never really seen a wolf up close. They were huge! She hadn't realized how big they were, or how dangerous they could look when they snarled.

Out of the corner of her eye she saw JL pull a long rifle out of a scabbard on his saddle. He shouldered it and looked down the sights, controlling the uneasy motion of his horse with his legs.

The wolf obviously thought he meant business, because it turned its head toward the others and loped away without a backward glance.

Cassie let out the breath she'd been holding. Or she tried to. She couldn't get the air out, which was the major problem with people who had asthma. Getting air in was easy. Getting it back out could be an issue.

She needed her rescue inhaler, but it was under her buttoned coat, in her purse. She swung down out of the saddle, a little unsteadily, and moved away from the horse, fighting to breathe.

"Here, now, it was just a wolf or two," he said, faintly irritated by her reaction. He put the rifle back in its scabbard. "Nothing to get so upset about."

She couldn't talk to tell him what was wrong. She was fumbling with her jacket, trying to get to her inhaler. She panted like a winded runner.

JL's dark eyes narrowed as he swung down out

of his saddle gracefully and moved toward her. His ex-fiancée had overreacted like that anytime she was upset. It was a painful reminder of what he'd lost, and it made him irritable. "Hell," he said with a scowl. "Don't be so melodramatic. You were in no danger!"

When she felt better, she thought dimly, she was going to kick him in the knee. Meanwhile, it was an ordeal just to get half a breath of air.

She finally worked her way into the purse under her light jacket and dragged out the rescue inhaler. She sat down on the ground, shivering, and held it up to her mouth. She took a puff and waited for the soothing spray to ease down into her tortured lungs and reduce the spasms.

He suddenly seemed to realize what had happened. He went down on one knee. "Here, are you all right?" he asked with belated concern.

She didn't answer him. She couldn't. One puff wasn't enough, and she had to wait a minute or two before she took another. It was frightening to smother like this. The cold air, the chill, the unexpected wolf sighting, all had combined to bring on an attack. She hadn't been using the preventative her doctor had prescribed. It was hard enough to afford the rescue inhaler. The other medicine was expensive, and she'd tried to do without it. Not a good idea, apparently.

He watched while she took a second puff and held it in. Slowly, the spasm turned loose, and she was able to get her lungs to work again. She leaned forward with her forehead on her knees.

He felt two inches high. He grimaced. "Can you ride?"

She nodded. She got to her feet, still breathing heavily, and let him help her into the saddle.

He turned his horse, watching her worriedly as she followed suit. They rode back to the stable in a tense silence. She was glad that she couldn't breathe properly, because she was really angry. So much for that kind attitude that he didn't really have. Apparently, it was all just an act. At least she knew now what sort of person he really was, even if it was a bad way to have to learn it.

"Would you like some coffee?" he asked.

She shook her head. "I need to go home," she said in a hoarse voice.

"Is your father there?"

She nodded.

He opened the door of the SUV, noting that she got in all by herself and fastened her seat belt without a word.

They drove in silence to the house she and her father rented.

"I'm sorry," he bit off when he pulled up at her door.

She forced a smile, although she didn't quite meet his eyes. "It's okay," she managed.

She got out before he could reach the door to open it for her.

"We forgot your clothes," he said, for something to break the tense silence.

She smiled again and just shook her head. "It doesn't matter. Thanks for the ride," she said, and turned away, walking slowly to the front porch.

He watched her go, feeling empty and guilty, and angry that he hadn't realized something was physically wrong with her. He'd made a mess of everything. He hoped he'd have the chance to make it up to her, when she had time to get over his clumsy accusation.

He climbed back into the vehicle and drove, reluctantly, away.

Her father knew something more than an asthma attack was wrong with her, but he didn't pry. She seemed uncomfortable talking about it. She pulled out her nebulizer and turned it on. It gave her something to do while she got over the misery of the afternoon.

She was going to cook supper, but her father insisted on making sandwiches instead. He sent her to bed early, worried about the sudden rattle in her chest. She'd gotten chilled, and her lungs were weak even on good days.

"You should have a heavier coat," he said worriedly. "I should have made arrangements to have our winter things sent out here."

"Too big a risk right now," she said. Their winter things were expensive clothing, stuff they wouldn't want anybody local to see. In retrospect, she thought, they should have put the furs and designer gowns into a consignment shop and they'd have had more money for incidentals.

Her voice was hoarse. She hated what she knew was coming. She'd had too many problems not to know what lay ahead. "I should never have gone riding in the snow."

"I should have noticed," he began.

"My fault, not yours," she said firmly. She patted his hand. "I'll be okay. Honest."

He didn't look convinced.

"Honest," she repeated. "I'll have a good night's sleep, and I'll be fine in the morning," she added brightly.

He wasn't smiling as he went out and closed the door behind him.

She wasn't better in the morning, but at least she wasn't any worse. She got dressed and went to work, shoving yesterday into the back of her mind so she wouldn't have to think about it.

In the meantime, at work, her father had two men walk onto the lot and peer at a huge new combine parked there.

One man was dressed like a working cowboy in denims and worn boots and hat and a denim jacket. His SUV was parked in front. The other customer was wearing a nice suit and had driven up in a fairly new luxury car.

Roger Reed went straight to the man in the suit,

bypassing the cowboy, and asked the man if he needed help.

The cowboy gave him an amused glance and walked back into the office.

"Hey, JL," the owner, Bill Clay, called to him as he walked in with a cup of coffee and a sweet roll from the town's only coffee shop. "I should have brought more coffee!"

"Mine's still out in the truck," JL Denton chuckled.

"What can I do for you?"

"I came to replace my combine," he said, glancing out the window. "I guess I should have worn a suit. Your other customer attracted your salesman."

Bill's face hardened. "Don Terrell. He never buys a damned thing. He comes over to see the new equipment so he can tell his grandson what to buy him. At a dealership down in Denver, at that."

"I guess your new salesman didn't know that."

"He'll find it out. Sorry about that."

"Who is he?" JL asked as he dropped into a chair in front of Bill's desk.

"Roger Reed. He's from back east somewhere. His cousin worked here until recently. I hired him as a replacement." He shook his head while JL wondered at the familiarity of that last name. "He's good with schematics, knows everything about the equipment so he can fill the customer in about its advantages. Not so good at deciding which customers to help first."

JL shrugged. "No problem. How about writing it up for me in between sips of coffee and I'll sign in the appropriate place," he added with a grin.

"Happy to!"

Outside, Cassie's harassed father was feeling less intelligent by the minute. He'd gone over all the pertinent information with his potential customer, but all he'd received in reply was a series of grunts. God knew what that meant.

Finally the man nodded. "Okay, I'm sold," he said. He grinned. "It sounds like a great piece of equipment." He pulled out a notepad and asked for the particulars. He wrote down the item number, the price, and the exact name. He snapped the notepad shut and slipped it back into his pocket.

"Can I write it up for you?" Roger asked the customer politely.

"Write it . . . ? Oh! No, sorry, I'm not buying it here," he replied. "My grandson buys all my ranch equipment for me. He works for an equipment company down in Denver. I just decide what I want and tell him." He grinned. "He gets an employee discount, you see. Sure helps my budget! Well, thanks again." He shook hands and walked off the lot, back to his expensive car.

Cassie's father stood there, blank-faced, watching his potential customer reverse his expensive car and pull out into the highway.

The man in denims was just coming out of Bill Clay's office when he walked back inside the building.

"Glad to help," Bill was saying. "I'll have it delivered tomorrow morning."

"Fine, fine," JL said. "No rush. We aren't going to be harvesting anything in the near future," he added with a laugh. He shook hands. "Thanks again, Bill."

He walked out, ignoring the salesman who'd ignored him.

Roger Reed just gaped after him. The cowboy he hadn't thought was worth a dime had apparently just purchased one of the most expensive pieces of equipment on the place.

"Missed a hell of a commission there," Bill told Reed quietly. "I would quote the old axiom about not judging a book by its cover, but I think you get the idea, don't you?"

The older man grimaced. "Do I ever," he said heavily.

"Old Don Terrell never buys anything here," Bill told him. "His grandson works for an equipment company down in Denver. Don comes over here to look at our new stock and pick out what he wants, then he calls his grandson with the information. He's never spent a dime here. On the other hand," he added amusedly, "JL Denton could buy this place and everything on the lot out of petty cash, if he wanted it."

Roger felt the blood going out of his face. "Denton?"

Bill nodded. "He owns a big Black Angus stud outside town. It's more of a hobby for him than anything else. He's a multi-generation rancher here. His money's mostly in oil and mining. He has a fortune in oil stocks that his grandfather left him."

And Roger had told his daughter that only a rich man could afford purebred cattle. He'd judged the man on old working clothes. What a lack of foresight. Lately it seemed to be his chief asset.

"I'm truly sorry," he said.

"We live and learn," Bill replied. "You're new here. It will take time for you to get used to the populace. No harm done."

Except there was. He'd made an enemy of the man his daughter was interested in, and he'd lost a huge sale. Neither thought made him particularly happy. He did still wonder what had happened the day before to bring his daughter home with an asthma attack and that aching sadness in her eyes. If he hadn't been such an idiot, he might have found out from JL while he was selling him a piece of equipment. But by slighting the rancher, he'd done himself no good.

He went back to work with a heavy heart.

Cassie was drooping. She had a cough that was productive and the sputum was colored, not a good combination, especially when added to what was most likely a fever. She kept going anyway. She couldn't afford to lose a day's pay.

Mary noticed that her newest hire wasn't feeling well. "You need to go home," she told Cassie early in the afternoon. She waved away the girl's protests. "I won't fire you for getting sick, for heaven's sake! I'll call Sarah and she'll come in and work the rest of your shift." She gave Cassie another long look. "I'm going to tell her to take over for you tomorrow as well. You need to see a doctor and go to bed!" she added firmly. "You're sick!"

Cassie drew in a painful breath. "I'm so sorry."

"Everybody gets sick once in a while," she said, her voice gentle. "It's not a big deal. You're a wonderful little worker. I'm happy to have you here. Now go home! And if you need anything, you call me, okay? I can send meals over for you and your dad if you can't cook supper."

Tears rolled down Cassie's cheek. "That's so kind. . . ." She choked up.

"Don't do that, or you'll have me bawling,

too," Mary teased. "Go home. I'll call and check on you in the morning."

"Thanks," she said.

She called her father at work. He had to ask Bill to let him off long enough to get his sick daughter and take her home.

"I knew you shouldn't have gone out in that lightweight coat," he said heavily when he saw how ill Cassie was.

"We all do dumb things," she told him.

"Funny you should mention that," he murmured as he helped her inside the house. "I lost a huge sale this morning. I had to choose between a customer in blue jeans and one in a suit. I chose the wrong one."

Cassie's eyebrows rose.

"The man in the suit was just looking," he said with a wry smile. "The man in blue jeans bought a brand-new combine from my boss while I was going over all the advantages of the equipment to a man who had no intention of buying it from me."

"Oh, dear," she said.

"It gets worse. The man I slighted was JL Denton."

Cassie's heart jumped. She bit her lower lip.

"Pity I didn't ask him to bring you inside when he dropped you off here yesterday, or I'd have known who he was," her father said sadly. "He didn't even look at me when he went out the door. I've made an enemy there."

"Just as well," she said, averting her eyes. "I'm not too keen on him, either."

"Care to tell me what happened yesterday?" he probed gently.

"There was a pack of wolves," she said. "I was already chilled. One of the wolves stopped and growled at my horse, who reared and unsettled me. JL had his rifle out and the wolf saw it and took off. But it brought on the asthma attack."

"I'm so sorry," he began.

"It gets worse," she interrupted. "He thought I was being melodramatic when I gasped for breath. It wasn't until I managed to get out my rescue inhaler that he stopped being sarcastic."

"No wonder you were upset."

"Just one of those things," she said. "But I don't care if I never see JL Denton again as long as I live."

He could see the pain in her eyes, in her face. She'd never cared enough about a man to be so angry at one. That alone told her father that she'd felt something for the rancher.

"Life hurts," he said.

"Tell me about it. You should go back to work before Mr. Clay fires you," she said, trying to smile.

"If he was going to fire me, he'd have done it already. At least he saved the sale I lost."

"I'm going to bed."

"I can bring home something for supper."

"Nonsense," she replied. "I can cook. I'm just going to lie down for a few minutes and use my nebulizer. I'll take some of that leftover cough syrup and I'll be fine."

"We can afford a doctor visit," he replied.

She made a face. "Sure we can. I'll do that, while they're filling up our yacht with diesel."

He laughed softly. "Okay. But I'd rather make payments on a doctor visit than lose my only child. Just saying."

"I love you, Dad."

"I love you, too."

She smiled and walked off toward her bedroom.

CHAPTER FIVE

JL was half out of sorts after being ignored by Bill Clay's salesman. He realized that the man wasn't likely to know much about local people since he'd just started at the concern. But it hurt to be ignored, as if he was of less worth because he dressed in working clothes.

He was curious about the newcomer. Hadn't Cassie said that her father was working for an equipment company? There was only one in town, and he'd just come from it.

He frowned. What if that had been her father? It made sense now that he'd have ignored the man who'd made fun of his daughter's asthma attack.

It shamed JL that he'd done that. He hadn't realized she'd had a health issue. He'd thought she was being overly dramatic about the wolf. In fact, his ex-fiancée had done the same thing over a similar incident. It had brought back painful memories. Of course, he hadn't said anything to the other woman about overreacting. He'd been kind and solicitous to his ex-fiancée, because he'd fancied himself in love with her.

He wished he'd been kinder to Cassie. No wonder she was mad at him. He didn't blame her, or her father. It hadn't been until she'd pulled out what looked like an inhaler that he realized she wasn't putting on an act.

He walked out to the barn to tell Drum about the new purchase and give him a time frame about delivery the next day.

"You look preoccupied," Drum noted.

"I did a stupid thing yesterday. I thought Cassie Reed was being overdramatic because a wolf growled at her mount and made it restless. She had an inhaler in her pocket, one of those things people with asthma use," he added. He sighed. "She was already chilled. Eastern tenderfeet don't know about Colorado winters, and she's from Georgia. She was wearing a lightweight coat. I guess she got chilled enough to bring on an attack."

"My mother had asthma," Drum replied. "She got pneumonia a lot. All she had to do was be around somebody with a cold and she'd get sick. It would always go right into her chest. We spent a lot of time in the hospital with her."

JL frowned. He hadn't thought that Cassie might get sick from being chilled. He felt even more guilty.

"She was barely speaking to me when I got her home," he murmured. "I hardly even had time to apologize." He scowled. "I made a worse mistake this morning. I think her father is Bill Clay's new employee. I snubbed him going out of the office. He'd passed me over for a man in a suit when I was looking at the combine I bought."

"In your favor, you didn't know," Drum pointed out.

He made a face. "That won't do much to help me." He pursed his lips. "I think I'll stop by the restaurant and see how much damage I did," he added. "It's getting on suppertime, anyway, and I'm hungry."

"Not me. I had a big lunch. Cook made pork chops and potatoes and onions. Not to mention, homemade rolls."

"I'm not living right," JL sighed. "I should have a cook full-time, instead of pleading with my house-keeper to do it three nights a week. This isn't one of those nights, and I'm sick of my own cooking."

"Your bunkhouse cook is awesome. You should come eat with us." Drum's eyes twinkled. "Of course, I do understand that it would work a hardship on you, eating with the peons . . . watch it!" Drum added, having just sidestepped a swat from that big hand.

"You watch it. I'm not a bad man."

"You sure about that?" Drum asked. "I haven't checked the FBI's most wanted list in a while. . . ."

"I'm going to town. Be back later."

"Good luck."

JL sighed. He was going to need some of that.

He sat down in a booth and waited for Cassie to come out. But she didn't. Sarah, a buxom middle-aged woman, came out instead.

"Hey, JL," she said pleasantly. "What can I get for you?"

"Where's Cassie?" he asked.

"Had to go home," she replied. "She was sick. Coughing her head off. Well, Mary made her go home," she amended. "She didn't want to. Mary promised she wouldn't fire her. She called her dad to come get her."

He was more concerned now than before. He glanced at the clock. "How about making me up three plates to go?" he asked, and chose the special.

"You going to take supper to her? That's nice," she said gently.

"I owe her a supper," he said. "She got sick riding around in the cold with me yesterday. She didn't have a proper coat."

"I told her that a week ago," Sarah said with a sigh. "She said she couldn't afford anything better right now. Proud, that one."

"Yes," he said, feeling small. His conscience was killing him. "Very proud."

"I'll get this ready as soon as I can. Want coffee while you wait?"

He nodded. "Please."

Cassie felt even worse as the afternoon wore on. She was going to have to try to get up and fix something for her father to eat, but she was too sick to stand at the stove and cook.

She dragged herself out of bed, wrapped in a pretty embroidered chenille housecoat that fell to her ankles. It was something from the old life that she'd brought along. It had been her mother's.

She held on to the wall as she wobbled toward the kitchen and prayed that she could make it that far. As it was, she had to stop halfway down the hall to pant for breath.

She heard a vehicle drive up and the engine cut off. She glanced at the clock. It was ten to five. Her father wasn't due home for at least thirty minutes. She grimaced. She didn't have dinner ready. . . .

There was a knock at the door. Surely that wasn't her father, she thought as she went to the door very slowly and opened it.

Her lips parted as she saw JL standing there with a big white bag in his hand.

He made a face. "You look like death warmed over."

"I'm not feeling up to company," she rasped.

"Good Lord," he said softly. He moved in past her. "I'll just put these in the fridge."

He opened the refrigerator door and grimaced at the lack of food in it. He slid the diner meals inside and closed it.

"What was that?" she asked from the doorway.

"Food," he said. "I brought supper. But you aren't eating anything until you've seen the doctor."

115

Her face flushed. "I don't need . . . !"

He picked her up gently and walked out the front door, pausing to pull it closed behind them with Cassie balanced on one powerful, raised thigh. "We can argue later."

She fought tears. She didn't want to tell him that she couldn't afford a doctor. She had health insurance, but she was afraid to use it. And it didn't cover office visits, even if she'd been willing to risk it. An enterprising reporter would be looking for things like insurance claims. Any good skip tracer would jump on the charges like a duck on a june bug.

"I can't afford—" she began.

He kissed her forehead. She felt feverish. "Just hush," he said gently.

She couldn't hold back the tears. He was being so kind!

He put her into the cab of his ranch truck and closed the door. He handed her his cell phone as he got in beside her and started it, checking to see that her seat belt was on before he fastened his. "Call your father and tell him where we're going," he added softly.

She wiped away the tears. She punched in numbers. "Dad? JL's kidnapped me," she rasped, "and he's taking me to a doctor." She frowned. "Turncoat," she accused. "Yes. Yes. All right. He brought supper, too, it's in the fridge." She gave JL an accusing look, which he ignored. "Okay,

Dad. Yes, I'll tell him. Good-bye." She hung up and passed the phone back to her companion. "He said to thank you and that he's sorry about this morning."

"It doesn't matter. Not his fault if he didn't know who I was," he replied, sticking the phone in his coat pocket.

She wrapped up closer in her robe. "I should have changed first."

"You're sick, and we're going in the back door, anyway," he replied.

"The back door?"

He nodded. "The doctor's a good friend."

"Oh."

He pulled up to the back of a one-story building with a big parking lot, pulled out his cell phone, and made a call.

He explained the situation. "Yes. I'll bring her right in. Thanks, Sandra," he added, a smile in his voice. He hung up.

"Lorna's receptionist said I could bring you in the back. The nurse will wait for us."

"Thanks," she managed weakly as he lifted her out of the truck and bumped the door shut with his hip.

"You look terrible," he remarked, searching over her pale face.

She laid her cheek against his coat. It was cold from the wind and it felt good against her fevered skin. "I feel terrible," she said in a hoarse tone.

"You'll be better soon," he promised.

He carried her in the back way. An elderly nurse was waiting for them with a gentle smile. She led them into a cubicle and went out to get the doctor.

JL deposited Cassie on the examination table and dropped into one of two chairs against the wall.

Before he could speak, a young woman with thick chestnut hair and dark eyes came into the room. She was wearing a white lab coat and there was a stethoscope draped around her neck.

She glanced at JL curiously and then at the redhead on the table. "I'm Dr. Lorna Blake," she introduced herself.

"Cassie Reed," came the hoarse reply. "Thanks for seeing me."

The doctor frowned. She put the stethoscope against Cassie's chest and had her breathe and cough while she listened. She looped it back around her neck, took Cassie's temperature, and asked questions, a lot of them.

"I'm pretty sure it's bronchitis," she said. "I need to send you over to the hospital for a chest X-ray. . . ."

"No. Please." Cassie's eyes were troubled. There was no way she could afford that.

The doctor sighed. "All right. I'll send you home with antibiotics and instructions, but if

118

you're not better in two days, I want you back here and you'll definitely get an X-ray then," she added firmly.

"Okay," Cassie said.

The doctor filled out a prescription and handed it not to Cassie, but to JL. "Go to bed," she added to Cassie. "Plenty of fluids. Take the antibiotic. Got cough syrup?"

Cassie nodded.

"Acetaminophen for the fever," the doctor added.

"Okay," Cassie agreed.

"Thanks, Lorna," JL said as he lifted Cassie from the table into his arms.

She grinned. "You're welcome."

He sighed. He knew what was coming later. He'd never brought a woman to his high school friend as a patient, not even that she-shrew he'd been engaged to. It was unusual to see JL so concerned about anyone's health. He was sure Lorna sensed a romance.

JL gave her a speaking glance as he walked out the back door with his patient. Lorna was still grinning when she shut the door behind them.

JL stopped by a pharmacy on the way home, leaving the engine running so that the heater would stay on, and Cassie wouldn't get chilled while he coaxed her prescription out of an amused pharmacist inside. He didn't have to wait. The pharmacist was dating Lorna, so they'd have plenty to talk about on their next evening out, JL was sure.

He drove Cassie home. By then, her father's car was parked at the door. Roger Reed opened it for them as JL carried her inside, straight to her bedroom. He deposited her gently on the bed.

"I heated up supper. You're staying for it, right?" Roger said pointedly.

JL hesitated.

"I made strong coffee," Roger added.

JL glanced at Cassie. "Okay," he said.

She smiled, her eyes bright with fever and delight.

"You can have yours in bed," her dad told the patient.

"Okay, Dad. Thanks."

He just smiled.

He punched the microwave, where the first of three plates was waiting to be heated. When it was done, he added utensils and a napkin and gave them to JL to take to Cassie on a tray he'd found earlier under the cabinet.

"Can you manage this?" JL asked her as he propped the tray on her legs.

"Yes, it's fine," she said.

He paused to read the directions on the antibiotic and shake a capsule out into her hand. She took it and he gave her a spoon and the cough syrup. She knew it was useless to argue. She took that, too.

He smiled. "You'll be better in no time."

"Thanks. For everything."

He brushed back her wild reddish-gold hair. "I'm sorry, about what I said," he told her with genuine regret. "I'm not good with people."

She managed a smile. "Me neither."

He stood up, searching for more words, but he couldn't find any. He smiled, turned, and went out to the dining room, where her father had two plates sitting on the table, along with two mugs of steaming, strong black coffee.

"I didn't know who you were," Roger told him in an apologetic tone as JL sat down. "I'm truly sorry. I'm not really good at working with the public. It's pretty much a life-changing experience," he added with a soft chuckle.

JL just nodded. The man had a very cultured voice, like that of a radio announcer. It sounded oddly familiar.

"Not your fault," JL said after he'd sipped coffee. "I never came inside and introduced myself when I took Cassie out to the ranch." He grimaced. "I should have realized she was getting too chilled. I didn't know about the asthma, either. I chided her for being melodramatic when she gasped for breath." He ground his teeth together. "I'll have hell living with that on my conscience, let me tell you," he added curtly.

"We all make mistakes," his companion said quietly. "God knows, I've made my share."

"Well, a friend of mine said that's why they put erasers on pencils," JL replied.

"I'd need a very big eraser," the other man commented.

They ate in a pleasant silence. The food was good. Mary had one of the best cooks in the county in the kitchen at her restaurant.

"This is really good food," Roger commented.

"Nobody cooks like Mary," JL replied. "We all know each other pretty well around here. Benton's only got a population of about two thousand souls. Only a few people ever leave, mostly kids who want more excitement."

"I've had all the excitement in my life that I care for," Roger said quietly. "The peace and quiet is comforting."

"I heard about what happened to you," JL said.

Roger felt the blood drain out of his face. "Oh?" he asked, trying to sound indifferent when he was churning with fear inside.

"Yes. From Cassie. It must have been very difficult, losing your wife in such a way."

Roger swallowed, hard, and felt relief at the same time. "It was traumatic, for Cassie and me," he said. "We were all close."

"You should sue the people who drove her to it," JL said firmly.

"I'm not that sort of person," Roger replied with a sad smile. "Besides all that, there would be too many to summon to court." He sighed. "Far too many."

JL frowned. It was an odd comment.

Roger realized that, just in time. "She had a page on Facebook," he added. "I hate social media."

"I know what you mean. Say one thing that offends somebody, and the world camps on your doorstep," JL chuckled. "Happened to my foreman a couple of years back. He's very political. Doesn't pay to advertise what party you support. Somebody's always waiting with smart remarks and threats."

"Tell me about it. We're too connected, I think sometimes. Cassie and I have a small TV set, but we don't watch it much. We get our news from the Internet."

"Me too," JL confessed. "I don't like getting news from a handful of people who own all the media in the country. They decide what's news and what's not."

"Too true. Back when I was young, news reporters were required to be objective and even-handed. Now, it's just a handful of executives pushing their own agendas and calling it news."

JL chuckled. "We think alike."

"On that issue, of a certainty."

"I'm sorry I let her get chilled," JL said,

nodding toward the bedroom and lowering his voice. "I knew that coat was too thin. I should have made her wear a heavier one."

Roger couldn't bring himself to mention that she didn't have a heavier one here. Actually, she did have one in storage back home; a very expensive one, but they didn't dare wear any couture stuff out here. It would stand out like a sore thumb.

JL noted the pained look on his companion's face and translated it as wounded pride. "You do the best you can when you're living on a budget," he said after a minute. "When I was a kid before we moved back here, my dad worked as a paleontologist and taught at a college in Texas. Times were hard, because my mother was fragile and couldn't hold down a job. It wasn't until my grandfather asked Dad to come back that we were able to afford good clothes and warm coats." He frowned because it sounded odd even to him that his father's salary didn't cover such essentials. "Funny," he said, almost to himself, "I never looked at it that way."

"Budgeting is new to me, and I'm not very good at it," Roger confessed. "But I'll get the hang of it. I want to get Cassie a gaming system for her birthday next month. She misses playing online."

JL's eyebrows raised. "She games?"

He laughed. "She games. She loves this space

game called *Destiny 2*. She played it all the time when she lived in Georgia."

"I thought Cassie said you lived in New York?"

"We all did, when Cassie was small. She went to Georgia State University in Atlanta and liked it so well that she stayed."

"Yes, she worked as a reporter, she told me."

"She was a good one. She worked for a weekly paper." He laughed. "She found the most unusual people to do feature stories about. Her columns were often picked up by major dailies."

"She might get on with our local paper," JL said thoughtfully.

"She gave it up," Roger replied. "The stress made her asthma worse."

"Oh. I see." He grimaced. "I'll have to be a lot more careful with her, when I take her out," he added, thinking ahead. "I'll make sure she's bundled up properly, even if I have to roll her up in one of my rugs."

Roger laughed at the picture that made in his mind. "She's a black belt," he reminded his companion.

JL grinned. "So am I."

"I heard about that."

"I'll take care of her, just the same. She's got a bagful of medicine. Make sure she takes it. And don't let her go to work tomorrow. Mary already tried to get her to go home today and she argued about it."

"I'll get a strong chain with a lock," Roger agreed, grinning.

"I can pick locks!" came a hoarse voice from the bedroom.

Her father just laughed. So did JL.

Cassie was flushed with excitement and joy when JL came in to say good-bye.

"You get better," he instructed.

"I'll work on it every day," she said in a hoarse tone, and smiled.

"Next time we go riding, I'll get you one of the old coats Nita left when she moved to Denver."

Her lips parted. She searched his dark eyes and felt warm inside, as if a fire had been kindled there.

He was feeling something similar. He reached out and brushed back her disheveled red-gold hair. It had been a very long time since he'd been needed by anyone. His mother was often ill, and he'd been attentive when she was. His father was never sick; his older brother had never even had a cold. But here was this little newcomer who needed nurturing and he felt a bond with her already.

He drew in a breath. He recalled what he'd told her, that he wasn't ready for a relationship. He was feeling surprisingly comfortable with her. "I don't think I've ever been around a redhead in my life," he teased softly.

"We're rare," she had to admit. She smiled. "It comes with freckles."

He chuckled. "I like freckles."

She drew in a rasping breath. "I don't, but it isn't as if I get a choice about having them," she laughed.

"You need to sleep," he said gently, getting to his feet. "I'll check on you in the morning. You can call me if you need anything."

She looked at him with wonder. "I can?"

"Where's your cell?"

"In my housecoat pocket, there," she said, pointing to the robe she'd draped around the back of a chair.

He lifted it, admiring the intricate embroidery. It looked very expensive. Definitely not something off the rack.

She could see the wheels turning in his mind. He was suspicious.

"It was my mother's," she said, noting the intent look he gave the robe as he searched for the phone. "It's one of the few things I have left of her. Dad gave her the robe three Christmases ago. She fussed because he splurged for it," she added quickly.

"Oh. I see," he said, smiling easily. His suspicions retreated. He opened her contact list and put his phone number into it. He put the phone on the table by the bed. "In case you need it," he said.

"Thanks," she said softly.

He grinned. "You're welcome. If you can't get your dad, and you need anything, you call me, okay?"

"Okay."

"I'll see you tomorrow, sprout."

She grinned. "Okay. Thanks for getting me to the doctor," she added. "I'll pay you back. . . ."

"Over my dead body," he said with a laugh. "This was my treat."

She bit her lower lip and fought tears. "It was so kind . . . !"

"Don't you start," he said, waving a finger at her. "You start bawling and your dad's going to go looking for a shotgun."

"Not likely," her dad said from the doorway, chuckling.

"Figure of speech," JL replied. He smiled at both of them. "I'll see you tomorrow."

"Thanks for all you did," Roger told him. "For supper, and for taking care of Cassie."

"My pleasure." He went out without another word or a backward glance, closing the door behind him.

Outside, he lifted his face to the cold wind and sighed. He was getting in over his head here, and he didn't know how to stop. Her vulnerability appealed to him as other feminine traits never had. His ex-fiancée had been a kind person, or seemed to be, until Cary told him the truth about her. He'd been badly taken in. He didn't trust his own responses. What if Cassie was playing a game? What if she wasn't what she seemed to be?

He dismissed the thought. She was as honest as the day was long, and why would she pretend to be poor, anyway? It was obvious that she and her father had very little money. She'd worried excessively about paying the doctor. She was proud, too, offering to pay him back when he knew she didn't have the money.

No, she seemed like the genuine article. But he'd do well to put on the brakes. He had enough to take care of at the ranch, with the improvements he was finally making. He'd keep close to home for a bit. But he'd check on her in the morning, because he'd promised.

He knocked on her door midmorning. She opened it with a big smile. She was wearing the housecoat, but her color was better.

"Those antibiotics work very fast," she said. "I can feel the difference already." She paused to cough into a tissue. "Well, I'm still coughing, but it's not as bad as it was. Come on in. Would you like coffee?"

"You shouldn't be up," he fussed.

"Yes, I should," she replied. "My doctor back home told me that it's never a good idea to stay in bed completely with a chest infection. You have to keep moving so that you're more likely to cough up the bad stuff. I've been in the kitchen."

He followed her in. On the counter was a baking sheet with several rolls just rising. They were covered with a sheet of plastic wrap.

"I made those for you," she said gently. "Let them rise for another hour or so, then bake them at three hundred fifty degrees Fahrenheit for about sixteen minutes. If they're not brown, let them put them back in the oven for another couple of minutes."

"I'll enjoy them," he said. "Thanks."

She grinned. "I love to cook. But I especially like to make breads. I love the feel of dough. It's almost alive."

"My mother could make bread," he said. "But it's been a long time since I've had any fresh from the oven. This was nice of you."

"Payback," she teased. "For your kindness yesterday."

"It's not hard to be kind to someone as sweet as you are," he said, and he wasn't teasing.

She searched his eyes and felt her stomach drop. It was new, the feelings she had with him.

He saw that and grimaced. Everything she felt was plain on her face. "Listen," he began worriedly.

"I can't get married this morning," she broke in, embarrassed by what he'd likely noticed, and desperate to change the mood.

He stared at her. "Excuse me?"

"I can't get married this morning," she said firmly. "Or this afternoon. Not even this year. And that's final. I'm sorry, but I have my heart set on climbing Mount Everest. I'll need an oxygen tank, of course, and the right clothing, and I'll have to save up. But I should have enough in about twenty years, so you can check back with me then."

It took him a minute to realize that she was teasing. He chuckled, deep in his throat. "Just when I think I've got you figured out, you throw me another curve."

"I'm quick, I am," she joked. "Sit down and have some coffee, if you've got time."

"I've got time." He tossed his hat into a spare chair and sat down at the table.

She poured coffee and sat down beside him. "I love coffee first thing in the morning."

"So do I," he said, sipping his. "Nice. I like strong coffee."

"Dad and I do, too," she said.

"I noticed. He makes good coffee as well."

"I forgot to offer you cream and sugar," she said suddenly.

"I don't take either. When you serve in the military, you get used to life without the frills," he chuckled.

"Reporters learn that early," she told him. "I was always on the run. It's a hectic sort of life."

"Your dad said the excitement made your asthma worse."

She nodded. "It did. I missed it, though."

"So, what did you do for a living before you moved out here?" he asked.

She just stared at him. That was the one question she hadn't anticipated, and there was no way she could tell him the truth.

CHAPTER SIX

JL scowled. She looked guilty, and he wondered why.

She thought for a minute. "I had a job as an assistant to a producer at a television station north of Atlanta," she said finally. It wasn't quite the truth. But it sounded better than confessing she'd been a top writer for one of the most successful network weekly shows in the country. She didn't dare admit that, because he might have heard about the scandal that involved her family.

"Assistant producer?" he asked.

"It's like being a research assistant," she continued. "I had all sorts of assignments and I didn't have to sit at a desk all day. Once I got to do a feature story all by myself with just a cameraman and a sound man with me in the van."

One of her friends had such a job, and she was able to recall what the other woman had told her about the assignments she got. It was like being a reporter, but with television cameras instead of a pad and pen—or, more recently, a notebook computer.

"It sounds complicated."

She laughed. "It's not. I covered news stories occasionally, too, but it was mostly feature stuff."

"We have a weekly paper here in Benton," he said. "In fact, the editor used to work in New York City."

Her heart stopped beating. She just sat and stared at JL, vaguely horrified. "Oh?" she asked. "Recently?"

"No," he said, wondering at the sudden paleness of her face. "About ten years ago. Are you okay? You look wan."

"I'm still weak," she said. She smiled. Ten years ago was a relief. The weekly editor wouldn't know about her father.

"I guess you are. I still feel bad that I let you get chilled like that."

"You made up for it," she told him. "It's okay."

He sipped more coffee. "What I was getting at, is that maybe you'd be happier working on the newspaper than waiting tables," he said hesitantly.

"I couldn't go back to it," she replied. "The stress would be too much."

"It's just a weekly paper. Not a daily," he teased.

"You don't understand. The stress on a weekly is much worse than on a daily paper. On a weekly, you're expected to do all sorts of things besides just report. On a daily, you just write your copy and turn it in to the city editor or the state news editor."

"Oh."

"Besides, I like being a waitress," she said, grinning.

"Almost anybody can be a waitress, with the right training. But it takes more than just training to be a reporter."

"Thanks," she said softly, searching his dark eyes.

"You're wasted, is what I meant."

She sighed. "It's not stressful, what I do now, and I love the people I work with," she said. "Besides, I don't have to sleep with a pistol under my pillow at night."

"What?" he exclaimed.

"Back when I worked for the newspaper, we had this reporter, Barney. He did a story about corruption in the county commission and ticked off members of one commissioner's family. He got death threats. He slept with a pistol under his pillow. He was run off the road one night and hit a telephone pole. The perp was never caught, and Barney decided he'd like to work in a happier place, so he got a job as a telephone lineman." She chuckled. "He said that it was a lot less stressful."

He laughed, too. "I guess so. I never thought of reporting as dangerous."

"It can be, depending on who you tick off," she replied.

"Did you ever get a death threat?" he asked easily.

She felt that question to the soles of her feet. She looked hunted suddenly, haunted. "Yes," she confessed. "Once or twice." It had been a lot more than once or twice. She and her parents all had death threats from people who supported the conniving woman who'd wanted her father's job. Social media had hounded them to the point of madness, cost her mother her life. It was unreal, how much damage people could do with just words.

He frowned as he saw how upset she'd become. His big hand slid over her cold one and curled around it. "Sorry," he said gently. "You were thinking about your mother, weren't you?"

He was amazingly perceptive. She took a deep breath and had to fight a cough. "Yes, I was," she confessed. "Sorry."

"I didn't think," he said apologetically. "I know it must be a hard thing to get over. Losing a parent is painful."

"Something we both know," she agreed. Her fingers curled around his. "It's still fresh."

"Life goes on," he replied softly. "It has to."

She nodded. She felt choked inside.

He squeezed her fingers and then let go. "I've got to go," he said. "We've got storm warnings for tonight. The boys and I have to bring the few remaining expectant mothers up to the shelters near the house. Calves are hard on heifers that are bred for the first time."

"I can imagine. I never did get to see the calves," she added suddenly.

"Next time," he said softly, and he smiled.

She smiled back, her heart in her throat. "Next time," she agreed.

"Just friends," he added firmly, even though he was feeling something that was definitely stronger than friendship.

"Just friends," she agreed pertly. "I've already told you that I have to climb Mount Everest before I can even think about marrying anybody."

He chuckled. "I'll remember that." He stood up and put on his hat. "You stay warm. I'm still on call if you need me. Don't go to work if there's ice on the road. Call Mary and tell her you can't get out. She has two other workers who live in town who can fill in if they have to."

His protective attitude made her feel warm inside. "Okay," she said softly.

"And don't go out unless the house catches on fire," he said firmly.

She laughed. "I won't."

He tilted his hat over one eye. "I'll be back by tomorrow. Just to check in."

"Okay. I'll have coffee ready. Oh, wait . . . !" she called as he started out the door.

She handed him the pan of rolls. "Three fifty, sixteen minutes," she repeated.

He smiled slowly. "I won't forget. I'll see you later."

137

"See you."

She watched him walk out the door with new emotions boiling over inside of her. He said they'd just be friends, but there had been a look in his dark eyes that made her giddy even in memory. They were building to something wonderful.

Her face fell. Something false. Because he didn't know the truth about her and her father. What would he feel, if he found out? Would he believe the lies people had told about her dad? Would he even listen if she tried to explain?

She bit her lower lip, hard. She didn't know what to do. In fact, there was nothing she could do, unless she wanted to tell him the truth right now. That was unwise. If he wasn't sympathetic and he told anybody, the media might be able to find them out here and start the persecution all over again. There would be no place left to go except maybe overseas, and they didn't have enough money for that anymore.

She poured herself another cup of coffee and turned off the pot, her face drawn with worry. Life had seemed so simple when she and her dad moved here. It was a small community, they'd blend in, nobody would know them. It would be fine.

Except that life was never static. You met new people and got involved with them, even superficially. Then you were hostages to fate.

Anybody might suddenly see a news item on television and connect it with the new man at the equipment store, or the waitress at the restaurant. It wasn't likely, but it was possible that her father could be recognized, even out here.

Then what would they do? She drew in a long, painful breath. Life was becoming more complicated all the time. She wanted to get closer to JL, but he didn't want a serious relationship. And even if he did, how would she tell him the truth?

She sipped coffee and put the worry to the back of her mind. She had to live one day at a time. It was no good anticipating trouble. That only made things worse. One day at a time, she told herself firmly.

JL went home, with snow falling softly on the back roads, on the tall sharp peaks of the surrounding mountains. He grimaced as he thought what a time they were going to have if the snow amounted to more than an inch or two. He was short-handed. Two of his cowboys had quit for no apparent reason. He was still trying to replace them, and not having much luck. It put more strain on the other workers, trying to absorb the overflow of routine tasks.

Pregnant cows, especially purebred ones, required a lot of work. No rancher could afford to lose many calves in this economy. It meant

139

checking on the herd several times a day to make sure they were sheltered and fed and watered, and safe from predators.

He thought about Two Toes and grimaced. That old wolf would be lounging in the tree line, waiting for his chance at another little lost calf. Just the thought of it made him irritated.

He parked the truck at his front door, went inside, and pulled out his cell phone. He had Butch Matthews, the wildlife rehabilitator, on the phone seconds later.

There was a long pause while he outlined his problems with the resident bad boy of the wolf variety.

"Only two toes?" Butch mused.

"Only two. Well, on one foot, that is. We can tell that much by tracking him through the snow. He limps. He's also old and he must be missing some teeth, because all he wants to bring down are little calves."

"I may be able to do something about that," Butch began.

"I don't want him killed," JL said at once.

There was deep laughter. "Neither do I. I have a special regard for them. A wolf saved my life once."

JL frowned. "You're kidding."

"I'm not," Butch replied. "I fell off my horse and rolled down into a ravine. Broke my leg. Somewhere along the line, my cell phone was torn out of its carrier and I had no way to get help. I heard howling close by. A big white wolf wandered up. It was old and grizzled and looked hungry. I thought my number was up. It wasn't. The animal came close, sniffed my leg, looked at me, and lumbered off. A couple of hours later, the wolf came back, sniffed my leg again, huffed, and trotted off. Not long after that, two men on horseback rode down the ravine to where I was. They made a makeshift travois of lodgepole pine trunks lashed together with rope and topped with a spare rain slicker. They got me back to their ranch, called an ambulance on the way there. I was barely conscious and in a lot of pain, but I remember calling it a miracle that they found me before I was buried in the snow. One of them laughed and said the damned wolf led them to me. They were riding along fence lines to check on pregnant heifers when the wolf came up to them and just sat down and stared at them. They moved toward him and he moved off a little distance. He sat right back down and stared at them some more. They finally got the idea that he wanted them to follow him. They did, and found me." He laughed. "That happened eight years ago, and people still tell that story. In retrospect, it really was something of a miracle."

"I guess so. I don't guess you ever saw the wolf again?" JL asked curiously.

"Not yet. But I might. The wolf that saved my

life had a track the men followed. A unique track. The front left paw only had two toes."

"Son of a gun!" JL exclaimed. "I'm getting cold chills down my spine," he chuckled.

"Me too. So no worries about how we'll cope with the old fellow. He can come and live with me. I'll feed him venison and turkey and let him watch television with me."

"I'll buy him a doggy bed," JL promised. "It would be great not to find any more savaged calves."

"There are other predators," he was reminded. "And it's still mostly winter here."

"I know. But most predators aren't quite as smart as that old wolf."

"So it would seem. I'll be around tomorrow after lunch, if that's okay. I'll bring a live trap with me."

"Good job. I'll expect you. And thanks."

"My pleasure."

JL hung up the phone. Well, that was a story he'd enjoy telling Parker and Drum. And maybe Cassie as well.

A few days later, he drove out to town and picked up Cassie after work to show her the growing calf crop.

"How about your wolf?" she asked curiously.

"Now, there's a story and a half," he chuckled, and related the story that Butch Matthews had told him.

"But you're going to lure him into a trap?" she asked, aghast.

"A live trap."

She just stared at him.

"It's called a humane trap. You put bait in it and wait for the animal to walk in. There's a spring that closes the gate and traps him inside, unharmed."

"Oh." She hesitated. "But what if you don't go back to check the trap and he starves to death?"

He shook his head with an affectionate smile. "Oh, tender heart," he teased.

She sighed. "I guess I am."

"It wasn't a complaint. Butch checks the trap every few hours," he added. "He's staying with us until Two Toes cooperates."

"What is he going to do with the old wolf when he traps him?" she asked worriedly.

"Take him home and feed him venison stew."

"Don't tease," she said gently.

"I'm not. He's going to take him home and feed him venison stew. Butch is the wildlife rehabilitator I told you about. He loves wolves. He had another one that was injured and couldn't be released into the wild. It lived with him for six years. He grieved for a long time after. Two Toes will be good for him."

"I see. That's not what I expected," she confessed, and laughed self-consciously.

"Not what I expected, either," he laughed. "We

143

usually trap animals like that and take them far up into the mountains and release them. We can't do that to Two Toes because he'd starve."

"He hasn't caught him yet?"

He shook his head. "Two Toes is wily. He's hard to fool."

"I can see why. He sounds very intelligent."

"Like some dogs," JL agreed. "We had a shepherd dog here a few years back, as a guard dog. He understood most of what you told him, and whole sentences, not just random words. You could tell him to go into another room, get a particular toy, and bring it back, and he'd do it." He sighed. "Never had another dog that smart."

"What happened to him?" she asked.

"He belonged to Drum, my foreman. Drum's girlfriend loved the dog to death and phoned every day to find out how he was when they broke up. In the end, Drum gave him to her. He said she'd grieve herself to death if he didn't."

"Poor Drum," she said.

"The dog was happy with her," he replied. "She took him everywhere with her. In fact, her next boyfriend didn't like him, so she got rid of the boyfriend." He laughed. "Tickled Drum to death."

"Think she might come back to him?"

"Anything's possible. But he's had several girlfriends. Women love him. He's just not easily lassoed. He likes being by himself. He doesn't mix well with other people. His girlfriend was making long-term plans, and it spooked him. He said he wasn't ready for all that."

"All that?" she wondered.

"Picket fences, kids, dinner at home, no more poker on Friday night with the boys. That sort of thing."

"Maybe it's just as well," she said. "I think it takes a lot of work to keep a couple together. My mom and dad loved each other very much, but even they had arguments and threatened to split up every so often. They compromised."

"So did my parents. Besides that, both of them were kind-natured. They never went out of their way to hurt each other, like some couples do today. I think compromise and tolerance are key parts of a good relationship."

"I do, too."

He glanced at her, a little concerned.

"I haven't climbed Mount Everest yet," she said abruptly and without looking at him.

He burst out laughing as he got the reference about when she planned to get married. "Stop reading my mind."

"Stop thinking absurd things," she shot right back.

He just shook his head.

They had a pasta salad and fruit for lunch, courtesy of JL's housekeeper, Bessie. The older woman was overweight and abrupt, but she had kind eyes and she seemed to approve of Cassie on sight.

"Heard you got sick?" she said as she poured hot coffee into their mugs as they sat at the table.

"Chest infection," Cassie replied. "I have asthma, so I'm prone to them."

"Had a grandma who was like that," the housekeeper said. She put the coffeepot up. "Back in a sec," she said, and ambled down the hall.

"This is wonderful coffee," Cassie mentioned to JL.

"Bessie likes it strong. So do I," he said.

Bessie was back in a minute with a long, heavy wool coat. She draped it over the back of an empty chair beside Cassie. "That belongs to my daughter," she told Cassie. "You wear that when you go out into the cold with him," she said, indicating JL. "Colorado is no place for a lightweight coat," she added with a kind smile.

Cassie's pride throbbed but she bit her tongue. "Thanks," she said huskily. "Thanks so much."

Bessie patted her gently on the back. "It's no problem, taking care of nice folks," she replied.

Cassie was fighting tears. The woman had a big heart.

JL saw those glistening eyes and he smiled tenderly. "That's what we're both doing," he added. "Taking care of nice folks."

"Thanks," she said softly.

"Eat up," he said. "A full belly makes traveling easier."

"Are we traveling, then?" she asked as she blinked away the tears and dug into her pasta salad.

"We are. To see the calves."

"Oh, boy!" she enthused.

He laughed out loud at her enthusiasm. "We've got a good crop this year," he told her. "Lucky for us that we only had an inch or two of snow. The spring grass will pop up, soon, just in time to feed the new babies."

"I can't wait to—"

The ringing of his phone interrupted her. It was playing the theme song of a popular new movie. She grinned as she recognized it.

He winked at her as he answered it. "Yes? Oh, hi, Butch," he added. "How's it going? Yes, I remember. Yes." His eyebrows arched. "You did? When?" He paused. "Sure, I can send Drum. I'll come myself. The three of us should be able to get him into the truck without any issues. We can go home with you, if you think . . . Okay. Well, you know wolves better than any of us. Sure. About ten minutes? We'll meet you there." He hung up.

"He got Two Toes," he told Cassie and Bessie, who were both waiting to hear what was said.

"Hooray," Bessie broke out. "Peace and quiet at last!"

"We hope," JL chuckled.

"Are you going to see him? Can I come?" Cassie asked at once.

He scowled, a little concerned.

"Please?" she added, and her blue eyes pinned his and pleaded with him.

He drew in a breath. "It might be risky. . . ."

"It won't be," she said with certainty. "I'll stay back and do what I'm told. Please?"

He was remembering how she'd panicked when the wolves had crossed their paths, the day she got sick.

"It was because they came up so suddenly," she said, puzzling Bessie, who didn't know what had happened that day. "It wasn't the wolves. Honest."

"Okay then. But, got your rescue inhaler with you?"

She pulled it out of her pocket and showed it to him.

"All right. You can come."

She grinned and grabbed the coat Bessie had brought out for her.

Butch Matthews was waiting for them at the edge of a section of lodgepole pines, with the snow-covered peaks of the mountains for a backdrop. A tall, lanky man, he was leaning up against the truck with his arms folded.

That was when Cassie, bundled up in Bessie's

daughter's warm, wool coat, noticed that one of his arms was artificial. That would explain why he couldn't lift the wolf into the truck by himself. She noticed something else when she looked past him at the trap. That wolf was twice the size of a large dog. He was huge. He was prone in the cage, just looking at the approaching humans without howling or making a noise of any kind.

"Has he been like that all this time?" JL asked, puzzled, as they approached the cage.

"Yep," Butch Matthews said with a grin. "Never tried to bite me, even when I gave him some jerky and a little water. I think he remembers me," he added, and took a minute to explain the remark to Cassie, who was fascinated by the story he told.

JL was staring intensely at the huge wolf. "I never get tired of looking at them," he said quietly. "They're magnificent creatures. I hate losing calves to them, but it isn't malicious, what they do. They're hungry and when they find food, they eat it."

"Except when they're old and their teeth are rotten and they can't half see."

"What?" JL asked.

"This old pet is just about blind, JL," Butch said, indicating Two Toes. "His eyes are milky, as if he's got cataracts. I'm going to get one of the wildlife service people over to look at him, to make sure. But I don't think he can see much. He must have been going on smell alone to find even a calf."

"What a shame," JL said. "Left in the wild, he'd die."

"He would. He could easily fall off the side of a sheer cliff, without being able to see where he's going. Starvation would probably be a better bet. I don't anticipate much argument over getting to keep him." He grinned. "Except he might have to just listen to TV instead of watching it with me."

"He's so pretty," Cassie said involuntarily. "I never realized wolves were so big."

"Most people don't, if they've never seen one in person. Native Americans have all sorts of legends about them."

"I've read some of those," she confessed.

"She was a newspaper reporter," JL told his friend.

"Really?" Butch asked. "That must be a high-pressure job."

"It was," she said. "I don't do it anymore. But if I did, what a feature story Two Toes would make," she added with a sigh.

"Feel free to interview me, anytime you like," Butch said with a twinkle in his eyes. "I can tell plenty of stories about wildlife that you'll never read in a book."

"I might take you up on that sometime," she said, but not with any great enthusiasm. In fact, she moved just a little closer to JL, although she still smiled at Butch.

JL felt oddly protective when she did that. His arm slid over her shoulder and drew her close. He smiled down at her. "She's softhearted," he said gently. "She was afraid we were going to kill Two Toes."

"We'd never do that," Butch laughed. "He's so well-known around these mountains that they'd probably ride us out of town on a rail if we even talked about it."

"People know about him?" she exclaimed.

"Sure they do," JL answered. "Benton's so small and thrives on gossip. Two Toes is a great conversation starter. People have spotted him all around town on government land and private land. He's recognizable."

"But they can't see from a distance that he has just two toes on one foot, can they?" she began.

They both laughed.

"That's not why. Come over here," Butch invited, and positioned himself right in front of the wolf.

She joined him, with JL, and caught her breath. "Well, for heaven's sake!" she exclaimed.

The big wolf was snow white except for a dark gray ruff around his head. But that was where he was most distinctive. His dark gray head had several white streaks through it, as if he'd had his fur dyed in a unique pattern.

"As you see," Butch continued, "he isn't hard to recognize, even at a distance. There isn't another wolf anywhere around with his particular coloring."

"He really is unique," Cassie said softly, staring at the big animal.

It turned its head and looked at her. It made an odd woofing sound and then whined. It cocked its head at her and sniffed.

She was fascinated. Without asking, she went closer to the cage, very slowly, and dropped down to one knee beside it.

"Pretty boy," she said softly. "Sweet old wolf."

He whined again and lowered his head to look up at her with big pale milky brown eyes.

She reached into the cage, slowly, and rubbed her fingers over his head, between his eyes. He whined again and sighed, making no move to bite or snap at her.

"Animals like you, miss," Butch remarked.

She laughed softly. "I've always had dogs," she said. "Well, until the past few months," she added sadly. "My last dog was very old. He developed cancer and we had to put him down."

"They can treat that, but it's massively expensive," Butch said.

"Massively," she agreed, not adding that she'd had the dog given chemotherapy in a hopeless effort to prolong his life. Finally, her father had convinced her that she was only adding to the animal's suffering. There was no hope of recovery. She gave in. Even the vet said that it was the kindest thing to do. "I still miss him," she added gently.

"What sort of dog was he?" JL asked.

She smiled. "A malamute," she replied.

"In Georgia?!" JL exclaimed.

She laughed. "Well, we had air-conditioning, you know. Although one day I came home from work and found him sitting inside the refrigerator. He'd opened the door after the air conditioner apparently failed." She shook her head. "It was a mess to clean up. He just laughed," she added, recalling the dog's happy expression.

"I had a malamute, and a Siberian husky once," JL said. "They're great pets. Lousy watch-dogs."

"I know!" She laughed out loud. "If you were ever robbed, they'd follow the burglars around, show them the best stuff, and help them carry it outside to their getaway car. At least, Ranger would have," she added.

"But they're great company."

"Yes," she agreed. "Ranger would sit outside with me on nights when we had meteor showers, and just lie down and be quiet the whole time, sometimes for hours."

"You like meteor showers?" JL asked.

"I love them."

"So do I."

She got to her feet. "Good luck, old fellow," she told Two Toes.

"He won't need luck. He's got Matthews," JL chuckled.

"Well, if you'll help me get him loaded up," Butch began.

A pickup truck pulled off the road and parked next to JL's SUV. A tall, powerfully built man with long black hair and a somber face joined them. "Caught him, I hear?" he asked.

"Caught him. Hey, Parker," Butch greeted, shaking the newcomer's hand. "I could use a little help. . . ."

"No problem." Parker walked over to the cage, knelt beside it, and passed something into the cage for the wolf. He patted it on the head and said something else. Then he got to his feet and, without asking for assistance, picked up the cage and slid it onto the bed of the pickup truck all by himself. He put up the tailgate and secured it in place.

"I didn't see that," Butch said.

"I didn't see that, either," JL added.

"I lift weights," Parker said, glaring at them. "You could do it, too, if either of you ever went to a gym!"

"Wouldn't do me much good," Butch sighed, indicating his mechanical arm, but smiling, as if making light of his disability.

"Wouldn't now," Parker agreed. "But you

154

couldn't have lifted him before you lost that arm, Matthews," he added with a grin.

"I guess not. I hate gyms. Nasty, smelly places," Butch said, making a face.

"Well, he won't build me a gym," Parker said, jerking a thumb at JL, "so I don't have much choice, do I?"

"Why should I build you a gym?" he asked the tall man.

"Because I can break horses like nobody else who works for you. And mostly, so I wouldn't have to go to town where there are nasty, smelly gyms and wandering gangs of panting women."

Cassie blinked. "Excuse me?"

"Panting women," Parker said, turning his twinkling black eyes and his infectious grin on her. "Every time I take off my shirt to work out, I have to fend them off with shields. A man with my assets gets harassed all the time by women."

"You should sue," JL said with a straight face.

"Absolutely," Butch agreed. "Or, at least, take me with you to the gym so that I can get the overflow."

Parker chuckled. "I might take you up on that."

"Thanks for the help," Butch said.

"No problem, Sarge," he replied. "I still owe you for that last deployment in Iraq."

"Yeah, well, I owe you a couple of favors, too," came the reply.

Cassie sensed the affection between the two men and wondered at it.

Parker threw up his hand and went back to his own truck. Butch thanked JL again, got into his truck, and drove away, leaving Cassie and JL alone.

"Why did he call Mr. Matthews 'Sarge'?" she asked.

"That's a long story," he replied. "I'll tell it to you, on the way to see the calves."

CHAPTER SEVEN

"Isn't Mr. Parker the man you said you had to keep away from people because he cussed so much?" she asked.

"He is."

"But he didn't cuss a single time," she pointed out.

"Must have a fever or something," he teased.

"Really?" She just laughed. "Were he and Mr. Matthews both in Iraq?"

"They were. Butch was his sergeant. They got into a firefight with insurgents and Butch was badly wounded. Parker dodged through a hail of gunfire to get to him, threw him over his shoulder, and dodged back behind our own lines. He was hit twice before he got there."

"A brave man," she said solemnly.

"Very brave. Butch lost his arm, but kept his life. Later on, he returned the favor by taking out an insurgent who'd sneaked into camp and had an automatic trained on Parker. Butch shot the man and saved Parker's life."

"I begin to understand," she said.

He nodded. "Combat makes fast friends of strangers."

She searched his hard face. "You were over there, too," she recalled.

He nodded. "I was in a different outfit than Butch and Parker were in, but in the same general vicinity."

She recalled that he never talked about it, so she didn't push.

He noticed that. He loved it about her. Most women would have tried to pry it out of him, become insistent. She didn't. She just accepted people the way they were.

He did wonder at Parker. The man was notorious for his blistering and politically incorrect vocabulary, yet he'd said not one bad word in Cassie's company. He was going to ask about that later. It was a real mystery.

Meanwhile, he took Cassie to the barn and walked her down the wide, paved aisle to the stalls where three calves were kept.

"These little ones have been sick," he told her. "So we brought them in here." He didn't add that taking her out in the pasture to see the calves could get dangerous. He didn't run polled, or dehorned cattle, and mother cows could be dangerous if they perceived a threat from human intruders. He'd seen one cow actually attack one of his cowboys for petting a calf on the head. That particular cow had been culled. It wasn't wise to keep an aggressive animal around his cowboys. But sometimes you didn't know a cow was aggressive until you found it out the hard way. He wasn't risking Cassie.

Polled cattle were less dangerous around cowboys and equipment, but in an area with predators, like JL's ranch, it was more profitable to leave the horns on, so that the cattle could defend themselves, especially when big snows made it difficult for workers to get to them.

"They're so pretty," Cassie remarked, leaning on the fence to smile over it at the calves. "Black as coal."

He nodded.

"Will they get better?"

He laughed. "Sure, they will. Then they'll go back to the herd with their mothers."

"I read that some mothers reject their calves. Then what do you do?"

"They become bottle calves," he said simply. "We bring them into the barn and keep them here until they're weaned. We always have a few of them."

"That's sad."

"That's life," he replied easily. "Sometimes mothers don't know what to do with their calves, especially first-time mothers. They walk away and can't find them again, or they just walk away, period. We check the herds several times a day during calving, so we'll find them if they're by themselves. Usually. Sometimes we have problems, like old Two Toes raiding our pastures."

"I like your Mr. Matthews," she said. "He's nice."

He chuckled. He liked it, the way she described his friend. He'd found over the years that women who thought men were nice didn't feel much attraction to them, except as substitute brothers. It pleased him that Matthews hadn't made an impression. Not that he was interested in her that way. Of course he wasn't!

On the other hand, Parker had been very interested in her. He'd never seen the man so animated.

"Mr. Parker lifted that whole cage into the truck by himself," she added worriedly. "I hope he didn't hurt himself. I imagine Two Toes is very heavy. He's a big wolf."

"Parker frequently amazes us," he replied. "We don't know a lot about his background. He never speaks of it. We only know about Iraq because Matthews was in his unit."

"Mr. Parker looks sort of different," she replied.

He laughed. "He's part Crow."

She nodded. "Yes. One of Custer's scouts was part Lakota; Mitch Bouyer, who died with him at the Little Bighorn. His best friend was Thomas Leforge, who wrote a book entitled *Memoirs of a White Crow Indian*. He lived with the Crow people. It was a fascinating book!"

He knew his jaw had dropped.

She glanced at him. She laughed. "I love that period of history," she explained. "I've read everything I could find on the Battle of the Little

Bighorn, including eyewitness accounts by the Native Americans who fought there. Isn't it amazing," she added, "that people of the period said there were no eyewitnesses left alive, when there were literally hundreds of Native Americans of many tribes who fought in the battle?"

"I know what you mean," he said. "It was a particularly sad period in our history."

She nodded. "It's painful to look too deeply into those fights. But I had a history professor who told me that we should never judge the past by the morality of the present. You have to judge by the morality of the time period. That's never easy."

"We learn as we grow," he agreed. "Our time period isn't perfect, but we're a hell of a lot better than we were a century ago."

She smiled. "I think that, too."

"I always loved history," he remarked. "I studied it in the military. Dad wanted me to go to law school, but I needed business courses to keep the companies operating in the black. I majored in business, minored in economics and marketing."

Cassie had majored in history, but she wasn't going to mention it. He might wonder why a woman who'd gone to college was waiting tables. "Dad said you deal more in oil than you do in cattle," she said.

"That's true. I inherited the cattle. But I made a

fortune in oil by speculating and taking chances," he replied, chuckling.

"I've never taken a chance in my life," she murmured. Actually, she had—coming out west incognito with her dad.

"I never used to. Then I went into the Army." He sighed and shook his head. "My dad and I fought it out, because he wanted me to go to college first. I wanted experience." He glanced at her. "I got my way. Wished I hadn't, too. I'd heard all these stories about combat, about how noble it was." He laughed. It had a hollow sound. "I had a buddy, Rick. We went through basic training together and ended up in the same company. We both came from rural backgrounds and we pretty much agreed on life and politics, so we spent our liberties together." His eyes had a faraway look as he stared over the fence at the little calves, as if he wasn't really seeing them. "We shipped out to Iraq. We were slated for an incursion into enemy territory, to take care of some insurgents who were standing off and taking potshots at us." He drew in a long breath. "It wasn't until we closed on them that I noticed one man was drawing back to throw something. Before I could say a word, Rick went up in the air, as if he'd been tossed by a giant hand. He died instantly."

"Oh, my gosh," she said softly.

"The insurgents moved up behind their

grenade-tossing front man. We had to call in reinforcements before we could recover our casualties." He winced. "There wasn't a lot of Rick left. . . ."

She slid her hand over his where it rested on the gate. His fingers curled around it. She could feel the tension in him. "So that was my introduction to the 'noble' art of war. There's nothing noble about it. There's fear and terror and grief and blood." He smoothed his hand over hers. "I took a round in the shoulder, fortunately not a fatal one, and got sent home because I was so close to being discharged. So Dad finally got his way after almost four years. I did go to college, after all."

She laughed softly. "I'm sure your dad was happy about that."

"Until I fought overseas, I wasn't sure I wanted to keep the ranch," he said, surprising her. "But when I came home, and settled back in, the very peace of it was comforting. Animals and people depending on me, needing me." He shrugged. "It was a new concept. I got used to it."

"I used to take care of Mama when she was sick," she said. "She never asked me to. She was always trying to convince me that she could take care of herself, even when she couldn't. She was a sweet, kind person. It wasn't right, what happened to her."

"I still think you have a potential lawsuit there," he remarked.

"It's like my father said, we aren't that sort of people," she said, heading off trouble. There was no way she could bring a lawsuit without going back east and blowing her cover. It would bring the weight of the media right back down on them all over again.

He looked at her with affection. "You feel things deeply, don't you?"

She nodded. "My dad always said I was too sensitive to live in the real world. I take things hard."

"Like ignorant men making fun of you for being overly dramatic, when you were gasping for breath," he said with a wry smile.

"Oh, I didn't blame you," she said, looking up into soft brown eyes. "I'm sure it looked like I was overreacting."

"I should have known better," he replied. He brushed back her disheveled red-gold hair with a gloved hand. "You hold things inside."

"I never wanted to worry Mama, so I had to. She was even more sensitive than I am." She sighed. "I miss her."

"You've still got your dad."

"Yes. My biggest blessing."

"He has a very cultured voice," he said abruptly. "I don't think I've ever heard one quite like it, except for radio announcers. I don't guess he ever worked for a radio station?"

She laughed and tried to make it sound natural.

"No. I've always thought he had the voice for it, too."

"What did he do, before he came out here?"

"He was a businessman," she said. "He worked for a corporation that marketed commodities." Well, it had, she rationalized, it marketed entertainment.

"And here he is in Benton, Colorado, selling farm and ranch equipment," he observed.

"It's an honest living," she told him. "At least he isn't holding up convenience stores to swipe chicken burritos." She recalled that last item from a movie she'd loved—*Battleship*—and she burst out laughing.

He looked down at her with howling amusement. "There was this movie . . ."

"Yes!" she laughed. "They ended up fighting aliens in a World War Two battleship, aided by the former crew!"

"It's one of my favorites," he confessed.

"Mine too, and nobody in my whole family was ever in the Navy. My people were Army all the way, through all the wars."

He laughed. "My family was strictly Marines."

"I won't hold it against you," she said with a wicked grin.

He sighed and shook his head. "I knew you'd be one of those, the first time I saw you," he mused.

"One of those?"

"Madcap people," he explained. "Outrageous and funny."

"Thanks. I think."

"Oh, it's a compliment," he said, turning back toward the aisle. "I tend to like outrageous people."

"So do I," she said, as she fell into step beside him. "Do you like superhero movies?"

"Love them."

"How about cartoon movies?"

He stopped halfway down the aisle and turned to her. "Cartoon movies?"

"*Moana*," she said. "*Lilo and Stitch. How to Train Your Dragon. Despicable Me.*"

"Oh, those." He chuckled. "I don't watch many of them. I did watch *Moana*. We had a guy from New Zealand who worked here when it came out, a Maori. He dragged us all into the theater to see it. He was right. It was spectacular. Besides," he added, "it had The Rock."

"The what?"

"The Rock," he repeated. "Don't tell me. You've never watched wrestling."

"Dwayne Johnson!" she exclaimed. "That Rock!"

He grinned. "Yes. That Rock."

"Isn't he awesome?" she sighed. "He could stand on a stage and read the telephone directory, and I'd buy a ticket. He's gorgeous."

"Women do love him. Men admire him because

he's so accomplished. An athlete and an actor, a very unusual combination."

"Dave Bautista's in *Guardians of the Galaxy*," she pointed out. "He was a wrestler, too, and he's a terrific actor."

"Nice, that we like the same ones," he returned. "Although, we have to keep in mind that you haven't climbed Mount Everest."

"Oh, I always keep that in mind," she agreed. "Do you have more calves?"

"Lots, but they're out in the pastures and I don't run polled cattle."

She stopped and looked up at him with wide, curious blue eyes.

"They all have horns," he explained.

"So?"

"So," he said, taking her gently by the shoulders, "mama cows are very protective of their babies, and some of them can be aggressive. We don't take chances our guests will get hurt."

"I see."

"But there's still the bottle calves," he added.

Her eyes lit up.

"Not today," he said, smiling. "I have a business meeting in Dallas on Monday, and I have to get to the airport early in the morning, so I'll have time to talk to some other investors over the weekend. How about next Saturday?"

"I'd love that," she said, her feelings spilling out of her like foam out of a latte.

"I would, too," he replied. He smiled. "I'll pick you up about noon and Bessie can fix us lunch."

She grimaced. "Saturday. I have to work!"

"Sunday," he amended.

She nodded. "Sunday's fine."

"I never mentioned how good those rolls were that you made me," he said. "Drum came in to ask a question, smelled the air, and promptly grabbed three and took them with him. They were delicious."

"I'm glad you liked them," she said, feeling warm inside.

"What would you like from Texas?" he asked.

"A longhorn?" she ventured.

He gave her a long-suffering look. "Something I can get on an airplane."

"Peanuts?"

That took him a minute. He burst out laughing. "Hell. I'll bring you something unexpected."

"Okay," she said, grinning up at him.

He was still laughing when he dropped her off at her home. He drove away feeling new, reborn. It was as if the past few months hadn't even happened. He was already looking forward to the next weekend.

"Did you have fun?" her father asked over supper.

"Lots," she replied. "They caught the wolf who's been bringing down their calves."

"Oh? Did they shoot it?"

"No. It's an old wolf, almost blind. There's a local wildlife rehabilitator who's going to adopt it."

"That's nice. Not what I expected from ranchers, I have to confess," he added.

"JL's not your average rancher," she said. "The rehabilitator only has one arm. He and this guy named Parker who works for JL were overseas in combat."

"So was JL, I hear."

She nodded. "He talked about it, just a little. He lost his best friend to a grenade."

"Damned shame, what young men and women have to go through when they join the military," he replied. "Not that I didn't try to join," he added ruefully and with a smile. "I had a bad heart valve. I tried more than once, but they wouldn't let me in." He grimaced. "The valve's still bad, and I've never had a minute's trouble from it. Go figure."

"Rules are rules."

"So they say."

"I'm going back over to the ranch for lunch next Sunday," she told him. "I'll make sure you've got something nice cooked before I go."

His eyebrows lifted. "Getting serious?"

"Trying not to," she said. "He isn't ready to get involved again, and I'm not sure I should. We've still got the scandal hanging over us. JL would think I'd been deceptive because I didn't level with him about why we're out here. But I can't risk telling him, in case he let it slip."

"I can feel your pain. I'm the same. I'm afraid to open my mouth."

"She's getting away with it all," she said angrily. "It's not right."

"I've got Jake working on things back in Manhattan," he said unexpectedly.

"Your attorney?" she asked, surprised.

He nodded. "He's asking questions. He thinks there may be a way to make her confess."

"That would take a miracle," she said.

"Don't ever discount miracles," he said affectionately. "Trudy Blaise has enemies. One of them used to be a television producer in Los Angeles. He got fired for harassment and she got his job."

"Why does that sound so familiar?" she asked with biting sarcasm.

"And it may not be the only instance of malfeasance. People who cause problems to get ahead generally use the same scheme over and over, because it works. But it can be a deal breaker if it gets found out."

"Oh, how I hope it gets found out!"

"Me too," he agreed. "At least, there's a little light at the end of the tunnel. All we have to do is be patient and wait for developments."

"Patience is hard," she said.

"I know. But we don't have much choice."
He grimaced. "I'm so sorry that I didn't see it
coming. I'll never stop blaming myself for what
happened to your mother. If I'd just given in, at
the very beginning . . . !"

"Don't do that," she told him firmly. "Neither
of us realized what she might do. She never told
us about the scathing things people were saying
to her on social media. She took those comments
to heart and let them eat at her. What she did
was in a moment of depression and madness. It
was an impulse that arose out of mental torment.
We'd have stopped her if we'd known. But she
never said a word."

"She was like that," he recalled sadly. "Always
putting other people first, in everything. I just
wish she'd told me."

"We can't go back," she replied. "We have to
go ahead, however difficult it is."

"I know. It's just . . ."

"I miss her, too," she said softly.

He managed a smile. "Yes. So do I."

They watched the evening news on the little
television set with no real enthusiasm. One
particular news item caught their attention. It was
just a quick note, running across the bottom of
the screen on the scrolling news items. It said
that one of the writers on the television program
Cassie used to write for had met with a terrible
accident on a snow-covered lane in Vermont,

where he was spending a week with his wife. He'd died instantly.

"Oh, poor Frank," she said, her face reflecting her sadness. "He was one of the best writers we had. And poor Essa, his wife. They didn't have children. All they had was each other." She sighed and lowered her eyes to the floor.

He patted her hand. "It's rough, what we're going through. But you know what your mother would say."

She nodded. "She'd say that God had a plan, that we were all part of it, and we'd realize one day why things happened the way they did. She was a fatalist."

"I'm sorry about Frank."

"Me too." She glanced at the screen again and noticed that the commentator was speaking about the writer's death. The producers were lamenting that their best writer, CN Reed, had given up "his" job. It was kept quiet, at least to the media, that CN Reed was, in fact, a woman. Everyone she worked with obviously knew she was female.

There was another news item about the *Warlocks and Warriors* weekly series—the one Cassie had written for—concerning its producer. He'd been accused of entertaining an underage girl at his apartment and executives with the network were discussing whether or not to fire him. Trudy Blaise, they added, had been discussed as coming on board at the show.

Gossip was that she might take a position, since the show she'd inherited from disgraced producer Roger Reed was failing in the ratings.

"Failing because she had a hand in it," Cassie said angrily. "She's like poison. She spoils everything she touches."

"Amen," he said quietly. "I'm sorry for your show," he added. "She'll send it to the scrap heap, if they give her that job. I can't understand why they would."

"It was an open secret that Matley Butler liked younger women," she said. "But he never entertained underage girls, and nobody ever accused him of anything. But Trudy could make a meal out of him. All she'd have to do is have someone trick him into a compromising situation and get photos of it and imply that his conquest was underage. The media would feed on the story and ignore anybody who tried to correct her lie, just like they did with you. She's sleeping with her attorney and he has an investigator who's known for dirty tricks," she added.

"So I've heard."

They listened again to the commentator. He was mentioning that a powerful network executive had stepped up to defend Mr. Reed and was adamant that he wasn't the sort of man to ever be indecent to any woman. He'd added an unflattering comment about Ms. Blaise, who seemed to inherit a lot of jobs from executives who were found in compromising situations.

"Kind of him," Roger said quietly. "But he's in the minority. Almost every executive on the network lined up to kick me out the door."

"They've mentioned both our names," Cassie said worriedly.

He drew in a breath. "We're safe out here," he assured her. "Nobody will connect us with the scandal. We're living in one of the smallest towns in Colorado. They won't look for us here."

"That's not what I meant," she said. "What if somebody local sees it on television and realizes it's us?"

"They only used your initials, like they used on the show's credits."

"Yes, but my last name is Reed and they gave your last name as well," she persisted.

He smiled sadly. "We'll have to hope we don't get connected with what happened in New York."

She bit her lower lip. "If JL sees it, he'll think I've been lying to him the whole time, about being poor and all."

"I don't think it would matter now," he replied. He smiled gently. "He's sweet on you. Maybe he doesn't want to be, but I don't think he'd walk away even if he knew the truth."

She grimaced. "I guess I can hope. Can't I?"

"Things will look up. I promise you they will," he said. "We just have to live one day at a time, sweetheart."

"You're right."

"We both have to stop trying to live in the past."

"That's harder."

"Of course it is."

She glanced at him. "Are you really happy out here, Dad?" she asked.

He shrugged. "It isn't as if I have a choice. Nobody in television in New York would touch me after what I've been accused of."

"That producer who defended you might."

"Hartman Spencer," he said, smiling. "He never believed Trudy in the first place. He called her a liar to her face. She just laughed."

"She'll get her comeuppance one of these days," she replied quietly. "You wait and see. Lies always get found out."

"Mostly."

"And that private detective may come up with something really nice to throw at her, especially if she's pulled that trick before."

He nodded.

"We should have made her take you to court," she said suddenly. "She'd have had to prove the charges and she couldn't. During the time she said you were assaulting her, you were in a meeting with the president of the film company and two of its directors."

"The president might be willing to testify to that, but I promise you that the two directors would run for their lives. Nobody sane wants to be sucked into this mess."

"It's not right, that one person can make such an accusation and suddenly get a million people yelling for blood."

"I do agree," he said. He smiled. "We've seen our share of them, for sure."

"What we have to do is fight back," she replied, meeting his gaze. "I don't know how to do it, and we don't have any money . . ."

"My attorney got paid before I got fired," he said. "So he's got the capital to pursue the case. A very wise decision on my part, I must say, considering that I didn't know what was about to happen."

"I like your attorney. He reminds me of those old *Perry Mason* episodes I like to watch on YouTube."

"He does bear a certain resemblance to Raymond Burr," he chuckled.

"He has first editions, and even an illuminated manuscript."

"Yes," he said. "He could retire to Europe and live like a king on what he inherited, but he practices law. He's good at it, too. Mostly he takes cases that no other counselor will."

She smiled. "He's dishy, too," she teased.

"My secretary used to think so," he chuckled. "She said it was fortunate that she was married, because otherwise she'd lie down on the floor in his office and refuse to leave until he took her to dinner."

"She'd have a long wait, from what I heard," she replied. "He went through a bitter divorce. He said he'd never marry anybody again."

"He probably means it. He says that his investigator is hot on the track of some vital information. He wouldn't tell me what it was. I hope it's coming from his investigation of Trudy."

"So do I. I would really hate to see her get away with what she did. Mama would still be alive, but for her!"

"We don't know that," he said unexpectedly. "We're all living on borrowed time, if you think about it. We know that we're going to die eventually. We just don't know when and how. Maybe she was right, and there really is a plan that God has in store for all of us. We die when we're supposed to."

"It's a kind way of looking at it," she said. "I just wish—"

"Yes," he interrupted. "Me too."

Cassie didn't sleep much that night, remembering the horrible accusations Trudy Blaise had thrown at her father in the news media. She'd made friends with one lonely reporter who worked for a major news agency, and she'd fed him pitiful stories about what that lecher Roger Reed had done to her.

It was all an act, all for show. The woman pretended to cry, but there were no real tears, no red eyes, no sign of true misery. Trudy had lied and it had cost Cassie's mother her life. She wasn't ready to talk about forgiveness even if her father was. She wanted to nail the woman's reputation to a tree. She wanted revenge.

But then she thought about how she wasn't telling JL the truth about her past. She sighed, and worried about what he would think if he ever found out. She just prayed that he'd understand that it wasn't malicious that she had to hide the truth.

CHAPTER EIGHT

Cassie went to work the next morning, still a little weak from her bout of bronchitis, but feeling much better.

She was nervous as she hung up her coat and looked around at the customers. She was hoping against hope that nobody local had seen the news last night and made any connections.

She went to work, forcing a smile as she thanked Mary for letting her have the days off to get better.

"I'll work really hard to make up for my lost time," she promised her boss.

"You always work hard," Mary teased. "And it was no trouble at all. We have people who can fill in for you when you're sick. I've never fired anybody for having bronchitis," she added with a grin.

"I appreciate that."

She went to work her tables. Two people were sitting at one of the tables, obviously businessmen. They looked at the menu and barely glanced at Cassie as they gave her their orders. Their accents were definitely New York ones. They must be passing through. Odd, that they'd be in such a small place on a business trip.

As she was turning to leave, she overheard one

of the men say that he'd heard some news last night about one of the writers for his favorite television show dying.

"Hell of a shame, he was really good," the man said. "Of course, I miss having CN Reed on the job. He was a hell of a storyteller. Nice sense of humor in what he wrote. The show hasn't been the same since he left."

Cassie wanted to wait and hear more, but she didn't dare. Eavesdropping could be deadly if the men grew curious about why a waitress was spying on them. She put their orders in and went to another table, where two senior ladies were sitting.

They gave her their orders and she took them down slowly so that she could hear more of what the traveling businessmen were saying. It relieved her that they thought the show's missing writer was a man. Cassie had always used just her initials, because she liked her privacy. Even in Georgia, fans of that show were resourceful enough to find out who she really was and where she lived. There had been a young man who actually stalked her, not for romantic purposes, but to try and wheedle the next month's developments in the show out of her. Fortunately, he'd been harmless and the local police had given him a nice talking to that resulted in no more midnight visits to Cassie's home.

The two men were now discussing a business

associate. Cassie wished they'd had more to say about the scandal. They seemed to know a lot about the program she'd written for. But maybe they were just fans. A lot of people were. The series was very well known.

She came back with their order. They hardly noticed her as they started to eat. She smiled and went back to the counter to get the elderly women's orders. As she walked to their table, she overheard one last remark from the businessmen.

"They say that Trudy Blaise may be replacing the producer who put *Warlocks and Warriors* on the air in the first place. Something about an underage woman he took home with him. She's also alluding to sexual harassment of some kind."

"I thought she was still spouting off about the Reed man . . . ?"

"No. He got fired, remember? She got all the news media involved, as well as several women's rights groups, acted the victim, and put it all out on social media. She got his job. Nobody knows where he went. After his wife's death, he just vanished. Poor guy. Now here's another poor sucker who's going to fall to Trudy Blaise's lies. It's a damned shame."

"Yes," the other man said heavily. "It is. She'll ruin that show. She has no experience at producing. Ratings are falling fast for the program she took over after Reed left. Nobody likes her. One of the stars has already said he's not renewing his contract if it means putting up with her. She interferes in every facet of production. Shame. It was a novel idea, having a weekly series built around a budding singing group's career rise. Not only that but setting it in the seventies with all the accompanying old songs that went with the era. Sheer genius."

"You can pin a rose on that. Reed was a man of vision. I hated seeing him go. I wish Blaise would get hers. I'd love to see it. I wish the media would eat her alive."

"Dream on," his companion said. "Pity about Matley Butler, the *Warlocks and Warriors* producer. She says he's got an underage lover."

"He ought to take her to court and make her prove it."

"Chance would be a fine thing. She's sleeping with one of the best lawyers in New York, and he's working pro bono for her. What a skunk."

"I can think of a better word," the other man replied.

Cassie, hovering, noticed one of the men glancing at her curiously. She smiled, grabbed the coffeepot, and moved beside them. "Can I warm up your coffee for you?" she asked pleasantly.

"Yes, thanks."

She poured hot coffee into their almost empty cups.

"Just passing through, are you?" she asked conversationally.

The older of the two chuckled. "I wish. We took a private plane to see a writer who lives up in Wyoming and it had mechanical failure. So we decided we'd hire a car and drive to the airport in Denver, where they have major airlines." He shook his head. "Give me New York any day! Sorry," he added.

"No offense taken," she said brightly. "Small towns aren't for everyone. A writer who lives near here?" she probed, worried that they might be looking for her.

The shorter man nodded. "Writes western novels. We work for the network that's producing a series based on them. Great writer." He named the man.

"Oh, I've read one of his books!" she exclaimed. "He's really good."

"We think so."

"Well, let me know when you're ready and I'll bring the check."

"Will do."

She smiled again and left them to talk. What an interesting story she was going to have to tell her father. And what an amazing coincidence, to find two New Yorkers involved in television production out here in the middle of nowhere.

"So now she's angling to take over the show you write for," her father said over supper. He shook his head. "She'll ruin it, too. My show has such low ratings that they'll probably never get them back up again."

"Your show was popular because you were the guiding force behind it," she replied. "You had a genius for hiring the best writers for the job, not on the basis of favorites."

"Thanks, sweetheart," he said. "But it was the writers who made the show. They were its heart."

"I'm so sorry about Frank," she said sadly. "I can't even send a card to his wife."

"I know." He made a face. "Not that we've got enough money between us to even send a small bouquet of flowers. When I think of how we used to live . . ."

"We still have each other, Dad," she reminded him. "And there's always hope. The men said that Trudy was probably going to get the executive producer spot on my show. She's got something on Matley. He's such a nice guy." She sighed. "I guess she'll micromanage things and my show will drop in the ratings like a rock, just like yours."

"Maybe we can do something about that in time," he said. "I need to call Jake and see what he's come up with. Think the budget will stand one phone call to New York?"

"Call him on Skype," she teased. "At least it's free."

"Got a point, kid. I'll do that."

• • •

She worried about their names being so prominent on a national news show, but except for the two businessmen—obviously not from Benton but just passing through—nobody had made the connection.

Her father had phoned his attorney, who wouldn't tell him anything except plans were in the works to bring a happy resolution to the problem. They'd have to be patient and let things develop.

Meanwhile, Cassie's phone rang Friday night and she didn't recognize the number. She hesitated and searched her contacts list and almost dropped the phone when she saw the new contact number and realized whose it was.

She fumbled the answer button on. "Hello?" she asked breathlessly.

There was a deep chuckle on the other end of the line. "Didn't recognize the number, I gather?"

"No! And then I saw it on my new contacts list. . . ." She swallowed. "Sorry." She laughed with self-consciousness. "How are you?"

"Lonesome. How about you?"

"Oh, I'm not lonesome," she said. "I have two movie stars and a bagger from the local grocery store sitting on my front porch right now, pleading for company."

"Two movie stars?"

"Yes!" She paused. "One of them plays the

hero's dog on that police show, and the other is the drug-sniffing dog from one of the SWAT reality shows."

He chuckled. "You nut."

"Actually, the bagger would like to take me out," she added. "His girlfriend threw him over last week and he wants to make her jealous, so she'll come back to him. I've been nominated because nobody else in Benton will date him."

He laughed louder. "Oh, the exciting life you lead."

"It's very hectic," she agreed. "I have to mark up calendars so I won't mix up my invitations."

"We still on for Sunday?"

"You bet!" she said.

"I'm looking forward to it. Not much going on here in the big city. Well, sirens, and loud music and whistles—the usual."

"I know," she laughed. She stopped suddenly. "Atlanta was like that," she added quickly when he paused.

"I'd forgotten you lived in a city," he said.

"Just while I worked for the newspaper," she replied. "I like the country sounds much better."

"Me too. I don't mind travel so much. I enjoy foreign places. But I'm always glad to get home."

"Are you still in Dallas?" she asked.

"Dallas? That was last weekend," he pointed out.

"Oh."

"I'm in Paris."

"Paris!" she exclaimed. She'd been there year before last with a girlfriend. They'd spent a week shopping and eating and enjoying the atmosphere. "It must be lovely," she added with a sigh.

"Most cities I visit all I do is end up in hotels and airports," he said wryly. "I did get to visit a vineyard, however, and they didn't even ask me to help stomp the grapes."

"I would love to have a vineyard," she sighed. "I don't even drink wine. I just love to watch grapes grow."

"Where did you see that in Georgia?" he asked, surprised.

"Up in the north Georgia mountains, there are vineyards," she replied. "The soil is really good for growing grapes. Some of the wines win prizes."

"We learn something new every day," he said.

"Yes, we do. Paris. You do get around."

"Business drives the money machine," he said. "I'm talking mergers with a man who lives here but owns refineries in Dallas. It's doing business the long way around," he laughed.

"I guess so."

"I miss you," he said suddenly.

She caught her breath. "I miss you, too," she said, and felt her heart jump.

"About that not getting involved thing," he began.

"But there's still Mount Everest," she interrupted.

He laughed. "Okay. We can talk about mountains when I get home. I'll see you Sunday."

"Be careful in foreign parts," she said. "You never know if you're having coffee next to a Russian spy."

"You watch too many old James Bond movies," he teased.

"No, no, it's the new ones, with Daniel Craig!"

"And they're espionage agents, not spies."

"Have it your way. Just don't get captured."

"We need to talk about spies."

"When you get home," she promised.

There was a lazy affection in his deep voice. "When I get home," he agreed. "I'll see you Sunday."

"Bye," she said.

"So long."

She hung up and caught her breath. She hadn't expected him to call her. It was a surprise, a very nice one. He missed her. She felt lighter than air, happier than she'd been in ages. Life was looking up. Way up!

She wished that she and her father could afford one of the nice cable packages that offered *Warlocks and Warriors,* so that she could keep up with the series she'd written for. She missed being part of it. She missed the other writers, the crew, the actors, she missed all of it.

She'd written for the show for three years. It had been quite a feather in her cap to become even an associate writer. Her father's contacts had given her a boost. Her writing skills had clinched the deal, of course. Even contacts would do nothing for a person with no literary ability. But her father's contacts had certainly helped.

She'd worked for a daily newspaper while she was in college in Atlanta. It had taught her a great deal about communities and how they worked. That insight also helped with her chosen craft. Even medieval communities had much in common with small towns, like the one she'd lived in while she was going to school. Human nature never changed, even if plenty of other things did.

It had been hard, giving up her work on *Warlocks and Warriors*. But the harassment wouldn't have stopped. Her father was leaving town. If she'd stayed, the brunt of the publicity would have shifted to her. It was a no-brainer, that she'd have to go with him. Waiting tables, she thought sadly, with two years of college and three years as a prestigious TV writer working on one of the top series on television. It was a comedown. But she had to be philosophical about it. At least she had a job, and a place to live, and food to eat. The necessities. It would be a learning experience, as much of life was.

She fixed a light supper for her father and herself Saturday night when they both got off work.

"My feet are throbbing," she laughed as they ate chili and corn bread. "I'm still not used to being on them all day."

"It's a comedown, I know," he said apologetically.

"Nobody made me come out here," she pointed out. "You're my dad. We're a matched set."

"Thanks, sweetheart." He finished his chili and sat back to drink coffee. "I wish we could afford satellite," he added wistfully.

She laughed. "I was just thinking how nice that would be," she confessed. "I miss seeing *Warlocks and Warriors*."

"You miss writing for it, too, I know," he said. He grimaced. "I miss being part of a hit TV show as well." He shook his head. "One mean-spirited woman and her lies, and look at the trail of misery she's left behind her."

"It sounds trite, but what goes around does come around," she pointed out. "She won't get away with it forever. Eventually, somebody's going to call her bluff."

"I wish I had," he said. "I could have produced witnesses, even if I'd had to have Jake browbeat them first into testifying. All she had for evidence was a big mouth and accusations."

"Mama always said that God never closed a door, but He opened a window. There's a benefit to anything, if you look for it."

"I'm short on benefits and long on misery," he laughed. "Sorry. It's been a long day. I missed another sale. This time, it wasn't my fault. The customer was willing to buy the machinery. But his bank informed us that he didn't have the price of a roll of paper towels." He sighed. "Just my luck. It would have been a very nice commission."

"There will be other ones," she said. "It's just now technically spring, even though we're still dealing in snow. People will need to replace equipment."

"I guess so."

"Don't get discouraged," she pleaded. "It's early days yet. We'll get through this. No matter how rough it gets, it won't be as bad as what we've already lived through."

"Your grandmother had a saying about that. She said life rewards us in the same measure that it punishes us. Bad things happen, then good things do. It all evens out."

"I'm so ready for good things," she laughed.

"Me too." His eyes twinkled. "I do believe you have a good thing due tomorrow."

She looked blank for a moment until she remembered. "Tomorrow's Sunday. JL's coming to pick me up," she said, and laughed.

"Definitely, a good thing," he teased.

"Definitely!"

JL was ten minutes early. Which didn't matter, because Cassie had been ready for an hour.

He came to the door to get her, carrying a bag from an exclusive store. "I brought you some peanuts from the airplane," he said dryly.

Her eyes widened at the size of the sack.

"A lot of peanuts," he amended.

"Hi, JL," her father said. "Have a good trip?"

"A long one," he chuckled. "I'm always glad to get back home. Well, go on, open it," he prompted Cassie.

She dug into the bag and pulled out a beautiful fringed leather jacket, with beadwork in a colorful and intricate pattern. "Oh," she whispered, admiring it. "It's beautiful!"

"It's warm," he said dryly, and grinned. "No more bronchitis."

Tears stung her eyes. Once, she would have taken such a thing for granted. Now, in her impoverished circumstances, it was almost too much for her. "Oh, JL," she began, her voice breaking.

"You stop that," he said firmly. "You'll be standing here bawling and somebody will come by and next thing you know, the newspaper will have big headlines and I'll be the talk of Benton."

She stared at him. So did Roger.

He gave them a droll look. "They'll see you crying and think I did something to hurt your feelings. Then they'll interview my foreman, who'll tell them what a bad man I am, and it will all go downhill from there."

"Why would your foreman tell them you're a bad man?" she asked blankly.

"Oh, he's jealous," he said easily. "I'm way handsomer than he is, and one of his girlfriends brought me a homemade apple pie once. He's still looking for ways to get even." He gave her an angelic smile.

She and her father burst out laughing, finally getting the joke.

"That's better," JL said. "Put on the jacket and I'll drive you over to see the kittens."

"Kittens?!" she exclaimed. "You didn't say you had kittens!"

"I didn't have them until four days ago. Bessie's got them in the kitchen, where it's warm, along with their mother."

"I love kittens," she remarked.

"You can't have a kitten," her father said firmly. "You're allergic."

"I am not!"

"You are so," he returned.

"I'm allergic to rabbit fur," she countered. "Not cat fur. That's why I was sneezing. It wasn't Ellen's cat, it was her coat."

"Oh." Her father looked perplexed. "Are you sure?"

"I'm sure." She slid into the jacket. "JL, this is the nicest thing anybody's done for me in a long time," she said softly. "I'll make you another pan of rolls!"

He grinned. "I was hoping you'd say that."

"Thanks," she said huskily, and flushed as she met his eyes.

"You're welcome. I'll have her home before midnight," he added to her dad, and chuckled. "But Bessie's working all day and everybody knows it. I'm not going to be the one to blemish Cassie's perfect reputation," he added, just to make the point.

"I appreciate that," Roger said quietly.

JL shrugged. "We should frame her," he mused. "Not many women with pristine reputations left in the world. Not these days."

"And you can pin a rose on that," Roger sighed.

"Stop it or I'm going to blush," Cassie chided.

"Okay," he said, but he was grinning.

"Have fun," Roger said as they were leaving.

"It will be. I'm going to teach her to play chess," JL said.

"Oh, but she . . ." Roger stopped abruptly. He laughed. "She plays checkers very well," he amended, having almost blown her cover. JL might wonder about a waitress who liked a cerebral game like chess.

"I've got a checkerboard," JL said. "We'll try a bit of both. See you later, Roger."

He herded her out to the truck and put her inside. She was admiring the jacket when he climbed in beside her.

She'd noticed that the beadwork wasn't machined. She flushed. This was a very expensive jacket. She'd thought at first that it was something off the rack. She almost remarked about the expense, but then he might wonder how she knew it was expensive. She bit her tongue.

"How was Paris?" she asked.

"Crowded," he sighed as he pulled out into the snow-lined road. "I'm not a social animal," he said. "I don't like high society. I hate brainy people with cocktail mentalities and city manners. You're a breath of fresh air," he added with a warm smile, missing the flush that flamed on her cheeks. "I can't remember the last time I was around a woman who didn't bathe in expensive perfume or wear couture."

She felt guilt all the way to her shoes. He was describing the real Cassie, not this pretender whom he thought he knew. "Not all brainy women wear couture," she said.

He laughed. "Care to bet?" He shook his head. "My ex-fiancée moved in those circles," he said with a cold smile. "She had to have the latest fashions, the most expensive purse. She paid hundreds of dollars to have her hair styled. She read all the popular novels. God, what a bore!"

"I see."

"You're nothing like her," he said, his eyes on the road. "You're a breath of spring. Unspoiled, natural. All I had to do was be around women in Paris at a cocktail party I attended to see the difference." He glanced at her with a warm smile. "I couldn't wait to get home."

"Thanks," she said, hating the guilt she felt.

"One of the attendees was a novelist." He made a face. "She'd just landed at the top of the *New York Times* best-seller list and readers gathered around her like flies around honey." He shook his head. "I don't mind a woman having a mind, I just hate women who think they have to flaunt how smart they are. I don't mean that in a bad way," he added quickly. "I know you worked as a reporter. But there's a world of difference between reporting news and swanning around in couture and preening because you can sell books."

"I like to read," she began.

"Me too. But I don't travel in those circles. I like living in the country, waking up to a rooster crowing, riding out early to see my cattle grazing in the pasture. Things like that. I guess what I'm trying to say is that sometimes rich, successful people live in an artificial world. They're removed from the simple things that make life worthwhile. They buy into a lifestyle that isn't real."

She'd never considered that. In a way, he was right. When she'd worked on *Warlocks and Warriors*, she was a world away from normal people. She'd associated with other writers, with business executives, with people who lived and worked in the city, in high social circles. Her whole family had lived like that.

It was only since she and her father had come to Benton, Colorado, that she realized how artificial that other world really was. She'd lost touch with everyday things, with normal people. And she hadn't even realized it.

"You're very quiet. Have I offended you?" he asked.

"Oh, no! No, of course not!" she said. "I was just thinking about what you said. I guess maybe people in those situations don't even realize how different the world is for those who have to struggle for a living."

"That's what I meant," he said. He laughed. "Nobody could accuse you and your father of being artificial. You live within your means and you don't put on airs. It's what I like best about both of you."

She smiled wanly. "Thanks."

"You're sure you're not allergic to kittens?" he added as he pulled up into his own yard. "Your lungs still sound a bit twitchy."

"I wasn't kidding. It was fur, not cats. Honest. I love cats."

He smiled. "Me too."

They stared at each other for a long moment. Cassie felt her heartbeat skyrocket as his dark eyes fell to her mouth and lingered there. It was so quiet in the cab of the truck that she could hear her own heart beating.

"It's been a long week," he whispered. His big hand slid into the hair at the nape of her neck and tugged, very gently. "And I'm starving. . . ."

She felt his lips, cold from the wind, settle gently on hers, tenderly, so that he didn't frighten her. He was slow, barely touching her as his mouth smoothed over her lips and began to part them.

Her fingers caught in the lapel of his jacket and tightened as he increased the pressure of his mouth. He heard her breath catch, felt her body stiffen, just a little. Then her lips softened under his and she shivered, just slightly.

He drew her completely against him and his mouth ground down into hers. She tasted him, drowned in him, as he explored her slowly warming lips in a silence that was static with feeling.

Finally, his mouth slid against her cheek and into the curve of her throat as he held her and rocked her in the silence.

"Maybe you should forget about climbing Mount Everest," he whispered.

Her heart was beating her to death. "Maybe . . . I should," she managed.

He laughed softly and drew away from her. He liked that little flutter in her breath, the flush in her cheeks, the light that grew in her eyes. "How about coffee and pound cake?"

"I'd love that," she whispered.

He just nodded. There was an expression on his face that made her feel warm and protected and valued. She felt as if her feet didn't touch the ground as they went into the house.

"Oh, my goodness," she exclaimed as they entered the kitchen and she saw what was in the cloth-lined box against the far wall. "They're beautiful! They're all white!"

Bessie chuckled. "White, with blue eyes," she agreed. "We've had white cats here forever."

"They're precious," she said, picking up one of the tiny creatures and cradling it against her cheek.

"They're handy, too," JL remarked as he slid off his jacket and looped it around the back of a kitchen chair. "They keep the mice down in the barn. So you could say that they earn their keep," he chuckled.

"I haven't had a kitten since I was ten," she remarked. "We had a Siamese cat. He was beautiful and absolutely dangerous," she laughed. "He hated dogs. He'd sit outside our apartment when he could get past us and wait for the neighbor to come by with her little Pekingese. Then he'd chase it, and her."

"A vicious cat," he laughed.

"Very. We named him Lucifer. The name really suited him, too." She petted the mama cat, who just looked at her with soft blue eyes and purred. "What's her name?" she asked.

"Should we tell her?" Bessie wondered.

He shrugged. "We call her Lady Godiva."

She frowned. "Why?"

"It should be obvious," he remarked. He leaned closer and said in a stage whisper, "She doesn't wear any clothes!"

Cassie burst out laughing. So did they. She'd never felt so much at home as she did here, in this bright kitchen with two of the nicest people she'd ever met. She thought about what JL had said, about artificial people, and she felt suddenly guilty. She was deceiving him. She hadn't meant to become involved with him, but now that she was . . . how in the world was she ever going to tell him the truth without having him perceive her as the biggest liar in town?

Her face looked stricken as she processed the thought.

He stared at her, frowning. "What's wrong?" he asked suddenly.

CHAPTER NINE

Cassie stared into his dark eyes and felt her cheeks flushing. She turned her attention back to the kitten. "I just had a sudden thought," she replied, and then tried to think of one that might divert him from her guilty expression.

"Something troubling?" he asked softly.

She drew in a breath. "Not really. We had a couple of New Yorkers in the restaurant recently," she added. "They were so glad to escape Benton. I felt sorry for them."

"I know what you mean," he said, relaxing back in his chair. "They can have big-city life, with my blessing. Come eat your cake and drink your coffee, before it gets cold."

"Okay." She put the kitten back with its mother and moved back to the table. "I love cats," she said. "I've always had them. But it wasn't until I went away to college that I was able to have a dog. Mama didn't really like them, but she agreed that I needed a watchdog. She was nervous about having me live off campus in a rented house."

"You didn't live in the dorm?" he asked curiously.

She sighed. "I was afraid I might get put in a coed dorm," she explained. "I guess I'm a throwback to Victorian times, but I don't think single men and women sharing a dorm is decent."

"I love you," Bessie said suddenly. "You can come and live with me and I'll feed you," she added with a grin.

Cassie laughed. "Thanks."

"So few women these days with that attitude," she sighed. She gave JL a speaking look. He gave her one back.

"I'm going to do the wash," Bessie said. "If you hear a big splash, come and pull me out."

"It's just a heavy-duty washer," JL repeated. "And it's not big enough that you can fall in."

"What do you know?" she retorted. "You've never seen it except from a distance. You're afraid of it," she accused with a grin. "Go on. Admit it."

"I don't do laundry," he said haughtily.

"Lucky you, that I do," she replied. "And lucky you, that you don't have to get grass stains and mud stains and cow poop stains out of your jeans!"

He gave her a long-suffering look. "I tell you how much I appreciate you, twice a day."

She shrugged. "I guess you do. Remember: big splash, come save me."

He waved a hand at her.

Cassie was laughing. "You two," she said with a tolerant look. "She's a treasure."

"I think so." He finished his coffee. "Want to see the bottle calves?"

"Oh, yes!"

"Finish up and we'll go."

The calves were big. She laughed as they bumped her and knocked her off-balance in their eagerness to get close to her.

"They're so sweet!" she exclaimed.

"They're pretty tame," he replied. "We all pet them."

She smoothed her hand over one's head. "I could learn to love cattle."

"Could you?" he asked with a secretive smile. "I'm going to have a party next weekend. Just a few friends, good food, dancing. Will you come?"

"Oh, yes," she agreed at once.

The smile widened. "I was hoping you'd say that."

"Were you? Why?" she asked absently, smoothing her hand over the muzzle of another calf.

"You'll find out," he said. "And I'm not telling."

Her eyes were a soft, curious blue. "It's a secret party?"

"Very much so."

"Special occasion?"

He pursed his lips. "I'm hoping it will be."

"Now I'm very curious!" she laughed.

"You'll have to wait and see."

She laughed. "Okay."

He drove her home after dark. They'd had fun, listening to music and finding that they had similar tastes in it, playing chess—although she pretended that she knew little about it. They even talked about television shows they liked, although his ran to old western movies, biographies, and nature specials. They had a lot in common. Even on tricky issues like politics and religion. She felt more and more at home with him. He didn't say much, but it was obvious that he was feeling something similar.

"I have to go to California for a meeting, and then to Dallas again, for another, and then to New Orleans," he said heavily. "I don't want to," he added gently, staring at her intently in the partial light from the house's porch light. "But business keeps the coffers full, so to speak."

"I understand," she said, not adding that she'd had to travel, too, while she was writing for *Warlocks and Warriors*.

He took her hand in his and drew the palm to his lips. "I didn't plan to get involved with you," he said softly.

"I didn't plan to get involved with you, either," she confessed. "There are reasons, good reasons, why. We need to talk about them."

"Okay. But not now," he chuckled. "I'm going to be running my legs off for a few days. We'll talk Saturday, all right? I'll pick you up about five." He frowned. "I told everybody semi-formal. . . ."

"I have one good cocktail dress," she interrupted. "I got it from the thrift shop at the college earlier this year," she lied. "It's very nice."

He hesitated to say what he was thinking, that if his cousin Cary brought one of those sophisticated women he liked to date, the woman might savage Cassie for a cheap dress. But he didn't say it. She was proud. He'd have offered to buy her a dress, but he knew already that she'd never accept it. "Don't worry about it," he told her. "You'll look fine. My pretty girl," he whispered, and drew her close to kiss her softly, warmly. "I'll miss you."

"I'll miss you, too," she whispered back.

He kissed her again, not softly, with a passion that started fires inside her, that brought her arms hard around his neck, propelled her close, as close as she could get, and yet still not close enough. She moaned under his devouring mouth.

He came to his senses just as he was sliding his hand inside her jeans. This was not the time or place. He drew back, breathing hard. "We really have to talk, soon," he said huskily.

She nodded, her eyes wide and fascinated, her body throbbing.

"When I get back," he said.

"Yes."

He touched her cheek gently. "Five, Saturday."

"I'll be ready."

"He's throwing a party?" her father mused.

"Yes. He said it was a special occasion, but he wouldn't tell me what it was," she added.

He chuckled. "People in small towns talk. A lot. Sometimes you overhear things they wouldn't tell you."

"Oh? Like what?" she asked as she put dishes of food on the table.

"Such as the fact that a certain reclusive rancher walked into the local jewelry store and bought a diamond ring."

Her heart jumped. So did her hand. She almost upended the gravy boat. "Oh?" she repeated, and felt like a parrot. "For himself?"

He shook his head and grinned. "It was an engagement ring. Rumors are flying."

"Was it JL?" she asked.

He nodded.

She sat down, hard. "Wow."

"So I have a hunch about the reason for that party next Saturday."

Her heart lifted. Soared. Crashed. Her face was tragic. "He doesn't know about us," she said miserably.

"You need to tell him the truth," her father said gently. "I don't think it will matter. Really I don't. But he should hear it from you. And soon, just in case anybody local did connect that news broadcast with us."

"You haven't heard anything . . . ?"

"No. We're pretty isolated here, and we don't stick out as famous people. I'd know, if anybody suspected. People are honest and straightforward here. Somebody would say something."

She relaxed, just a little. "Okay. I'll tell him Saturday."

He smiled. "It will be all right. I know it will." He cocked his head. "Can you live in Benton, Colorado, you think?"

She laughed. "Oh, yes. Even if I went back to writing scripts, I could still go to New York when I need to. He's not a controlling sort of man. It will be a good life. What about you?" she added.

"I may go home and put up a fight," he said solemnly. "Something I should have done before. I was too distraught after your mother's death to do that." His face set in hard lines. "Trudy Blaise shouldn't be allowed to get away with what she's doing."

"Jake will help you expose her," she said firmly.

"We'll see how it works out. Your happiness is the most important thing to me. JL's a good man. He'll take care of you."

She smiled. "I'll take care of him, too."

She went to work, cooked, cleaned, talked to her father, and watched the days go by with maddening slowness. Time stood still, she thought, when you were anticipating something wonderful.

Her mind was on JL so much that he seemed to be with her all the time. He phoned her at least once a day, just to talk. Sometimes twice a day. She walked around feeling as if her feet weren't even touching the ground. She'd never really loved a man until now. It was overpowering with its intensity, its sweetness. The idea that she could live with JL, sleep in his arms every night, give him children, made her feel complete, as if she'd been only half a person before.

That Saturday, she fussed over her one good cocktail dress. Her father overheard her talking to herself and peeked in, chuckling. She had the dress on a hanger and she was picking it to pieces.

"He's inviting you over, not the dress," he emphasized. "If he'd wanted to concentrate on the dress alone, I'm certain that you wouldn't have been included in the invitation."

She laughed helplessly. "You're right. It's just, I want everything to be perfect. Mary even gave me the day off, and she had that same secret smile I saw on Agatha's face. It seems to be an open secret."

"I imagine it is," he replied. He glanced at the clock on the wall. "Two hours to go," he said.

She let out a sigh. "I've been grinding my teeth all week because time was so slow. Now I'm going to have to hurry to get dressed in time!"

"That's life," her father said dryly, and left her to it.

He smiled with pure delight when she came into the living room. The cocktail dress fit her nicely, but it was conservative and still in style. Her long red-gold hair was swept up in an exquisitely tricky hairdo that was held in place with jeweled hairpins. Her feet were in dainty black leather high heels with ankle straps. She wore a thick, black, wool crocheted shawl over it because she didn't have a good coat, and the beautiful fringed jacket JL had brought her wasn't quite dressy enough for this rig.

"Will I do?" she asked her father.

He chuckled. "You certainly will. You remind me so much of your mother's mother. She wasn't a redhead, but she had the same grace and poise that you do. Your mother would be proud tonight."

She smiled sadly. "I wish . . ."

He kissed her forehead. "Me too, sweetheart. I hope you have the time of your life tonight. And I won't expect you early!"

She laughed and kissed his cheek. "I'm so excited, I can hardly bear it!"

"I'd wish you luck, but you won't need it." He lifted his head and listened. "And I believe your enchanted carriage is coming up the driveway."

"Disguised as a pickup truck," she laughed wickedly.

He parted the curtains and whistled. "Apparently not."

She looked out over his shoulder and caught her breath. "Well!" she said.

"Unexpected. But not entirely," he replied, and grinned.

She walked out the door. JL was getting out the back door of a super-stretch black limousine, its liveried driver holding the door for him. He had a box in his hand. He was wearing evening clothes, no hat, and he looked devastatingly handsome.

He was doing some looking of his own. Cassie looked beautiful, and very sexy, in the nicest sort of way. He smiled and couldn't stop.

"Here," he said, handing her an orchid. "It's going to be an enchanted evening, however trite that may sound."

"Not trite at all," she assured him. She took the orchid out of its box and slid it onto her wrist. "I'll press it in a book, afterward," she said with breathless delight, and met his eyes. "I'll keep it forever."

His breath caught. She was so real, so innocent, so honest. He couldn't believe how perfect she was. And she was all his, if he wanted her. He did. He'd never wanted anyone so much, least of all his ex-fiancée.

"We can talk about that forever thing, after the party," he said softly. He brought her hand to his lips and kissed it lightly. "Shall we go?"

Her whole face smiled at him. "Let's."

It was the sort of gathering she was used to. She'd been to numerous cocktail parties in New York, and she was used to eating in five-star restaurants, sipping champagne, having the most expensive hors d'oeuvres. She mingled with his guests, most of them businessmen who were his friends, and she fit in effortlessly.

He saw that, and it disturbed him. She was too much at home here. How could a waitress from a small Georgia town feel so comfortable in what was an alien environment?

Cassie didn't notice his expression. She was meeting people, socializing as she was used to doing, drawing out people by asking them to talk about themselves. Authors were, by nature, introverts. But she'd had to learn to be outgoing when she started work for the weekly newspaper outside Atlanta. It had been a good preparation for what came afterward.

JL nursed a whiskey and soda and frowned as Cassie mingled with his guests. One was missing. He was still uncertain about inviting Cary, after the slight run-in his cousin had with Cassie, but he took the chance anyway. Cary was, after all, the only family he had left in the world. It was fitting that he should be here when JL announced his engagement to Cassie. It would also be a way of letting Cary know that he held no grudges about Cary's part in breaking his former engagement.

He was growing certain that Cary wouldn't show up when the man walked in the door with, of all the damned people in the world, JL's ex-fiancée. He pushed away from the bar, where he'd been leaning, and glared at his cousin with flaming brown eyes. Damn the man!

Cary approached them with a nervous smile. What had seemed like a neat little stab in the heart to pay his cousin back for taking Cassie away was feeling more like Waterloo. JL glared at him. Cassie, unaware, at first, of who the sophisticated woman with Cary really was, smiled as she joined JL.

"Hi, Cuz," Cary said. "Marge was in town on business so I thought I'd bring her along." He smiled at Cassie. "This is Marge Bailey," he said. He pursed his lips with a faint glint in his eyes. "JL was engaged to her a few months ago."

Cassie felt all the joy and excitement drain out of her with the words. She knew the name. She recognized the woman, and not because she'd been JL's fiancée. Marge Bailey was in advertising. Cassie had been in a meeting with her and network executives about advertising for *Warlocks and Warriors*. She felt her stomach drop. So far, Marge hadn't recognized her. Hopefully, she wouldn't.

But even without that unexpected complication, she knew how hard it had been for JL to get over the woman. And here was Cary, throwing her in his face. What a dreadful thing to do! Why was he doing it?

"Hello, JL," Marge said with a tight smile, ignoring Cassie.

"You're here on business?" JL replied tersely.

"An advertising campaign for a new client. I was . . ." She stopped and stared at Cassie, recognizing her all at once. "My gosh, I know you! My company did the advertising for *Warlocks and Warriors*! It's my favorite show! You and I met at a meeting in New York," she said, stunned. "They were talking about you on a news show a few days ago. Well, it was about your father, of course, but they mentioned that you'd resigned as a writer for *Warlocks and Warriors*. Now that Frank's dead, they have to be missing you!"

JL seemed to turn to stone. His eyes slid around to Cassie. "Writer for *Warlocks and Warriors*?" he asked with a bite in his deep voice. Like most television viewers, he knew the show. It was in its sixth season, one of the most successful dramas in the history of cable.

Cassie felt her heart fall to her feet. The jig was up, it seemed. She glanced at Cary and saw the guilt in his face as he averted his eyes. The beautiful woman at his side was more surprised than guilty as she glanced from JL to Cassie. Cary had told her about JL's new friend and the engagement rumors before they arrived.

"Surely you knew?" she asked JL. When he didn't answer, she looked at Cassie. "I can't imagine how your father thought he'd outrun the scandal, even by coming all the way out here to a small town in Colorado. I read all about the case. He was charged with sexual harassment of several women, of trying to force himself on Trudy Blaise. . . ."

"He did nothing of the sort," Cassie said sharply. "Trudy Blaise has played that hand one time too many. After the accusations were made, my mother was hounded to death by the media, by so-called friends on social media as well. The pressure was too much for her. She committed suicide because of Trudy's lies. People who cause tragedies incur tragedies. Ms. Blaise's moment is coming," she added icily. "And it's coming soon! My father can prove his innocence. His attorney is already working on it."

"Your mother committed suicide?!" Marge's face closed up. "I knew that she died. I didn't know how. I honestly didn't know. I'm sorry."

"Well . . . this is awkward," Cary began slowly.

"Not so awkward for you, I'm sure," Cassie told him with heat in her tone. Her blue eyes were flashing like lightning in her pale face. "You planned it right down to the last detail, didn't you?"

Cary flushed. He tugged at his collar. "Listen, I never meant—"

"I wish we were in a less public place," Cassie said. "I'd put you on the floor and stomp on you!" Her lower lip trembled. "You worm. You despicable worm!"

JL's dark eyes were full of ice. "Cary isn't the one living a lie," he said to her. "I think it's time you went home, Ms. Reed."

Cassie wanted to argue, to plead, to explain. JL was so rigid that she knew it was hopeless. The light went out of her eyes. The evening that had begun with such promise had ended in tears.

"Okay," she said quietly.

He moved away and signaled the driver, who was sitting with a book in the corner.

The man came at once.

"Drive Ms. Reed home, if you please," JL told the man. He didn't look at Cassie. He didn't offer to go with her. He didn't say another word.

Music was playing and one couple was already on the makeshift dance floor. JL took Marge by the hand and led her out into a two-step. He smiled at Marge, his attention completely on her.

Cary drew in a breath. "I'm . . ." he began.

"Spare me," Cassie said coldly. "Someday you'll get what you deserve, Cary. I won't be around to see it, but your day's coming."

She turned on her heel and walked out the door, with the driver right behind her.

When she walked in the door, her father knew immediately that something terrible had happened.

"What is it?" he asked gently.

She fell against him, tears blinding her. "Cary brought JL's ex-fiancée to the party," she sobbed. "I know her. She works in advertising and her company did a campaign for *Warlocks and Warriors*. She told JL all about us."

"I should hire a hit man for JL's cousin," he muttered, patting her on the back. "I'm so sorry!"

She had to get through the tears to speak rationally. When she was calmer, she made coffee and they sat at the kitchen table together.

"We have to go back," he said after a minute. "I spoke to Jake just before you came home. He's got solid evidence that Trudy's done this before, and he has witnesses who'll testify. He's filing suit against her in my behalf for defamation of character and making malicious false allegations that cost me my job and held me up to public embarrassment. One of her victims is coming all the way from LA to testify." He smiled sadly. "The network has also been working behind the scenes to substantiate her allegations and their investigations have cleared me. It looks as if I'll go back to work. If that happens, you can also go back to work. With Frank gone, you'll be welcomed with open arms. I'm sure of it."

She thought of the restaurant where she'd worked, the nice people who'd been so good to her. She thought of JL and Bessie and the dreams that had made a silver web around her as she contemplated a beautiful future on that ranch with the man she loved. All of that would be left behind.

JL, of course, wouldn't miss her. He was hurt and angry and wouldn't even speak to her. He'd gone straight to Marge, probably to wound his cousin for bringing her. Maybe they'd end up back together after Cary's mischief. Maybe they'd be happy.

She hoped sincerely that someday Cary fell in love with a woman who tore him up like Marge had torn up JL. There had been too many lies. Too many false statements and cruel words.

None of that helped her situation. She couldn't stay here. Not now. Everybody would know the truth. It would be hard to live down in a small town. First her father had to prove his innocence, beyond a shadow of a doubt. When he did, and it was publicized, perhaps people here would think kindly of the strange Easterner and his daughter who'd lived among them for such a short time.

"I'm going back with you," Cassie said quietly. "There's nothing left for me here."

"JL might listen to you when he cools off."

She laughed hollowly. "He looked at me as if I were dirt, and then he made a beeline right back to his ex-fiancée, if only to put the knife in his cousin's ego. No," she added softly. "He'd never trust me again. He'll think I lied about everything deliberately. You can't build a life on lies. We've certainly found that out, and so will Trudy Blaise. Besides," she said firmly, "it will be nice to get back to work, doing what I do. JL thought of me as a plain, no-frills country girl. I'm not. He never knew the person I am. It's just as well." She forced a smile. "If we can get Trudy Blaise in as much trouble as you were in, that will be worth giving up Benton, Colorado," she said with a cold laugh.

"That much, I think I can promise you." He grimaced. "I'm so sorry, Cassie."

She fought tears. "Me too. Life happens. Then we pick up the pieces and go on."

"Yes," he said. "We do."

After all the turmoil of the past few months, the solution to Cassie's and Roger's problems came quickly and all the furor died abruptly. Trudy Blaise was actually arrested on charges of embezzlement, of all things. She'd created a false vendor account, with the help of her attorney (who was facing disbarment), and pocketed assets to which she wasn't entitled. As it turned out, she'd done the same thing in LA, as her former boss testified to a grand jury. She hadn't been prosecuted for that crime, but she would face charges for it after an investigation had uncovered her illegal enterprise as producer of another program originating in LA.

Not only was she facing jail time for conversion of property, but she was also looking at defamation charges from both Roger and three other men. As part of a plea deal, she agreed to go on the air and refute her charges against Roger and her former boss, and make apologies on air as well as in all her social media accounts.

Roger was cleared in a firestorm of political activism. At least one group made a public apology for its part in the death of Mrs. Reed. The others, of course, conceded only that occasionally, very occasionally, charges were made erroneously. It was politics as usual.

Cassie did return to work as a writer for *Warlocks and Warriors*, but she moved back to Atlanta, into an apartment complex where she'd lived before she bought the house that she'd put on the market when the scandal broke.

Sadly, she had to part with her dog, whom she'd left with a neighboring family once the scandal forced her to leave town. The apartment allowed only for dogs under thirty pounds, and hers had been a beautiful purebred neutered German shepherd named Josh who weighed over ninety pounds.

Happily, however, the family who adopted her pet promised to let her visit Josh when she wanted to.

She settled back into her job and watched spring become summer without any particular enthusiasm. She hadn't kept in touch with people in Benton because she didn't want to hear about JL and Marge. She was certain that they were back together now, if only to pay Cary back for his interference.

It had been such a sweet dream, thinking that she and JL would get married and live happily ever after on the ranch. A silly dream, as it turned out. She should have told him the truth in the very beginning. But they hadn't been headed for anything more than friendship when it started, and she was reluctant to clutter up their relationship with painful revelations about her father's past.

She was lonely. Lonelier, now, with memories of happier times stabbing her in the heart. She'd been so excited when her father told her about JL buying a diamond ring.

Marge was probably wearing the ring by now.

She had to go to New York for a writers' discussion about *Warlocks and Warriors*. She arranged to have lunch with her father at the Four Seasons near his office. He was back in charge of the hit show about a seventies singing group's rise to fame. He'd been completely exonerated of any charges relating to Trudy Blaise, who had plenty of problems of her own making, and he told Cassie that he wasn't even speaking to women on his staff unless it was work-related and in the company of coworkers. She thought how sad the world had become. Harassment was terrible. But so was creating an atmosphere of artificial coldness that denied any warm human feelings at all, in the effort to head off charges of misconduct. Lies and malice were toxic, and could ruin everything. She'd seen it with Trudy Blaise, with Cary lying to his cousin . . . and worst of all, she blamed herself for not being upfront with JL.

Cassie sat listening to her colleagues go over a necessary plot change because one of their actors had been injured in an accident. They'd have to write around him while he got through the aftermath of the mishap and into a cast for his broken leg. They solved the problem with a created injury in the series to compensate for his lack of mobility.

"And aren't we the creative geniuses?" Derry, a female coworker chuckled as they finalized the change.

"We're writers," Cassie said with a wicked grin. "It's who we are."

"Most of us," Ted, another writer, murmured dryly.

Angela, the live wire of the group, gave him a mock glare. "I am so a genius," she shot back. "In fact, I can prove it. Only this morning at a coffee shop, I instructed a barista in how to make change from a five without taking off her socks."

Everybody roared.

"And for that," Ted countered, "you could be sued for character assassination."

He realized belatedly that Cassie was in the group, and remembered what she and Roger had been through. "Sorry," he said at once, and grimaced.

"I am not politically correct," she assured him with a warm smile. "And I haven't ever sued anybody in my life. Yet."

He stood and bowed. "Thank you, my lady, for your kind regard."

She stood and curtsied. "My knight!"

Everybody groaned.

"Peasants," Cassie said huffily.

"And on that note," Angela, who now led the writers' room, said with a grin, "we'll adjourn to lunch. Cassie, coming with us?"

"I'm meeting Dad at Four Seasons," she replied. "But thanks! Rain check?"

"Next time you come to New York," Ted said. "Why don't you move up here? Hot as hell in Atlanta!"

"You get used to it," she said with a lazy smile. "Besides, we have a huge lake nearby. Sailing, hiking, picnic spots, fishing . . ."

"Fishing!" Angela groaned. "Who goes fishing, for God's sake?"

"Me," Cassie said, laughing. "Actually, it's great fun. Yellow flies, mosquitoes, water moccasins, copperheads, smelly worms . . ."

"Please," Angela said. "I'm headed for a restaurant!"

"And speaking of restaurants," Cassie said, "I'm going to have fish!"

"You can't reform misplaced New Yorkers," Ted said, shaking his head. "Fishing!" He rolled his eyes.

"To each his own," Cassie said with a flash of white teeth.

CHAPTER TEN

Four Seasons was crowded, but her father had reservations, so they went right in. Cassie was wearing navy blue slacks with a perky white-and-blue silk blouse and a white sweater. Her hair was up in a complicated hairdo, her small ears dripping gold earrings in a medieval design. She wore small stacked high heels, because everything in Manhattan was a long walk, even after riding around in a company-provided limo.

Roger Reed, in a blue business suit and patterned tie, looked every bit the producer as he rose to greet his daughter, smiling. She hugged him and sat down.

"How's it going?" he asked after they'd ordered.

She smiled. "Fine, fine. We're looking forward to the next season. Lots of twists and turns and surprises for the fans." She glanced at him. "How's your show going?"

He chuckled. "Better than ever. The staff was so happy to have me back that they bought a cake and party hats."

She smiled. "I could almost feel sorry for Trudy Blaise."

"I couldn't," he said flatly. "Her lies caused

your mother's death and tainted the reputations of several of us. She'll get what's coming to her. In fact, she's already had to close down her social media accounts. The people who attacked us are now attacking her."

"Tit for tat," she said quietly. "But all the hate in the world won't bring Mama back."

He nodded, his face sad. "It's been an ordeal. I'm happy things are back to normal. Although, I have to confess that I do sort of miss Benton, Colorado."

Her fork slipped at the mention of the town where she'd left her heart. She picked it back up and didn't look at her father. "I miss Mary and Agatha," she said. "They were kind to me."

He nudged a perfectly cooked piece of steak with his fork before spearing it into his mouth. He sipped red wine before he spoke. "I had a phone call today."

"Did you?"

"From Colorado."

The fork jumped again, but this time she didn't drop it. "Oh."

"From Cary, of all people."

"Cary?" Disappointment welled up in her. Cary had called her father? "How would he have your number?"

"His friend, JL's former fiancée, gave it to him."

The mention of Marge Bailey closed her up like

a sensitive plant. She didn't say a word. "What did he want?"

"To apologize."

She laughed shortly. "He's always sorry after he does something unspeakable."

"This time, he's really sorry. He's living in Denver. His cousin, who really is his last living relative even if not by blood, won't speak to him or have him on the ranch. He's lost his livelihood, his job, his prospects, pretty near everything he had."

"JL didn't seem that vindictive to me," she replied, surprised.

"It wasn't JL. It was the citizens of Benton."

She stopped eating and just stared at him.

"When the truth got out, about what Cary did to you and JL, the whole town turned against him. Nobody in Benton would sell him so much as a cup of coffee. He left in self-defense."

"Well!" She hesitated and lowered her eyes. "What about JL? Are he and Marge married now?"

"Marge is back in New York," he said. "She's still with the advertising agency, but your executive producer and the higher-ups at the network have switched their account to a rival agency."

Her lips parted on a shocked breath.

"You have friends in high places," he mused. "It wasn't Marge's fault, really, but they couldn't get to Cary."

"This gets stranger and stranger," she remarked, sipping wine. "Did JL come with her to New York?"

"He went off on an extended business trip to the Middle East, to talk to his partners in the oil business. At least one major newsmagazine has carried photos of him being entertained by some members of Arab royalty."

"I suppose he'll make even more money," was all she said.

"He phoned me, too."

She dropped the glass. It was unfortunate, because she was wearing a lacy white sweater over her silk blouse and it stained at once. She wiped at it and just gave up, when she saw the hopelessness of it all.

"He said he might come back to the States if he thought there was any chance that you could forgive him for the way he treated you," he continued, as if the accident hadn't happened. "He said it wasn't all Cary's fault. He should have realized that Cary was getting even. He should have spoken to you before he sent you home."

"Yes, he should have," she said with some heat.

"He did mention that if you hadn't kept secrets from him, none of it would have happened the way it did. I was forced to agree with him. I did suggest, if you remember, that it wasn't a good idea not to tell him."

"I was afraid to," she replied. "You know I was, and you know why."

"Yes, I do. But he didn't."

She drew in a long breath. She'd missed JL terribly in the time she'd been back at work. She was empty and cold and alone. She lived in Georgia, all by herself. She came to New York when she had to, for her job, which was why she was in the city right now. She came to see her father. But even writing, which she loved, was no substitute for the tall rancher who'd been a part of her life for such a short time.

"New York and Colorado aren't that far apart by plane," he said. "You could commute from there as easily as you can from Georgia. JL has a private jet, which would make the trip even easier."

She bit her lower lip.

"I'm not pushing," he said gently. "But JL is a fine man. He has wonderful qualities. He was shocked and upset by what Cary said and did that night. It doesn't excuse it, but it does explain it. Nobody's so perfect that they can't be allowed a second chance. That is, if you wanted to give him one."

She looked up, her eyes sad and quiet. "Maybe he just wants to apologize and nothing else, you know," she ventured.

"He could do that in a letter. He wants to see you."

She drew in a long breath. It was a terrible chance to take. She might get over him, in time. She had her work. It was almost enough.

She looked down at her hands and thought how happy she'd been the day her father relayed the gossip that JL had bought a diamond ring for her. She thought about her finger being ringless for the rest of her life.

"You can always tell him to go home."

She looked up at his amused expression. "Yes. I guess I could."

"There's a nice symphony concert tomorrow night. They're playing Debussy. I understand that he likes Debussy very much, and that he has two tickets up front."

"Oh, he does, does he?"

"He only lacks the right partner for the event. And I believe you bought a new gown to wear to the opening of the arts center next month . . . ?"

She laughed, the first humor she'd felt in a long time. "Yes, I did."

"So he said that, if you were willing, he could pick you up at my apartment about six tomorrow evening? He mentioned supper at the Plaza. He has reservations for that, too. And he also mentioned that he was going to look really stupid with empty seats beside him at both those events. He'd be such an object of pity that he might never recover."

Her eyes grew bright with humor. "Well, I suppose I could listen to what he has to say."

"Exactly what I told him."

"Turncoat," she said, but she smiled affectionately when she said it.

"You've been miserable since we got back. So has he. Take a chance."

"I guess I'll have to. But if things don't work out . . ."

"You can have me paged at the airport."

"How would that pay you back?"

"You could tell people that I was a famous movie star traveling incognito, and have me mobbed for autographs," he chuckled.

"In that case, I'll do it."

"That's my girl!"

She tried several times to talk herself out of the date. But she couldn't help herself. She wanted to see JL so much that it was like a fire burning in the pit of her stomach. He was all she thought about, all she dreamed about, all she wanted in life. She pictured herself living on the ranch, traveling with him, rocking their children to sleep at night by a fire in the fireplace. She was miserable alone. Perhaps he was, too. There was only one way she was going to find out, and that was, as her father had said, by taking a chance.

She dressed in her new gown, a pretty beige couture one that fell in folds to the ankle straps of

231

her leather pumps. Her red-gold hair was up again in a complicated coiffure, with her jeweled clips. She wore just enough makeup, without overdoing it. She wore pearls around her neck and in her ears. A gold designer watch was fastened around her wrist. She looked expensive and cultured, which she was. For once, she wasn't in disguise.

The phone rang. The clerk informed her that a gentleman awaited her in the lobby.

She picked up her purse, wished her father good night, and walked out the door.

JL was near the elevators, waiting. His first sight of her produced an expression of pride, of faint possession, of approval.

He smiled slowly. "The real Cassie," he said softly as he approached her.

She smiled back, trying to contain her excitement. He was wearing designer clothing as well, evening clothes in which he looked debonair and very cultured. His thick black hair was uncovered. His face was tanned and handsome. His dark eyes ate her from head to toe. She had to fight to breathe normally.

"The real me," she replied.

"If I start apologizing here," he said softly as he escorted her toward the front door, "maybe by the time we get to the symphony, you'll be in a forgiving mood."

"It was my fault, too, you know," she replied quietly. "I should have told you the truth. I was afraid to. It was so horrible here—"

"It's all right," he interrupted. "You don't have to say a thing."

He paused at a super-stretch black limo, whose driver was waiting with the back door open.

JL helped her inside, and followed her, the driver shutting them in before he went around to get in under the steering wheel.

"I hope you're hungry," he said, smiling. "I came straight here from Saudi Arabia."

"I had a nice salad and light fish for lunch," she replied. "It's worn off."

He chuckled. "I had peanuts."

"You can get those on airplanes!" she exclaimed.

He glared at her.

She laughed. "Sorry."

He laughed softly. "I missed you."

"I missed you, too."

His hand slid over hers and curled into it. "It's going to be the best date we've ever had."

She caught her breath. "Yes."

His hand tightened. Hers tightened, too.

"Marge wasn't any happier with Cary than I was, when she knew who you were," he said. "She gave him the rough side of her tongue. So he turned around and called your bosses, to get even with her. He told them that she'd been rude and obnoxious to you."

"Is that why she lost the account?" she asked, shocked.

He nodded. "She wasn't even sorry about it. She felt guilty about what she let Cary talk her into. She called me and told me what happened. She said she felt even more guilty when she knew how your mother died. There have been too many lies, and mixed messages. Too many deceptions by both women and men. Trudy lied about your dad, Cary lied about Marge, and about you. But justice prevailed." He squeezed her hand. "Trudy is in jail, and Marge will be fine. Cary won't. He's living in Denver now, and nobody back home will speak to him. Especially me."

"He's done a lot of damage," she said quietly.

"More than you know. It's about time he faced the music. I'm not letting him back on the ranch again, ever. He almost separated us for good out of jealousy."

"Who was he jealous of?"

"You and Marge, because you both ended up with me and he felt jilted," he replied. "He's got some real ego issues. Maybe he can deal with them. Whether he can or not, it's not my business anymore. I've had enough of his mischief."

"I can see why." She shook her head. "Maybe I'm lucky that I don't have any extended family living nearby!"

He laughed. "Maybe you are, honey."

She felt her heart expand at the endearment.

She felt warm and protected. She looked up at him with her heart in her eyes and found him staring back at her hungrily. It was a moment out of time, when everything was perfect. Just perfect.

All too soon, they arrived at the exclusive restaurant. When they were seated, poring over the menu, he glanced at her.

He smiled. "I suppose French dishes on a menu aren't intimidating to you."

She laughed. "I speak it and read it. My grandmother was French."

"My great-grandmother was French-Canadian," he told her. "I speak it, too." He lowered his voice. "I know some really sweet words in French."

She flushed.

He laughed. "Sorry. I couldn't resist it."

She laughed, too. "I'm educated, but I'm not worldly."

"And that delights me," he said softly. "It may be a sophisticated world, but innocence has a cachet all its own. I love it that you can still blush."

"I'll bet you can't," she returned.

He chuckled, deep in his throat. "No, I can't. And one day, you may be very happy about that."

She didn't dare reply. She concentrated on her menu instead.

The symphony was delightful. She held hands with JL and soaked up every sweet minute of "Afternoon of a Faun" and *La mer*, two of her Debussy favorites. Afterward, they walked slowly down the sidewalk toward the waiting limousine.

Stars twinkled in the sky above, visible despite all the lights of the city. The faint breeze blew tendrils of her hair around her face.

"It's been a magical night," she said.

"Right out of a fantasy," he replied. "How did you end up writing for a hit television series? Were you really a reporter?"

She nodded. "I loved my job. But Dad mentioned me to a friend, who had a friend, and I submitted some samples of my work. They hired me on the spot. I was terrified. I'd never written scripts, I had no idea what working for a series entailed, and I was scared to death."

"But you adjusted."

"Yes. I adjusted. It's been exciting, maddening, nerve-racking, and horrifying, all at once. But I've loved every minute of it."

"You know, I own a private jet," he remarked, sliding his fingers so that they meshed with hers.

"Do you?" she asked, breathless all over again at the slow, caressing contact.

"So if you lived in Benton," he continued, "it would be easy for you to commute."

She could barely breathe. "Yes, it would."

"We have bitter winters in Colorado, but I have a nice big fireplace and plenty of wood for fires."

"Do you?"

"Not to mention, central heat and air-conditioning as well," he chuckled.

"I see."

He stopped and turned to her, towering over her, even though she was wearing fairly high heels. "I bought you a ring," he said huskily. "I was going to give it to you that night, before Cary came in with Marge and ruined everything."

"I knew."

"How?" he asked, surprised.

"Everybody in town knew. The jeweler told people."

He touched her soft cheek with his fingertips. "I bought one for Marge, but it was different. It was a fever, quickly quenched, even if I did think it was like dying at the time when she left me. But when you left, that was the desert after the oasis. I couldn't eat or sleep. I couldn't rest. I left town, because I couldn't bear to see the places I'd seen you in. So much pain," he added huskily. "And I brought it on myself, because I didn't trust . . ."

She put her fingers over his firm mouth. "We were both at fault. You didn't know me. I didn't try to explain. But that's in the past. That's over."

He turned her hand and kissed the palm hungrily. "I still have the ring."

Her breath caught at the passion in his tone. "Do you?"

"And I got information on getting a marriage license this morning."

She gasped.

"We could go down to the Office of the City Clerk together and get one."

"We could?"

"I've got everything arranged already for next Friday," he added. "Think of the embarrassment if I have to call it off. I mean, I invited total strangers to the event. I'm having Mary and Agatha and your dad's former boss, Bill Clay, flown up here. I'll never live down the shame if you say no."

She just gaped at him. "But, JL, I don't have a wedding gown . . . is it a civil service?"

"It is not. And we can get a wedding gown. I had a couture boutique put several on hold, just for you. I've been shopping." He grinned.

"But . . . but . . ."

He bent and kissed her, very softly. "Just say yes. Everything else will work out. Honest. I have the best wedding planner in the city. She's amazing."

She just shook her head. "Oh . . . okay!" She gave up. It was probably going to be a disaster, but she loved him and she didn't care. She threw her arms around his neck. "I love you," she said huskily. "We can get married by a beachcomber, I don't even care how."

He lifted her and kissed her hungrily, oblivious to passersby and cars and cabs and the whole world.

"Get a room," someone yelled humorously.

"I'm getting a room, after I marry her!" he yelled back.

There was raucous laughter.

Cassie laughed, too, and snuggled close in his arms.

The wedding planner was truly amazing. She had it all arranged, right down to the wedding gown, the bouquet, the church, the minister, the works. Two little girls who belonged to one of the series' stars of *Warlocks and Warriors* were flower girls. The ring bearer was the son of another. Roger Reed was JL's best man and the show's female star was Cassie's matron of honor. The wedding was covered by the media. And Mary and Agatha and Bill Clay, along with Bessie and her daughter, from Benton, Colorado, sat in the front pew and watched with utter delight and a little bit of shock. They'd had no idea who their new friend actually was. All of them were fans of *Warlocks and Warriors*.

JL lifted the delicate, lacy veil from her face and kissed Cassie with exquisite tenderness. His eyes were full of love. He hadn't said the words, but he didn't need to. She knew. She'd always known.

She smiled up at him with her whole heart in her own eyes.

"My beautiful wife," he said gently. "Mrs. Denton."

She flushed and laughed. "I like the way that sounds."

"Me too."

He shook hands with the minister, took Cassie by the hand, and they walked back down the aisle towards the exit.

The reception was held in the Bull and Bear restaurant at the Waldorf Astoria. There were more people than Cassie could account for. JL mentioned that he'd invited several members of his board of directors and at least one Arab prince. He pointed the man out to Cassie, who would never have guessed his identity because he was wearing an expensive suit, not robes.

"You have some amazing friends," she remarked later.

"Yes, I do. I don't pick them because of their bank accounts, either. They're just plain people. They don't put on airs or equate wealth with character."

"The prince is nice," she remarked.

He chuckled. "He's a big fan of *Warlocks and Warriors*," he informed her. "Never misses an episode. In fact, neither do I. I'll have to show you one of my T-shirts when we get back home. It's black with 'Here Be Dragons' in white across the chest."

She grinned. That phrase was the watchword of the show. Most people recognized it instantly. "I didn't come up with that," she said. "It was Frank's." She sighed. "We all still miss him. He was a great writer, and a sweet man."

He bent and brushed her cheek with his lips. "For years to come, people will murmur that phrase and think of him," he said comfortingly. "He'll have a taste of immortality."

"I didn't think of that. It's nice."

"So am I," he drawled with a grin.

"And now I have a son to go with my daughter," Roger Reed chuckled as he hugged JL and Cassie. "Welcome to the family."

"Thanks," JL said. "I'm happy to be part of it. And very lucky that she has a tender and forgiving heart," he added dryly.

"I didn't think to ask, where are you two going for your honeymoon?" Roger asked.

JL looked down at Cassie with mischievous eyes. "It's a surprise. But we'll send you a post-card eventually," he promised her father.

"I'll have to talk with my bosses. . . ." Cassie began worriedly.

"Already taken care of," her father said easily. "I play poker with your producer. I told him I'd let him win a hand and he said you can have a week off."

She hugged her father. "You're the best father on earth."

"Yes, I am," he chuckled. "Now go have a happy honeymoon and don't worry about things back here. By the way," he added softly, "you were a beautiful bride. Your mother would have been so proud." He had to stop and fight tears.

"She would have," Cassie agreed, and hugged him in a moment of shared sadness.

Before things could deteriorate, the photographer JL had hired interrupted them for a shot of Cassie and JL with her father. They obliged and smiles replaced sad faces.

JL and Cassie posed for pictures and then said their farewells to the Benton natives who'd come so far to see them wed. JL was sending them home in business class on commercial airlines. He apologized but added that he and Cassie would be taking his jet on their honeymoon. Nobody had a problem with that, especially when he added that the guests would be spending the weekend in New York City with prepaid credit cards, prepaid hotel bills—at the Plaza—and all the food and entertainment they could wish for, also prepaid. Cassie was delighted that he was so generous with their friends. But, then, that was the way JL was. Happiness was spilling out all over.

Cassie had thought they might spend the night in New York City, but JL had them driven to the airport after they said their good-byes.

"Not a thing to worry about," he assured her. His eyes twinkled mysteriously. "I have a very special wedding surprise in store for you. We're going to join an exclusive club."

"We are? Which one?" she asked, wondering if it was a restricted area in the airport where members of certain groups got VIP treatment.

"Wait and see, sweetheart," he said softly, and held her hand tightly.

"Oh, my gosh!" she exclaimed just as they reached the airport. "JL, I forgot my suitcase! It's still at Dad's apartment! I won't have anything to wear!"

"Already taken care of," he said easily. "Your dad packed it and I had it picked up. It's already on the jet."

"The jet?"

"My own jet," he said. "Big, roomy, comfortable, with a pilot who's the best in the business. We even have in-flight meal service." His eyes twinkled. "You're going to love it."

She did. She'd been on an executive jet just once, when she was needed urgently for a story conference and the CEO of the company that produced *Warlocks and Warriors* had sent his own jet to pick her up in Atlanta. But even that luxurious jet wasn't a patch on JL's.

"This is absolutely unreal," she said as she looked around. There was TV, a bar, a comfortable sitting area with tables, and a male steward, who greeted them at the door.

"This is Dennis," he introduced her to the pleasant man. "He's been with me for eight years."

"Nice to meet you," she said, shaking hands and smiling.

"Nice to meet you also, Mrs. Denton. Will you be wanting to eat soon?"

JL looked at his watch. "In about two hours, I think. Until then, no phone calls, okay?" he added, and tossed his cell phone to Dennis.

He held out his hand. Cassie got the idea. She handed him her cell phone, which he also tossed to Dennis.

JL took Cassie's hand and led her toward the back of the jet. The engines were just revving up for takeoff.

"Shouldn't we be strapped in or something?" she asked worriedly.

"We're about to be," he assured her.

He opened a door and nudged her inside. He followed her. It was a bedroom, complete with television, stereo, a computer, a desk, and the biggest, cushiest bed she'd seen in a long time.

He picked her up and put her gently on the bed

as the jet began to speed up and rise into the air.

"Have you ever heard," he asked her amusedly, "of the 'mile high club'?"

She flushed. "Everybody has," she stammered, referring to those who'd had sex in flight, high above the earth.

"Well, darlin'," he whispered as his hands went to the fastenings on her beautiful wedding gown, "we are about to join the club!"

CHAPTER ELEVEN

Cassie had no experience of intimacy. A few kisses and some groping, yes, but nothing really intimate. So what JL did to her came as a shock.

"It's all right," he whispered. He'd removed her gown between soft, tender kisses and put her under the covers while he removed his own clothes. She hadn't watched. It was pretty intimidating already, this initiation into true adulthood. But he hadn't made fun of her shyness. It had delighted him. Now he was touching her in ways and places that embarrassed her, and she caught his wrist worriedly.

"It's really all right," he said again, brushing her mouth with his. "Just relax. There's no reason to be embarrassed. This is part of the process. You have to let me touch you. It's how I can be sure that I won't hurt you, when the time comes."

"I don't understand," she whispered back, and she really didn't. Her few girlfriends had been mostly like her, uninitiated, and what she heard from experienced people was general rather than specific.

He chuckled. "Okay." He whispered it to her, so that she understood what he was doing, and why.

Her faint gasp indicated how new to it she

really was. She swallowed, hard, and let go of his wrist.

"That's it. Yes. Shhhhh." His mouth opened on hers, tasting her, arousing her, while his hands were doing the most incredible things to her body.

She began to writhe on the sheets, shivering with each new touch.

"It won't be hard at all," he said huskily. "And by the time we start, you won't be afraid anymore."

She was barely hearing him now. Her body was throbbing with new sensations, new experience. She opened her legs for him without coaxing, gave him back the hungry kisses with new passion, arched up to his hands and then, unbelievably, his mouth!

She wanted to protest, but all at once, she shot up into the sky, exploding, throbbing, dying of pleasure. She cried out helplessly, a sound she'd never heard from her own lips.

"Oh, yes," he murmured just as he went into her.

His mouth covered the faint little cry that was less protest than enticement. She was sensitized now, so that the joining of their bodies was warm and sweet and welcome. She wrapped her long legs around his and held on, shuddering as he moved, feeling him swell in her, feeling her own body respond urgently to the slow, deep movements of his hips.

Then, all at once, it became something else, something primitive and devouring, a throbbing need that ached to be fulfilled, that demanded heat and motion and passion. She bit his shoulder in her ecstasy, crying, sobbing as she begged him not to stop.

His mouth buried itself in her throat as he pushed harder, harder, and then suddenly went rigid above her and cried out. She found her own fulfillment at the same time, riveted to his hard body, shivering and convulsing in a pleasure she'd never known existed. It was almost unbearable at the last, a sweetness so volcanic that she thought she might pass out.

Finally, she was able to relax, to flow into his body as she felt him go heavy against her. He started to pull away, but she held him there, coaxed him back to her mouth so that she could kiss him hungrily, with new and sweet knowledge of him as a man, as her husband.

He lifted his head and looked down into her soft, sated eyes. He smiled at her expression. His big hand brushed back her unruly red-gold hair. "Now you know," he whispered.

She nodded. "Now I know."

He covered her mouth with his and kissed her hungrily. "That exclusive club I mentioned?"

"Umhmm," she murmured lazily.

"We are now members in good standing," he chuckled.

Her eyes laughed as they met his. "Yes, we are. So. Where are we going?"

"Jamaica," he said. "Montego Bay, to be precise. We can be beachcombers for a week."

"Maybe enlist on a pirate ship and raid small villages?" she suggested.

He pinched her bottom and laughed when she flinched and grinned at him.

"Maybe sit around drinking piña coladas and enjoy the swimming pool," he countered.

"Spoilsport."

He smoothed back her damp hair. "My darling, if you wanted a pirate ship for real, I'd go right out and get you one. I'm the happiest man in the world right now."

"I hope to keep you that way," she replied. She touched his hard mouth. "What does JL stand for?"

He smiled. "John Lewis," he said. "But I've gone by JL for so long that it's pretty much my name now."

"I have a better one."

"You do?"

She nodded. "My sweetheart."

He grinned from ear to ear. "I like it."

She tugged him closer. "Me too. And this is where we live happily ever after, right?"

He rolled over, taking her with him. "Happily ever after and after and after."

"Promise?"

"Cross my heart."

She smiled with her whole heart and kissed him again. "I love you," she whispered.

"I love you more."

She beamed. It was the first time he'd really said it. "You do?"

"I loved you when you were standing in the rain holding a protest sign, with your hair all wet," he confessed. "You stole my heart, when I didn't think I had one left. If I'd lost you, I could never have gone home again, you know," he added solemnly. "I'd have been a wanderer for the rest of my life, rootless, useless."

She touched his mouth with her fingertips. "You stole my heart when you took me home and dried my clothes and made me coffee."

He smiled. "And here we are, married."

"Married." She looked at the beautiful diamond, set in gold, with its beautiful wedding band. "Now I feel married," she added with a wicked look.

He chuckled. "So do I." He pursed his lips. "Hungry yet?"

She moved under him. "Yes. But not for food. . . ." she whispered against his mouth. "Suppose we have another go at that exclusive club you mentioned?"

He smoothed his body over hers. "We should have just about enough time before we land," he said with a grin.

And they did. Just.

• • •

Nine months to the day later, a little boy was delivered in the community hospital in Benton, Colorado. His name was Cole Reed Denton and he had so many godmothers and godfathers that they couldn't all fit into the waiting room. They spilled out onto the parking lot and some were left sitting in stretch limos until they could get into the building.

It was talked about in Benton for many years to come. The rancher and his famous wife, who were just JL and Cassie locally, no matter how famous she got or how much richer he got. The lovebirds, as they were referred to, were just part of the big family that was Benton. And they did live happily, ever after.

Dear Reader:

I started this story with little more than the opening scene, which is how many of my stories begin. I see something in my mind, a tableau of two characters, and the book builds from there. In this case, I saw a poor, thin, straggly girl standing in the rain alone with a placard. There was a ranch nearby. That was all I saw. The rest developed from that one little thing.

Writing has always fascinated me. I sit down at the computer and I never know what's going to appear on the page. It is a magical process that never loses its mystery or its delight. Every story I craft is like the first one I ever wrote, and I enjoy them all.

I am so happy to be working with Tara, my Kensington editor, once more. I love writing about Colorado, and I feel privileged to be included in these anthologies with such talented other writers. I hope you enjoyed JL and Cassie's story. I truly adore these characters.

Love,
Diana Palmer

Wind River Wedding

Lindsay McKenna

*To all the men and women in the military
and those who are vets.
Thank YOU for your sacrifices for all of us.
Freedom is never free.*

CHAPTER ONE

October 1964

Steve Whitcomb was serving from behind the steam tables at the Helping Hand Center in Cranbury Township, New Jersey, when his buddy Jose leaned toward him.

"Hey, here comes one of the richest women in the world, Maud Campbell." He lifted his head in the direction of the doors. This was a huge hall, alive with talk, at least a hundred people and children, coming in for breakfast from around the area. Some were homeless, but many were families with low incomes, bringing their young children in for a hot meal on Saturday morning. "And," Jose added, "you're new, but you need to know Maud is special. Everyone loves her. Her mother started on Wall Street about twenty years ago and she's worth millions. Maud is a freshman at Rider College, the school in Lawrenceville. She has volunteered on Saturdays and Sundays every week since she started college."

"No, I didn't know that," Steve murmured, serving a young mother with a baby in her arms as she pushed the tray to where he stood.

He barely glanced in the direction of the double open doors on the warm October morning, but he still caught sight of her. Maud Campbell looked like a lot of the young women going to Rider College, which had admitted women to the school back in the late 1800s: tall, lithe, her black hair short and shiny, and she was about four inches shorter than his six-foot height. She had a square face, but he couldn't tell the color of her eyes as she hurried toward the kitchen behind where they were standing. If she was rich, it didn't show in her clothes. She was wearing a scruffy-looking denim jacket, a red T-shirt beneath it, jeans that looked very worn, along with a pair of sensible white tennis shoes. She looked nothing like a privileged heiress.

Steve smiled, said hello to the mother, and spooned several helpings of scrambled eggs and added four pieces of bacon to her plate. She wouldn't keep contact with his eyes, looking down, and he understood. No one wanted to find themselves taking handouts in America, but there were plenty of people who needed just that. Especially their children who sometimes went hungry for a day without food. It was nothing to be ashamed of. He watched Maud waving, saying hello to a few patrons in the hall who hailed her by name, who smiled and waved back to her as she hurried through the kitchen and disappeared.

"Her mother," Jose added, giving the mother two large, steaming, flaky biscuits, "gave Helping Hand millions of dollars after Maud arrived.

We're all sure she told her mother about this place. Things have changed since then. Reverend Annie Culver is dancing because with that donation, we've been able to add a soup kitchen. Before? We were just a food pantry. Now, Rev has three meals a day, seven days a week, children and families." He motioned up and down where they stood behind glass counters and the steam food trays. "We had children going hungry, but not anymore. Maud is gung ho, just like my mother." He chuckled. "You'll find out soon enough."

Steve smiled and nodded. Like all food servers behind the glass cases in front of them, he wore gloves. "I'm kind of surprised someone with that kind of money would have a daughter volunteering her time here."

Jose nodded. "When Maud first came to New Jersey, she told us that she was used to volunteering back in New York City where she lives. She and her mother would visit soup kitchens and food pantries all around the city, donating to them. Maud grew up standing where you and I are standing right now. Like I said, the Campbell family is real special. They might have millions, but they didn't forget the rest of us struggling to make ends meet every day of the week."

"I know that one, coming from a ranch out west," Steve said, keeping an eye out toward the swinging doors of the kitchen. There were a lot of positions for volunteers to fill. His curiosity about Maud was piqued. He liked her lanky grace, her shoulders back, and she was a fast walker, like she was in a hurry to get where she was going.

"Yeah, Cowboy," Jose said, pointing to the black Stetson hat he wore. "I think you go to bed in that hat and cowboy boots on, Steve."

"Almost," he laughed.

"You're probably the only cowboy at Princeton. How are they taking to you refusing to fit in with the Princeton blazer and slacks gang here?"

"Oh," he said, deadpan, "they're gradually getting used to me dressing in my Wyoming finery."

"I wish I could be a fly on the wall and see all their mouths drop open when you come by with that hat and dungarees. Never mind those boots of yours." Jose was going to Princeton, a sophomore.

"Hey, I'm comfortable in my clothes. Besides, going to Princeton is about education, not what I'm wearing, thank God."

"Oh! Here comes Maud! And she's got her eyes on you, Cowboy! It's gotta be your hat!" Jose laughed. He stepped back, waving hello to Maud as she drew on her gloves and approached them.

Steve watched the warmth between Maud and Jose. She hugged the hell out of him, spoke in

262

fluent Spanish to him, which made him glow with pleasure. Steve caught her fleeting glance in his direction. He knew she was attracted by the black cowboy hat he wore. She reminded him of an outdoors kind of woman, her hair a bit mussed, framing her spring green–colored eyes that missed nothing, her clothing comfortable and the type a hiker might wear. The soft shape of her lips made him wonder if she had a significant other. Steve was sure she did. If she was rich? More than likely she was engaged to some rich guy. He saw no ring on her hand, though.

Still, he smiled a little as she took her place next to him. Jose patted her on the shoulder and left for the kitchen. His time on the food line was over. He was one of the important people in Rev's organization and Steve was sure Jose was needed elsewhere. There was a large shipment of canned food coming in today via an eighteen-wheeler truck and Jose was a manager and a good leader here at the busy center.

"Hi, I'm Maud Campbell," she said, and held out her hand in his direction.

"Steve Whitcomb." He tipped his fingers to the brim of his hat as he released her hand.

"You must be new?"

"Yes, ma'am, I am."

Her eyes sparkled as she looked him up and down. "Haven't I seen you on the Princeton campus? The other day I was taking a back way to my college, Rider, and I saw someone in a black cowboy hat. It had to be you. No one else would dare wear a cowboy hat on the campus."

Grinning sheepishly, Steve saw a Hispanic mother with two five-year-old twins in tow. He quickly filled her tray with plenty of scrambled eggs. He spoke to her in Spanish. Her smile was shy, but she appreciated him trying to speak her language. He wasn't as fluent as Maud was. "Probably was me. I don't see too many people from Wyoming going to Princeton."

She tittered, broke out in Spanish, leaning forward and greeting the young mother with genuine affection.

Steve liked the husky warmth of Maud's voice. She was respectful to the mother. The twins stared up at her, as if mesmerized by her sincere greetings. If she was wealthy, it sure didn't show. In his world, that was a checked box. Not that he knew many rich people out on the Wind River Ranch that his family had owned for three generations in western Wyoming. For the next five minutes, they were busy doling out food for ten families who came and stood in line.

Still, he was drawn to Maud, and he was curious about her. She laughed often, was sincere with everyone who came through the line. And she knew all of them! She remembered every mother's name, plus the names of their children.

That was pretty amazing to Steve. People didn't remember people's names unless it was important to them. Another box checked. So? Why was he checking boxes at all? He was here at Princeton to get an AB with a concentration in architecture. After that, he would apply for admission in a graduate program for his master's degree. He had a number of years to go at this place, and it was a dream come true for him. He'd always wanted to build, to design and create sustainable homes for people in third world countries. Unlike Maud, who didn't have to worry about money to pay for this expensive education, his parents had saved the first eighteen years of his life to fund his studies at a college of his choice.

Even now, at eighteen, he understood how much his folks had given up to give him this lifetime opportunity. There was no way he was going to squander it by becoming interested in a relationship. Every time their gazes met briefly, he felt his chest tighten.

There was a lull between clients. Maud turned to him. "You look like a commercial for that cowboy on TV," she said, and she flashed him a wide grin, teasing in her eyes. "That Marlboro cowboy cigarette ad."

"Yes, ma'am, you aren't the first to tell me that since landing here in New Jersey. And I don't smoke."

Rolling her eyes, she said, "Stop the ma'am,

will you? You make me feel old! I'm eighteen! And I don't smoke either, although it's the rage right now. Hate the smell of the stuff."

He laughed with her, that husky tone riffling through his heart once more. "What are you thinking of majoring in, Maud?" She reminded him of the fierce feminists who had risen in 1960, and wondered if she was a member of one of the women's protest groups at the university. There was a refreshing air of confidence and individuality with her. Maud was not like the girls he'd gone through high school with. No, this filly was wild and undomesticated in an exciting way. He wanted to know everything about her. Everything.

"Math. My mother graduated from here," she said, and she hooked a thumb over her shoulder in the general direction of where Rider College was located.

"You're here for six years?"

"Yep, I am."

"So am I."

Tilting her head, she said, "What are YOU thinking of majoring in? Being a cowboy? I haven't seen any classes on that!"

They laughed.

"I want to get my AB and then a master's in architecture."

"Really?" She gave him a bold look, sizing him up from head to toe and back to his eyes.

"Aiming to be another Frank Lloyd Wright, are you? A western version?"

He felt heat in his cheeks, looking away for a moment. "Oh no, nothing like that." Lifting his hand, he gestured toward the hundred people sitting at the tables. "My goal is to create sustainable, but good housing for people in the third world countries."

"Really?" She rocked back on her heels, giving him a long look. "You aren't what you seem."

"Is anyone?" he teased.

She snorted. "Touché."

"How long have you volunteered here?"

"Since I came earlier in the summer. My parents believe in giving back. Last summer I came here to Cranbury Township and worked with Reverend Annie before entering college. My mother is going to send a yearly donation to her, as she does about a hundred other food pantries and soup kitchens around the US. Since I had been accepted to college, I wanted to find the nearest facility and volunteer. I just love this place. Rev Annie is a force of nature, just like my mother. She gets things done and everyone is better off because of it." She sighed and smiled softly. "This has become a second home to me. I love having family around me."

"It looked like you knew everyone when you came through those doors."

"Yeah," she chuckled. "I like people and

animals. The better you know someone, the more you find similarities between you and them. My parents took me with them on long trips around the world, and I learned very quickly that what we have here in the US is rare. We have it good here, but most of the rest of the world doesn't. I don't like inequities. All people deserve a roof over their head, clean water to drink, and food to eat."

"It sounds like your mother is very focused on women and children." He looked up. "When I arrived, they showed me a huge building that's being constructed right now near the food pantry. It was housing for families who were living out of cars in this area."

"Yes, that's my mother's donation money at work." She wrinkled her nose, becoming sad. "No one in the world should have to live in a car with their family. No one . . ."

Hearing the grit in her voice, he admired her sincerity. "It's good that your parents can afford this type of donation."

"Mom says she wants everyone to have a chance to fulfill their dreams. I agree with her."

"I like your attitude," he said.

"What about you? Are you a real cowboy?"

His heart expanded with unexpected joy over her question. "I'm the third generation of a ranching family at the Wind River Ranch. It's located in the Wind River Valley, fifty miles south of Jackson Hole, Wyoming. The Grand Teton National Park is a little beyond that town."

"So, you ride a horse?"

"Grew up on one. I like throwing a leg over a good horse and doing a hard day's work at the ranch."

"I love horses," she sighed, lifting her hand, waving to a new family coming down the line.

He was going to say something sexist, but stopped, rethinking it all before he spoke. Since Gloria Steinem's exposé of the NYC Playboy Club fired up the feminist revolution in 1963, that had made him start looking at how men treated women. His own mother, Lydia, was a highly outspoken and independent Wyoming-bred woman. She didn't get cowed at all by men, or it was a man's world. In fact, it dawned on him that his mother ran the ranch; his father, Sam, didn't. She was the chief manager of the 150,000-acre ranch, did the accounting, and did a darned good job at it. Since he was ten years old, he'd seen the ranch prosper as never before in the multigenerational family. Lydia had visionary plans for the ranch and by the time he was eighteen, they had more money in the bank than ever before.

Smiling a little as he served the families coming through his line, he thought that Maud would love to meet his mother, Lydia. They were like two peas that came from the same pod. Powerful women who each followed a vision and put it into action.

Maud tried to keep her attention on the people she was serving. Steve Whitcomb stood out from the rest of the men due to his hat, but from what she could see, he was nice to everyone and that counted a lot in her book. He wasn't arrogant, acting entitled, attitudes that she'd come to expect from the rich sons of rich parents. In fact, she was turned off by them, despairing of ever finding a young man with manners, with respect toward women and children, and who wasn't a Neanderthal jerk. That was important to her.

Keeping one ear keyed to Steve's quiet conversations with their clients as he served, she found herself liking him more and more. He was handsome in a rugged, cowboy kind of way. Most of all, she liked the devilry that danced in his light blue eyes, that short blond hair of his more like a Vietnam War military haircut, unlike the hippie men who insisted upon wearing their hair long. And that well-shaped mouth of his, the way he crooked one corner of it when she knew he was teasing her or a client, was a turn-on, not a turn-off.

Her mind raced with questions about this enigmatic cowboy from Wyoming. He insisted upon wearing his western clothes, not dressed in expected Ivy League clothes like every other young man attending Princeton. No sport coat, pants, shirt, and tie for him! She liked his sense of self. She had always dreamed of living out west; the books on cowboy heroes, horses, and cowgirls she'd read growing up filled her with a burning desire to see that part of the USA.

In another hour, breakfast was over. The steam line was closed down, and soon she and Steve were carrying the huge aluminum trays back to the kitchen area where twenty other volunteers were working nonstop. She liked the way he walked, that boneless kind of grace, confidence, and most importantly, always alert and sensitive to others. What was there NOT to like about this guy? Really?

After they delivered the last of the huge aluminum trays, she pulled off her gloves. Sensing that he wanted to be with her, Maud took it as an opportunity.

"Hey, you like horses. So do I. My car's out in the parking lot and I've got a riding lesson at a nearby stable in about forty-five minutes. Are you doing anything right now? Would you like to come with me? It would give you a chance to be around horses again." How she wanted him to say yes! He halted outside the swinging doors, standing out of the way of the people going in and out.

"Sure, that would be nice. I don't have a car.

The apartment I've rented is about half a mile from here."

"Can I drive you? If you trust me to drive?" She saw him grin and slide her a knowing look.

"Somehow, I think you drive just fine."

"Well," she huffed, "men always call women bad drivers, but in reality? If you asked the insurance company who has the most accidents? Turns out it's men, eighteen to twenty-five years old, not women."

He walked with her to the front doors, opening one for her. "I can believe that."

Outside, she gestured for him to follow her. She had a blue Ford Falcon station wagon that had some wear and tear on it. If she was as rich as Jose said her mother was, her taste in cars went to common sense and practicality, not status. Another box checked. He saw several bales of timothy grass hay in the rear of the car. As she slid into the driver's seat, he settled into the passenger side.

"Hay for the horses?" he asked.

"The Pegasus Horse Center is where we're going," she said. "It charges an arm and a leg for a bale of alfalfa or timothy hay. I get mine from a local farmer about fifteen miles from here for half the price."

"You have a horse stalled there?"

She put the car in gear, a stick shift, and they

took off. "I've leased a thoroughbred gelding for a year."

"So, you're a rider?"

"I've been around horses all my life," she confided, giving him a glance. He seemed pleased. "What? You don't think Eastern women can ride horses?" she said, and she laughed heartily, as if it were an inside joke. She put the car in gear and they were off.

Steve drank in the multicolored fall trees that lined the highway. The sky was a deep blue and it made the rich, vibrant colors even more intense. "I guess my way of looking at the East is a bit off," he admitted. "No, I didn't think of women riding horses back here."

"Have you traveled much?" she wondered.

Shaking his head, he said, "Well, I've been to Utah, Montana, and Idaho. Does that count?"

Her lips pulled upward. "Sure, it does."

"What about you? It sounds like you've traveled the world."

"My parents are globe-trotters. I was born in New York City. They live there to this day." She shrugged. "Most kids who have rich parents, with some exceptions, are raised by nannies and kept at home when their parents travel. Mine didn't do that. I did have a nanny, but they always took me with them when they traveled. It gave me a bird's-eye view on how people around the world struggle to just eat or find water to drink."

"Why did your parents travel?"

"My mother has charities around the world that she donates to. She loves all people and is a stickler on giving women a chance to run their own business like she does."

"Tell me about that. My mother, Lydia, is the boss of our ranch. She doesn't have a college education, but she has a vision for our ranch. She's helped us make more money in the last twenty years with her innovations and seeing how to make the ranch prosper far more than anyone in the family before her."

"Sounds like my mom," she agreed. "I don't think you need a college education to be a good businessperson. Many people learn it hands on. Their experience is actually better than going to college. It sounds like Lydia is one of those rare birds."

"What about your mother?"

"My mother is a chip off the old block of Gloria Steinem long before she became associated with the feminist movement. My father owns a seat on the Stock Exchange and my mother wanted to start an investment firm of her own. She got an MBA from Rider University. She went around the world investing in corporations owned by women. She has nothing but women's companies in her portfolio, and everyone on Wall Street said she wasn't going to make a plug nickel. But she did." Maud filled with pride. "My mother has been making good money at it. Every year she attracts bigger investors. And the women who own these businesses are prospering as a result, too."

"And you don't want to work on Wall Street, too?" he asked. "You're going after an MBA like her."

Maud liked his remembering those details. Opening and closing her fingers around the steering wheel, she turned off to a two-lane highway outside the town limits. They were now in green, rolling pastures with groves of trees here and there. "Originally, Mom wanted me to take over her company, but I got cold feet. It wasn't that I didn't feel up to it, because I was. Like her, I wanted to help the women's businesses continue to prosper. I want to learn how to help people create a business, thereby lifting the entire community I lived in. That would mean helping women and men. I think when a small town prospers with mom-and-pop businesses, everyone prospers. Then the county they are in is lifted economically, as well. It's a positive domino effect."

"A small town? I thought you were a city girl."

"I guess I'm far more limited in how I see myself, Steve. I don't like traveling very much. I love being in one place forever and knowing and making friends with those who live around me. Community is vital to me. Knowing everyone is very important to me."

He rubbed his chin. "You've never lived in a rural community, though?"

"No, and I really want to. I love New York City, but I pine for greenery, grassy hills, and dales, not concrete, glass, and steel skyscrapers." She slowed, turning into a white-fenced lane, several huge riding rings along with an indoor arena sitting on two hundred acres before them. "I feel my heart is in the country," she said, and she made an expansive gesture with her hand.

"A city girl with a country heart?" he teased her gently.

"Oh," she said, giving him a brilliant smile, "I love that thought! Yes! Yes, that's who I am at heart. I really want to live in the country. That's one reason I love the Princeton area so much. It's got a country feel to it. My mom doesn't understand, but I'm hoping after I get my degree and then my MBA, I'll be looking for a small, rural community to go live in and help the people prosper."

"If you want to see country," Steve said, "on summer break you should visit our ranch. THAT is rural country. Have you ever been to the West?"

"No," she said, pulling into the parking lot that was filled with Mercedes-Benz vehicles. "The closest I got to your state was New Mexico one time, and I just loved Santa Fe!"

Getting out, he settled the Stetson on his

head, glancing around at the riders on tall, sleek thoroughbred horses, wearing English apparel and sitting on English saddles. He came around and opened her door for her and she thanked him. He'd never seen such an odd-looking little saddle before. The only one he knew about was the western saddle that all ranchers used out west. Glancing up, he saw Maud waving for him to follow her.

"I've got to get the hay manager, Julie. I have my own stash of hay for Peppy, my leased horse."

Following her, he smiled to himself. Maud took off like a rocket, calling to her friends riding in some of the rings, waving hello to them, and then diving into the cavernous riding arena. Steve increased his stride. She was a woman on a mission, no question. There was nothing aggressive or mannish about Maud, in his opinion. She wore loose-fitting jeans, but it couldn't hide her curves or her long, long legs. Maud was all energy, focused, committed, and he kept up with her as they entered the stall area on one side of the long building. He saw several women dressed in English riding togs look up and stare at him as they walked past them in the aisleway. His hat always drew attention and he chuckled to himself.

East meets West.

That pleased him for no discernable reason as he slowed and watched Maud dive into a door with a sign over the top of it that said: OFFICE. Looking around, he saw a number of horses, some bay, a gray, and a sorrel, were all in ties being either saddled or unsaddled by their attentive riders. There were a lot of young women here, he guessed in their late teens or early twenties. All were dressed spiffily in proper English garb. Even the long stovepipe black leather riding boots that snugged to just below their knees. He knew the cost of a good pair of cowboy boots, and there was a lot of money in the English variety, he was sure.

He wondered if Maud was going to ride. He missed his horse, Tiger, a blood bay quarter horse. It had been a long time since he'd been riding, and he acutely missed it. And clearly, there was some very nice, but expensive horseflesh here in this barn.

Inhaling deeply, Steve filled his lungs with the sweet scent of the alfalfa and timothy hay. The smell of a horse was euphoria for him. And the scent of freshly cleaned saddle leather was wonderful, as well. All those fragrances wafted around him, reminding him sharply of home, which he missed so much. Both ends of the arena, where there were box stalls on either side of the concrete aisle, were opened to allow not only light, but fresh autumn breezes in.

There were horses of varying sizes and colors sticking their heads out from their roomy box stalls and into the busy aisleway, watching the comings and goings of horses and riders. He knew horses had a very low threshold for boredom and relished constant distraction. They were also herd animals and needed their own kind around them. Even the way the eyes on a horse were set in their head was for maximum vision of the world around them.

"Hey! Steve!" Maud called from the opened door. "Come on in! I'll only be a few more minutes and then, I'll show you around."

Maud's smile was infectious, and he appreciated her being sensitive to the fact he was a stranger here in their midst, in more than one way. Her light green eyes were large, fringed thickly with black lashes, like a frame for a gorgeous painting. As he turned and walked toward her, he kept sternly reminding himself that he had years remaining at Princeton to make his architecture degree a reality. He couldn't afford to fall in love with the first woman he met.

CHAPTER TWO

August 1, 1966

"I just love your ranch, Steve," Maud sighed, looking up from where they rested their elbows on the pipe rail fence of the corral. She lifted her face to the overhead sun. August was the hottest month of the year in Wyoming, Steve had told her. Since she came to the ranch, the bright red baseball cap his father, Sam, had given to her to wear was on her head all the time. She tipped the bill upward. "I love the smell of the grass, the sound of cattle mooing, and the horses whinnying . . ." she said, and she tilted her head, catching his glance. As always, he wore his black Stetson, jeans, a blue chambray cowboy shirt, and boots. It was just who he was and that was more than enough for her. She melted beneath his warming smile, her body running hot, remembering how, over a year ago, they agreed to live together off campus. Her love for him had only increased over time. This was her second summer at the Wind River Ranch.

"I do, too," he admitted, watching as wranglers vaccinated bawling, struggling buffalo calves from their growing herd. His mother, Lydia, had gotten a grocery store chain in the West to start buying buffalo meat as a low-cholesterol product. It was working, and each year more and more meat was being ordered. It was starting to make the ranch far richer than anyone could have ever dreamed that it could be.

"There's your dad," she said, gesturing toward the other side of the stout, ten-foot-tall corral. This fenced-in area, she found out, was for buffalos since they could push over a cattle corral with no problem at all with their height and weight. She watched as Sam Whitcomb, riding Ace, his big black quarter horse gelding, was working a stubborn calf toward the pen to get its vaccinations from the team waiting for him. He was blond-haired like Steve, had dancing blue eyes, and wore a black Stetson on his head, too. Like father, like son, and she grinned, already feeling comfortable with the forty-five-year-old rancher. To her left, she saw Lydia, his mother, on a pretty gray, feminine-looking quarter horse mare, riding in another corral, working with wranglers to move a herd of Hereford cattle to another grass lease area.

This place was a beehive of activity from dawn to dusk, from June through late September. The ranch was comprised of mostly grass leases bought by ranchers who trucked in their herds from other western states to fatten them up on the rich, nutritious green grass.

She loved eating dinner with the family in their

log cabin home after dusk came every night. If there was any light outside? Wranglers were still working. Everyone always had stories to tell at the dinner table about their day. It was exciting to Maud. This was the kind of home she had envisioned in her girlish dreams while growing up in New York City. She'd never dreamed, however, that she'd fall in love with such a handsome Wyoming cowboy like Steve!

"Hey," he said, touching her shoulder, "I got something to show you. Come with me?"

Curious, she smiled. "Sure. What do you have up your sleeve, Whitcomb?" Steve was a clown at heart, teasing her, making her laugh and always surprising her in nice ways with his intelligence and architect mind. He was doing great at Princeton, getting a 3.9 average. She wasn't doing too bad herself, with a 3.8 average toward her MBA.

"Oh," he said, giving her a mysterious look, catching her hand and leading her toward one of the huge three-story red barns on the ranch. "You'll see. . . ."

Giving him a gleeful look, she shook her finger at him. "This had better not be a joke you're going to play on a city girl!"

Holding up his other hand, he solemnly promised, "Scout's honor, it isn't. I'm just not sure you'll like it or not."

Catching the seriousness that came to his eyes,

she lost her smile. "It's not something bad, is it, Steve?"

"I hope not."

She removed her red baseball cap, jamming it into her back pocket as they entered the cool shade of the barn. Their boots clunked along the old, roughened oak floor. He led her to a ladder that would take them up to the second floor, the hayloft. Once there, she sat down on a bale of timothy that he gestured toward. She watched him with full attention. Something serious was up. What?

They were alone, the warmth of the afternoon surrounding them. This was one of their hidey holes where they could neck and kiss in privacy. At their rental apartment off campus in New Jersey, they lived together, even though it was frowned upon by society. With the hippie movement, living with a woman was acceptable, but the rest of her parents' generation frowned mightily upon it. Martha, her mother, knew she was living with Steve and they'd had several talks about it, but her mother respected her choice. Out here at the Wind River Ranch, they did not talk of their living arrangement with Steve's parents, who would probably object to it. Instead, when they came here over summer vacation, they had separate guest bedrooms in the main log house where his parents lived. As a result, Steve got creative and they had several places where they could kiss, make love to each other, and still keep it a secret.

Steve pulled a small box from the pocket of his long-sleeved shirt. He turned toward her, their knees meeting. "Now, I wanted to give this to you in private for a lot of reasons." He became somber, holding her gaze. "Maud, I've never been happier in my life. I didn't know what love was until I met you." He opened the box and it showed a diamond engagement and wedding ring in it. "I want to marry you. But first, I know we have more years of classes before that happens." He heard her gasp, her hands flying to her lips as she stared down at the rings.

Pulling the engagement ring from it, he gently took her left hand, sliding it on her finger. "Will you marry me? Even though it's a long ways off, I think we have a good chance of making that date in the future. This engagement ring is my oath to you that I love you, that I want you as my best friend, my partner, wife, and anything else you can think of." He sought her gaze. "I love you, Maud. What do you think?"

Stunned, she stared at him and then down at her hand, which he held with his roughened one. She took her other hand away from her lips, love rising in her, expanding her heart, suffusing her with a joy she'd never felt except with him. "Yes . . . a thousand times, yes . . ." she said, and she pulled her hand from his and threw her arms around his broad shoulders, meeting his mouth, kissing him with everything she had inside her. His mouth was strong but tender, cherishing and sliding across her lips, worshipping her as he always did.

Finally, they came up for air, giving each other a silly grin, gripping each other's hands, the silence settling around them like a warm blanket.

"Why now?" she asked, her voice off-key and wispy.

"Because we've spent two years living together. We get along, we have so much fun, we laugh a lot, and we like each other. I didn't know what real love was until I ran into you, Maud. I thought I did, having a few relationships during high school, but that was puppy love in comparison. Not the real thing." He squeezed her fingers. "You're the real thing to me. You're my heart and I think you know that."

Nodding, she watched the glint of the small solitaire diamond set in yellow gold move with the light. "I do. You know I'm crazy about you. I was from the day I met you. It just took me six months to work up to letting you know how I felt," she said, and she flashed him a wry smile.

"What do you think Martha and your dad will say about our plans?"

She heard the concern in his low voice, saw the worry in his shadowed blue eyes. "They know we're serious about each other. And Mom knows we live together, although she's never said anything to Dad about it."

He grimaced. "I haven't built up the courage yet to tell my parents."

"They live by a different generational code, Steve. It's okay. I'm fine with keeping what we do back in Princeton our secret. Okay?" she said, and she tilted her head, catching his gaze. Steve's worry lifted beneath her softly spoken words.

"Yeah, okay . . . People out west, the ranchers in particular, have a pretty strict code of how to treat a woman. And part of that code is"—he caressed her hand that held the engagement ring on it—"you go through a long engagement before marrying."

Laughing in a low tone, she said, "You think they'll be okay with a multiyear engagement? Even the Victorians didn't wait that long!"

He laughed with her, keeping his voice low, not wanting to be discovered by anyone who might walk into the barn. Steve didn't want a curious visitor coming up the ladder to see what was going on. "Yeah . . . four years. Seems long, doesn't it?"

"No, not to me. We have many years to get the degrees we want. It's worth it. We're both doing well and we have good grades. Plus, we know how to study and we have a wonderful personal life with each other, despite all of the stresses at the universities."

"I like going riding with you on weekends." He'd brought his western saddle back East with him after the first time they visited his family.

"Yeah, I think everyone around the horse center likes seeing you riding in your western gear."

"I stand out like a sore thumb," he agreed, giving her a wolfish smile.

"Not that you care."

"No, I don't. I don't think you do, either."

She chuckled. "We like each other just the way we are. Neither of us has tried to change the other. We fit well together, Steve."

Caressing her cheek, he placed a warm kiss on her lips. Maud always tasted good, like honey, sweet and soft. He broke the kiss reluctantly, a lot more on his mind. "Are you okay if we tell everyone at dinner tonight that we're officially engaged?"

"Sure. I think Lydia, especially, will breathe a sigh of relief, showing everyone that we're serious about each other."

"So do I. She's been hinting pretty baldly that if I'm serious about you, we should become engaged."

"Well, this is the second summer I'm spending with you and your family. I can see her concerns."

"Me too. That's why I'm asking you to marry me."

She sighed and snuggled beneath his arm, resting her cheek against his shoulder. "We haven't really talked about any future after school. You want to travel the world helping third world countries create cheap, good housing for the poor. I know my mom hasn't dropped her dream of me staying in New York City and taking over her business. I love that Rider and Princeton are located in beautiful, rural New Jersey. Coming to this area freed me up and it's like new life has been breathed into me as a result," she said, and she pressed her hand against her heart.

"What do you REALLY want after we graduate, Maud? We need to talk about this. You keep avoiding it with me when I ask."

Giving him a guilty look, she murmured, "You deserve the truth. I have been evasive, but there's a good reason why. When I met you, Steve, you felt like someone I'd known from a past life, coming back to be with me again. Oh, I know you don't believe in reincarnation, but I'm spiritual in my reality. My mother thinks it poppycock, and so does my dad."

"I don't think it is," he said, frowning. "I can't prove it, but you can't prove gravity exists either, except by the fact we aren't all floating around."

She laughed a little. "Always pragmatic, Whitcomb, another plus to loving you. You always bring things into perspective."

"Sometimes," he protested, "not all the time."

"But you try." She took a deep breath and then released it. "Okay, here's my truth. When you invited me out here last summer for the first time, I fell utterly in love with the ranch, the whole valley and tiny town of Wind River that struggles daily to survive. I see the world I always dreamed of, right here, Steve, as crazy as that might sound. The valley is a hundred miles long and fifty miles wide, bracketed by two parallel mountain ranges, one east of the valley, the other west. It's perfect," she said, giving him a rueful look. Holding up the engagement ring, she added, "When we marry? I want to live out here, with you. I want to learn how to run a ranch, be taught the business end by Lydia, and pick her brain on how we can help the people of this valley prosper, because they aren't right now. And be taught by Sam, as well. I want to understand how a ranch works, inside and out."

Nodding, he digested her impassioned words. "I was worried that you might want to go back to New York City, to be near your parents. I know Martha has really been pleading with you to come home after graduation." His brows fell. "She didn't like the idea of you spending your summer out here with us for a second time, either, but I can't blame her. Maybe we can divide our summer break between both families from here on out?"

"My mom can be a real prodder when she wants to be," Maud admitted apologetically. "Yes, I like the idea of dividing our time. You'll hate the city, I know."

"While we're being brutally honest with each other?" he said, holding her gaze, "I know your parents don't think much of me. I'm a working-class man, Maud, not the rich bachelor from another well-known Eastern family that they'd probably like to see you marry. Maybe, by being around them more, they'll see why you love me and I love you."

She snorted derisively, standing up, pacing a bit. Turning toward him, she said, "My mother has unrealistic expectations for me. She always has. I just keep telling her 'no' and eventually, grudgingly, she backs off, but I can feel her still wanting me to step into her shoes and take over the business she's built. I've made no secret of my dream to take a little rural town and give it a makeover where everyone does well. I know I can do that. But she loves the city. I don't. I love the country. That's never going to change. And yes, I think if we spend a month with them each summer, they'll get to know you and realize how wonderful you are."

"How do you think they'll take our engagement?" he asked warily.

Halting, Maud crossed her arms across her chest, studying him. "I think they'll be disappointed at first, but over time, I'll wear them down and they'll come around."

"I worry what it will do to you, Maud."

"What do you mean?"

"Your mother is a woman who doesn't take 'no' for an answer."

She smiled a little and allowed her hands to fall to her side, coming over and sitting down close to him once more. "Neither do I, but I know you've noticed that. I'm a lot like my mother. She's one of the most successful women on this earth right now precisely because she's stalwart in whatever challenges she takes on. So am I, for myself and my dream, not hers."

"I'm a different kind of challenge to her," he pointed out gruffly. "I'm not from an old money kind of East Coast family heritage. In fact, I'm from a no-money family. Ranching life has always been hardscrabble until the last few years. And now? We're making good money thanks to my mom opening up a grocery market for our buffalo meat."

"But your family is worthy, and something to be proud of, Steve." She slid her arm around his broad shoulders, giving him a squeeze and then releasing him. "Money can't buy honor, values, morals, or integrity. Your family has all those things. They passed them on to you."

"And money can't buy love, either," he reminded her, leaning over, pressing a kiss to her mussed black hair.

"My parents know that," she said softly, giving him a kind look. "They have worked hard for what they have. My family aren't snobs and understand working on the land. They get that, and I don't think my parents are going to be terrified of me being engaged to you. The world has changed and is changing around us right now. We have the passage of the Civil Rights Act to protect against segregation, and all citizens have the same federal and legal rights. in this country. The power of women is rising via feminist marches and protests. We're in the middle of the Vietnam War, which is costing us a generation of young men and it shouldn't be happening. There's so much change going on around us. Nothing is the same and we don't know how it will end up, either."

"Yes, and I'm asking to marry the daughter of great wealth even though I'm a pauper in comparison."

"We'll handle it together," she whispered. Holding up her hand, the ring sparkling upon it, she added, "Love can't be bought or sold. I think your parents will take our engagement with hope and happiness. My parents will get over the shock that I'm marrying you. Someday"— she gave him a proud look—"they will see that you're going to become a globally famous architect. We won't always be poor. We'll be building our own empire in our way. I've always believed that if you do what you love to do, you will not only be successful at it, but you'll make good money from it, as well. Whatever your heart is invested in, Steve, it will bud, blossom and grow."

He brought her up and onto his lap, her arms going around his shoulders, head against his. "I have dreams of helping the world. I know it's not going to be easy, but I see how our own people in Wind River struggle daily, too. We can both help them in our own ways."

"Well," she said wryly, "if all goes well I'll be living out here while you gallivant around the world creating homes to keep people warm and safe. I'll learn the ranch business from your parents. That will take years of education on my part. But I'm looking forward to it, Steve. Then, we can turn around and start helping the town and the people of the valley."

Looking deeply into her eyes, he rasped, "You're sure this is what you want? Running a ranch? With an MBA? I don't think Martha will be very pleased that it's all that you're doing. You've got a lot of brainpower, Maud. Will she think you're wasting it by living out here with me?"

She shook her head, sliding her fingers through his hair. "I fell in love with you, not because you were a cowboy, not because you come from the working class, darling. Remember? A long time ago I told you my dream of living in a rural part of America. Helping not only ourselves, but those around us. Wind River Valley is my dream come true." She looked over at him, smiling softly.

"And you're my dream come true, too. I'll be happy and I'll be content."

"Okay," he grumbled, frowning. "I know Martha well enough by now that she's going to ask you the same questions I just did."

"Yes, over and over again."

"This is a beautiful area," he agreed.

"And Wind River Valley is a very economically poor area, Steve. Lincoln County has massive potential. And from where I sit, this valley is ripe to be infused with new ideas, ways to bring tourists who are driving through and not stopping because they want to get to either the Tetons or Yellowstone parks that are fifty miles north of here. This is the second year I've been here and I've spent a good amount of time with the local mom-and-pop businesses. I've asked them what they need, how they see the area growing, and how we can get those tourists to stop and spend their money here and not always north of us. I even have put a regional airport into my business plan for the area. Right now, the closest airport is fifty miles away, in Jackson Hole, Wyoming. The big airport is in Salt Lake City, Utah. We have nothing here for people. And putting in a regional airport with federal help, which my mother is very educated about, could lift so many out of poverty around here, and give so many jobs. I have big, vast dreams."

"It's a great business plan you're developing,"

Steve murmured, caressing her back. "And I like it. But in reality, it could take decades to build."

"I'm not going to come in here and pull the rug out from under your parents. I figure it will take me many years to learn the ranch business. I'm already starting to create a long-range business plan for the valley, like you said. Your parents want to retire at sixty years old. It will be a gentle handoff from them to us." She gave him a hopeful look. "And while I know you are planning on having your company office on the ranch, you will stay here in between the architecture projects that take you away. And while you're out of the country for months at a time, I will be managing this huge ranch by myself. I feel fully capable of running it without you around."

"Mom and Dad want to retire to Tucson, Arizona, where there's no snow during the winter, but they'll be available by phone in case you have a question. I know they'll support you. And yes, you're fully capable, Maud. I have no worries whatsoever."

"We'll be fine," she said, giving him a tender look. "You and I have big dreams, but there's nothing wrong with that. We can both have them and fulfill them. I know we can. Love will support us and give us the wings we need to fly."

Maud wasn't sure what would happen at dinner as they gathered around a large, round table made of oak. She sat next to Steve, with Lydia on her right and Sam across from her. The scent of spaghetti, and garlic toast, wafted through the air.

"Mom," Steve said, standing next to her chair, "come sit down for a minute? Maud and I have something to share with you two."

Sam, dressed in a clean white cowboy shirt, grinned up at his son. "A surprise?"

Lydia hurried in from the kitchen, wiping her hands on her blue apron. "The spaghetti has about ten minutes before it's ready to take up." She smiled and thanked her son as he pulled the chair out for her.

"Good timing," Steve murmured, sitting down next to Maud, giving her a look that he hoped made her feel calm. He could feel the tension radiating off her, her hands clasped tightly beneath the pink tablecloth, hidden from sight. He looked first at his mother and then his father.

"I've asked Maud to marry me," he told them quietly.

Maud pulled her hand above the tablecloth, showing them the engagement ring.

"Oh! My!" Lydia said, beaming. "Oh! Wonderful!" and she looked at her husband. "Sam, this is wonderful!"

He smiled proudly, looked at Maud, and said, "You okay marrying this hombre?"

Laughing a bit nervously, Maud said, "Very much so. I love your son, Sam. I think I started falling in love with him the day I met him."

Lydia pushed away, coming around, capturing Maud's hand, looking at the ring closely. "That's so beautiful, Maud! Do you like it?" she asked, and she looked at her, flushed with happiness.

"I love it. I love this guy sitting next to me."

Releasing her hand, Lydia hugged her fiercely. "Welcome to our family, Maud! I was so hoping this would happen!" She released her, embarrassed by tears running down her cheeks. Turning, she gave her son a fierce hug and big kiss on the cheek. "I'm so glad! She's the right girl for you."

Touched, Steve smiled up at this mother, who was taking the edges of her apron and dabbing her eyes, giving them a look of apology. "I think so too, Mom."

Sam got up, came around, and gave Maud a quick hug. He then extended his hand to Steve. "You do realize this filly is gonna be wild for the rest of her life. She's not someone you can tame."

Shaking his father's hand, Steve grinned up at him. "Yeah, I got that the day she came in the door of the soup kitchen where I was volunteering. We've been the best of friends the last two years and I think we've stood the test of time. And I don't want her tamed. I want her to follow her dreams just like she's allowing me to follow mine. We're a good team."

Nodding, Sam pushed his fingers through his

gray and blond hair, giving his wife a tender smile before he sat down. "You know, Lydia and I were born here in Wind River. We became the best of friends in the first grade and she's still my best friend to this day." He turned to Maud. "We married at eighteen, shortly after graduating from high school. She made my life complete. I can lean on her when I'm weak, and she can lean on me at those times she feels that way."

Maud gave them both a warm look, placing her hands on top of the table. "Lydia told me one day about how you two just fell all over each other in the first grade, how you were her hero. She always called you 'twinkle toes' because your blue eyes sparkled like stars in the sky."

Snorting, Sam colored. "Lydia? Did you have to tell her that?"

Tittering, Lydia arched an eyebrow imperiously. "I know you don't like that name I gave you then, but it was the truth. Heck," she said, waving her hand in his direction, "to this day you have the most beautiful, sparkling blue eyes that I've EVER seen. And, you still are, to this day, MY knight in shining armor!"

"Oh," Sam demurred, embarrassed, "when you fell head over heels for Paul Newman, you said his eyes were as pretty as mine were."

"And who did I marry, Mr. Samuel Whitcomb?"

Laughing with Steve, Maud felt comforted when he placed his hand over hers. "I once was on a plane, in first class, a United flight, and Paul Newman was sitting across the aisle from me," she told them. "And Sam, I have to tell you, the first time I met you? I was so struck by the beautiful color of your eyes, how they shined with such life, that I almost told you this story of meeting Mr. Newman, and that your eyes were better looking than his."

Ruddiness tinged Sam's cheeks and he raised his thick brows over her compliment. "That's a right nice compliment, Maud. Thank you."

"See?" Lydia teased unmercifully. "See? I was RIGHT! Now? Will you finally, after all these years, believe me?"

Steve grinned at his parents. "So, you two are okay with Maud and me being engaged?"

Sighing, Lydia clasped her hands beneath her chin, giving them a joyous look. "This is so funny, because last night before I fell asleep, I told Sam that you two were meant to marry each other. Everything you do, there's a kindness shared between you. And I love that you support each other's dreams. That's so rare. It's something precious that you two have."

"And respect," Sam said in a gravelly tone, nodding. "Both of you are truly the best of friends and there's respect between you. I can't tell you how many times and situations, Maud, when you come for a visit to see us, that Lydia and I would sometimes sit back, shocked, at how much you reminded us of us," he said, and he placed a thumb against his barrel chest. "I couldn't be happier to hear this. I believe you were meant for each other, just as Lydia and I were."

"Sam! I got five minutes till I gotta get that spaghetti out of the stockpot! Let's ask them about when they want to get married after I sit back down!"

Steve laughed. Maud smiled.

"It's going to be a very long, Victorian era engagement, Mom. We want to get married shortly after we graduate from getting our degrees."

"Oh," Lydia whined, "that's YEARS AWAY!!!!" She pushed the chair away, smoothing her apron.

"Now, Lydia," Sam said gently, "the kids are right. It's not a bad idea. They are in very demanding fields, and if they got married sooner, it might detour one or both of 'em from finishing up their degrees. Don't you think?" and he gave his distraught wife a gentle look.

"Oh . . . oh, well, I guess."

Maud's heart fell, seeing her disappointment. And it was real. "Lydia, I think we have some good news." She turned to Steve, and he nodded.

Steve squeezed his mother's hand. "Our summer vacations will be spent out here and divided up between being with Maud's parents for a month. And then the rest of the time, we'll be out here in Wind River. Maud, tell them what you'd like to do with your time spent here with us."

"I want to learn all about how to run the ranch, Lydia. I know that you two want to retire and go to Tucson, Arizona, at age sixty. Steve and I want to take over the ranch, understanding that it belongs to you until you pass it on to us. But we can caretake it until that time. I know nothing about ranching, so I wanted to spend the time with you and learn. Really learn. That way, I can carry on all your wonderful ideas that are making you a lot more money, as a result."

"That's a wise plan," Sam congratulated. "Don't you think, Lydia?"

Lydia lightened up a bit, feeling somewhat better. "Well, yes, yes, that sounds like a good plan, Maud. I'd love to teach you what I know."

"And I'll teach you the rest of the work, Maud. I know Steve has already told us he'll be in and out of the ranch, somewhere in the world building economy homes for third world countries from time to time. And you'll be here at the helm by yourself. You'll need ten or fifteen years to really learn it all and then build upon your experience."

"Plus," Maud said, anxious to make Lydia feel better, "Steve and I want to start taking Thanksgiving and Christmas break with you. We think it would be nice to split the holidays and we can be with my mom and dad, and we can be with you at the other time. We can switch them around every other year."

"Plus," Steve said, "during our spring break, we'll be out here with you. Maud needs to see this ranch run in all four seasons."

"Sound judgment, Son. That's a fine idea," Sam said, and gave his son a look of pride.

"But, won't your parents be unhappy about that?" Lydia asked.

"I don't think so. Honestly? I find myself not wanting to be in a big city anymore. I need to talk to my parents about the engagement, and our long-range plans. They lead SUCH a busy life, Lydia, they travel so much, that I don't think they'll miss having me in New York. I'm hoping my mother will understand why we'll be out here with you two-thirds of the time. I have to learn how to keep the ranch solvent when Steve is away on business. And if nothing else, my mother is the ultimate businesswoman and she will understand that."

"See?" Sam said archly to Lydia. "The kids are gonna spend most of their time with us. So, don't look so glum, honeypot. This is all good."

"Yes," Steve said, "and I'm relying on you both to help Maud when I'm gone. We don't like the idea of many months of separation when a new project starts up, and she'll be lonely."

Lydia reached across her son and patted Maud's arm. "Don't you worry, sweetheart, we will make

SURE you aren't lonely. We'll take such good care of you! Now, I gotta get to that spaghetti!" She hurried toward the kitchen, a big smile on her face.

Steve winked at Maud, who nodded. This was going to work. He hid his worry over Maud's parents and what they would think of it. That would be the next hurdle.

CHAPTER THREE

August 29, 1966

Maud tried to quell the butterflies in her stomach as she and Steve rode in a taxi from the New York City airport into Manhattan where her parents had a multimillion-dollar penthouse apartment that overlooked the city. Steve had been here four times in the last two years, for a weekend each time. Like her, he was glad to get out of this bustling global city and into the quieter backwaters of Princeton and their apartment in New Jersey. Like all New York City taxi drivers, the man wove in and around traffic with a fierce passion whenever possible. She hated it and kept her eyes closed a lot, always afraid that someday, she would be killed in an accident caused by one of these kamikaze pilot drivers.

Steve placed his large hand over her fisted hand resting on her white linen slacks. His flesh was warm, skin roughened against hers, but it felt good. She appreciated his silent sensitivity to her hating this wild-eyed drive from airport into city. Her mother wanted to have her picked up in the company limo, but she declined the offer. It wouldn't be any better in a limo, either.

"Do you think your parents will be there?" he asked her.

She opened her eyes, focusing on him. As always, Steve dressed the same for her parents as he did everyone else, the symbolic black Stetson on his head. "They said they were coming in from Paris, France, landing two hours ahead of us. I hope their plane hasn't been delayed."

"Well," he said, looking out the window, watching the canyon of skyscrapers blur by, "if they are late, we'll just make ourselves at home." A teasing grin came to one corner of his mouth. "We've already been assigned two guest bedrooms, a hall apart from each other. We'll get our luggage and put it in the bedrooms and wait for them."

"Mom has a live-in maid, Selene, so she'll have lunch waiting for us."

"That's right," he said, "I forgot about that." Giving her a smile, he said, "I guess that puts us in the maid's place, right? We have to do all the daily stuff on our own. Make our own breakfast? Lunch? Dinner?"

"Well," she muttered, "Mom tried to hire a cleaning service for my apartment before I met you. I told her no. She just doesn't understand 99.9 percent of the people of the world can't afford to have a maid living in their apartment like they do."

"It's another reality," he agreed. "I'm not surprised you turned her down."

She turned her hand over, squeezing his. "I guess I'm embarrassed by my family's wealth. Not that they didn't earn it the hard way, they did. They worked for every penny they've made. But"—she shrugged—"I don't look at money as buying a five-million-dollar penthouse apartment or hiring a live-in maid, as necessary. Even as a kid, when I could understand their wealth, I thought it was supposed to be given to those who had hardly anything in order to survive. I always asked my mom about that and eventually, when I was nine years old, she took me to a soup kitchen in the Bronx to show me that their donations kept it open to feed the hungry and poor. I loved my parents so much for that, and I loved being in that soup kitchen. From then on, she allowed me to go with her every Saturday, unless she was out of town on business, to work at the soup kitchen and help others."

"Your parents have a big heart and they're generous," he said, nodding. "And kudos to your mother for seeing how you felt, and she showed you what money could do for the needy."

"Yes, as I grew up, she showed me more and more of what her and my father's hedge funds were doing to help the poor around the world. Instead of being forever embarrassed by rich parents, I began to change my attitude and be proud of all they did for others."

"Did you ever lose your embarrassment over their penthouse apartment?"

"No . . . never did. I just don't see extravagant use of money—just because you have it—to feather your own nest. All I had to do is walk anywhere in the Bronx and see horrible poverty. But I never said anything more about it to them. They have their lifestyle, and mine is different from theirs and that's okay. They respect my choices and I respect theirs."

"You said the other day that your parents donate millions of dollars a year to major charities around the world. That makes my head spin. I can't imagine, first of all, making that kind of money."

She snorted. "Tell me about it! Yet, my parents have MBAs and they were fascinated with finances. For them, it's a challenge they love to pit themselves against. They're both risk takers and if you own a hedge fund, you are the quintessential high stakes gambler. They both started up their own hedge funds and eventually moved back to their penthouse, had two offices with a staff, and made over a billion dollars a year at it. For them, they love to make or lose money. I'm not like that. I like putting money into something that isn't so much as a risk, as it is a long-term investment that will eventually pay off."

"I guess you didn't get that enthusiastic money challenging gene?" he teased.

She laughed a little. "No. But I love what they DO with the money they make."

"Oh, we're here," Steve said.

He paid the taxi driver and got out. He walked around and opened the door for Maud, holding out his hand to her. She gripped it and eased out of the yellow taxi as the driver got their luggage from the trunk and set it on the curb. The doorman to the apartments came out, tipped his hat to them, welcomed them, and picked up the two pieces of luggage. He smiled at Maud, knowing her by name. She went over and hugged the black man in a neat gray uniform.

"Henry! So good to see you again," she said, releasing him, smiling up at the tall man who was Steve's height.

"Thank you, Miss Maud. I'll take your bags up to the lobby, and have Timmy, our new elevator boy, carry them into your parents' penthouse apartment." His brown eyes sparkled as Maud walked with him to the doors that whooshed open. "Your parents arrived an hour ago, just for your information."

"Oh, good!" Maud said, walking inside the white marble entrance. Timmy tipped his hat, welcomed her. Henry asked the young man to take the luggage up to her parents' apartment.

Maud smiled, shook Timmy's hand because he was new, welcoming him to her parents' world.

Turning, Maud gripped Henry's hand. He was

in his sixties now and had been a fixture in her life since she was born. He always had a stash of candy beneath his desk, on a particular shelf, and when she'd come down from the apartment, he'd sneak her a piece. Her mother wasn't keen on a lot of sweets for her, but she forgave Henry. "How is your family doing? Is everyone well?"

"Yes, ma'am, they are. Everyone is fit, but my wife complains of being a tad overweight since I last saw you."

She laughed with him, because both of them were what people called "string beans": tall and thin. Releasing his hand, she dug into her pocket. "Here's something for Millie, your wife." She pressed the cash, a hundred dollars, into his hand. Henry opened his mouth to protest.

"Nope," Maud said firmly, "take it. Go take Millie out for a nice dinner or something."

Henry shook his head, looking at the wad of cash. "You're kind, Maud. Just like your parents. Thank you. I'll do that. Millie says thank you, too."

She hugged him fiercely. "I'll be seeing you later. I want to come down and catch up on how everyone is in your huge family."

Glowing, Henry stepped back and tipped his hat. "I'd like that a lot, Miss Maud. Now, skedaddle! Your parents were excited that you were coming for a visit."

Steve entered, shook Henry's hand warmly, thanking him for his genuine and sincere welcome. He walked Maud to the elevator, following her in. Taking off his hat, he pushed his fingers through his hat hair that always got squashed beneath the Stetson. Maud turned, quickly pushing some strands here and there off his brow after the doors shut.

"You look fine," she said, as the elevator sped upward.

"So do you," he said, and he leaned over, hooking his arm around her waist and gently drawing her against him, his mouth closing over her smiling lips. The kiss had to be quick because the elevator didn't wait for anyone. In no time, the doors opened directly into the penthouse apartment.

Maud relished the supportive kiss Steve gave her. He always seemed to sense when she needed his strength or his quiet, calm demeanor. Not much of anything ever flustered him. In the two years they had been together, she never saw him get overly dramatic or wigged out on some issue or event. "I love you," she whispered, giving him a quick peck on the cheek as she moved away from him and stepped onto the white marble floor, which was variegated with pink and mostly black spidery lines where fractures had occurred.

"Maud!"

She saw her mother, Martha, come hurrying

toward her. To say that Martha was a fashion plate was an understatement. She wore Coco Chanel suits when working, which she felt was the epitome of a conservative businesswoman, but now she wore low white leather heels with her pink linen suit and a white silk blouse with ruffles around her neck.

"Hey, Mom," Maud said, smiling and opening her arms. Martha was five feet ten inches tall, a model's body and beautiful. Maud was the height of her father, James, who was five feet eight inches tall.

Her mother's arms enclosed her, and she smelled the faint scent of Chanel No. 5 perfume around her. Martha loved Chanel, but it hadn't rubbed off on her daughter, however. She made a quick hug, kissed Maud's cheeks, and held her at arm's length.

"It's wonderful to see you!" She released her and went over to Steve, offering her manicured hand to him, shaking it with warmth and sincerity. "So nice to see you, Steve!" She laughed a bit. "Ever the cowboy in New York City. Right?"

Steve held his hat in his left hand. "Yes, ma'am. Spots don't change on a leopard."

Tittering, she placed an arm around their waists, drawing them forward. "James is in the dining room. Selene is putting the final touches for a lunch for the four of us."

Maud smiled as they walked through the five thousand square foot mausoleum, as she called it. The furniture was the best money could buy. There were handwoven silk rugs, tasteful and colorful, here and there. "Henry said you arrived an hour ago. Are you unpacked?"

"Heaven's no!" Martha laughed. She led them to the huge dining room. It had a pale peach rug beneath a long teak-colored wooden table that would easily seat twelve people. Her parents threw dinner parties twice a month and the rich and famous were always invited. Above the center of the table was a huge, glittery crystal chandelier. "We'll worry about that later. James! They've arrived!"

James was standing by the chair at the end of the table. Maud liked that her dad dressed down when he could. He preferred Izod, more in keeping with a yachtsman kind of clothing. Her father's blue eyes crinkled with happiness and he stepped toward them. She liked his short black hair, and the Izod white polo shirt he wore with a pair of white pants and deck shoes. "Maud!"

His welcome was warm, followed by a huge bear hug. She melted in her quiet, introverted father's embrace. He smelled of Old Spice aftershave lotion, something she loved to inhale and always associated with him. He shaved twice a day because his black bristles grew fast. He bussed her cheek and held her at arm's length. "We're so glad to see you." He released her and then turned, shaking Steve's hand. "Welcome back, Steve."

"Thank you, sir. Nice to see you again, too."

Martha gasped, her eyes rounding. "Maud!" She grabbed her daughter's left hand, staring at the diamond flashing on it. "You're *engaged?!*" she said, and she stared down at her. *"Really?"*

Steve came to Maud's side. "I thought it was time to ask her to marry me, Mrs. Campbell."

Martha stared at it, gasping. "Oh, this is so beautiful, Maud! Do you like it?" James came over, admiring the ring, too.

"I love the guy who gave it to me," Maud said, her voice low with feeling. She was sure her mother probably thought the solitaire was too small for her. Martha, when she dolled up, wore glamorous, flashy jewelry. Maud didn't like wearing any jewelry, but then, her father tended to wear not even a watch, unless he had to. She was sure her fashion sense was her father's genes, not her mother's.

"A great answer," James said. He beamed. "Congratulations, Sweet Pea," he said, and he kissed his daughter's brow. He moved to Steve, pumping his hand. "We always thought that you two would someday get married."

Martha sighed and gave Maud a watery look. "I think you make a beautiful couple." And then she looked over at Steve. "I think you know how special Maud is to us."

"I believe I do, ma'am."

"Come on, let's eat," James said, and gestured for them to come and sit down.

Selene had prepared a simple lunch of salad with thin slices of beef and a vinaigrette on the side. She smiled warmly, pulling their chairs away from the table for the four of them.

Steve thanked her and seated Maud and then he sat opposite her, near James's left elbow. Martha sat with her daughter, her eyes shining with excitement over the discovery her daughter was now engaged.

As they ate lunch, Maud noticed the questions she was asking of Steve and herself. Like his parents, they were surprised that there would be a four-year wait until after they graduated with their master's degrees.

"You know," James said, giving a sage look toward Steve, "I've often thought if couples would marry around twenty-eight or so, the marriage would have a better chance of success. You see these girls at eighteen getting out of high school and marrying right away."

"Because our society wants it that way," Martha growled, her thin brows dipping. "We didn't get married until we were twenty-seven, James."

"Well, I'm glad to see Maud and Steve following the same pattern. Of course, I realize not every marriage is made in heaven, but Martha and I were longtime friends before we married. We shared similar interests."

"I don't see Steve as an architect globetrotting and Maud like an anchor running a cattle ranch," she said, slight distaste in her tone.

"You and Dad need to come out and meet Steve's parents, Sam and Lydia," Maud coaxed. "You've always valued hard work and you won't find two more hardworking people than them."

Lifting her hand, she patted her daughter's shoulder. "But just think, Maud. After graduation you could come and live in New York City. You have a job waiting for you worth millions of dollars. And you'll have an MBA and will catch on quickly to handling my company."

Squirming uncomfortably inwardly, Maud continued to slowly eat the salad. "Remember how I always loved going out into Central Park? That I was always happiest out in the woods, near the pond and lying on the grass?"

"That's true," Martha murmured, sipping her white wine. "You've always been a nature child, Maud."

"She got that from me," James said, winking at Maud. "I love golf. I love being outdoors in the sun and fresh air."

"Yes, and you own four golf resorts within a two-hour drive from the city," Martha reminded him tartly.

"I don't like golf, Mom."

"No, you never did, that's true. I think trees and ponds run in your veins, instead."

Everyone chuckled.

"We've been talking about how to split our summer vacation between the two families," Steve told them. "We know how busy you are, and you do a lot of traveling. Maud and I thought if we stayed no more than a month here with you, that we'd take the month and a half out at my parents' ranch."

Martha was pleased. "I'm so happy to hear this! I was whining to James the other day that for the last two years, Maud, you've spent it entirely in Wyoming."

Reaching out, Maud squeezed her mother's hand. "I just needed that green space, Mom. It had nothing to do with us not wanting to be with you, because we did."

Steve saw that Martha was mollified by Maud's soft explanation. The mother was trying so hard not to put her own wishes and dreams on her footloose and fancy-free daughter. Maud was untamable, and he'd known that from the first. She was just as headstrong as her super-successful mother was. And he could see Martha doted upon Maud. He was proud of Maud for being sensitive and caring toward her struggling mother. There was nothing but love in their expressions for each other. Despite all their wealth, this family understood what was really important and it was something money could never buy—a loving family. He and Maud were very, very lucky in that regard, to have two such sets of parents who loved their child enough to allow them to be who they were. Not stamp the child in the guise of the parents.

Martha leaned over, kissing Maud's cheek. "You've shared some ideas over the last year with us about Wind River Valley. We think your ideas, the growing business plan you're developing, will really work."

"Really?"

James nodded, finishing off a warm homemade biscuit slathered with butter. "Really. You're just like your mother, Sweet Pea. Your business plan, as you're developing it, is grounded in practical economics. Your plans are modest, but straightforward. You've provided jobs for at least a hundred people in the valley, from what I can tell so far."

"Lincoln County is one of the poorest, economically speaking, in Wyoming," Maud said. "The biggest issue is that it's a hundred-mile drive from the border to Jackson Hole, the Tetons park ten miles outside of it, and another forty miles is Yellowstone. No one stops in Wind River Valley except, maybe, to gas up and take off for the north."

Martha looked confused. "Steve? You said you had a family ranch?"

"Yes, we do."

"The pictures you sent to us showed buffalo in some corrals."

"We have a herd of them."

"I didn't see any cows."

"Only during the summer."

She frowned. "What do you mean, only in the summer?"

Maud said, "They lease grass pastures to other ranchers across the West who want to fatten up their cattle."

"Cattle don't survive our winters," Steve explained. "They die of exposure. It's too cold for them, so we have a small herd of Herefords we do keep at the ranch, but only a dozen or so."

"And buffalo do survive?" James surmised.

"Yes, they have really thick coats and have lived in the Plains states for hundreds of thousands of years. If you put a Hereford up in our area, it doesn't have the coat to survive the weather."

"I always thought ranches meant you had scads of cows on it."

Steve smiled a little, finishing off his salad and opening the last biscuit he'd taken from a nearby tray. "Ours doesn't. None of the ranches in western Wyoming do. So? We sell grass leases."

"They've got some of the most luscious and nutritious grass in the US," Maud told them. "It's amazing. It grows so fast. And it's so thick and abundant. It grows two or three feet long, depending upon the species."

"We're going to have to invite ourselves out to meet your family," James said. "I'm sure your father would be more than happy to squire Martha and me around and see the family ranch."

"He'd like that," Steve said, pleased that he made such a request. "We have log cabins on the property and we rent them out to tourists during the summer months. And that's the time you should come, July or August. We'll put you up in one of them, but I warn you, they aren't like your apartment."

"No," Maud said, "they're rustic."

Martha smiled and blotted her lips with the orange linen napkin. "As long as it has a toilet and hot and cold water, I'm happy."

"Oh, they're a lot nicer than that," Maud put in.

"I think, if I recall," James told his daughter, "that part of your business plan was to expand the number of cabins for tourists?"

"Absolutely. Once we get them to stop and play in our area, we want to provide them with a western experience by renting a log cabin. I want to build them big enough for a family of four and even the family dog coming along."

"I just think that the geography of the area is working against you," Martha said, giving her a sad look. "How can you compete with the Tetons, Yellowstone, and Jackson Hole? It's like a nature lover or anyone interested in the Wild West will have it all within fifty miles of these three grand tourist destinations."

"Well," Maud demurred, "my plans are to create places where the tourists driving through will WANT to stop." She gave them an earnest look. "I want family stops. Things for children to play on, to explore and take part in. I know that's years away, and I know tourist destinations always evolve and change. What it is today, it won't be, necessarily, in twenty years."

"It will probably take you that twenty years," James said. "If you're relying on the ranch to be the base of income that means saving a lot of money."

"It does," Steve agreed, "but my mother worked a year to make inroads into a western grocery chain to buy our low-cholesterol buffalo meat. That was five years ago. Demands for the meat have risen over two hundred percent a year. For the first time in our family's history, we've gone from always being in the red, to deep into black territory."

"I need to meet Lydia," Martha said, smiling broadly. "She sounds like a businesswoman like myself."

"Oh," Maud laughed, "she is! Steve and I think you two are like two peas from the same pod!"

"Well, now that they're engaged, Pet, I think it's time we put them on our appointment schedule and get out to meet Sam and Lydia," James suggested.

"Absolutely," she agreed. "I've never really been on a ranch and sadly, I haven't done much western travel, except to the West Coast."

"I'd love you to see their ranch," Maud whispered, suddenly emotional. "It's like a dream come true for me, Mom. The sky is so big! There's so much clean air, trees, and grass. I love the horses and the other animals they raise. I always look forward to going out there. It's like shedding my skin and I renew myself."

Martha gave her daughter a warm look. "You have always been happiest when we were out in the woods or out on the land."

James smiled. "She's taken a lot from me on that. I'd rather be out on the golf course, hunting in the weeds for a ball, as I've gotten older."

"Both of you two birds," Martha declared, "are rural people at heart." She patted Maud's hand. "Over dinner? Let's talk more about when we might come out. And oh, you must tell me what to wear out there!"

Steve gave Maud a one-eyebrow-raised look, but he said nothing.

"Well," Maud said, trying to remain serious, "maybe we can go shopping and I can show you the type of clothes you might want to wear."

James laughed. "You know there are NO five-star restaurants out there in Wind River Valley, Martha?"

She frowned. "Seriously?"

"Seriously."

"But, what about Jackson Hole?"

"None." James's grin widened and he leaned back in his chair, chuckling. "Probably the closest five-stars would be Salt Lake City, Utah."

"But, that's so far away!"

Maud giggled. Steve gave her a sour grin, again, not volunteering to say anything. James laughed deeply, enjoying Martha's sudden discomfiture.

"My mother is a darned good cook," Steve said, trying to ease her worries.

"I've been working with Lydia in the kitchen and she's a wonderful cook, Mom."

"Oh, well, that's good. I'm honestly not worried about the home cooking at Steve's ranch. I trust Lydia's cooking."

"She'll be happy to hear that," Steve said, a grin crawling across his mouth.

James roared with laughter.

Maud saw her mother's cheeks turn bright red. "Mom, it's okay. Really. You will love the food Lydia serves for dinner."

"Just don't expect dinnerware like this," Steve said. "My mother's silverware and china are almost a hundred years old. We're kind of simple that way, Martha."

"That doesn't bother me at all," she told Steve. "I'm truly sorry if I sounded like a shrew about this. I'm just used to New York City. I don't expect the same type of restaurants out in Wyoming."

"It's the Wild West," Steve said, giving her a kind look that he hoped made Martha feel less embarrassed.

"You like a good steak," James teased her. "This is where your beef comes from: Wyoming."

"You're quite right," Martha said, touching her hair in a nervous gesture. "I'm sure it will be a wonderful experience."

"You just can't wear any of your Chanel outfits on the ranch," Maud counseled, patting her mother's shoulder. "And you love to ride horses. Steve's parents have a lot of horses used by wranglers that you can choose from."

"Except," James said, waggling his brows at his wife, "these horses are used to a western saddle and not an English saddle. They use different types of bits, too."

"But I can help you with all of that," Maud said. "There's so many trails to ride! We'll do as much as you want, Mom. Even pack a picnic lunch, if you want."

Martha smiled. "I would love to do that, Maud."

"There's always something going on at the ranch. Never a dull moment."

"I like activity. Now, Steve, tell me. Is it possible to loan me an office while I'm out there visiting? I must be on the phone a lot when Wall Street is open."

"Of course. Lydia has a huge office, two phone lines, and all sorts of machines."

Pressing her hand to her heart, Martha breathed, "That's so good to hear!"

"What? You thought we lived so far out in the country there were no phone lines?" Steve said, and grinned.

Touching her cheek, Martha said wryly, "You're probably surprised I didn't ask if you had the wheel invented out where you live."

Maud cracked up, slapping her hand on her thigh, seeing Steve and her dad roar with laughter. "I was wondering," she giggled, giving Martha a laughter-filled look, "if you thought I was marrying a Neanderthal and we were still in the Stone Age."

"No, no," Martha protested, joining the laughter. "Honest, I did not think that, Maud!"

Rolling her eyes, Maud patted her arm. "It's okay, Mom. Don't worry, I'll make sure you have the right clothes, shoes, and that phone lines are available to you! You won't miss New York City at all."

CHAPTER FOUR

June 15, 1970

Martha sighed, giving her daughter a loving look of pride. "You look so beautiful in that wedding dress, Maud. It fits perfectly this time. Lydia put in those tucks and it just flows from your bodice down to the tulle skirt!"

Maud smiled over at her mother, who stood with Lydia. Both of them had a pleased look in their eyes. She smoothed the white tulle nervously with her hands. "I just don't like getting dressed up, but you're right, I do feel pretty. More like a fairy princess." And she did. The wedding was set for June twentieth at the Unity church just outside of town. Her parents had arrived a week earlier, now comfortable and like old friends with Sam and Lydia.

It was a happy event, all around.

Lydia had asked her years ago if she could make her a wedding gown, and invited Martha to help her. Not a seamstress, Martha employed a wonderful woman who created flower embroidery and then sewed it into the simple lace behind it for the top of the dress to the waist. Lydia had sewn the skirt and the separate parts together and today was the final fit. Maud felt humbled that they had done this for her. The wedding dress took on far more meaning than if she'd had her mother purchase one from a major Paris or Italian designer.

Lydia moved forward and caressed her strands. "Your black hair has grown and with it barely touching your shoulders, it brings out the color in your cheeks as well as making the dress come alive." She touched the shoulder of the dress here and there, making sure the fit was perfect. And it was.

"That's nice to know." She pointed to her shoes. "I like the low white heels I'm going to be wearing," she said.

"You'll be more comfortable," Martha agreed. "And no one is really going to see how high or low your heels are anyway because the dress is designed to barely wisp along the floor."

Lydia picked up the white headband that would fit across the top of Maud's hair. "Martha, I just love that you chose our Mule's-ear yellow daises to cover the headband."

Martha nodded. "My daughter loves nature. She adores wildflowers. These huge yellow daisies will be blooming through their date for the wedding. I think it's a nice touch to honor where she's going to live for the rest of her life."

Maud heard a nearly veiled sadness in her mother's voice. She was trying so hard to be positive about her living on the ranch and not in New York City. At twenty-four years old, she was now a far more mature woman than when she first went to college at eighteen. She and Steve had grown even closer over the years as they lived together in their apartment near the universities. Their visiting schedule worked well for both their families. Best of all? Her father, James, got along swimmingly with Sam. And her mother, Martha, adored Lydia. They were both strong-willed businesswomen and admired and respected each other. Over the years and the visits, Martha had come to understand Maud's desire to become a ranch woman and not a hedge fund owner.

"When Steve sees you coming down the aisle of the church," Martha said, her voice rising with emotion, "he's going to think you are a dream. That dress makes you look ethereal, Maud, like a dream coming to life in our world. Truly."

Feeling heat steal into her cheeks, Maud nervously patted the tulle fabric over her hips. "I just never got comfortable with high fashion, Mom."

"It's all right. This is your day." She beamed, coming over and giving her a peck on the cheek, her way of trying to make her daughter feel calmer about the wedding. She smoothed the embroidery of flowers in the lace across her shoulder and down the sleeves. "I love that the flowers are across the bodice."

"Me too," Maud said, touching the white embroidery on her other sleeve. "I'm wearing nature."

Martha held her luminous gaze. "Steve already knows how lucky he is to love you and you love him." She squeezed her daughter's hand. "You two are truly made for each other."

Lydia came over to stand on the other side of Maud. "And just think, after your honeymoon in Hawaii and you come home to the ranch? You'll begin your PhD in learning how to run this place."

"I'm really looking forward to that," Maud said, eagerness in her tone.

"And Steve, because he won several architectural awards over the past two years for these ecological designs," Lydia said proudly, "he's already got five jobs overseas confirmed and lined up. My son is going to be busy."

"And gone a lot," Maud said, frowning.

"But he has to establish his name," Martha soothed. "The first couple of years will be rough on both of you. As Steve's type of revolutionary designs becomes known, and James and I are going to help him in that regard, he will be able to spend more and more time here at the ranch with you. And one day, sooner, not later, he'll be home all the time and able to coordinate his designs around the world. He's already famous! Everyone wants him."

Maud rallied. "I've gotten so used to him being in my life that it's kind of a jolt to realize we'll be spending more time apart for two years than together."

Lydia patted her shoulder. "You'll be so busy from dawn to dusk that you'll fall into bed, dead to the world every night, Maud. Ranching life is hard, physical, everyday work."

"You're right," Maud said. "And I love being physical and active. I'm so looking forward to you and Sam helping me learn how to run your ranch on a full-time basis."

Martha smiled. "Another PhD, for sure. Armed with your MBA, Maud, Lydia and I will be there to help you complete your business plan for the ranch and this gorgeous valley."

"So?" Maud teased her mother, who was dressed in pink slacks and a short-sleeved silk blouse, "you've fallen in love with western Wyoming?"

"I have," Martha admitted ruefully. "The last four years of coming out here for weeks at a time during the summer have convinced me this is a little slice of heaven."

Giving a sharp laugh, Lydia added, "You won't be saying that about the nine months of winter we get here, Martha. You've visited only when it's warm and sunny."

"True," Martha groused good-naturedly. "New York City isn't much more fun in winter, either."

"That's why you and Dad always winter in Florida at your penthouse in Miami."

"Yes," Martha said, "guilty as charged. I don't care for snow at all."

"That's why I sew during the winter months," Lydia said. "There's not a whole lot to do outdoors. The ranch work slows down, but in the barns and hay mows, it doesn't. We get all our tack equipment cleaned up, repaired, or replaced at that time. We do indoor repairs to all the buildings, too. Replacing a roof or painting the outside of our buildings has to be done in that three months of summer."

"A lot of continuous work," Martha agreed, giving her daughter a concerned look.

Maud held out her long, spare hands. "When you see us next summer, Mom, I'm sure I'll have calloused palms and my hands will be stronger and maybe a little rougher feeling to you."

Martha picked up her daughter's hand. "No fingernail polish, either."

Laughing, Maud hugged her mother. "You know I've never been into makeup or nail polish."

Glumly, Martha nodded. "You've always been a tomboy, Maud. I agree with James: You take after his side of the family."

"But I'm happy out here, Mom. And I love Steve with my heart and soul. We're looking forward to this new chapter in our lives. And I know you will be the lead cheerleader for us."

Perking up, Martha smoothed some of the tulle at her waist. "That's very, very true."

"Besides," Lydia put in, "having two women with MBAs in our expanding family can only help our ranch grow, make more money, and then, Maud can make her business plan for the valley, and make it start taking shape for the people who live here."

"Absolutely," Martha said, giving Maud a smile. "Start a charity out here, too?"

"Oh, that's already in the works," Maud promised, turning around, asking her mother to unbutton the wedding dress. "There's a lot of Vietnam vets coming home and they've got battle fatigue. They can't hold a job and they need help. I was talking with the Becker family in town, who owns the hay and feed store, about that. The first thing I'm going to do is create a soup kitchen and food pantry for the town, Mom."

"Good to hear. Tell me how we can help. We can put your charity on our yearly list."

"That's all I need to know," Maud said, slipping out of the gown, standing barefoot in a long silk slip. Lydia took the dress and hung it up, smoothing it out and then placing a garment bag over it so it couldn't be seen if Steve accidentally walked in. Grooms were not meant to see the dress until the bride walked down the aisle.

Shimmying out of the slip, Maud got rid of

the hated bra that she never wore under any circumstances and dropped it with utter disgust on the couch. Martha handed her a bright red short-sleeved T-shirt and she pulled it on. She was not big breasted, just the opposite. She had hated it when her mother urged her to put on her first bra at twelve years old. She cried. It felt like a cinch around her upper chest, and she saw no reason to wear that awful contraption. She'd had to wear it in high school but just as soon as she escaped to college, Maud got rid of the bra permanently. Except for this wedding.

Giving the bra a dark look, she grabbed her jeans and sat down, pulling on a well-worn pair of cowboy boots that Steve had bought for her four years earlier. These boots were old friends and comfortable to wear, despite all the dings and scraps across the cow leather.

"There," Maud said, standing and smoothing her jeans into place over her long, curved thighs, and then running her fingers through her hair, quickly capturing it into a ponytail. She knew her mother wasn't crazy about her ranching clothes, but she loved them. "It's almost noon. Let's go have lunch in the kitchen. Maybe Dad and Steve can join us."

Brightening, Martha nodded. "Sounds like a good idea!" She slipped her arm around Maud's and they walked to the door, opening it. Lydia followed behind them. Joy flowed through

Maud's heart as the three of them walked down the oak hall toward the central area of the huge log cabin. She missed seeing Steve, but she knew he was out with his dad and wranglers, building another huge buffalo corral, which took a lot of male muscle and at least half a dozen of them working on it during daylight hours. Would they be coming in for lunch? She hoped so.

Steve held Maud's hand as they slowly walked down a well-used dirt trail that would lead them to the red barn where they routinely met for some alone time with each other. He'd come back midafternoon and he'd found Maud in her room, her business plan spread out across the queen-size bed. He'd gotten a quick shower then, wishing she was with him but knowing it was impossible under the circumstances until they got married.

"How did the last fitting on Mom's wedding dress go for you?"

Maud smiled softly. "Your mom is amazing. She put two small darts in at the waist and it fits so comfortably. I'm ready to marry you now."

He winked at her. "Good to know, Tonto."

She giggled. "Right, Kemosabe." Early on in their relationship she referred to Steve as the Lone Ranger, the 1950s TV cowboy hero who wore a black mask and his sidekick was an Indian named Tonto. And she was happy to be his sidekick. The Lone Ranger went around protecting good people from bad people. She saw Steve in the same way. He had soared with his architectural degree.

Many architectural firms were interested in his award-winning low-cost housing for people who could not afford homes that were more expensive. They wanted him to do that, but also to turn his creative and innovative eye to building billion-dollar skyscrapers, as well.

Turning them all down because that was not his vision, he proceeded to create his own company and since then, had so many jobs lined up that she knew she wouldn't see him but four times a year, a month each time. All the work was going to be in different African countries, and he loved that continent. And she wouldn't be able to leave the ranch to join him. A ranch was a full-time job, just like his. In her eyes, he truly was the LONE Ranger, going out to rescue impoverished people, protect them from the baddies of the world, and give them a roof over their head for the first time in their lives. She was so proud of Steve and loved him fiercely for his compassion and humanity toward those who had so little. He was her hero.

"Do you like how the dress fits you now?" he asked, and he cocked his head, holding her gaze as they walked, brushing each other's elbows.

"I love it. I was just thinking earlier that the

top of the dress was created by my mother's seamstress, at her direction. And Lydia, being a seamstress herself, put it all together and created the lower two-thirds of it. That dress means so much more to me because they both worked on it, a team mission, for me . . . for us. It's better than Mom's original idea to employ Chanel to create a wedding dress for me. My mother is great at carrying off and wearing clothing by the best designers in the world, but I couldn't handle the thousands of dollars that would be spent on such a dress that would be worn only once. I told her at the time I'd rather see that money go to a charity instead. She grudgingly agreed."

"Well, the times you've worn a dress or skirt and blouse, you looked pretty to me." He grinned. "However? You can wear nothing at all and you look dynamite, too."

Heat crawled into her cheeks. Steve was raised with rough and tumble, highly independent wranglers, his language salty and reflecting that environment that he grew up in. She'd never heard her mother or father curse—ever. And it was expected a young lady would never speak such epithets, either. "You'd think after all these years, I'd get over your bald language," she teased, laughing and pointing to her reddened cheeks.

Giving her an apologetic look, he said, "I can't

help myself, Maud. You are a looker, no question about it. And you can't hide that great bod of yours no matter what you do or don't wear."

They walked into the coolness of the shadowy barn. Taking the ladder, they climbed up to the second floor where the hay and straw bales were kept. Having a favorite seat, they sat down opposite the opening. As always, they kept their voices low as they spoke to each other.

"Just think," Steve said, giving her an evil grin, "four days from now? We won't have to do this anymore. It will be okay if we live and sleep together."

"That will be nice."

He looked around the cavernous barn, the scent of alfalfa and the sweet, dried timothy hay surrounding them. "Still, this is a nice place to be at times."

"Yes." She snuggled beneath his arm, resting her cheek on his shoulder, her hand resting over his heart. "I'm going to miss you, Steve. I know you need to go, but I will miss you terribly."

He squeezed her shoulders and kissed the top of her head. "No more than I'll miss you."

She caressed his upper chest beneath the denim of his wrangler's shirt. "We'll have phone calls. That will help."

"You're going to be so busy you won't miss me," he said, and he chuckled.

"That's not true!" And she slapped his chest

playfully, lifting her chin, meeting his dancing, laughter-filled eyes. "Snot."

"Yeah, I do tease you unmercifully," he admitted, giving her a look of semi-apology. "I'll be as busy as you. Out in the field, at the sites where the construction is going to take place, I won't be able to talk with you. Once I get back to a major city, I can."

"Do you think after these first two years that you can stay home? I know you have to get everything in order. But after that? Maybe it can be managed from a distance?"

"That's what I'm hoping. I'll be working with local construction companies and after they get the hang of things, I can hire a construction manager from the area to do the heavy lifting so I can fly home and live with you."

His words floated softly into the silence surrounding them. Below, Steve could hear the snort of horses from the stables on the first floor. Someone was walking a horse into the barn, the hooves clip-clopping echoes on the concrete aisle area wafting upward to where they sat. "I'm going to miss you and I'm going to miss my parents and Wyoming."

"Well, where you're going is over a hundred degrees in the summer and seventies in the winter. You're going to sweat a lot, guy."

He smiled and enjoyed her hand moving across his chest. Maud was a toucher and he valued that highly. She always let him know that she loved him in so many small, but important ways.

"I think we deserve a break," he murmured, resting his cheek against her hair, the strands tickling him. "We spent many years of our lives pursuing our degrees, a foundation that will serve us for the rest of our lives. And we were lucky: We lived together for that time. That two-week honeymoon in Hawaii is going to be a godsend."

"Which is why," Maud drawled, poking him in the chest with her index finger, "after that wonderful vacation, I'll feel like I'm being abandoned. Everyone who marries dreams of settling down, having their partner, having children, and being with them all the time."

Sighing, he squeezed her shoulders. "I know. I'm going to use this first construction mission as a template for future ones. As I get to know the global construction industry, the players, and who are good at building structures, I can then turn around and hire those companies and their experienced people. But it's going to take some time, Maud. I don't like it any more than you do."

"I know," she whispered, sliding her arm around his torso, squeezing him. "Don't mind me, I'm just whining. A down day. I'll bounce back by tomorrow morning."

Laughing, he said, "You're allowed. I know my mom and dad love you dearly and they'll see to it you're not lonely. They love you like the daughter they never had. You know that, don't you?"

Nodding, she closed her eyes, content with his warm strength surrounding her. "I do know that. And my parents want to come out for visits at least four times a year, to keep tabs on me." She chuckled. "I'm grateful they will fly out to be with me. I love them and I want to be a part of their lives, too."

"Well," he said huskily, kissing her temple, "soon we'll be Mr. and Mrs. Steve Whitcomb."

She poked his chest. "Hold up, pardner. Feminism is in, patriarchy is out. I want my last name to be Campbell-Whitcomb on all our major and important documents."

"A done deal," he said.

"A woman's place is NOT being barefoot and pregnant and in front of a stove, doing all the cooking. My mother showed me early on that she could run a household, have a kid and a career. That time has come."

"Your best friend, Molly Stewart, graduated with her master's in architecture this year and she's going to be your matron of honor. She should be coming here with Brad Truelove, my best friend, tomorrow. I can hardly wait to see them."

"Me too. I'm so glad Molly and Brad are going to Africa with you. She's interested in ecological architecture, too." Maud loved Molly. They both had very rich business parents and she'd gone to school with her in New York City from the first grade through the twelfth grade. And then, they'd both gotten into college. Molly was a no-nonsense Easterner with loads of practicality and visionary ideas to help people in low economic levels just like Steve. Her best friend had met another architecture student, Brad Truelove, and they'd eventually fallen in love and gotten married three years ago. And with Steve at the helm, they had created the concepts that he eventually won awards for. Now, they were a part of his company and they'd be going to Africa with him. "Are they ready to fly out with you?"

"Yes, they've already got their tickets, their shots, and everything in order."

"I'm so glad because the three of you are best friends and you all love the same thing: architecture," Maud congratulated.

"I am lucky. We've worked well together in school," he agreed. "Once we get to Africa, we all know what jobs we're going to fill. They are eager to see it work and so am I."

She gave him a sly look. "I hope that Molly is getting the same salary any man would for the same position?"

"Molly gets equal pay. I never believed women should be paid less."

"Good to hear." She saw him wink down at

her. He was a rare man in the patriarchy where males ruled the world and women were treated as second-class citizens. There was a streak of fairness in him that spoke volumes. He had never treated her as anything but his equal, proud of her accomplishments and supporting her own vision for her life. They were a two-career couple, an oddball to the woman marrying a man, getting pregnant, running the family, and staying at home. She couldn't see that for herself or for the many other feminist women friends she had, Molly among them. They all wanted a career in a passion that they wanted to pursue. Marriage and children, if any, could come later. Finally, women were putting themselves first, not last, as her mother would often say. Maud was so glad her mother had led the way for women in the world of money, stocks, and bonds. There were many following her, opening up Wall Street firms so it wasn't a hundred percent men working there.

"Speaking of family," he said, giving her a warm look, "are we still on track for what we've planned?"

Maud nodded. "If you're going to be gone for two years, I don't see getting pregnant. I want you home, Steve. I want you there for the birth. I'll be twenty-six by that time and I'll have the ranch management pretty much learned by that time."

"It's a good time to start a family," he agreed.

She bit her lower lip, frowning. "I know I've talked to you about this before. My mother had several miscarriages before she had me. My grandmother did, too. We've been a one-child family. I worry about that. What if I can't carry a baby to full term? What then?"

He slid his arm around her shoulders, hugging her. "Look, like we've said before, if you can't have a child, then we'll adopt. There's plenty of kids who don't have parents or a family. Are you still thinking the same thing?"

Nodding, she sighed. "My period has been a mess all my life. My gynecologist has his concerns. I just don't know, Steve. It eats at me. You know my dream to have three or four kids running around, being part of our lives. I've always wanted a large family. I was an only child and I hated it. I always wanted brothers and sisters, but never got them. I'd really like to break this awful genetic family trait and have those children."

"And I've always pined for brothers and sisters, too. We both come from a one-child family, which is sort of a rarity in our society today."

"That's my only worry," she said, and she lifted her lashes, holding his warm gaze. "Can I have kids?"

"It's two years away. You have other important things to do." He kissed the top of her head. "And it doesn't matter to me, Maud. I love you. I want to marry you. If we have kids, that's fine. If we don't? We'll adopt. We'll love them just as much, regardless. Hold that thought, huh?"

She forced a small smile she didn't feel but didn't want to upset Steve with her greatest fear. She normally kept it deep within herself. "You're right. . . ." He kissed her cheek and she could feel him trying to make her feel better. She had not confided in her mother about it, either, or to Lydia. Somehow Maud knew they would be very accepting of adopted children and love them just as much as she and Steve would.

"Four days until we're married," he rasped, sliding his finger beneath her chin, lifting it slightly so he could fit his mouth across hers.

"Mmmmm." The word vibrated in her throat as she eagerly met and slid against his, the masculine warmth and worshipping of her lips making her focus only on him—and them.

Lifting her hand, she slid it across his broad shoulder, fingers curling around his nape, relishing the sweet contact between them. At the same time, her lower body bloomed and the ache that told her how much she wanted him in every way began as it always did when he kissed her.

As they slowly broke their kiss, breathing a little ragged, Maud smiled up at him. "It's hell not being able to sleep with you every night. I'll be glad being married will make it okay for us to share the same bedroom."

Chuckling, he threaded his fingers through her hair. "We could meet out here after dark when everyone is gone for the day. Our favorite spot? Just you and me?"

"I'd like that," she replied, her voice smoky with desire. "We'll steal out here after everyone goes to bed."

"Better believe that. I wonder if they know?"

"If they do, no one is saying anything. We've never made anything of the fact that we were living together. Dad calls us hippies, and that's okay with me."

"Well, his generation would never have done what we're doing," he agreed, smoothing the strands behind her shoulder. "I think my mom knows."

"I know my mother is well aware, too. I'm not sure about Dad."

"I think both women are street-smart and have known for a long, long time," Steve said. "My guess is that neither father knows."

"Women know how to hold secrets."

He laughed. "That's true. The look my mother gives me sometimes, sorta tells me she knows what's going on."

"Is she judging us?"

Steve shook his head. "No."

"My mother isn't either. That's such a relief."

"I think women are far more flexible and better at dealing with changes, large or small, than men. . . ."

Maud snorted. "I'll agree with that ninety-nine percent. You're the one percent of men in the world who can change and are flexible. Just more reasons why I love you."

"I like being your role model," he murmured, caressing her cheek, holding her fiery gaze. No mistake about it, Maud was a bra-burning feminist. And she didn't brook any of what she called "Neanderthal" males giving her grief, either. No, she went toe to toe with them. He liked that his young wife-to-be was a warrior. Running a 150,000-acre ranch in some of the worst winters in the USA would take a warrior spirit and someone who wasn't cowed and would remain undaunted by the challenges he knew she would have to battle. And he loved Maud fiercely. Steve couldn't wait until the wedding date rolled around. It would be a new chapter, a wonderful one, in their lives together.

CHAPTER FIVE

"Are you ready?" Lydia asked Maud as she nervously smoothed the white tulle skirt one more time. Martha stood nearby, taking photos, enthusiastic and smiling. There was also a young woman photographer, Diana, taking the official wedding pictures. There was a male photographer, Terry, out front, taking photos of everyone coming into the church for the wedding.

Maud nodded. "Yes. I just want to get started." Outside the room, she could hear the organist playing soft, classical music for the overflowing crowd. Peeking out of the door, she saw the entire church was filled with people, and at least fifty were standing around the sides and clustered in the back.

"I think half the valley came," Lydia said, glowing with pride. "I'm not at all surprised."

"Steve said he thought there would be standing room only because there's not that many people in the valley and everyone knows everyone else," Maud said.

"He's right," Lydia confirmed, touching the freshly picked Mule's-ears daisies that had been chosen just outside the church's door by Molly, her matron of honor. The June daisies were everywhere, making the valley a golden carpet for everyone to appreciate. Many of the men gave up their pew seats for older men and women who were coming in late, so they could sit down and let their joints take a rest. That is what Maud loved about Westerners: they were so thoughtful toward children and the elderly, without fail. Up front, she saw her family in the front row of one section, and Steve's family across the aisle, in the other. She didn't have many relatives who were still alive, but Steve's side was filled with a lot of relatives who had traveled from near and far to see him married off. Not to mention old friends he grew up with.

This was a Unity church and the Reverend Sheila Parsons, forty-five years old, her bright red hair in a French twist, blue eyes sparkling, stood at the doors, welcoming everyone. It was very, very rare to have a woman in the clergy at all, no matter the denomination, but Sheila's father, Andy Parsons, had been the leader of the flock until he suddenly died two years ago of a heart attack. The parishioners knew Sheila well and she had graduated from a Unity college and was working as an assistant pastor to her father. When Andy died, it was a seamless transition to ask her to lead the church. No one seemed to care if Sheila was a woman. Still, in Maud's eyes, she saw the woman as a role model, sending the signal to society that within religion, there could be women leaders, as well. God loved everyone. She was so happy that a woman would preside over their marriage vows!

Maud, over the last four years of their academic chase, looked forward to coming out in the summer to the ranch and helping Sheila run their church charity, Harvest Food Bank. It was a soup kitchen, plus a food bank, and she often was in the back, cooking up meals for those who had so little. This church was dedicated to its members as well as anyone else, without fail, and there was a wonderful sense of happiness in the air that she could literally absorb.

Her mother was dressed in a specially designed gold silk Chanel suit. Lydia had made a silk suit of pale green with gold trim—both business-type suits. The mothers had agreed they didn't want bell sleeves, empire waistlines, or puffed sleeves, which were the rage right now. Martha had given Lydia a gift of a bolt of the pale green silk that she'd bought in China months earlier on another visit. Maud thought it was a wonderful gift. And so did Lydia, who adored the sleek, expensive fabric.

Molly Truelove slipped through the room's other door. She was wearing an apple-green gown with an empire waistline that fell to her ankles with low-heeled shoes of the same color. There was a large, flat bow across her blond hair.

"Hey, how are you doing?" Molly asked, coming up to her, assessing her keenly.

"Wishing it was starting. This waiting is killing me."

Martha chuckled and so did Lydia, giving each other a wise look.

Patting her shoulder, Molly said, "I just talked with Brad. He's over in the groom's room. Steve is pacing like a wild animal caught in a cage. He's mumbling the same words!"

Laughing with her, Maud said, "Poor guy. How many people are here? The place is packed!"

"Rev Sheila said everyone has arrived now and there's close to two hundred people. They're playing musical chairs with the elders, and a lot of the guys are giving up their pew seats so that others have a place to sit. Rev Sheila is having about thirty chairs walked over from the annex to here, so everyone is going to have a seat. A lot of the guys are pitching in to help."

"All heroes," Maud said, pleased. "Where are our cascade bouquets of Mule's-ears?"

"Oh, I have everyone's bouquets in Sheila's fridge in the basement. I'll bring them out just before we have to walk down the aisle. I've been spraying them with water every once in a while, so they stay perky and fresh."

"Ever the engineer," Maud teased her architect friend. She saw Molly's eyes light up with laughter.

"I'll tell you, every wedding needs an engineer. There's so many moving parts. Poor little Sherrie Muir just threw up. The poor thing, only seven years old and she's our flower girl."

"Oh no, the poor tyke," Maud said, concerned. "A cold? Flu?"

Molly shook her head. "No, nerves, excitement, and too much of both. She's okay now. Her mom, Pattie Muir, got a 7 Up from down in the basement and her daughter took a few sips of it, and it calmed her stomach down. Thank goodness she wasn't wearing her dress for the wedding yet!"

"That was close," Maud agreed, "but I'm more concerned for her. Maybe we should not let her throw daisy and rose petals down the aisle? What do you think? I want the poor little girl to enjoy this, not be throwing up because she's overly excited."

"She's okay now. But I'll be checking back with them later. Her brother, Todd, who is eight, is doing fine. He's cool, calm, and collected."

"Good to hear."

"He's playing around with the guys. He and his father, Dick, are with Steve and his friends. It's a party in there because they have a neon orange little plastic football that they're throwing back and forth. Everyone's having fun!"

Rolling her eyes, Maud muttered, "Unbelievable."

Tittering, Molly nodded. "You know Steve is a big kid, Maud. He was always playing jokes on all of us."

"Yes, and you're a glutton for punishment, going to work with him in Africa!" she teased back.

Molly gave her a smile and buffed her green fingernails against her dress, shining them up. "Hey, I'm really excited about it, Maud. Brad, Steve, and I have always worked well together. We'll be a good team over there in Africa to help the poor. It's in keeping with the Peace Corps vision that President Kennedy created in the 1960s. We feel like them! Doing something good for humanity."

"It's true, you are and I'm proud of all three of you. Me? I'm looking forward to working with Lydia and Sam and learning the ranch business."

"They'll be great teachers. I want to kick around the world with Brad. We're young and we don't want to start a family until we're around thirty. Everyone thinks we're crazy because women get married at eighteen and by the time they're our age? They have four kids!"

"Not us, either," Maud said. "We're putting off our family for two years while Steve gets the template for his economical home designs in place."

"Yes, I think it will take two years, for sure. But once we get the template nailed down, and pardon the pun, we can then replicate these homes very quickly anywhere they're needed. Steve has tasked me with going to major lumber companies around the world and getting bids from them for producing the various hardwoods, the plyboard, and other items necessary to build a house. And then I'll put it in a package, contracts signed, paid for, and then these folks who don't have homes will have one."

"That sounds really exciting," Maud said. She glanced at the watch on her right wrist. "Ten minutes to go."

"Yep, we're getting there," Molly said. "Your dad will be knocking on the door in about a minute before you walk down the aisle. He's excited and so proud of you, Maud."

"He's super excited!" Maud said, smiling. "I'm so glad he'll be with me."

Once her dad arrived, the photographer asked if the three of them could stand together for some impromptu pictures and they complied. Afterward, Molly said, "I'm going down to the fridge and get all our bouquets. I'll be back in five minutes! You look beautiful, Maud!"

Maud smiled a little, her stomach tight with anticipation. Not one who craved the limelight and attention, she wished for a justice of the peace at the courthouse instead. But her mother would have had a conniption over that idea. She wanted a big wedding, and her parents had paid for the whole shindig. Smoothing the dress, her mother came forward and blew her an air kiss.

"Soon, darling girl!" She squeezed Maud's hand. "You're so beautiful in that dress!"

"Our dress," Maud said, giving Lydia a fond look of gratefulness. "It gives this dress so much more meaning to me that both of you have worked on it."

"Indeed. Well, I'm going to get my seat. Lydia? Coming?"

"Yes," she said, picking up her small white beaded purse.

"Molly will put the flowers in my hair," Maud told them. "Skedaddle!" They all hugged one another and then left.

For about three minutes, it was silent in the room. Maud slipped into her low white heels, hating to even wear them. She'd much rather be in a pair of her old cowboy boots or her work boots. At least her toes wouldn't be pinched in her boots with the severely pointed toes on these darned heels. What a pain!

Molly came whizzing in, arms full of two cascade bouquets and her hairband ornament. Breathless, she grinned, pushed the door closed, and settled the flowers in place on a couch. Grabbing the hair spray nearby on a table, she quickly placed the hairband over her head, the flowers fresh and in place.

"Perfect! The guys are already up there at the

altar! Everyone's excited!" She turned, handing Maud her cascade of the huge yellow daisies that had been placed with orange carnations and cream-colored roses. The same flowers were in her hair. "You look gorgeous! Steve is gonna faint when he sees you! He's never seen you so dolled up," she said, and she laughed, grabbing her bouquet, which was about half the size of Maud's.

"There's our cue," Maud whispered, her voice squeaky with nerves, listening to the organ song now starting to play.

"I'll get the kids out in front of me right now! Just peek out the door once we get them about a quarter of the way down the aisle."

"And that's my cue to come out."

"Yep!" Molly said, and squeezed her hand and slipped out the door, leaving it open for James to enter. It was Molly's job to get the children lined up, give them a last-minute reminder of what they were to do, and then send them down that white-carpet aisle. Maud smiled, peeking and seeing cute little Sherrie Muir with a large willow basket full of daisies and cream rose petals. She was having a ball throwing them into the air. People along the aisle laughed and smiled hugely at the child as she passed by them.

"Are you ready?" James asked her, giving her a kiss on the temple.

"More than ready, Dad. You look great in your tuxedo!" she said.

"Are you disappointed I'm not in western gear?" he asked, giving her a grin.

"Not at all. You and Mom represent the East Coast. Steve and his friends and family represent the West. I think it's fine."

Her gaze drifted up to the front. Rev Sheila was in her cream-colored robe, a bright red mantle around her neck and hanging halfway down it, the black Bible in her hands, smiling beneficently at everyone.

Her heart pounded to underscore how handsome Steve looked. He wore a black light wool western tuxedo. The coat had two buttons, showing the white cotton shirt he'd chosen and the thin black tie around his throat. With that black Stetson on his head, he looked dangerous, sexy, and all hers.

His best man, Brad Truelove, was dressed in the same type of tuxedo, but wore a green silk vest beneath the coat, the same color and fabric as the maid of honor's dress. Next to him, Steve's groomsman, Chris Cooper, another student he'd met at Princeton, was dressed the same as Brad. They'd grown very close over the years. Both guys, she knew, were from the East Coast. She wondered how they felt wearing western duds, cowboy boots, and Stetsons. She grinned and giggled. It was nerves. Her father smiled at her.

Little Sherri Muir got the hang of throwing flower petals around and started skipping and dancing about halfway down the aisle. The church erupted with laughter and clapping.

Maud's throat tightened as Sam stood up when little Todd, the ring bearer, drew closer. He held out his large hand to the boy, who was looking all around, tripped, almost fell, but held on to that green pillow that had a pair of fake wedding rings on it.

Once Sherri was at the altar, standing next to Todd, and he was standing next to Sam's tall, calm side, the organ music changed.

Molly looked back at Maud, grinned, turned, and then became solemn and stepped forward, her movements measured with the beat of the slow music. Maud slipped her arm around her father's waiting arm. Her heart started beating so loudly she could hardly hear anything. She held the bouquet in front of her and waited until Molly made it up to the front of the altar.

Maud felt her father gently tug her arm as a signal to start walking down the aisle with him.

The organ music thundered, sending vibrations throughout the packed church, as the wedding march filled the area. Everyone stood, turned, and faced her.

Oh! She felt like a fly pinned to a piece of cardboard in a science class! But she knew most of these people. They were her friends, and her neighbors. Her father glanced down at her, and she melted beneath his look of love.

Suddenly, all her nerves dissolved and, in their place, she felt a lightness entering her heart, appreciating that all these people took pains and care to come in their best finery to see her married to Steve. It brought tears to her eyes and she swallowed hard and kept doing that slow step forward. They were all celebrating her and Steve's coming happiness. How could she be nervous about that? Maud just wasn't used to such intense scrutiny, an introvert, a shadow who quietly walked through life and liked it that way. It could have been overwhelming if she hadn't focused on the wonderful celebration that was here, in this church.

When her gaze moved to Steve, she no longer heard much of anything else. It was as if her whole life, her reason for existing, was standing and waiting for her at the altar. She saw the warmth in his pale blue eyes that reminded her of the wide sky during the heat of August in Wyoming. She clung to his gaze, feeling an invisible warmth reach out and encircle her in an embrace. It dissolved all her nervousness and anxiety.

In its place was a wonderful, flowing happiness sweeping through her chest, her heart swelling with such joy she thought she might faint from the euphoria now enclosing her. She saw nothing but Steve. As she approached the altar, Molly took her beautiful cascade of flowers, smiling broadly.

James moved forward, taking her elbow and guiding her to where Steve stood. Her father gave her a watery smile, and she knew he was just as emotional as she was. Maud reached up, kissing her father's cheek, seeing tears glimmer in his eyes. She saw Steve's parents wiping their eyes, too.

Steve's hand was warm, solid, and calming to Maud. He stood so tall and proud beside her. Rev Sheila was beaming broadly at them.

James shook his hand. "I know you love my daughter and she loves you. Welcome to our family."

Steve nodded. "Thank you," he choked out.

James turned and sat down in the first pew next to Martha, who was dabbing her eyes with a white linen handkerchief. The organ music began to fade away.

Maud faced Steve. They reached out, claiming each other's extended hands. The pastor began reciting the ageless words that so many couples had heard before, but for Maud, as she repeated them, they were brand-new and she meant every word she spoke. She drowned in Steve's moistened eyes. His voice shook with emotion as he spoke those same words back to her. Their whole world anchored to a sweet halt, embracing them as their many friends and families listened intently with their eyes, ears, and hearts. When it came time for little Todd to hold the pillow up toward Steve, the child beamed proudly. The real wedding ring was already in his hand, but Steve went through the motions of taking the one on the pillow. He thanked Todd, patting him gently on the shoulder and then aiming him toward Sam, who took him back to his side once more.

Maud lifted her hand and Steve took it, saying the words he meant with all his heart as he slid the simple gold ring onto her finger. And then, Maud took a larger plain gold ring for him, whispered the words, tears leaking from her eyes, as she slid it on his finger.

"You may kiss the bride," Sheila pronounced, her voice husky with feeling.

Maud stepped forward, Steve cupped his hands around her shoulders, drawing her near, guiding her to him, and she relaxed. It was over. It was real. This was forever.

As he leaned down, his mouth brushing hers, she felt a flare of such overwhelming joy that tears were running down her cheeks, trickling into the corners of her mouth. He kissed her with all the tenderness he had inside him, her tears melding and connecting them.

Tears of joy.

"I have one more gift to give you before the day's over," Steve confided to Maud. They had spent four hours at the annex, dancing and chatting with their friends and relatives. The photographers were everywhere. Five hundred people showed up and all the wives had brought casseroles, and a feast was had by everyone. They managed to slip out about five p.m. and drove back to the main house where they had one wing of the log cabin that they would call home for now. Tonight, they could sleep together, make love with each other, and no longer have to hide how they felt from anyone. It was a day of freedom as far as he was concerned as he pulled out a long, thick roll of paper from the nearby closet in the living room.

Maud poked her head out the bedroom door, pulling on a favorite old pink T-shirt that hung over her hips and had short sleeves. She had traded in her beautiful wedding dress for a pair of gray sweatpants and comfy old tennis shoes. Taking the hair ornament out, she had brushed her hair so it rested once more on her shoulders. "Really?" She wandered out into the living room where he was unrolling the papers. Looking at them, she realized it looked like architectural drawings for a house. Sitting down next to him, she said, "Is this the surprise you were hinting at last week in the barn?"

Steve grinned. "Yeah, it is." He slid his arm around her waist, pulling her close. "This is going to be our home, Maud. I worked with Sam on these months earlier. My parents have given us ten acres of land about a mile down the road. It's away from all the busy areas that their home is a part of around here. Lydia thought you'd appreciate the grove of trees, with the house built on one side of them, and it will protect it from the hard west winds of winter."

"That's wonderful!" she said, blossoming into a smile. "Ten acres? I know where that grove of pine trees is, Steve. It's one of my favorite places to go ride and have a picnic. It's such a quiet place. I just love that area!"

"Well, it's all ours now," he said, spreading out the blueprint. "I've drawn up the plans, but I want your input and ideas." And he laid out the two-story log cabin. It had a total of five bedrooms. Maud had often wished out loud to have four children; two boys and two girls. He knew that because of his career, which had made him an instant global architect star, they could afford a large family. He absorbed her excitement as he showed the lower part of the home would be wide open and not hidden behind walls or partitions, as most homes were nowadays. Anyone in the L-shaped kitchen could look up and see the family in the dining room or living room. It was a huge and masterful project that must have taken him weeks to figure out the underlying construction to make it structurally sound.

For nearly an hour, they were bent over the coffee table and the many drawings he had labored over for nearly a month. Maud had good ideas, things he could change in the blueprints. Things she wanted in her kitchen, or in the four bedrooms that they hoped someday would be for each of their children.

Finally, Maud sat up and leaned back, taking his hand, kissing the back of it. "You're so visionary, Steve. How is it a kid of a Wyoming rancher has such an incredible and creative mind?"

He flushed. He liked the pride in her eyes over his efforts to create their new home that would be built starting a week from now. "I honestly don't know. My family has always been ranchers here in Wyoming for over a hundred years. You know from being out here in the summer for the last four years that being a rancher means having to be super creative. We make do with things or create tools or fixes, from whatever we have lying around."

"That's common sense talking," she agreed.

He glanced at the blueprints. "Building and designing need total common sense."

She moved and tucked her legs beneath her. She slid her arm around his shoulders, resting her head against his neck. "I love it. I love you."

"My dad is going to work with the local contractors. He'll be managing the whole project."

"Yes, and winter comes early in September. They don't have much time to bring everything in. And who is going to build it in the winter?"

"Sam has several construction companies lined up and they plan to have the shell up and enclosed with a tin roof by mid-October. Then? All the inside work, the drywall, the stringing of electric and putting in the plumbing, can be done. The main contractor, Ryan Collier, out of Driggs, Idaho, just across the border from the valley, will be managing the crews who are coming and going. Getting the cabin enclosed means everything. Usually, if we're lucky, mid-October will bring some snow, but not the five-foot blizzards of December onward."

"That's an amazing time line, Steve. You're leaving at the end of September for Africa."

He gave her a sad look. "Yeah, even though I'm excited about going to Africa to put my plans on the ground, I'm going to miss you, and miss the building of our home."

She squeezed his shoulder, commiserating with him. "I'll miss you so much. . . ."

"I'll be calling you every night when I'm in the city. But five days a week I'll be out in the boondocks where there's no electricity or phone lines."

"We'll deal with it," Maud whispered, kissing his cheek. She could feel the heaviness around Steve. They had had four happy years living together. Now, they were going to endure two years apart, off and on. It was hard on both of them. "And I'll send you photos every week so you can see how the cabin is taking shape."

"I'm going to look forward to them," he said, emotion in his voice.

"We can look forward to the rooms, the paint colors we'd like, the type of furniture you and I want. I'll be cutting out a lot of magazine pictures on these things and stuffing them into the envelope as well."

Steve leaned back, placing his arm around her shoulder. He kissed her slowly, sliding his hand along her cheek, holding her in place to absorb the sweetness of the woman he loved more than his life. He nibbled on her ear and she giggled, lifting her head away, giving him a chastising look.

"That's not fair!"

"No," he admitted, sliding his fingers through her loose, shining hair, "it's not. I'm going to miss sneaking up on you and doing it."

"Joker!" she said, and she laughed, kissing him hard and swiftly.

"I like making you laugh, sweet woman. Your eyes are incredibly beautiful when you do it."

"You're a silver-tongued devil, Whitcomb," she said, and she slid her hand along his jaw, leaning forward and whispering against his smiling mouth, "but I love you anyway. . . ."

CHAPTER SIX

September 30, 1970

Steve moved quietly, rolling onto his side, watching Maud sleeping deeply next to him. Outside the window, he saw the autumn dawn peeking around the edges of a blanket put up over the glass. The construction work on their cabin had accelerated because he'd wanted their bedroom in the house completed before he left for Africa. Everyone involved had worked hard and on weekends to enclose the shell of the cabin to protect it from the coming snow, which had already fallen three times earlier. His father had gotten several men to complete their bedroom on the second floor, put in the electric, the plumbing, drywalled it, and painted it so he and Maud could have this night in their own home before he left for Africa. He could dream, when alone, of this night together with his wife. It would sustain him over the months that he'd be gone from her warm, loving arms.

He watched the slow rise and fall of her chest beneath the pink flannel granny gown she wore, and the purple goose down comforter that lay across her shoulders, which kept them toasty on the below-freezing night. There was no heat in the cabin yet. Their master bathroom was off the bedroom, and they'd enjoyed a hot, steamy shower together in it last night. But no heat in the cabin meant piling on the blankets, plus the comforter. They'd made love and then slept. And woke up again around three a.m. and loved each other a final time. Each had fallen into an exhausted sleep in the other's arms after that.

The windows did not have drapes on them yet, but that would come with time. The blankets would do. The queen-size bed was the only thing in the room, along with two small braided brown, cream, and yellow rugs on either side of it. The floor was still in its plyboard phase, the oak flooring not yet due for arrival. Still, it was their bedroom and Steve would carry this special memory in their lives with him to Africa. From the time they had been married in June, to a few days ago, they had gone over every detail of what color each room in their cabin would be painted, the appliances to be ordered, the furniture chosen for each room; and it was all placed in Maud's thick, growing scrapbook, along with ordering information for each piece.

Her dark, straight hair hid half her face from him and he wanted to wake her with a kiss, but wanted her to sleep, too. They hadn't exactly gotten much rest last night and his mouth twitched with self-deprecating humor as he quietly eased out of the bed. Turning, he tucked the bedding against Maud's long, graceful back and over her shoulders to keep her warm. Tiptoeing out of the room, he gently closed the door to the bathroom. Time for a shower, a shave, and start preparing to leave around noontime for Africa.

By the time he'd washed his hair, taken a good, bracing hot shower, and was towel drying off afterward, Maud came stumbling sleepily into the bathroom. A huge cloud of steamy humidity rushed out of the open door. She shut it quickly, wanting to keep the warmth inside the huge room. She smiled and pushed hair away from her face.

"Did I wake you?" he asked, hanging the towel on a hook and retrieving his dark green flannel shirt, pulling it across his shoulders.

"No, I just woke up on my own. What time is it?" She located his watch on the counter, picked it up, and squinted to see the clock hands. "Eight a.m. We overslept."

Chuckling, he pulled on his Levi's. Sitting on the edge of the tub, next came a pair of thick, dark cotton socks. "We didn't exactly get eight hours of sleep, did we?" he said, and he smiled up at her. Maud had pulled on her fuzzy purple bathrobe, which fell to her slippered feet.

"No, but it was really, really nice," she said, and she reached out to touch his damp hair. "No regrets."

"Want a shower?" he asked, standing and then leaning down to kiss her lips.

"I need coffee first," she muttered sleepily.

"How about I get the coffeemaker downstairs, load it up, and bring it up here and plug it in. It's the only place where we have electricity."

"That would be wonderful. . . ."

He placed his hand on the brass doorknob. "I'll bring up the Coffee-Mate and sugar and spoons, too."

"Good," she murmured, shucking out of the robe and hanging it on a hook on the door. "Thank you, lifesaver. . . ."

He smiled, slipped out of the door, and shut it.

Maud sighed and stepped into the shower, shutting the glass door. In no time, she had a lovely, very warm stream of water against her skin. She washed her hair, luxuriating in the warmth of the water pouring across her face and closed eyes. Her heart lingered on Steve, and that he was leaving her at noon today. A small pain went through her as she stepped out of the shower, placed a towel over her hair, and grabbed a second one to dry herself off. As she was using a hair dryer and brush, the door opened. In came a cup of coffee and Steve behind it.

"Oh, my hero," Maud whispered, setting the hair dryer down, turning and taking the cup from his extended hand. She took several sips, made a humming sound in the back of her throat, closed her eyes, and savored the coffee that had creamer and sugar in it.

Shutting the door, Steve leaned against it, thumbs in his pockets, smiling. "You are now officially saved, my lady."

Opening her eyes, Maud grinned grudgingly, her hands warming around the tall white ceramic mug. "You are my knight in shining armor, Sir Steve. Thank you. This tastes so good!"

He looked at his watch. "We promised Mom and Dad that we'd join them for breakfast. Can you be ready to leave in half an hour?"

"Oh, yes, no worries." She set the cup aside and slid her arms around his shoulders, kissing him soundly and for a long time.

"You taste like coffee and honey," he murmured against her lips, sliding his arms around her waist and hips. "I'm going to miss this."

"Me too."

He stared down into her sad-looking gaze. "It's not forever. Just two years. And I'll be back home four times a year, for a full month, each time. You're going to be busier than a one-armed paper hanger, Maud. There's so much to learn about ranching."

"I'm sure I will." She caressed his shaven cheek. "When our home is finished, it's going to be awfully large and awfully lonely. It will be just me here."

"I know," he murmured. "We're both going to be lonely for each other."

She moved back, turned, and looked in the mirror, fluffing her recently dried hair. It was straight, so it always fell nicely, barely brushing her shoulders. It took her another fifteen minutes to get dressed and put on her snow boots. She stepped out and saw Steve taking down the blankets from across the windows. She spotted their heavy winter coats lying at the end of the bed. Glancing at the rumpled bedcover, knowing that she would no longer feel his male warmth against her at night when she went to bed, Maud picked up her coat. Her heart ached already with the loss of Steve in her everyday life. She'd grown so used to having him around. And now this. Steve helped her into her coat. Deciding not to dwell on how she was feeling inwardly, Maud thanked him. They hurried down the stairs, still unvarnished wood.

The entire lower area was chilly, her breath like little clouds ejecting from her mouth as they left the cabin and moved into the attached garage. Climbing into the pickup, Steve drove them down the wintery road toward the main staging area of the ranch where his parents lived.

The morning was like a million diamonds glistening beneath the sunlight, each conifer wearing a glowing snow gown magically sparkling against the white of the covered earth and blinding light blue of the cloudless sky above them.

As they drove up to the U-shaped drive and parked in front of the house, there were lots of winter birds at Lydia's huge seed feeder. A number of woodpeckers were at the nearby suet container. Maud decided she wanted one of those bird feeders at their home, too. The cold went to thirty below on some days, which could pretty much kill any bird in the area.

Tramping through the snowpack across the graveled area, Steve opened the white picket fence gate leading to red bricks that had been swept clean. In no time, they were inside the toasty warm house. Sam met them and helped Maud off with her coat, hanging it on a nearby peg. She thanked him and hurried to the kitchen, seeing Lydia was busy making many stacks of buckwheat pancakes. The kitchen smelled wonderful!

"What can I do to help, Lydia?" she asked, leaning over, giving her a kiss on the cheek.

"See all that food on the counter? Just take it to the dining room table. I'm just about done here."

"Gotcha," Maud said, scooping up a casserole of eggs mixed with chopped bacon, onion, cheddar cheese, and red pimentos, plus a large platter with at least fifteen hot, steaming pancakes on it.

Steve came in and picked up the butter and

syrup, and followed her. Sam brought a cold pitcher of orange juice from the fridge.

Steve drew out the chair for his mother. Sam pulled out the chair for Maud, and then they sat down. They all clasped hands, bowed their heads while Lydia said a short, heartfelt prayer. He always liked that he'd been taught to be grateful for everything put on their table because out in this harsh, demanding country that was so beautiful, people and animals lived and died—a stark reminder that life was tenuous at best. He'd grown up appreciating every meal, the smell of it, the taste of it, and had been raised on this mind-set by his grandparents, who struggled to survive the Great Depression. It hadn't been lost on his parents, who were raised to value every morsel of food, and to make something out of it to eat. Nothing was ever wasted. Nothing was ever thrown away. A roof overhead wasn't taken for granted, either. His grandparents had lived in a canvas tent as they escaped the Dust Bowl and went west to California.

"Did you like your freezing night in your bedroom?" Lydia asked, passing the syrup after she poured some on her two pancakes.

"My nose was cold," Maud admitted, taking the bottle. "But I was warm under that comforter you gave us."

Sam nodded, buttering six pancakes in a stack on his plate. He was going to be going outside and work in the harsh cold even though the sun was shining. Cold stole a lot of energy away from everyone and a top-notch breakfast protected him from that loss. "Maud, did you know that Lydia made that comforter you used ten years ago?"

"No," she said, passing the syrup across the table to Steve.

"Well, you can have it," Lydia said. "I have another one that I made two years ago on our bed. A goose down comforter just can't be beat."

"And you have heat in your house," Maud said wryly, cutting into the fragrant pancakes, her mouth watering. For several minutes, all she could hear was the clink of silverware against the plates. The casserole of eggs was a great pairing as far as she was concerned. Amazed that Sam ate such a huge meal compared to her own, she had come to realize over the summers just how hard and constantly wranglers work outdoors. Steve had three pancakes on his plate. She and Lydia had two apiece.

Halfway through the breakfast, Lydia brought a coffee cake out of the oven, placing it on a trivet and cutting it up. That would be dessert. The scent of cinnamon wafted into the air. When Sam was done with his towering stack of pancakes, he got up and brought over coffee cups and poured strong black joe into each cup. Maud inhaled deeply, loving the scent of the freshly percolated coffee. Lydia gathered chicory, a weed with blue flowers that grew around the area, and pulled up the roots. She cleaned the roots off and dried them and cut them up into fine little chunks. This was coffee for the Depression Era poor. No one could afford to buy ground coffee and her grandmother had discovered it made a tasty cup of non-coffee. It was free and anyone could pick it, dry the roots, and crush them, and then "coffee" could be drunk. She had shared that trick with Maud, who genuinely liked the coffee-chicory mixture. Last year, Lydia had shown her the chicory growing in the area. They'd pulled a bunch from each huge patch around the ranch house, and then Lydia showed her how to dry the roots. After they were dried, Lydia cut them up almost as fine as coffee grounds. Now? She couldn't think of coffee without chicory in it, the tastes all enhanced and delicious. She also found out that in New Orleans, chicory was mixed with coffee.

"You packed yet?" Sam asked his son.

"Not yet. Getting there."

Lydia frowned. "We're going to miss you terribly, Steve." She reached over, patting Maud's forearm. "But we'll make sure she's cared for and has lots to do."

Sam said, "Why don't we have our dessert and coffee in the living room?"

Great idea, Maud thought. She looked forward to sitting with Steve's parents. Every time they did that, she learned more and more about Steve and his growing-up years through the stories they shared with her. Maud helped Sam clear the table. Steve took the coffee cups down to the coffee table. Lydia cut up the coffee cake and Steve took the saucers and forks down, as well. By the time Maud and his father were done clearing the kitchen table, everyone gathered on the two couches that faced each other, the red and gold cedar coffee table sitting between them.

Maud sat down, looking to her left at the roaring blaze in the main fireplace. She would never tire of the crackle, snapping, and pop of the wood that wranglers had chopped for their three fireplaces in the house. She'd even tried her hand at chopping wood and found it a lot tougher than she realized. Over the past summer, she'd join Steve out at the huge woodpile and put in an hour's worth of chopping with him every few days. Everyone worked; there were no lazy people on a ranch, that was for sure!

She loved sitting next to Steve, enjoying the discussion, the cake and coffee. When they were done, Steve said, "Stay here. I've got something for you . . ." and he rose, giving his parents a smile. They smiled back like they were sharing a well-known secret that she didn't have a clue about.

Curious, Maud watched Steve walk down the

hall toward the end where the washer-and-dryer room was located.

"Now, Maud," Lydia urged, "close your eyes. Steve has a surprise for you. . . ."

"Really?"

"Close your eyes," Lydia urged excitedly, beaming.

Maud nodded and put her hands over her closed eyes. She could hear the sound of Steve's boots thunking down the hall, and then heard a door being opened and closed. His boot echoes were coming closer to where she sat. What was it? What was the surprise? She heard Lydia giggle and Sam chuckle. How bad she wanted to open her eyes! She felt Steve sit down next to her, the cushion dipping slightly next to hers.

"Open your eyes, Maud," Steve said.

She did so, now wildly curious. As soon as he set the fuzzy, warm, wriggling thing into her hands, her eyes flew open.

"A puppy!" she gasped, her eyes going wide as her fingers curled around the fluffy, curled white hair.

Steve cupped her hands around the puppy. "This is Gracie. She's a very rare, white golden retriever and she's eight weeks old." He looked deeply into Maud's gaze. "I didn't want you to go home to an empty cabin, sweet woman. Every rancher has at least one dog, and usually more than one, in their home. Gracie was born in a litter of my father's friend Hector. She was the only white one. The rest were gold colored." He gave her a wobbly smile, his eyes glistening. "Gracie is as rare as you are. And goldens are known far and wide for being loyal and loving people dogs. She will keep you company so you won't be lonely, Maud. This is my parting gift from me to you. . . ."

Gracie yipped and leaped from Maud's cupped hands, landing on her chest. She licked her jaw and neck, nuzzling beneath her chin, wanting to be cradled and held. Maud didn't disappoint her. Sniffing, she saw the tears in Steve's eyes, knowing the parting was just as painful for him as it was for her. She held the wriggling puppy, who stopped whining once she cossetted her against the warmth of her body.

"She's perfect, Steve . . . just perfect," she managed, her voice cracking. "And beautiful . . ."

Steve caressed her hair. "Like you. And I bought Gracie from Hector precisely because that pup's color was different. You're different, too, but in the best of ways." He stroked Gracie's head with his index finger. "She'll be a good friend to you, Maud. She'll take some of the loneliness away from you while I'm gone."

Lydia came over, making clucking sounds as she leaned over, gently petting Gracie's head. "We just got her yesterday, Maud. Steve was having a heck of a time keeping her a secret. She's such a cute little tyke!"

Sam chuckled. "Maud? Lydia is already spoiling Gracie."

Everyone laughed.

"I'm sure I will, too," she said, leaning upward and giving Steve a kiss. "Thank you," she whispered to him. "This is just the best gift," she said, and she looked down at Gracie, who was utterly at home in her hands, snuggled up beneath her chin.

"That pup knows home," Sam said, nodding sagely. "She's going to be a good companion for you, Maud."

Lydia stood up, giving her son a loving look. "Gracie will be wonderful with any children you have, too. They are such people dogs. They live to be with humans."

"That's good to know. I wasn't raised around dogs and cats like you were." Maud gave Sam and Lydia a searching look. "You'll help me with Gracie?"

"Of course, honey," Lydia said, patting her shoulder.

"We're old hands at having animals around us," Sam assured her, a twinkle in his eyes.

Steve gave her a warm smile. "In a year's time, Gracie will become your best friend."

"She can't replace you, though," Maud said, kissing the top of Gracie's fluffy white head.

"No, but she'll make your life feel more whole," he said. "I've always had a dog since I could remember."

"You went six years without one," she reminded him.

"Not because I wanted to," he admitted. "Dogs completed me. I truly yearned to have one at Princeton, but there was no way to make it happen."

"Well," Sam said, his voice deep with confidence, "when you come home for visits from Africa, I'm sure Gracie will be happy to include you in her family."

Maud laughed. "That's probably truer than we know, Sam."

"Steve and Sam bought a nice, woven willow basket for Gracie from the Beckers' Feed and Seed store. It's on the service porch. It's nice and warm for her and I put one of my very old towels in it so she had something to snuggle into."

"You might want to have her in your bedroom," Steve said. "Gracie will feel abandoned if you lock her in the service porch every night and she's away from the person she loves."

"Okay, I can make that happen. But you don't put her in bed with you, do you?"

"No," Lydia said. "She'll be happy to be in her willow basket bed near your bed. She just needs to feel you're not that far away from her."

"Makes sense," Maud whispered, giving Steve

a loving look. "She's priceless. And perfect." Reaching out, she gripped Steve's hand, watching the love burn in his eyes for her alone. His thoughtfulness of getting her a puppy who could grow up with her here at the ranch as she learned how to run one was a brilliant idea.

"I'm sure Gracie will keep you fully occupied," Steve said, lifting her hand and kissing the back of it.

"It will be great to write to you about how Gracie is doing. I'll be sure to send photos, too."

"I'd like that."

Maud knew that Steve would be very busy over in Africa. He was setting up an empire of sorts, a global one, where his house designs could be used everywhere. Two years was a long time, but his visiting during those years, eased her sadness over him leaving her. He loved her so much that he'd thought of a way to short-circuit some of her loneliness.

Her heart swelled fiercely with love for this man who was selfless and loving toward her. Maud didn't know what kind of life lay ahead for them, but she was hopeful because his parents, as well as her own, loved both of them without question. Who knew what was in store for her and Steve? She was excited to find out.

Dear Reader:

It was a joy to be able to get some of the "back-story" on Maud and Steve Whitcomb. Kensington gave me a chance to do this and I leaped at it! And better? To do it with my sister writers, Diana Palmer and Kate Pearce.

Maud Whitcomb comes from a very rich family from the Hamptons of New York. She had everything a little girl could have growing up. Every opportunity because her parents had the money to get her into the best schools and excel. Beneath Maud's exterior lurked a child who daydreamed of a day when she could live out in the wild, wonderful West. She yearned for wide-open spaces, the sky so large over her that it went on forever. She never liked the heavily populated New York City, with its type A energy that never slept and wore on her sensitive nerves.

Little did she know that she'd run into a REAL cowboy at college in New Jersey, where she was spending the next years of her life going after her degree and then an MBA. And she met the handsome wrangler who wore a black Stetson hat at a charity food kitchen nearby! The day they met, she started to fall in love with Steve Whitcomb, a confident eighteen-year-old who grew up in Wind River, Wyoming, and learned the family ranching trade.

The rest is magic! City girl meets country cowboy! Their lives were poles apart, yet their hearts beat in time to the same yearnings: love, wide-open country, and the wild, untamed West! Enjoy!

Warmly,

Lindsay McKenna

The Cowboy Lassoes a Bride

Kate Pearce

*To all the Morgan Ranch readers
who were worried about HW and Sam—
this one is for you.*

CHAPTER ONE

Morgan Ranch, California

"Samantha Bernadette Kelly, you come right back here!" HW Morgan bellowed at her retreating form. "I'm *talking* to you!"

Sam took a quick look over her shoulder as she booked it to the barn. Her beloved blond cowboy was standing in the center of the drive in front of the ranch house, and he definitely wasn't happy. If she could reach her horse, she could get away from him for a few hours and let him cool off.

Not that he'd do a thing to her, but she wasn't ready to answer his question yet. She needed time to think. She hurried into the barn, where she'd already saddled Dollar, and went into the stall.

"Where exactly do you think you're going, Sam?"

She almost squeaked as HW spoke from behind her. He must have moved really fast and was now regarding her over the half door of the stall. He wasn't even breathing hard. She peered at him over Dollar's back with renewed respect.

"I'm going for a ride."

"Right *now?* When I just went down on one knee, and asked you to *marry* me?" HW asked.

"Yes."

"But—"

She held up her hand. "I need to think about it, okay? I'm not saying no. I'm just . . . having a hard time getting my head around the idea."

"Because last time you got engaged the marriage was called off?" HW was trying to be reasonable, and she loved him even more for the effort. "Okay, I get that."

"I do love you, though." Sam added reassuringly.

He stepped back, his hands held high. "Okay. I'll get out of your hair then."

He walked away leaving Sam clutching Dollar's reins and staring after him. She'd expected him to talk her out of it and argue it through until they reached an agreement like they always did. But maybe she was asking too much this time?

She patted the horse and squeezed out of the stall behind his rump. "Don't go anywhere, I'll be back."

Dollar snorted as if he didn't believe her and whisked his tail. She carefully locked the door and went looking for HW. It didn't take her long to find him. He'd gone up into the hayloft and was sitting on a bale of straw, blond head down, hands twisted in front of him staring out over the ranch his family had owned for 150 years.

Her heart actually hurt at the sight of his dejection. Sam bit her lip and approached him, taking the seat next to him on the prickly bale.

"I'm sorry." Sam put her hand on his denim-clad thigh. "I panicked."

He didn't speak, but he managed a nod, so Sam pressed on. "I'm not afraid of loving you, I'm just scared that the moment I commit everything will go wrong. And I know you're nothing like that jerk who two-timed me, and that your word means something, but I guess I'm gun-shy."

"Please go on." He waved a hand at her. "You're winning my argument for me."

Sam took a deep breath. "Okay, then."

"Okay to what, exactly?" HW turned to face her, his expression wary. "Us being on the same page, or okay to marrying me?"

"Both." Sam stared into his stunned hazel eyes and flapped a hand in front of her face. "Oh God. I think I might pass out."

"Well, that's hardly reassuring." His smile warmed her heart as he dumped her in his lap and wrapped his arms around her. "I promise I won't back out, let you down, or screw this up."

"I'm the one most likely to do all of those things," Sam protested as she kissed him. "But it's going to have to be a quick, simple ceremony, and none of that fancy stuff, okay?"

"I'd marry you in a barn, you know that." He

hesitated. "Do you want to do it here at the ranch, or would you rather elope?"

"Here." Sam kissed his nose. "And soon, before I lose my nerve."

HW stood up, brought her to her feet, and with a whoop, swung her around in a circle, laughing like a fool.

"It's a good job I love you so much, Sam Kelly, because your enthusiasm is killing me."

She thumped his shoulder until he set her carefully back down on her feet. "Now what's wrong?" HW sighed.

"Don't say that."

"Which part?" HW asked.

"The dying part." Sam cupped his chin as his smile disappeared. "I can't . . . deal with that again." Her former fiancé had ditched her just before their wedding and been blown up in the same military convoy where she had lost her foot.

HW winced. "Sorry, I wasn't thinking." He kissed her very thoroughly and stared deeply into her eyes. "I'm not going to die on you. I promise."

"You can't promise that," Sam whispered.

"Then I promise to do my best to stay alive until we're celebrating fifty-plus years of marriage."

"Okay. That sounds awesome." Sam nodded. "I'll hold you to that."

HW took her hand. "Then let's unsaddle Dollar and break the news to the family."

"This is awesome!" Nancy, the bartender at the Red Dragon, thumped Sam on the back making her wheeze. Sam had gone to the only bar in Morgantown to celebrate the news of her upcoming wedding with a few of her girlfriends. "Leave all the details of your bachelorette night to me, okay?"

Dubiously, Sam studied her purple-haired, pierced and tattooed companion. "You don't have to do anything *too* radical, okay?"

"Don't worry." Actually, Nancy's confidence was making Sam worry a lot. "I know all the best bars and places to take you. We'll start in Bridgeport and work our way back here to Morgantown."

"Sounds like fun," January Morgan, Sam's soon to be sister-in-law, chimed in. "But I don't think I'll be able to make it with the baby."

"Leave the baby with Chase. He won't mind," Nancy encouraged her. "He *dotes* on that kid."

"It's his kid, of course he dotes on him." January smiled. "He's a fantastic father."

"I know, and who would've thought that a few years ago? He was such a nerd at school." She paused. "You could bring the baby with you? He might enjoy a night out."

"I think I'll leave him with Chase, actually,"

January said firmly. "He's a little too young to be out on the town."

"Well, I'll definitely come," Yvonne from the coffee shop piped up. "Rio's in Vegas, so I'm all alone. If you make it a Friday or Saturday, I won't have to get up too early in the morning to start baking."

"I know Marley and Jenna would love a night out," January added enthusiastically, "And Sonali, Lizzie, and Daisy—"

Nancy nudged January. "You're making Sam nervous. How about we talk about this when she's not around? We don't want her changing her mind or anything."

"Sure!" January agreed. "We're having the wedding the week after next at the ranch. We had a cancellation on the Sunday, so the timing was perfect, wasn't it, Sam?"

Sam nodded, her mind still wrestling with the speed at which everything was coming together. She'd told HW she wanted to get married *quickly,* but hadn't counted on the entire Morgan family mobilizing into action, and actually making it happen within two weeks. She focused on HW, her demanding, gorgeous man, and her heart rate slowed down again. He was worth it. She knew he was.

Avery, who was engaged to HW's identical twin brother, Ry, touched Sam's sleeve. "It's all going to be okay. I'll make sure nothing gets out of hand,

and we get you back safely for the wedding."

"Thanks, Avery." Sam smiled at her friend. "You're probably the most sensible person I know around here."

"*Sensible?*" Nancy said, one eyebrow raised. "You do know Avery was once a competitive barrel racer?"

"Of course I do." Sam grinned at her friends. "Which says a lot about the rest of you, doesn't it?"

No one disputed her assumption, and they went back to toasting her health, and whispering to one another when they thought she wasn't listening. At nine o'clock, Sam rose to her feet.

"I'm going to bed. See you all later."

"Already?" Nancy looked pained. "It's still early."

"I got up at five this morning to help Roy with the pigs," Sam said. "He says I'm the only person on the ranch apart from Jenna who understands them."

"I've got some theories about that, but I'm not going to share them right now." Nancy blew her a kiss. "Off you go, bride-to-be, and I'll speak to you tomorrow."

Sam walked back through the quiet streets of the small town to her apartment above the health center. HW hadn't liked it when she'd moved out of the ranch guest cabin, but had eventually conceded that he had to do a lot less creeping around avoiding his grandma Ruth. Sam enjoyed the drive up to the ranch every morning where she oversaw the equine therapy program with HW, but she also appreciated being able to come home by herself occasionally.

She and HW had what some might call a *tempestuous* relationship. They were both outspoken, stubborn, and liked to get their point across. After almost two years of dating and working together, Sam was ready to concede that they got along well enough to make things permanent.

She checked the parking lot behind her building just to make sure HW hadn't decided on a nocturnal visit. He usually sent her a text if he was planning on turning up, but occasionally when he got stuck in town, he'd just appear, sweep her off her feet, and make wild, passionate love to her all night.

After she got inside her apartment and put all the lights on, she made herself some cocoa and sent a text to her best friend, Cam, in Sacramento.

Hey, are you around?

Yeah ☺☺ Just finishing my shift. What's up?

Sam smiled as she texted back.

Nothing much. I'm just getting married. Can you get time off in two weeks?

Her phone rang, and she winced as Cam screamed in her ear.

"Yay! Go you! That's awesome!"

Sam held the phone away and shouted back. "Thanks! I'm terrified!"

"I bet you are," Cam said. "But I really think this is a good thing, and I'm definitely going to come out there and support you through it."

Sam let out a relieved breath as she eased off her cowboy boots, socks, and then her prosthetic left foot. "That would be so nice of you. And by the way, they are looking for a pediatrician for the new health center if you want a job."

Cam laughed. "I'll think about it. Can you put me up if I come to the wedding?"

Sam gulped and considered the chaotic state of her spare room.

"Sure!"

She'd get that sorted in the next week or so. HW loved showing off his muscles lifting heavy things.

"Then I look forward to it," Cam said. "In fact, I can't wait!"

CHAPTER TWO

"Sam, stop arguing with me, and go and try it on," Yvonne said patiently. "Trust me."

They were currently sitting in what Sam might once have called her worst nightmare— an exclusive bridal boutique in San Francisco. Chase Morgan had let her and Yvonne hitch a ride on his private jet to the big city, and here they were—trying on bridal gowns. Well, she was trying them on, and Yvonne, who had the best taste ever, was advising her. Sam had looked online and in the more local stores, found nothing she liked, and was still not feeling hopeful.

Sam went into the fitting room with Janet, the lovely woman assigned to help her get fitted out, and reluctantly shed her clothes. While she was changing, Yvonne added a few more dresses to the rack.

"Put your arms up, dearie," Janet advised her. "And I'll slip this over your head."

The fabric rustled and whished over Sam's face, and settled around her like the lightest froth on coffee.

"Wow." Sam breathed out hard. "I look . . . *okay.*"

"You look lovely, like a flower." Janet smiled

at her in the mirror as she buttoned up the back of the fitted bodice. "Come and show your friend."

Sam gathered up the skirt and stomped back into the main shop where Yvonne was fussing around with tiaras and veils.

"Oh, *Sam* . . ." Yvonne gasped, "You look *beautiful!*" She dropped the tiara and rushed over to Sam, taking the delicate, many-layered skirt out of her hands, and displaying it properly with Janet's help. "Come and see yourself in the big mirror."

Sam studied herself before turning a slow circle. "It's really pretty, but with my dodgy foot, I don't want to trip up and embarrass myself. I'm thinking that maybe I should choose something ankle length?"

"What are you going to wear on your feet?" Janet asked.

"Cowboy boots. Fancy ones," Sam said. "I'm getting married on a ranch."

"She might need them." Yvonne sighed. "Goodness knows what she could step in."

"And no veil or tiara," Sam said firmly. "I'm wearing a cowboy hat. I don't want Nolly chewing my ear off."

"Is Nolly the bridegroom?" Janet asked, uncertainly.

"No, he's one of the horses up at the ranch, and he likes to get involved in all the weddings, and eats anything he can get in his mouth," Sam replied, and paused. "Rather *like* my bridegroom, actually, but not *exactly* the same."

Yvonne stifled a laugh. "Okay, try on the second one. It's much shorter."

Sam picked up her skirts, hung them over her arm rather like Doris Day tromping through the creek in the old western musical, and went back to the fitting room. HW wouldn't recognize her without her jeans and cowboy boots on, so she'd better keep the boots.

She didn't like the second or third dresses, and neither did Yvonne or Janet, so her hopes rested on dress number four, or some drastic alterations to the first one, which she secretly loved.

The last dress had a boat-shape neckline very similar to the first one, with the addition of embroidered flowers on the bodice and a simple handkerchief skirt that didn't quite reach the floor. Sam took an experimental twirl as she exited the fitting room, and nothing caught under her heels.

"This is also beautiful," Yvonne said. "It shows off your figure, and has that lovely green and yellow embroidery. What do you think?"

Sam smoothed her hands over the skirt. "I like it a lot." She twisted herself in a knot and attempted to find the price tag. "How much is it compared to the other one?"

"Chase said not to worry about that," Yvonne

reminded her. "He's worked out some deal with HW."

"But *I'm* paying for my dress," Sam said. "It's very kind of Chase but I don't expect the Morgans to pay for everything. It's not fair."

Janet stepped forward and checked the price tag. "This one is about five hundred dollars less than the first one you tried on."

Sam gazed longingly at the pile of fluffy goodness, aka the first dress, and tried to be practical. "This will work much better with my boots and cowboy hat, and won't trip me up." She nodded. "I'll go with this one."

"Are you sure?" Yvonne asked. "They are both lovely, but—"

"It's all good." Sam smiled at her, and then at Janet. "You know I'm getting married in less than two weeks, right? Will that give you enough time to get the dress altered and sent on to me?"

"Yes, of course. We pride ourselves on our quick turnaround. We can alter any of them," Janet said. "Why don't you get changed, and I'll make sure I've got all the measurements accurately recorded."

"This getting married is *hard,*" Sam complained to HW as he sat next to her on her couch in her apartment. He'd helped her clean out her guest bedroom, and they were both pleasantly tired from their exertions.

"I hadn't noticed," HW said gloomily. "Every time I ask if I can help organize something, they all tell me not to worry my pretty little head about it."

"Lucky you." Sam poked him in the ribs. "I've had to try on millions of dresses and have a makeup and *hair* consultation of all things, *and* talk to Daisy about my flowers. . . ." She sighed. "All you have to do is pick out a new shirt and turn up."

"It's a tough job, but someone has to do it," HW agreed.

"So there's no excuse for you not to be there, right?" Sam asked.

"Don't worry." HW kissed the top of her head. "I can't wait. No more creeping around." He wrapped an arm around her shoulders and nuzzled her throat. "You, in my bed, finally, and legally."

Sam allowed herself to be thoroughly kissed and reciprocated in kind. When HW slid his hand up inside her T-shirt, she drew back.

"None of that, remember? We agreed."

HW groaned but kept his palm flat against her skin. "You sure?"

"Yes." Sam firmly removed his hand. "It's only a couple of days now." She kissed his nose. "Is Ry taking you out for your bachelor party?"

"Apparently so." HW shrugged. "I have no idea what he's got planned, but he and BB have been grinning and whispering about it all week."

"You behave yourself, okay?" Sam met his amused golden gaze.

"*Me?* You're going out with Nancy," HW pointed out. "Make sure you have your phone with you, and remember the name of Chase's hotshot lawyer."

"Will do." She kissed his mouth and then got off the couch. "Speaking of which, I'd better get ready. Nancy said to meet her at the bar at six, and Cam's due in at five."

She shoved her horny beau out the door, had a quick shower, and was ready to greet her bestie, Cam, when she finally arrived after getting lost a few times driving down from Sacramento. Cam had never had much of a sense of direction, and was deeply suspicious of her car's navigation system, which she called Agnes, and swore was trying to kill her.

Cam had majored in psychology, and then went on to become a pediatrician. She'd helped Sam through the worst of her PTSD after the bomb blast killed the rest of her team, and had ended up becoming a good friend. She was dark-haired like Sam, but way more petite, and totally put together in a way Sam would never be.

"I swear that Agnes was trying to send me to some place called Morgansville about four miles away from here." Cam sipped her coffee and sat on the side of the bed. "She insisted she was right, so I had to turn her off, and work it out for myself."

"There is an abandoned ghost town called Morgansville up on the ranch, so she wasn't far off," Sam said.

Cam shuddered. "Imagine if I'd ended up there. I'd probably have turned around and run all the way home."

"It is pretty spooky," Sam agreed. "Do you think you'll be okay coming out again so soon? We're supposed to be meeting Yvonne and the gang at six."

Cam glanced at her watch. "Give me a few minutes to take a shower and unpack, and I'll be right with you. I wouldn't miss this for the world."

Sam put on a red Morgan Ranch T-shirt, her fancy red boots, and her favorite brown cowboy hat. She'd left her black hair to curl by itself, and even put on mascara and lipstick. Cam also wore jeans, but her boots had stiletto heels and her tight green T-shirt had *Yes, I am a Genius, ask me anything* on it. She'd met the rest of the ladies on her previous visits to Morgantown, so Sam wasn't worried that she'd feel left out.

As she opened the front door, Cam turned and took a picture of Sam with her phone.

"Why are you doing that?" Sam asked suspiciously.

"Just in case we lose you somewhere tonight." Cam winked. "Or for the WANTED posters."

"So not funny," Sam grumbled as they went down to the first floor. She pointed at the health center that took up all the ground-floor level. "You could work right here *and* rent my place after I go live on the ranch."

"That's a short commute." Cam studied the closed door. "Are the staff nice?"

"Dr. Tio is awesome, and he's young, hot, and single."

"Sounds perfect." Cam grinned at her. "Maybe after the wedding you can introduce me to him."

"He'll be there so I'll definitely do it," Sam agreed.

They walked out of the building and along Main Street to the corner where the Red Dragon Bar was situated. Sam stopped to stare at the endless length of a stretch limo that took up half the row of shops. The car was metallic blue and had flashing neon strip lights around all the windows.

Cam grabbed her arm. "Is that for *us?* Cool!"

"Hey, Sam!" Nancy appeared beside a guy in a peaked cap and waved enthusiastically. "Come and meet Ian, our driver! He's originally from Scotland and he has the *best* accent!"

Nancy wore a metallic dress, thigh-high silver boots, and had dyed her hair to match her outfit. All the other ladies had gone for skirts, dresses, or tight pants, and for a second Sam wondered if she was underdressed. It didn't last long. She was happy and with her friends, and that was the most important thing.

Yvonne came over to hug her and Cam. She wore a chic black dress and a beautiful chunky, scarlet, woolen shrug that Sam actually coveted.

"I haven't got my wedding dress yet," Sam casually mentioned to Yvonne before the rest of her posse engulfed them. "It was supposed to have been delivered yesterday, but the tracking says it's still en route."

"That means it has to get here by tomorrow, for the wedding on Sunday." Yvonne frowned. "That's not good. Do you want me to call the wedding place and see if there is anything they can do?"

"I've already left them about a hundred messages, but no one is picking up." Sam tried to stay positive. "January offered me her dress if I get stuck, and it fits me pretty well."

"So much for them being ready to alter anything and get it to you in time." Yvonne pulled out her cell phone and started typing furiously. "I'll see if there is anything I can do."

Sam was almost glad for the distraction provided by the arrival of the Morgan Ranch ladies, Avery, Jenna, and January, who had left the baby with his great-grandma Ruth. By the time Sonali and Marley turned up, the limo was full to bursting.

Nancy decided to sit up front with Ian and poked her head through the glass divider to grin at them all. "First stop, the laser tag place in Bridgeport!"

"Can I take the blindfold off now?" HW inquired as his brother's private jet landed at some unknown destination.

When he'd gotten back from helping Sam clear out her spare bedroom, he'd been ambushed by his groomsmen, hogtied, and put on the plane. He hadn't struggled. Even though he knew they were going to make him sweat, he trusted them to get him back home by the end of the night.

Well, he hoped they would. . . .

"Not yet." That was his twin, Ry's voice.

"You wait until your bachelor party, Bro," HW said. "You'll get yours."

Ry chuckled. "Yeah, right." He took hold of HW's elbow. "Come on. We've got stuff to do."

As soon as his feet hit solid ground, the tinkling and clattering of slot machines reverberated around him. Las Vegas had a sound all its own, and HW knew it well from his days as a professional saddle bronc rider. He wasn't allowed to linger, his brothers and friends sweeping him along, and into a waiting limo. He considered trying to take his blindfold off, but decided it was more fun to just go along for the ride.

He wondered what Sam was getting up to at her

bachelorette party. Nancy had promised him that they weren't going far, and that she would make sure Sam got back safely. But Nancy and Sam out together was a slightly terrifying proposition. He'd once watched them take down a biker in the Red Dragon Bar. He reminded himself that Sam was retired military police and could take care of herself.

"Here we are," his older brother Chase spoke up for the first time. "Let's get into the elevator."

The next thing HW knew, he was being marched out into the open. Wind battered at his Stetson, and someone took it off his head, making him feel vulnerable.

"Stay there, Bro. Let the man do his job," Ry advised.

HW stiffened as he was stuffed into some kind of body harness. What the hell had his brothers come up with? Was he about to be picked up by a crane and dangled over the Strip?

"Walk forward, please." Someone new with a very calm voice spoke in his ear. "You'd better remove his blindfold now."

HW blinked as his sight was restored, and then looked down, and frantically tried to back up.

"What the *hell?*" he said hoarsely. He was literally standing on the edge of an extremely tall building looking down at the city. "I'm not—"

He didn't even get to finish the thought as he was eased over the edge. He plummeted

411

downward until the harness creaked and gathered him up again. He might have screamed. He hoped no one was videoing it, but suspected he was going to be disappointed.

Eventually, he was hauled back up and set on his feet surrounded by a circle of his guffawing friends. He scowled at each of them in turn, and none of them stopped laughing even for a second.

"Welcome to Sky Jump," said the guy with the quiet voice who was busy unhooking HW from the harness. "Did you enjoy that?"

HW found his famous smile somewhere. "It was great. Thanks."

"Wanna do it again?" Ry wheezed. "You screamed like a baby."

HW shot him a death look, which made his twin laugh even harder.

"Come on, HW." Chase patted his arm. "Let's get you a drink. You look as though you need one."

"Hi!" Sam wiped the sweat from her brow and counted her tokens before presenting herself to the bored teenager at the desk. She'd beaten everyone at laser tag and was feeling pretty good about herself. "What can I get for these?"

The boy pointed silently at some hideous stuffed animals.

"I'll take the blue monkey." Sam handed over her tokens, collected the googly-eyed, badly stuffed limp monkey, and tied it to her belt by its tail.

She walked back over to where her posse awaited her and grinned at Nancy. "What's next?"

"Dinner and a show." Nancy winked at her. "Come on."

Three hours later, they were back in Morgantown. Well, Sam thought they were, although her vision was a little blurry, and she had hiccups from the spiced tequila shots at the bar they'd ended up in. She climbed out of the limo on her hands and knees, and was assisted to her feet by an anxious-looking Avery.

"Are you okay, Sam?"

"I'm great!" Sam beamed at Avery and flung her arms wide. "This is the best night out I've ever had!"

Marley, who was something of a Dudley Do-Right, frowned at her. "You need to drink lots of water and go to bed."

"But I don't feel like going to bed," Sam countered. "Unless HW is there all naked and pleased to see me and everything." She winked lasciviously, making Marley blush, and looked around the silent street. "Where is he?"

"I believe he's in Vegas." January chuckled. "But don't worry, Chase promised me they'd bring him home safely."

Sam pouted. "But I want him to be here." She dug her phone out of her pocket and started texting.

Avery looked over her shoulder and cleared her throat. "Er, Sam, you're texting your mother. You probably don't want to send her that."

Sam blinked at the screen and giggled before deleting the text. "Oops! Sorry, Mom."

"I don't think HW has his phone on him anyway," Avery said. "They were planning on a lot of physical activities so Ry thought he might drop it."

"Physical?" Sam frowned. "I hope he's not stripping or anything."

Avery grinned at her. "Nope, just some mechanical bull riding, craft beers, and jumping off a building."

"Wow . . ." Sam put her phone away. "I really wish he was here though."

"I can text Ry, and see whether they are on their way back if you like?" Avery offered.

"Thanks. That would be awesome."

Sonali, Yvonne, Lizzie, and Marley came up to wish Sam good night, and Avery went to speak to January and Jenna, leaving Sam by herself. Cam and Nancy were chatting up the limo driver while settling the bill.

She really missed HW. . . . Sam started walking, her gaze on the recently erected water feature in the center of the street, which commemorated the first Morgan who had founded the town. It had a circular stone base filled with about six inches of water that flowed down from a rocky-type pedestal on which stood the figure of a cowboy, which the Morgans insisted looked nothing like their ancestor William. He stood, booted feet wide apart, one hand shielding his eyes, and a pickax in the other.

Sam stared at him for a long moment. There was something wrong with him, but it would be an easy fix. She waded into the water, giggling as it sloshed over her boots, and clambered awkwardly up onto the stone plinth using the statue's legs to hoist herself up.

"Sam!"

She heard the shouts, but ignored them, too intent on her mission. She stood upright, grinning as she embraced the cowboy and put her arms around his neck. When she felt steady, she carefully took off her hat, and stuck it on the statue's head.

"There," Sam shouted. "Fixed it."

She took out her phone, found HW's number, checked she had it right this time, and held the phone up. She pressed her cheek against the cold stone features of the Morgantown founder, and smiled as she took a selfie and sent it to her lover.

"Sam! Get down from there!"

She looked down to see Cam and Nancy

gesticulating at her, and waved at them, almost losing her grip.

"It's okay!" she yelled. "It's all good!"

"Sam . . ." Nancy took a step closer. "You need to get down. You're going to wake people up."

Sam nodded obediently, and stared down at the gushing water, which seemed to be churning up into a storm.

Nancy held out her hand. "You're coming down, right?"

"Got to get my hat first," Sam said as she put her cell in the pocket of her jeans. She reached up to take the hat, and almost slipped again, making her friends on the ground gasp.

"Be careful!" Cam said in the calm voice she used in her professional life. "Just take it slow, Sam. You can do this."

"I dunno." Sam was now clutching the statue like a lifeline. "I'm not sure about that. Everything's swirling around. . . ."

She looked up as a vehicle came around the corner, blue lights flashing, and stopped right beside the fountain. Nate Turner, the local sheriff, got out of his car, put on his hat, and strolled over to look up at Sam.

"Hey, I've had some calls about you causing a disturbance." His smile was full of encouragement. "Do you want to come down and tell me what's going on?"

Sam swallowed hard. "I'm not sure if I can actually do that."

Nate sighed and rolled up his sleeves. "Then stay put. I'm coming in."

HW cursed out loud, waking his twin, who was sleeping beside him on the plane.

"What's going on?" Ry groaned and rubbed at his eyes.

HW showed Ry his phone, which his twin had returned to him later in the evening.

"What the hell is Sam *doing?*" Ry peered at the image. "Who's that guy?"

"That's the new statue in Morgantown," HW growled. "And she's up there taking a selfie with it."

"Well, at least she's almost home." Ry relaxed down again, and then sat bolt upright when his cell buzzed in his pocket. He took out his phone "What's going on, now?"

"Avery wants to know when we'll be back," Ry called out to Chase, who was sitting at the front of the plane with BB.

"In about five minutes," Chase confirmed. "We're landing on the ranch strip."

After the Sky Jump, they'd taken HW to a microbrewery, and then on to the PBR Rock Bar and Grill, where they'd met up with his best friend, Rio Martinez, and other old rodeo buddies. He'd tried out the beer, rode the bull, and generally had a great night. None of them were big drinkers so HW was quietly buzzed, but definitely still standing.

His bride-to-be was obviously up to something far more worrying, but why was he surprised? Sam's specialty was getting into trouble.

All the cell phones on the plane suddenly buzzed except HW's, and then everyone looked at him.

"What?" HW stiffened his spine. "What's Sam done now?"

Chase came back to speak to him. "Don't stress, Bro, but Sam's been taken to the sheriff's office for causing a disturbance."

Gosh, the sheriff's office was loud . . . Sam wished everyone would just go away and leave her in peace. She closed her eyes, but she could still hear her friends arguing with Nate about his decision to put her behind bars. Had he actually charged her with anything? She couldn't remember. He'd helped her down off the plinth, carried her across the water and straight into the sheriff's office with her friends tagging along behind.

He'd taken her cell phone, so she couldn't contact HW and tell him where she was. Not that it was a problem. She was fairly certain that this being Morgantown, her beloved would be brought up to speed quite rapidly.

Finally, it got quiet, and the room stopped swirling around. Nate came back to take a look at her.

She opened one eye as he handed her a bottle of water and sat on the edge of her bunk. "What did you do to make them go away?"

"Well, I offered to put them all in here with you, and that seemed to do the trick." He fought a smile. "You have a very loyal bunch of friends there."

"I know." Sam sighed and sat up. "Thanks for saving me."

"You're welcome." This time his smile was more obvious. "First drunk who's ever said thank you, rather than taking a slug at me, or vomiting all over my uniform."

Sam made a face as she sipped her water. "I couldn't get down. My boots were soaked, and I wasn't able to get any grip."

"Which is why you don't climb up statues," Nate said. He stood up. "I think I hear your rescue party."

"My what?" Sam said, but he was already on the move, locking the cell door behind him, which he hadn't done before. "Wait—what are you *doing?*"

She heard a familiar voice and lay back down on the bench, pulling the towel she'd used to dry off over her head. The door was unlocked; she heard the sound of booted and spurred feet on the concrete floor, and then silence.

Eventually, Sam couldn't stand it anymore, and lowered the towel to see HW looming over her.

"Eew . . . You smell like spirits." Sam wrinkled her nose.

"So do you," HW pointed out. "But I'm not the one in jail for being loud and obnoxious, and fondling public property."

Sam slowly sat up and waited for her head to stop spinning. "Did you bring a lawyer?"

"For what?"

"To get me out of here."

HW stared at her, shook his head, and held out his hand. "Come on."

She allowed him to help her to her feet and clutched his muscled arm for support. "I can just *go?*"

"Yeah, I'm breaking you out. I tied Nate up in the front office."

"Really?" Sam looked worshipfully up at him.

"Wow, you really are drunk, aren't you?" HW chuckled. He wrapped his arm around her shoulders. "Come on, Billy the Kid. I'm taking you home."

HW paused long enough to thank Nate for not pressing charges, and then walked Sam down the street toward her apartment. He'd spoken to Cam and Nancy, and sent everyone home, assuring them that he'd take care of Sam, and absolving them of any blame. Sam was uncharacteristically quiet on the way back, which was a first, and made the laughter bubbling up inside him even harder to hold back.

In the apartment, Cam's door was discreetly shut, and everything was quiet. He helped Sam out of her clothes and maneuvered her into the shower, getting totally drenched when she refused to let go of him. After toweling her dry, he found her a fresh T-shirt and settled her into bed.

She looked up at him, her green eyes soft and luminous in the lamplight.

"I love you, HW."

He smoothed her dark hair out of her eyes. "I know."

"I really, really do." She squeezed his fingers. "When I'm with you, everything is better. I'm not scared, or lonely, or afraid of going to sleep because I know you will keep me safe from the nightmares."

"Yeah?" He swallowed hard at the trust in her voice. He knew all about her nightmares, which always involved a version of the ambush that had almost killed her and ended her military career. "I'll always do that for you."

"Because even though you are totally hot on the outside, you are also a really nice person on the inside." Sam nodded. "And if anyone says any different, you just send them my way, and I'll sort them out, okay?"

"I will, my fierce little warrior." He kissed her nose. He'd never seen her with a buzz on before. It was quite entertaining.

"I mean it, HW. I'm not putting up with it."

"And I respect that about you," HW reassured her. "But right now, I want you to go to sleep."

"You won't go away?" Sam opened her eyes again.

"No, I'll stay right here." HW reassured her with another kiss. "I just need to let Chase know what's happening and get out of these wet clothes."

She wrinkled her nose. "Why are you wet? Did you fall into a pond as well?"

"Something like that." He stood up. "Now, just stay put, and I'll be back in a minute, okay?"

"Okay, I love you."

He left the bedroom door slightly ajar as he took a quick shower and hung his damp clothes over the back of one of the chairs in the kitchen to dry out. Luckily, he kept a few clothes in the apartment so was able to don boxers and a T-shirt of his Sam had somehow acquired. He also liberated a bucket from the closet and set it next to Sam's side of the bed—just in case.

As soon as he slid between the sheets, she scooted over and put one hand on his chest. Her bent knee rested on his hip. She smelled like a tequila factory, but he wasn't going to let it bother him. She was his woman, and he was grateful for every contrary, beautiful inch of her.

HW gathered her close, and she murmured his name, her fingernails scratching down over his chest toward his abs.

"We could have sex?" Sam suddenly said, making HW jump.

"No thanks. Remember our promise?" HW said hastily.

"Oh, yes, right." She lapsed back into apparent unconsciousness. HW settled down again, watching her like a cat with a mouse until she started snoring.

She might think that he'd saved her, but the feeling was mutual. She was the only woman he'd ever met who was one hundred percent in his corner. When Sam Kelly loved you, you darn well knew it. She might argue everything out with him toe to toe, but he knew in his soul she would never abandon him. And that was the most amazing thing in his whole world. . . .

HW's last thought as he succumbed to sleep was that they'd both survived their bachelor parties, and that in two days' time, barring any more accidents like his fiancée ending up in the town jail again, they would finally be married.

CHAPTER THREE

"Here you go, Sam. Try this."

For some reason Cam's voice was incredibly loud this morning. Sam groped her way over to the table and sat down with a thump. A glass full of something fizzy awaited her, and even that was too noisy.

"Drink up," Cam said. "It really will help."

"Thanks." Sam picked up the glass, braced herself, and drank it down in one. "Gah . . ." She shuddered.

"Exactly." Cam looked way too smug as she ate her granola and yogurt.

"I swear I will never drink tequila again," Sam croaked as her stomach rolled uneasily.

"You're not a big drinker, and last night was a special occasion," Cam reminded her gently. "Just take a day to rehydrate and relax, and you'll be all set for Sunday."

"Is HW here?" Sam looked around, but there was no sign of her cowboy.

"He left about six this morning." Cam grinned. "I caught him coming out of the bathroom, which was a bit embarrassing."

"Was he naked?' Sam asked with interest.

"Not quite. He had a towel around the important bits." Cam ate another spoonful of granola and chewed extra slowly. "But what I did get to see was pretty spectacular. Well done, you."

"Thanks," Sam said. "He is pretty fit. Was he embarrassed when you bumped into him?"

"I think he actually blushed and then he stuttered a bit, held on to his towel like it was a lifeline, and skedaddled for your bedroom."

"Sweet." Sam contemplated Cam's granola. "I think I want to eat something, but not that rabbit food."

"I saw waffles in the freezer. You could have them with maple syrup."

"What a great idea!" Sam perked up. "And lots of whipped cream."

She made herself a plateful of fat, sugar, and carbs and ate her way through the whole lot while Cam sipped green tea and answered e-mail.

"Is there anything we have to do today?" Cam asked.

"Loads." Sam sighed. "I have to go and see Daisy at the flower shop to make sure my bouquet is how I want it, and then check the post office in case my dress has ended up there."

"Your dress?" Cam looked up from her phone. "Not your *wedding* dress?"

"Yeah, that one. I had a message this morning from the store saying that they sent it five days ago and have no idea what has happened to it."

"That's not good." Cam frowned. "Did they give you the tracking information?"

"I think so. I didn't read the whole thing I was too busy hyperventilating." Sam got up to unplug her phone from the charger. She didn't remember Nate giving it back, so HW must have got it. She scrolled through her messages and found the one from the shop.

"There is a tracking number. I'll check it out." She copy-and-pasted the number into the relevant site and frowned. "It just disappears around Friday. I suppose I should call them."

"Check the address as well," Cam suggested. "Sometimes they get it wrong. Maybe it went up to the ranch?"

Sam sent a text to January to see if that had happened and finished her coffee. "I'll still call at the post office. They might have been the ones to make the final delivery, and that's why we can't track it."

Cam put all the breakfast things into the dishwasher and Sam got ready to go out. It was weird worrying about the nonappearance of her wedding dress when she knew HW wouldn't mind what she wore. But trying on the dresses and looking so different had secretly made her want to surprise him. She still had her beautiful white embroidered boots, and a new white cowboy hat with a veil. What she wore in the middle might turn out to be January Morgan's wedding dress. . . . She reminded herself not to worry. It was all good.

She zipped up her fleece, followed Cam out the door and down in the elevator. As they exited the elevator, the outside door of the building opened, and Dr. Tio came in. He smiled when he saw Sam and waited for her to reach him.

"Hey, it's my favorite patient." He looked her up and down. "What have I told you about wading in fountains?"

Sam felt herself blushing. "Oh jeez . . . does everyone know?"

"Pretty much." Dr. Tio grinned as Sam groaned. "Most exciting thing that's happened in Morgantown for years."

By way of a desperate diversion, Sam turned to Cam. "I'd like to introduce you to my friend Dr. Cam Lee. She's a pediatrician in Sacramento."

"Nice to meet you." Dr. Tio shook Cam's hand. "If you ever want a change of scenery, please consider the exciting, bustling metropolis of Morgantown. I'd love to find a great pediatrician to add to my team—preferably one who would stick around for a while."

"Yeah?" Cam smiled at the doctor. "I'm always willing to check out new things. Do you have a website or contact number?"

"I have them," Sam intervened, seeing as the other two were still busy shaking hands and making the most blatant eye contact. "I'll give them to you before you go back, Cam."

"Okay." Cam finally stepped back. "Nice to meet you."

"Right back at you." Dr. Tio winked at Sam. "See you tomorrow at the wedding."

Sam hustled Cam out through the door and onto Main Street. "I told you he was cute."

"You were right." Cam sighed. "Cute and smart. The perfect combination."

"And he loves his grandmother," Sam added. "Which means extra points in my book."

"And in mine." Cam linked her arm through Sam's. "I'm up for a challenge. Maybe I'll move here after all. . . ."

Ignoring the siren scent of coffee drifting out of Yvonne's café, Sam went to the post office and found out that they hadn't received any rogue parcels. The woman in the back did promise to let Sam know if anything turned up, which was helpful. Worried, but trying not to show it, Sam went into Daisy's flower shop, which was next door.

"Hey!" Daisy, who was small and curvy with long brown hair, greeted Sam with a smile. "I hear you were painting the town red last night. I'm sorry I had to work and couldn't come to your bachelorette party. It sounds like it was a lot of fun."

"It *was* fun—until Nate Turner stuck me in the slammer," Sam said.

Daisy chuckled. "Poor old Nate. He gets all the

worst jobs. It's a good thing he's such a nice guy."

"He usually is—except he called HW to come and bail me out," Sam said gloomily. "You can imagine how that went."

It was Cam's turn to laugh. "Yeah, he rescued you from jail, brought you home, helped you shower, and put you to bed. What a big meanie."

Realizing she wouldn't win because Cam was right, Sam turned to Daisy. "Did you want me to look at some flowers?"

"Yes! Come in the back and tell me what you think of this arrangement for your bouquet," Daisy said. "I know you said you didn't want anything fancy, but I wanted to make sure it would go with the design of your dress."

Sam winced. "Well, as to that . . ."

She followed Daisy into the rear of the shop. The smell of flowers and greenery settled around her, making her think of a drenched rain forest. Daisy was also making the corsages for her attendants, and Cam was thrilled with hers.

After Daisy promised to have everything up at the ranch early the next morning, Sam took her best friend into Yvonne's café for a cup of coffee, and possibly something sweet. There was no sign of Yvonne, but Lizzie was busy working the register and making coffee like a pro.

"Is Yvonne here?" Sam asked as she paid for the drinks and Cam's strawberry tart.

"She's in the back. Do you want to speak to

her?" Lizzie asked. "She's got a bit of a headache this morning, which she entirely blames on you by the way."

Glad to hear that someone else was suffering, Sam sat down at the table and sipped her excellent coffee while Lizzie went to speak to the boss. She idly checked her phone as she waited, and Cam did the same.

"Oh, *no,*" Sam breathed.

"What is it?" Cam looked over at her.

"My dress," Sam said. "It's been returned to the shop. It just turned up there as undeliverable."

"What?"

Yvonne joined the conversation. "What on earth happened?"

Sam continued reading the e-mail. "Apparently, the dress and box were badly damaged in transit, and the address label wasn't clear, so the barcode wasn't scannable, and by the time it got to Morgantown, the deliverer didn't know where to drop it off, so he returned it to the store."

Sam sat back. "Well, that's that, then, isn't it?" For some reason she wanted to cry, which wasn't like her at all. Maybe the wedding was getting to her. "I'll *have* to go with January's dress."

Yvonne sat down and took Sam's hand. "We could drive to one of the bigger towns today, and try and find something there?"

"I doubt I'll find anything I liked as much as those two dresses." Sam said. "I looked everywhere before we went to the city. And to be honest, I'm not sure I have the heart to do this all again." She found a smile somewhere. "It's fine, *really,* and you can't leave your business on a Saturday, Yvonne."

"But I could take you," Cam insisted, her brown gaze serious. "Just tell me where to go, and I'll get you there."

"It's *okay.*" Sam met her friend's worried gaze. "It's just a white dress. No one is going to remember what it looks like anyway. Do you want to come up to the ranch with me so I can check out how everything's going, and make sure January's dress is going to work for me?"

"Of course I'll come with you." Cam nodded. Yvonne still looked worried as she rose to her feet.

"And don't tell HW about this, okay?" Sam finished her coffee. "He'll just want to fix everything for me, and I don't want him worrying about anything."

Yvonne didn't look convinced as she went back into her kitchen, but Sam knew her friend wouldn't say anything. HW was way too worried that she wouldn't turn up. She didn't need to give him anything else to fret about.

HW came out of the ranch house and went down the steps to greet Sam and Cam as they got out of Sam's truck.

"Hey." HW smiled at his beloved and her best friend. "Isn't it unlucky for you to see me?"

Sam frowned. "Is it?" She kissed his cheek and gave him a bright smile. "Then maybe you'd better go away."

"I'm not going anywhere." HW kissed her back. There was something up, but he wasn't going to mention anything yet. He'd learned with Sam that sometimes the less said the better because at some point she usually blurted it out all by herself.

"Everything okay?" HW asked casually as he held the screen door open for her and Cam to go past him.

"Yes! Everything's great!" Sam said, avoiding his gaze, which really set his alarm bells ringing. "Is January around?"

"She's upstairs with the baby. She said to tell you to go on up when you arrived." He leaned against the doorframe as she and Cam took off their boots and coats and hung them in the mudroom. "You sure everything's good?"

He caught the glance between the two friends and silently groaned.

"Everything is great!" Sam said enthusiastically. "Can you tell Avery I'll be over to speak to her at the guest center after I'm done with January?"

"Sure." HW stepped back as Sam went by him and marched up the stairs. He touched Cam's shoulder. "Are you sure everything is all right?"

Her smile was about as genuine as Sam's. "Absolutely! Nothing to worry about at all!"

HW walked down the hall to the kitchen, and sat at the table where his grandma was reading the local newspaper and sipping tea.

"What's wrong?" Ruth asked from behind the paper.

"I didn't say anything was wrong," HW objected.

"You're sighing like someone let all the air out of your tires." Ruth studied him over the top of the newspaper. "Is something up with Sam?"

"Ah, the million-dollar question," HW muttered. "When *isn't* there something wrong with Sam? She's acting weird, and I don't like it."

"Have you asked her what's going on?"

"Of course I have." HW scowled at his grandma. "I'm not a complete idiot."

"Could've fooled me." Ruth set the paper aside. "Do you want me to talk to her?"

"No! Because then she'd know I was worried, and that would just make things worse. It always does."

Ruth shook her head and tutted. "Why do you boys always make everything so complicated? Maybe she's just a bit nervous about the wedding tomorrow."

"It's more than that," HW said slowly. "I feel it in my gut."

"Maybe you're the one who is nervous and

you're overreacting?" Ruth met his gaze. "Getting married is a big commitment for both of you."

HW let out another sigh. "I suppose Sam will let me know one way or the other at some point what the heck is going on."

"I'm sure she will." Ruth reached over and patted his hand. "She loves you very much, HW. Don't forget that."

"Hey, Sam!" January grinned as Sam and Cam came into her bedroom. She was sitting in a rocking chair close to the window nursing her son and looked so happy that Sam had to smile back at her. "Hope you don't mind me feeding Chase William. The dress is hanging up in the bathroom. I washed and ironed it last night when no one was around, so feel free to try it on again."

"Thanks." Sam gestured at Cam, who was smiling fondly at the baby. "Why don't you two chat about baby things while I put on the dress?"

"Okay, but give me a shout if you need any help with the fastenings," Cam said.

"Will do."

January had also put out the fancy petticoat that went under the dress, so Sam put that on first, and then the dress. She was a little taller than January so the length was perfect for her. She checked herself out in the full-length mirror on the back of the closet door. The dress fitted her nicely, it didn't drag on the floor, it was white, and it would do just fine. She wasn't going to waste another second bemoaning the fate of her first choice, which had actually been her second choice, because she was being practical and frugal.

"Come and show us!" January called out.

"Okay." Sam walked out into the sitting area where her two friends awaited her. "Ta-da!"

"It's very nice, Sam." January nodded. "You look better in it than I did. Your coloring is much more striking in white."

"Thanks." Sam took a few experimental steps. She had left her boots downstairs but guessed the tips would just show beneath the skirt, which suited her just fine.

"HW is going to be blown away," January said happily.

"I hope not," Sam cracked back. "Can I leave the dress here with you, and come and get changed in here tomorrow?"

"I was just going to suggest the exact same thing." January beamed at her as she expertly patted the baby's back, impressing Sam with the loudness of Chase William's burp. She wasn't used to being around babies and would now be an official auntie to this one, and to BB's teenage daughter, Maria. "This is the biggest room, so we can all get changed in here."

Sam carefully hung the dress back on the hanger and stepped out of the petticoat, mentally reviewing all the other things she needed to bring with her before she married HW. Avery had arranged for someone to come in and do the hair and makeup, and Daisy was bringing the flowers. Was there anything else she'd forgotten?

"My parents!" Sam shrieked, startling the baby and making his lower lip quiver.

"What about them?" Cam asked.

"They'll be arriving here at the ranch around four o'clock, and I haven't checked in with them!"

January handed the baby off to Cam and came over to pat Sam's back. "It's all good. I spoke to them this morning. They have directions, they are on their way, and looking forward to seeing you."

"Thank goodness for that," Sam exhaled. "With all the drama over the dress I completely forgot about my family."

"That's what I'm here for," January joked. "I coordinate things. We're hosting a dinner over at the guest center tonight for all the guests who are staying at the ranch. You *are* coming, right?"

"Of course!" Sam nodded as though she hadn't completely forgotten about that as well. "I'm looking forward to it."

"We can run through our plans for the actual wedding at the dinner, make sure everyone knows what time the ceremony and reception are taking place, and where they are sitting."

January sounded so calm and competent that Sam wanted to hug her, so she did.

"Thanks for doing all this."

"You're going to be part of our family." January hugged her back. "We *love* you. And don't forget to bring everything with you tonight so you and Cam can sleep over in one of the guest cabins."

"I'll get her organized, don't worry," Cam chimed in as she handed the baby back to his mother.

Sam smiled dubiously at Chase William and received a toothless grin in return. From what she had seen, he was a very happy baby who didn't cry much, but that might be because so many helpful pairs of hands and so much love surrounded him.

"Did you tell Chase about me borrowing your dress?" Sam asked. January's husband was a lovely man, but he was famous for his total inability to keep a secret.

"Nope." January shook her head. "You know what he's like."

"Won't he wonder why the dress is hanging in your bathroom?" Sam asked.

"I'm going to hide it away as soon as I put Junior down for his nap," January reassured Sam. "He probably won't even notice that you are wearing it at the wedding tomorrow."

"I hope he doesn't, because being Chase he'd probably point it out, and then HW would be all over me asking why I'd borrowed a dress rather than buying my own." Sam sighed. "And, *then* I'd have to explain it to him, and we'd be well on the way to having our first row as a married couple."

Cam stifled a laugh. "I can see that all too clearly."

Sam smoothed a finger over the blond fuzz of the baby's hair and smiled at January. "He's going to be fair like you."

January groaned. "Another blond Morgan. Just what we need." She walked over to the door and opened it. "I'll see you later tonight, okay? Now go and talk to Avery. She wants to go over the menu for tomorrow, and all the other stuff."

"Yvonne's baked the wedding cake." Sam remembered that at least.

"I know. She brought it up early this morning. It's safely in the refrigerator." January made the baby wave good-bye with his pudgy starfish hand. "Text me if you need anything, okay?"

Sam went down the hallway, and then the stairs, and instead of heading out the door went toward the kitchen.

Ruth Morgan, HW's indomitable grandmother, greeted her with a smile.

"Sam! How are you?"

"Great!" Sam gave Ruth a hug and introduced

her to Cam again just in case. She was missing so many things worrying about the wedding that she'd decided it was better to be safe than sorry.

"I'm just going over to see Avery and talk through the final arrangements. Is HW around?"

"I think he's already on his way over there." Ruth offered them coffee, but Sam declined. "He's worried about you, though."

"What's new?" Sam countered. She had a sense that if the Morgans had their way she'd be confiding the story of the missing dress to all of them, and eventually someone would tell HW. "He knows that if anyone is going to mess up his big day it will be me."

Ruth studied her with all the uncanny observational skills of an almost eighty-year-old woman—which basically meant she had X-ray vision as far as Sam was concerned. Sam concentrated hard on looking like a very happy bride-to-be, but suspected she wasn't fooling anyone.

She held Ruth's gaze. "Everything between me and HW is fine. I swear."

"Okay, then." Ruth nodded. "Maybe you should tell *him* that."

"I will." Sam kissed Ruth's cheek. "I'll see you later at the dinner."

CHAPTER FOUR

HW took hold of Sam's hand, and dragged her out of the dining room where most of the guests for their upcoming wedding were having a great time chatting and getting to know one another. It was the first time that Sam's grandparents had been to the ranch, and they were enjoying sharing long, boring stories of the good old days with his grandma and Roy, the ranch foreman.

Sam grumbled a bit but didn't stop him leading her out into the inky blackness of the clear night sky.

"Where are we going?" Sam asked.

"Down to the barn." HW winked at her. "I know how much you love it in there."

She blushed and looked down at her boots. "It's all very nice until you get pricked by the hay."

"Pricked?"

Sam frowned at him. "Behave yourself."

"I *said* you should've let me be on the bottom." HW grinned. He tried to study her expression, but she wasn't giving much away, which was unusual for Sam.

"Next time, I'll take your advice, okay?"

Sam squeezed his fingers, which made him feel a whole lot better. All through the dinner he'd sensed that something was troubling her, and his unease still hadn't gone away.

"I offered to do Dad's final rounds tonight so he could spend some time with Bella," HW said. "It won't take me long."

He flicked on the lights in the old barn, and several of the horses immediately poked their heads out of their stalls to see what was going down. Sam went over to Dollar and made a big fuss of him while HW got on with the task of making sure all the horses were secured for the night. After a while, Sam started to help without being asked, and they were soon done.

HW washed out the sink in the tack room and stacked the feeding bowls belonging to the barn cats ready for the morning. He also made sure the chickens were locked in their pen and that there were no escapees to tempt the local coyote pack.

When HW returned to the barn, there was no sign of Sam, but he knew where she'd be. Even though it was hard for her to climb the ladder up to the hay store, she loved the view looking out at the Sierra Nevada mountain range as much as he did.

He went up and smiled as he located her sitting on one of the hay bales, her jacket firmly under her butt.

"It's beautiful out here tonight," Sam whispered.

"Yeah." He put an arm around her shoulders

and she leaned into him. "Not half as beautiful as you are though."

"Flatterer." She elbowed him in the ribs.

"I mean it." He put a finger under her chin and raised her face until he could stare into her green eyes. "What's up, Sam?"

She swallowed hard. "Nothing."

He continued to study her, weighing up the risks of challenging her the day before he was expecting her to walk down the aisle to him. But wasn't that the whole point? If he didn't feel she was being straight with him now, wasn't it better to have it out before the big day?

"What if I said I don't believe you?" HW asked slowly.

"About which particular part?" Sam was hedging now, and he wasn't sure whether to laugh or cry.

"So there *is* something wrong." HW hesitated. "Can you just *tell* me?"

"It's nothing worth telling," Sam blurted out. "It's just a stupid thing, which won't make any difference to the day, and I can't even believe I allowed myself to get worried about it."

"If it's worrying you, I'd still like to know what it is," HW persisted. His grandma had always insisted his middle name was *stubborn*.

"Then *you'll* be worrying about it *too,* and the whole point of not telling you is so that doesn't happen!" Now Sam sounded exasperated, and suddenly everything was *his* fault. "It really is okay. In fact you probably won't even notice."

HW considered his options. His gut was telling him to keep asking questions, but experience told him to shut the hell up.

She touched his cheek. "Don't make that face."

"Which face?"

"The one when you look all worried, and then I feel bad, and want to hold you tight, and tell you that everything is going to be okay," Sam whispered. "I'm not going to leave you at the altar, HW. I swear it."

Sometimes she knew him far better than he was comfortable with. Knew that inside him, the fears of a little boy who'd been abandoned by his mother sometimes got out and took hold of him.

"Sam . . ."

She stopped his words by scrambling into his lap and kissing him. She kissed him with all the intensity she was capable of, wanting to erase the look in his eyes that expected to be kicked back again and left behind. He tried to pretend he was such a bad boy without a care in the world, but she knew better. But if she told him about the dress, he'd move heaven and earth to sort it out for her, and it really wasn't worth his time.

"My mom thinks you are adorable," Sam told him in an attempt to head him off at the pass. "My dad, not so much, because I'm still his little girl."

HW's expression relaxed a little as he wrapped his arms around her waist so that she straddled him. "Your parents are great, and nothing like you at all."

"Yeah, I know. They are really *nice,* aren't they? I'm a throwback to my wild Irish granny who came over to New York from Ireland without a penny to her name, a head full of dreams, and a drive to succeed."

"She sounds just like you."

"She also wore out four husbands," Sam noted.

"Wow." HW shuddered. "Maybe not." He kissed her again. "Are you and Cam staying up here tonight?"

"Yes, we are. January said she'd come and wake us up at eight so we can have breakfast, and then start getting ready. She said it would take *hours.*" Sam grimaced. "I'm worried you won't recognize me after they've all gotten their hands on me."

"You'll be the one wearing white, and coming down the aisle, right?"

"Yes, that one." She smiled at him.

"If it's too much pressure," HW said carefully, "we can just get in my truck, drive to Vegas, and get married there."

She petted his chest. "That's very sweet of you, but my mother would kill me."

"So would my grandma." HW sighed. "But I just wanted to put it out there for you." His hand slid over her ass and her hips rolled toward his. He groaned and gathered her closer until the zipper of her jeans pressed against the hard bulge in his. "I miss you."

"Mmm . . ." Sam sighed as she rubbed herself shamelessly against him, her nipples hardening against his chest as she bit and sucked on his lower lip.

"Let me . . ." HW murmured in her ear. "Just let me in, let me make you feel good, okay?"

His work-roughened fingers slid under her T-shirt making her shiver as he bit down on her throat, distracting her as he unzipped her jeans and fitted the palm of his other hand over her mound.

"You're wet for me." He stroked her through her panties. "Yeah, you're soaking."

Sam whimpered as his thumb settled over her most sensitive flesh, and he gently caressed her. She wasn't even aware that she was rocking into his touch, inviting him deeper.

"Oh, yeah," HW crooned to her as his fingers slipped beneath the cotton and slicked through her wet welcome. "That's my girl. Give it up for me."

She shuddered as his touch turned from playful to demanding and his fingers penetrated inside her. He placed his thumb firmly on her bud, driving her on until she climaxed so hard she froze, dug her fingernails into his scalp like a startled cat, and yelped his name.

He reached up and gently removed her hand from his hair. "Ouch."

"Sorry," she gasped against his lips. "It was just so good."

"Thank you."

She eased back a little so she could see his face in the darkness. "No, thank *you*." She ran a hand down over his stomach and tapped his belt buckle. "Now, it's your turn."

"Nah, I'm good." He eased his hand free and set her on the bale beside him. "We're not supposed to be doing this, are we?"

Sam glared at him. "You just remembered that *now?*"

"Yeah. Aren't you glad I took my time to stand my ground?" HW smiled at her. "Tomorrow you can have your way with me, okay?"

"I will," Sam said darkly. "I'll tie you up and torment you all night."

"I can't wait." His cell buzzed, and he winced as he took it out of his jeans pocket and stared at the screen. "January says Yvonne's not answering her phone." He looked over at Sam. "What the hell does she expect me to do about *that?*"

His phone chimed again. "Oh, she says to tell *you* that because apparently you left your cell on the table next to your plate."

It was Sam's turn to wince. "I hope Yvonne is okay. Do you think we should drive down and check?"

"No, I don't." HW frowned at her. "January says she'll get Sonali and Lizzie to report back. They both live right across the road from the café, which makes me wonder why January's telling *us* about this. Aren't the bride and groom supposed to be stress-free for the big day?"

"January probably knew I would worry if I tried to get hold of Yvonne, and she didn't answer me." Sam sighed. "She is one of my attendants. I do hope she's okay." She stood and quickly fastened everything HW had undone. "We should get back."

"Yeah. HW rose and made some adjustments to the fit of his jeans. "By the time we get back to the guest center, the whole thing will probably have blown over."

Sam hesitated, her gaze fixed on his face. Should she tell him about the dress after all? It seemed really unimportant now.

Before she could speak, he turned away and headed for the ladder. "I'll go first."

"Good thinking," Sam rallied, and called after him. "Then if I trip I'll have something soft to fall down on."

His chuckle came back to her. "Nothing soft about me right now, darlin'."

"Well then I'll be really careful, because I wouldn't want anything important to snap off," Sam said.

His choke of appreciative laughter made her

smile as she followed him down the ladder.

When they reached the door of the guest welcome center, HW drew to a stop and faced Sam. It was a cold night, but it wasn't snowing or too windy, so she didn't feel the need to run inside.

HW cleared his throat. "Seeing as this is probably the last moment we'll have alone together in the next twenty-four hours, I want to say something."

Sam nodded encouragingly. "Go ahead."

He poked her gently in the chest with his index finger. "Turn up. Or else."

"Wow, that wasn't very romantic," Sam complained.

His golden eyes glinted. "I love you. If you don't turn up, you'll break my heart."

"Got it." Sam held his gaze. "And right back at you."

"Then we're good." HW stepped back. "Now let's go in and find out what's going on with Yvonne? Rio will kill me if something's happened to his fiancée."

Cam walked up the path ahead of Sam and unlocked the door to their cabin. Sam's parents had already been installed next door, and her grandparents were on the other side. It was kind of nice having them all at the ranch she had started to call home. She'd had a lovely evening introducing her family to HW's and seeing how well they'd all gotten along. It had definitely reinforced her sense that she was doing the right thing.

All the lights in the other cabins were out and it was almost midnight. Sam had stayed behind to go over some last-minute catering issues with Avery, and to take a quick look at the seating plan for the wedding luncheon. Sometimes, she still couldn't quite believe that tomorrow she would be the one getting married. It had all happened so fast.

"January says she'll come down and knock on the door around eight." Cam took off her boots and left them by the front door. "I'll set my alarm as well just so we're covered."

"Cool." Sam removed her fleece and sat on the couch. "Not that I'm going to sleep at all tonight anyway."

"You really should try." Cam joined her on the couch.

Sam checked her messages and frowned. "My brother just texted me."

"Which one?"

"Carter, the only one who still talks to me? He's supposed to be out on an oil rig somewhere, and now he wants directions to the wedding." Sam exhaled. "Talk about short notice. I didn't even bother to send him an invite because I knew he wasn't due back for months. Avery isn't going to be very happy if he turns up and ruins her seating chart."

"It's great that he wants to come, isn't it?" Cam asked. "Why don't you give him the information, and if he arrives at some point it'll be a lovely surprise for your parents, and a bonus for you."

"As I said, maybe not so much for Avery," Sam commented. "But I'm fairly sure she'll just smile, wave her wand, and somehow make everything right again."

Cam nodded. "She is amazingly good at organizing stuff."

Sam found a copy of the invite and pasted it into her message along with driving directions, and received a thumbs-up in reply. She waited another minute, but that was all she got.

"Typical." Sam set the alarm on her phone. "Now I have no idea whether he's going to make it or not."

"I wouldn't worry about it." Cam yawned. "Did anyone get hold of Yvonne?"

"Lizzie said the last time she saw Yvonne, she was on the phone with Rio, and dashing off to her apartment. She's not there anymore, but no one knows exactly where she's gone. She left a note for Lizzie that said not to worry anyone, and she'd definitely be back in time for the wedding."

"Maybe something happened to Rio?" Cam said. "He is a bull rider, and they do get injured a lot."

"That's possible." Sam got off the couch. "I can't deal with anything else tonight. Let's go to bed and hope it all resolves itself by morning."

Sam opened her eyes into complete darkness as her cell phone buzzed right in her ear. She checked the time, which was almost six in the morning, and read the series of texts from her younger brother, Carter.

Sam muttered, "How did he end up near Morgansville with a flat tire? How did he even get onto the *ranch?*"

Knowing her brother was a laid-back version of herself, she wasn't surprised he'd ended up in the wrong place. Squinting at the screen, she replied.

Stay put and I'll come to you x.

She received another thumbs-up in reply.

Sam got dressed in the clothes she'd worn the night before and tiptoed out into the silent kitchen. Should she leave a note for Cam? Hopefully, she'd be back in an hour.

Deciding not to alarm her friend, Sam put on her boots and went out, shutting the door against the cold. The faintest hint of the approaching dawn showed up above the Sierras, illuminating the blackened snowcapped tops. Sam paused to appreciate the amazing sight, then made her way up the slope to the barn.

The route to Morgansville from the ranch was much quicker on horseback than by truck. She knew Carter could ride, because they'd learned together as kids. She decided to take one of the older horses, Sugar, with her and Dollar just to make it as easy as possible for him. The last thing she wanted was a brother with a concussion on her wedding day.

She saddled both horses and led them outside, tying Sugar's reins to the back of Dollar's saddle. One of her favorite things about riding a horse when it was cold was the warmth they generated. It was like having heated seats in your truck. She glanced back at the ranch house as she mounted up, but the whole place was in darkness. She pictured HW sleeping in his bed and couldn't believe that she'd be right there with him later that night.

Smiling to herself, she clicked to Dollar, and they moved out. Luckily, she had a good sense of direction. She only had to follow the old mule road up to the ghost town. The terrain wasn't that difficult after you crossed Morgan Creek, which wasn't running very high at this time of year.

As Dollar splashed through the uneven rocky bottom of the creek, Sam hung on for dear life, allowing her body to move with the horse, yet avoid sliding off. As soon as they reached the other side, she took out her cell, and sent a text to Carter.

On my way. See you in 20. x

She followed the road upward and took the right-hand fork, which would take her to the highest point of the ranch where the original silver mine and the town of Morgansville had stood. After cutting down all the trees and destroying the topsoil, both the silver haul and the creek had dried up, leaving the stamping mill with not enough work or waterpower. At some point, the entire population had voted to move down the valley to the site of the current town and had never looked back.

Sam settled down in the saddle and focused on the narrowing path, and the eerie silence that pervaded the barren landscape. After her experiences in the military, she never felt comfortable in enclosed spaces, where she still feared an ambush. She concentrated on the mission at hand—finding her brother—and on how thrilled her parents would be to see their elusive youngest son.

Eventually, the ground leveled out, and Sam rode alongside what used to be the iron rail tracks that had taken the silver ore from the mine to the stamping mill to be pulverized into a thousand pieces. At one end of the ghost town there was a parking lot created by the historical society so that visitors could get out and walk along what had once been Main Street. Sam could already see a rental car sitting in the otherwise vacant lot, which she assumed belonged to her brother.

She set Dollar off down the slope and leaned back in the saddle as a figure emerged from the vehicle. Carter had black wavy hair just like hers, but his eyes were more hazel than green.

"Hey, Sis. What's up?"

Carter sounded like he'd just popped out for a quick coffee rather than disappearing on her for three years.

"Hey yourself." Sam grinned down at him. The last time she'd seen him, she'd just gotten out of the hospital and hadn't been a pretty sight. "I'll just tie up the horses."

She dismounted and made sure the horses were secured before turning back to her much taller brother. He wore a thick ski jacket, jeans, and decent boots, so he wasn't too underdressed for the cold.

He drew her into a hug and gave her a noogie, which was just like him.

"Long time no see, shrimp." He drew back and looked down at her. "You haven't changed a bit."

"I have!" Sam protested. "I have a whole new foot and everything."

"Yeah?" He studied her boots. "I can't tell which one it is."

"Which is the whole point." She pointed at the car. "How on *earth* did you get stuck up here?"

He shrugged. "I drove all night, got tired, and

just kept following the damn navigation. I went through some wire, damaged the front of the car, and just kept bouncing along until the tire exploded under me."

Sam took a walk around the car, wincing at its banged-up appearance, and stopped to view the shredded back left tire.

"Wow, you really did a number on this. Next time you want to go off-roading, try a horse."

"Can you help me change the tire?" Carter asked. He'd never been the most mechanically minded member of the family. "I'm so tired after trying to sleep in that tiny space that I can't get my fingers to work properly. If we can get the car moving, I'll follow you down to the ranch."

"Seeing as I came on a horse it's not quite that straightforward, but I can certainly show you the most suitable route for a vehicle. It will take you quite a while," Sam said. "The easiest thing would be to come back to the ranch with me on horseback, and we'll send someone up later to pick up your car."

She reached into her pocket for her cell phone to see what the time was and ended up searching through all her pockets.

"Oh crap." Sam breathed slowly through her nose to set off her rising panic. "I've lost my phone."

"Dude." Carter raised a laconic eyebrow. "That's not good."

"I took it out to text you after I crossed the creek. Maybe I didn't put it back in my pocket securely enough." Sam groaned and smacked herself in the head. "I'm such an *idiot*." She held out her hand. "Can I borrow your phone?"

"I hate to be the bearer of bad news, Sis, but mine ran out of juice just before you got here," Carter said. "I brought the wrong adapter with me, and it won't charge."

Sam stared at her brother, who didn't seem to appreciate just how badly her wedding day was going so far.

"I've got to get back to the ranch, Carter."

"I get that." He nodded. "You could just leave me here, ride back, and get help."

"Everyone is busy preparing for the wedding. No one has *time* to come and get you."

"I could start walking and meet them halfway," Carter suggested.

Sam just stared at him until the impulse to scream died away, and she straightened her shoulders.

"No, we're going to work this out. Together."

CHAPTER FIVE

"HW?"

HW turned around and found Cam hovering anxiously at the entrance to the barn.

"Hey, what's up?" HW mentally counted heads as he doled out the daily vitamins, noting Dollar wasn't in his usual place by the open door.

"It's Sam." Cam advanced into the barn after him.

HW put down the bottle. "What about her?"

"She's . . . gone."

Even though it felt like someone had just knocked the wind out of him, HW desperately tried to stay calm.

"Come again?"

"I set my alarm for seven thirty, got up and showered, and then knocked on Sam's door to make sure she was up," Cam said. "When she didn't respond, I went in, and found the bed was empty."

"Okay." HW nodded as if she was making sense. "Did she leave you a note?"

"No." Cam's hands twisted together as she faced him. "Nothing, but her clothes and boots were missing."

"So she obviously got up and went somewhere." HW turned back toward the stalls. "Hold on a minute."

He walked over to Dollar's stall and looked inside. "Her horse has gone."

Cam joined him, her expression hopeful. "Maybe she couldn't sleep, and just went out for a ride?"

"It's possible," HW agreed even though every instinct was telling him no. He checked the time. "Maybe she'll be back soon then."

Cam touched his arm. "She was fine when she went to bed last night, no worries about the wedding, or anything."

"Good to know." HW couldn't stop mouthing stupid platitudes while his mind was racing in panicked circles. "I've got chores to do in the barn. I'll let you know when she comes back, okay?"

Cam still hesitated, her expression uncertain, and HW summoned a smile.

"Why don't you go and have some breakfast, and tell January what's going on?"

"I'll do that." Cam finally nodded as if pleased to have something concrete to wrestle with. "Are you okay?"

"I'm good." He watched her walk up to the house, and then picked up the plastic container filled with vitamins, gazing unseeingly at the contents.

"Hey, Bro."

He turned to find his twin brother behind him. He wasn't surprised. He and Ry had an uncanny ability to know when the other was hurting.

"Sam's disappeared."

Ry blinked once, and then nodded. "Okay. Did you two have a fight or something?"

"No." HW took a quick breath. "I have no idea what the hell is going on."

"I'm sure there's a good explanation, HW. Just stay calm, and—"

"What if she doesn't come back?" HW interrupted his twin. "What if she *never* comes back? It's not as if that hadn't happened to us before, has it, Ry? Our own damned mother walked out on us never to return when we were *five*."

"HW . . . snap out of it." Ry grabbed HW's shoulder and slowly shook him back and forth. "Sam loves you, and she's not the kind of person who would disappear without a word. If she had a problem, you'd hear about it. She's probably just gone out for a ride and will be back soon. Have you tried texting her?"

"Not yet," HW said.

"Then do it right now." At this point, Ry's calm voice was the only thing stopping HW from outright panicking.

HW found his phone and forced his shaking thumbs to text Sam. She didn't immediately reply, which didn't make him feel any better.

"What did she say?" Ry asked.

"Nothing. She's not responding." HW stared intently at the screen, willing her to reply even if it was just to tell him off for bothering her. "If she was going for a ride, why didn't she *tell* someone?"

"Maybe it was a last-minute thing." Ry shrugged. "Look, we've still got hours before the official wedding, so don't get too worked up. Yvonne isn't back from wherever she went to yet either."

"I'm not *marrying* Yvonne," HW objected. "Rio wouldn't like it."

"True, but Sam will be back. I'd bet the ranch on it." Ry smiled encouragingly at his twin.

"I've got chores to do," HW said numbly.

"Great idea." Ry clapped him on the back. "Keep busy, and I bet she'll be back in no time."

"I still think we should change the tire," Carter said stubbornly.

"Why?" Sam faced him down. "It really would be much quicker to ride." The loss of her phone wasn't helping her deal patiently with her laid-back brother. "You do realize I'm getting married today, right?"

"Today?" Carter blinked at her. "Is it Sunday already?"

"Yes," Sam said. "And in a few hours I am *supposed* to be walking down the aisle and marrying HW Morgan."

"What time *is* it?" Carter got into the car and turned on the ignition. "It's almost eight. When's the wedding?"

"Midday." Sam had a hollow feeling in her gut. It had taken her way longer than she had anticipated saddling the horses and then riding up to Morgansville. By that reckoning, it would take at least an hour to get back down. "We really should get going."

"So let's change the tire."

Sam pointed at the gas indicator. "Carter, you're almost out of fuel. Even if we *fix* the tire you won't get far. What's going on?"

He sighed and got out of the driver's seat, shoving a hand through his long hair. "I'm scared of horses."

"What?" Sam stared at him. "Since *when?*"

He shrugged. "Since I fell off, broke my arm, and got knocked out when the thing kicked out at me."

"When was that exactly?" Sam demanded.

"About five years ago."

"Then it's about time you got over it." Sam pointed back toward Dollar and Sugar. "Just get on the damned horse, Bro, *please.*" She widened her eyes at him. "I really don't want to miss my own wedding."

"What about my bags?" Carter asked. He sounded resigned to his fate, and Sam secretly cheered.

"We can tie them on." Sam hustled around to the trunk and opened it. "You don't have much, thank goodness." She grabbed one of the bags and walked it over to the horses. "See?" She set it behind Sugar's saddle and tied it on. "Where's the other one?"

Carter put the larger bag on Dollar and secured it with the leather ties Sam gave him before dubiously eyeing the two horses. "Which one do you want me to ride?"

Sam patted Sugar's neck. "This one. She's an old lady, and she never goes above a trot even when she sees her favorite food. All you have to do is sit on her back, hold the reins, and let her find her own way back to her stall at the ranch."

Carter still looked worried, but stepped up into the stirrup, and onto the horse's back. Sugar didn't even flick her tail and stood solid as a rock.

"Do you remember how to hold the reins?" Sam asked.

"Yeah, like an ice cream cone." Carter gathered them awkwardly in his right hand. "I don't suppose you have a hard hat in those saddlebags, do you?"

"You work in the offshore oil fields, you're a *badass*," Sam pointed out. "Even if you do fall off with your long legs, you won't go far."

Carter looked down and shuddered. "Looks a long way down to me, but as I'm not intending to fall off, I'm not going to think about it."

"That's the spirit!" Sam said brightly. "Is there anything else you need to bring with you from the car? Paperwork or anything?"

"I'm not getting down again until we reach the ranch, Sis," Carter said. "So if you want to check out the car and make sure I haven't left anything behind, be my guest."

Sam stomped off toward the car, took the rental agreement and a pack of gum out, and handed them over to Carter. She returned for one last look and discovered a brightly wrapped present in the back seat.

"Is this for me?" Sam held it up, and Carter's face broke into a smile.

"Yeah! I forgot! Happy Wedding Day thing!"

"Jeez, it's heavy." Sam shifted the box in her arms. "Maybe we should leave it here, and get it later?"

At Carter's nod, she put it in the trunk, locked the car, and went to mount up. The sun made a brief appearance between the clouds, which Sam took as a good omen as she untied the horses and pointed at the far end of the parking lot.

"We'll go back the way I came, okay?"

"Sure. Go slow and just don't lose me," Carter said.

"I promise I won't." Sam clicked to Dollar. "So, what's in the box?"

"Your wedding gift."

"Yeah, I know that, but what exactly is it?" Sam asked. She turned her head to see her brother grinning at her.

"If you get me there in one piece, I'll tell you when we arrive at the ranch."

"Okay." Sam grinned back. "It's a deal."

HW was just finishing his chores when Chase, his oldest brother, came into the barn whistling and looked around as if he didn't have a care in the world.

"Hey, HW, did Sam get back?"

HW stared at his brother. "Yeah, she's hiding in one of the stalls."

"Really?"

"Nope." Sometimes it was way too easy to wind up his very literal, nerdy brother, but HW wasn't into it today. "She's not come back, Sugar's missing as well, and I haven't heard a peep from Sam."

Chase let out his breath. "Okay, I have an idea, but you might consider it an invasion of privacy, so—"

"What?" HW demanded. "Tell me."

"Do you happen to know how to get into Sam's laptop?"

"Of course I do," HW said. "We share a lot of our stuff."

"Then you could find out where her phone currently is if she has the lost and found app."

"Genius!" HW started toward Sam's cabin. "Thanks, Chase!"

He was already knocking on the door before

his brother caught up and silently handed him the key. He'd forgotten that Cam was up with January in the main house.

The place smelled of coffee and Sam. For a moment HW halted and just breathed her in. He went into the first bedroom, realized it was Cam's, and backed straight out again. The second bedroom still had the shades drawn. He opened them up and stared at the unmade bed where his bride-to-be should've been sleeping.

Her laptop was plugged in and recharging up against the wall. He picked it up and set it on his knee. Sam always forgot her passwords, so he'd made her set up autofill on almost everything. He clicked on the Find My Phone app and waited a second for it to start up.

It took another second for him to ask the million-dollar question, and then a map flashed up showing a very familiar landscape.

"It's here on the ranch." HW let out a breath he hadn't realized he'd been holding. He squinted at the map and clicked on the satellite link, which showed the actual terrain. "It's right next to Morgan Creek."

"Maybe she's up there just contemplating life before the big wedding?" Chase came and sat beside him. "By the way, you can ping her phone if you click on that icon."

HW did what Chase suggested, but Sam still didn't pick up.

"I'm going up there." HW got to his feet. "I know you're going to tell me I'm stupid, but I can't just sit here and worry."

"I'm not going to tell you anything, Bro." Chase looked up at him. "If that were January out there? I'd do exactly the same thing."

HW was halfway to the barn when something else finally registered in his brain. In Cam's bedroom her wedding finery had been hanging up on the door of the closet, her shoes set underneath. There hadn't been anything in Sam's.

He stopped walking. Had she already gotten dressed? He tried to imagine her mounting a horse dressed like a bride and couldn't make it work. Had she *changed her mind?*

Realizing that worrying about it was just making him feel a whole lot worse, HW went into the barn and saddled up Messi, his brother BB's favorite horse. He was just about to head out when Ry shouted his name.

"Wait up! I'm coming with you."

HW didn't bother to stand around while his twin got himself organized. If he insisted on coming, he'd find HW by the creek.

Sam pulled up Dollar for the umpteenth time and glanced over her shoulder to find Carter a long way behind. Sugar had obviously realized that the person on her back was not in charge and was having a lovely time dawdling along at minimum speed. Sam had no idea what the time was, but as the day brightened around her, it felt like the return journey was taking hours.

Carter also tended to stop and ask questions about the landscape whenever something occurred to him, which wasn't helping at all. Sam was trying to keep her nerves in check, but her answers were getting shorter. If she didn't get back to the ranch soon, HW would find out she wasn't there and probably suspect the worst, seeing as his own mother had run out on him.

Carter finally came alongside her. "This place is weird. Why aren't there any trees?"

"They cut them down for fuel and to expose the mine workings," Sam said. "Do you think you could increase your pace just a little bit?"

"I dunno." Carter patted Sugar. "Ask the horse."

"I could tie your reins to the back of my saddle, and you could just sit there, and let me do the driving," Sam offered.

"No thanks. I've seen you drive." Carter shuddered. "And I hate not being in control."

Sometimes it was a real shame that he was so like her. . . .

"We've still got hours, Sis, so take a chill pill," Carter reminded her.

"I have to get ready," Sam reminded him.

"How long does that take?" He studied her

carefully. "It's not like you're one of those high-maintenance women."

"I will be on my wedding day—if I get back in time, and my bridegroom hasn't given up on me, and left for a life of sin and debauchery in Las Vegas."

Carter frowned. "You sound a bit stressed, Sis."

She glared at him. "I wonder *why?*"

He raised his eyebrows. "Then maybe you should stop talking, and we should get moving?"

For a second, Sam contemplated abandoning him to the local coyotes, and then gathered her reins. "Okay, let's get going."

"It's somewhere around here." HW dismounted and walked over to the bank of the creek. There were only a couple of places where it was safe to cross, and all the ranch riders used them. "She definitely came this way. I can see Dollar's hoofprints."

Ry joined him. "And it doesn't look as if she came off or anything. There's no sign of a disturbance in the rocks or in the creek bed." He spoke into his cell. "Chase? You there? Can you activate that signal on Sam's cell?"

Seconds later a high-pitched beeping noise had both men scrambling over the rocky terrain.

"There!" HW got back on his horse, forded the creek, and spotted Sam's pink phone case wedged in between two of the rocks. He dismounted and gingerly picked it up. "It doesn't look in bad shape. I wonder if it slid out of her pocket when she was coming up the side of the creek bank?"

"That's certainly happened to me before," Ry said. "Crossing the creek can be a bit of a roller coaster."

They retreated to level ground, HW guarding the cell phone like a priceless jewel.

"Do you know her password?" Ry asked.

"Yeah." HW stared at the phone, his reluctance growing.

"Then punch it in," Ry suggested.

"What if she was texting someone to come and get her?"

The rushing water of the creek filled Ry's silence.

"You won't know that unless you look," Ry suggested carefully. "It's way more likely she was texting you or Cam."

"Okay." HW took a deep breath and typed in her password. Her last two text messages to someone with the name CKOilz5 flashed on the screen.

Stay put and I'll come to you x.

On my way. See you in 20. x

HW stared at the screen and then read the messages aloud to his brother, stumbling over the

471

words as it suddenly hurt to breathe. "She's gone, hasn't she?" He slapped his Stetson against his thigh. *"Goddammit."*

Ry tried to take the cell out of his hand, but HW wouldn't let him. He stuffed the phone in his pocket and went back to his horse.

"HW . . ." Ry said.

But he was done listening. Wheeling Messi about, he set off. As soon as he gained level ground he just rode until the landscape became a blur, and nothing else mattered.

CHAPTER SIX

"Oh, thank goodness!" Sam gasped as the ranch and barn finally came into sight. "We *made* it!"

"I'm not sure my ass did," Carter grumbled. "It's so numb I can't tell if it's actually still there or I left it behind in Morgansville."

"Don't worry, you're still an ass," Sam reassured him. "Wow, look at all the cars. I wonder what time it is?"

She dismounted outside the barn, helped Carter down, and left him wobbling around complaining his legs were like Jell-O. She set about taking the tack off the horses and rubbing them down. For once the barn was completely quiet. She assumed that everyone was off getting spruced up for the wedding. A glance at the barn clock showed her it was almost ten, which meant she had two hours to get ready for the wedding.

Cam and January were not going to be pleased with her. . . . But she was back, and considering everything that had gone down that was an achievement in itself.

She took Carter up to the main house and went through into the kitchen. There was no sign of Ruth, who was probably getting ready, but Chase was sitting at the table, his laptop open while he talked on the phone. He glanced up as she appeared, and then startled and did a double take as if he'd seen a ghost.

"Sam!"

He held up his hand, as if she was going to do a runner, and then spoke into the phone. "Yeah, she's here. Where is he?"

Sam pulled out a chair for Carter and helped them both to a mug of coffee, which her brother gulped down with all the fervor of the caffeine addicted. She studied the back of the laptop, which looked remarkably familiar, and stiffened.

"Why are you on my laptop, Chase?"

He set his cell down on the table and stared at her. *"Where have you been?"*

Slightly put off by his unusual intensity, Sam blinked at him. "I went to pick up my brother." Carter waved at Chase over the rim of his second mug of coffee. "He's an idiot. He ended up in Morgansville with a flat tire."

"You didn't drive up there," Chase stated.

"No, I took Dollar and Sugar. I stupidly thought that would be quicker than driving on the proper road past the silver mine, and round the back of the ghost town." Sam raised her eyebrows. "What's going on? I lost my phone somewhere so I couldn't get in touch with anyone."

"Jeez." Chase let out his breath. "What a mess."

"What do you mean?" Sam asked slowly. "And why are you using my laptop?"

"We didn't know where you'd gone," Chase explained. "We were trying to ping your phone."

"When you say 'we' who exactly are we talking about here?" Sam asked.

"Me, Ry, and HW."

Sam groaned. "Oh, no."

"Oh yeah." Chase sighed. "I was just talking to Ry. He and HW rode out to see if they could locate your phone. They found it by the creek."

"Did HW think I'd fallen in the water?"

"No." Chase grimaced. "HW read your last texts out to Ry. I guess HW misread them or misunderstood the context."

Sam frowned. "I can't even remember what I said."

"Something along the lines of you going to meet someone—which I now assume was your brother, but apparently HW didn't make the same connection."

"He thinks I've gone off with another man." Sam didn't make it a question. She knew HW would immediately imagine the worst. She shot to her feet. "Where is he? I need to talk to him."

"That's the other thing I was going to tell you." Chase sat back and looked up at her. "Ry said HW pocketed your phone, and then rode off on Messi. We haven't heard or seen him since."

Sam set off for the barn again, ignoring Chase's plea for her to wait. She had to find HW and explain. Just as she reached the barn, Ry and his horse arrived back, and he rode toward her.

"Sam. Thank goodness. I told HW he was being a fool, but he wouldn't listen to me."

"Of course he wouldn't listen." Sam choked back tears. "He's as stubborn as the rest of you. Which direction did he go in?"

"Hold your horses," Ry said. "What are you planning to do, go haring after him so we lose both bride *and* groom?"

"*Yes,* you big dope!" Sam actually stamped her foot. "You know what he's like. I have to make this right with him!"

"How about we try it my way?" Ry smiled, which didn't help, and only reminded her achingly of HW. "I'll send him a text to get him coming back this way, and then you can ride out to meet him."

"Will he stop to read a text from you?" Sam asked suspiciously.

"Seeing as he's probably still hoping you'll show up, then yes." Ry held her gaze. "Despite what you think, he can't really believe you'd do that to him."

"Why not? You of all people know how much losing his mother hurt him."

"Yeah, but I also know you're nothing like her. HW just needs to calm down and remember that," Ry said.

"Okay." Sam nodded. "Send him a text."

Ry took off his gloves, extracted his phone

from the back of the pocket of his Wranglers, and typed away, his smile widening.

"That should do it."

"What did you say?" Sam asked.

Ry read it out to her. "Sam at ranch. Wants to speak to you. Come back now before it is too late."

"Do you really think that will work?" Sam said dubiously. "It sounds super dramatic."

Ry shrugged. "It's worth a shot. He's had half an hour to cool off and start thinking things through. That's usually enough time to get some sense into his thick skull." He dismounted and walked his horse toward the barn. "How about we cool this guy off, and wait and see if HW's the man I think he is."

HW stared at the text from Ry and couldn't decide whether it was relief he was feeling or something much more complicated that he couldn't even begin to untangle. He stared out across Morgan Valley toward the Sierras noting how utterly small and insignificant he was in the big scheme of things. Should he go back and face Sam? If she'd had the nerve to come and find him, surely he owed her the same favor?

He tried to run through all the possible scenarios of how it might go, and almost drove himself crazy. If he loved her—and he did with all his heart—he had to at least hear her out. She might just have gotten scared again. Maybe there was something he'd been missing, and she had good and valid reasons for dumping him on their wedding day.

"Bullshit," HW muttered. "She *loves* me!"

It dawned on him that in his heart he had already decided to go back and have it out with her. Sam was nothing like the mother who had walked out on him and she deserved better. Whatever happened between them next, at least this time he'd get closure.

With one long, last look at the mountains that surrounded and protected the valley he loved and called home, HW mounted up and turned around.

He was just coming into the fenced home pastures when a rider approached him waving frantically. He slowed to a stop and waited. The only sign of his tension translated into the fidgety sidestepping of his horse.

Sam rode up to him. She'd lost her hat, her face was red, and her hair all over the place, and she looked absolutely frantic. She slid down from the horse, grabbing onto the saddle to steady herself, and looked up at him.

"I lost my phone! I had to go and pick up my really stupid baby brother who ended up in Morgansville of all places, with no gas, and a deflated tire! And then he wouldn't get on the bloody horse, and I had to *make* him, and *then* he took hours to get back, and I didn't know what the time was because neither of us wears a watch, and—"

HW dismounted, walked up to her, and pulled her roughly into his arms. The feel of her pressed against him made him bury his face in her hair and just breathe her in. He didn't pray often, but he was making up for it now. After a little while, she thumped on his chest, and he eased back just a little so he could see her face.

"Aren't you going to shout at me?" Sam asked.

"Maybe later." HW swallowed hard. "At the moment I'm just . . . glad you're here."

She cupped his chin. "You thought I'd walked out on you."

"For a little while, yeah, I did." He sighed. "But somehow I couldn't convince myself of it, even when all the signs pointed that way."

"What signs?" Sam asked.

"You not telling me stuff, the lack of any wedding crap in your bedroom . . . that kind of thing."

"Oh, HW." She kissed his mouth. "That's the other thing I didn't want to tell you."

"What?" HW tensed again.

"The wedding dress bit." She met his gaze. "My dress was lost in the mail. I'm going to have to borrow January's. I was . . . a bit upset about it, and I didn't want to bother you about something so trivial."

He regarded her for a long moment. "I'd marry

you right now with your hair all mussed up, and your jeans covered in dirt."

"I *know,* which is why I didn't want to worry you about the dress." She bit her lip. "It was stupid. I just wanted to look . . . *nice* for one day in my life."

HW let out his breath. "What time is it?"

"I don't know, why?" Sam asked.

HW took out his phone. "It's eleven o'clock. One hour before we get hitched." He took Sam's hand. "Do you think you can stay out of trouble for that long?"

By the time they got back to the barn, it was ten minutes after eleven. One of the ranch hands shooed them both away to get changed and handled the horses. At the top of the stairs of the ranch house, Sam gave HW one last kiss and walked along the hallway to January and Chase's suite.

The moment she opened the door, everyone started shrieking at her. Sam gave up the effort to answer them all individually and allowed herself to be thrown in the shower. She then sat in front of a mirror where the extremely unhappy makeup and hair people promised to make her look as pretty as possible in forty-five minutes.

She let the ebb and flow of chatter roll over her as she considered what had happened so far that day. Her attendants were already dressed and made up, and Avery was distributing the fragrant posies and corsages Daisy had created for everyone. The smell of spring flowers fought the various perfumes making a heady brew Sam happily breathed in.

"Drink this."

Sam blinked as Nancy handed her a glass of wine.

"Thanks, I need it." Sam took a huge gulp. "What a day."

Nancy grinned at her. She wore a silky dress in her favorite teal and had blue flowers entwined in her silver pigtails. "And they say I'm the troublemaker in Morgantown. I've got nothing on you, girl."

"I'm retiring from troublemaking and intend to become a very well-behaved, happily married woman," Sam said piously.

"Right," Nancy snorted. "Good luck with that."

"Has Yvonne turned up yet?" Sam suddenly thought to ask.

"Apparently, she's on her way," January chimed in from the window seat where she was nursing Chase William. "She's got Rio with her."

"Where did she find him?" Sam wrinkled her nose making the makeup artist sigh. "I thought he was in Vegas."

"Yvonne said something about Rio's father's company plane, so maybe he picked her up from wherever she went and is bringing her home."

Sam sighed. "It must be nice to have a fiancée with a billionaire for a father."

"I guess." January chuckled. "But I can't complain myself really, can I?"

The door opened behind Sam, but she couldn't look round because the hairdresser was directly behind her, and currently had a handful of Sam's hair.

"*Bonjour*!" Yvonne called out. "I made it! How's everything going?"

Sam was fairly certain everyone in the room would be more than happy to enliven Yvonne's day with their various accounts of how Sam had accidentally almost ruined her own wedding day and sent her fiancé into flat despair. She couldn't quite believe she'd managed it herself, but now all she had to do was hang in there for another half an hour or so, and it would all be over. . . .

So much for a stress-free small wedding. If she'd eloped to Vegas with HW, what damage might she have done there? She might have taken out the whole city. It didn't bear thinking about.

"Close your eyes, please."

Sam did as she was asked and let the professionals do their work. She was surprisingly sleepy and incredibly calm. The emotions of the morning had driven out all her worries about the actual wedding. Her fear of not making the ceremony had made her realize how devastated she would've been if she'd *not* got back in time. Everything else—all the fuss about the dress, and her family, and the *occasion* meant nothing compared to how much she loved HW. She was looking forward to getting married to her beautiful blond cowboy.

"Okay, I think we're almost done."

Sam opened her eyes and viewed herself in the mirror. She still looked like herself—but like the best polished, prettiest version of herself there had ever been.

"Wow. Thank you." Sam smiled at both the ladies. "Thank you *so* much!"

Avery appeared by Sam's side. "Come and get dressed, and don't worry about the time. It's traditional for the bride to be late."

"But I don't want poor old HW getting all nervous again," Sam objected. "He'll probably pass out. How long have we got?"

"About fifteen minutes," January called out as she dressed the baby in a sailor suit. "You'll be fine."

Sam went into the bathroom to pee and put on the important basics before she got into the wedding dress. She took off her bathrobe and changed her woolen socks for a pair of long white knee-high ones Ruth had knitted specially for her. She needed something between her prosthetic foot and the leather of the boot, and nylon wouldn't hack it. Her white cowboy boots with silver embroidery were beautiful. She didn't really look sexy, but HW wouldn't care.

She added a new bra and the under petticoat January had obviously ironed for her and went back into the bedroom. Some of her friends had gone down to the wedding venue leaving just her main attendants all wearing dresses in their favorite colors and carrying coordinating posies.

"Ah, there you are," Yvonne said. "Come over here by the mirror and close your eyes so I don't damage your makeup when I put the dress over your head."

"Okay," Sam obliged, shivering as the cold fabric of the dress slipped over her skin. She opened her eyes and blinked hard. "Hey! This isn't January's dress."

"I know." Yvonne was beaming at her. "I couldn't bear to see you trying to be so brave about not having your own wedding dress, so I went and got you this one."

Sam smoothed down the frothy skirts as she fought the strange urge to bawl like a baby. "This is the *first* dress I tried on. The one I *loved*." She turned to Yvonne, her skirts swirling around her. "How on *earth* did you manage this? It's even the right length."

Yvonne made an airy gesture. "I just commandeered my father-in-law-to-be's private jet, made a stop in Vegas at a shop that stocked the same dress, and got them to alter it immediately. Nothing much."

Sam rushed over and gave Yvonne a hug. "Thank you," she whispered. "That was the most awesome thing to do for me *ever*."

Yvonne kissed her cheek. "You're welcome. Now, let's make sure it fits properly. Avery is standing by with her needle and thread if you need to make any last-minute alterations."

"And I'm quite good at it," Avery piped up. "I've literally sewn people into their wedding gowns." She helped Yvonne fluff out Sam's skirts, and took a slow walk around her. "I think this looks good to go."

"How does it feel, Sam?" Yvonne asked.

Sam looked in the mirror. The boat neck of the dress sat nicely over her collarbones and the half-lace sleeves hid the scars left by the explosion on her upper arms. The bodice was fitted, but the skirts were wide with several layers of chiffon, lace, and silk panels cut like the petals of a flower. It was the most beautiful thing Sam had ever seen.

"I love it," Sam said in a hushed voice. "I look like a cowgirl princess." She turned to grin at all her friends, some of whom were actually shedding a tear. "Enjoy it while it lasts because I doubt I'll ever look like this again!"

Yvonne clapped her hands. "Then perhaps we'd better take some pictures so we don't forget."

• • •

HW fiddled with the collar of his new shirt again and Ry nudged him.

"Stop it."

"I'm not doing anything," HW muttered. "What time is it?"

"Five minutes after twelve. Plenty of time for the bride to arrive," Ry said soothingly.

"I'm not sure what's taking so long," HW said. "She only has to walk across the yard."

"She'll be here. Don't worry. Everyone else is in place now."

Ry sounded way too confident, but HW couldn't keep turning around and staring at the assembled guests every ten seconds. He guessed he'd just have to be patient.

As it was a family wedding, and it was such a beautiful day, Avery and January had decided to hold the ceremony outside in the garden attached to the guest center at the ranch. Rows of chairs framed a center aisle that was laid with a blue carpet. Fragrant flowers surrounded the space, both in the flowerbeds, and in the beautiful arrangements Daisy Miller had provided. Soft music played in the background and everything was perfect.

Maybe too perfect . . .

The hairs on the back of HW's neck rose, as there was a small disturbance at the back of the space. Moments later, the music changed, and an arrangement of "She's a Little Bit Country" started playing, which made HW want to laugh out loud. He suspected he wasn't the rock and roll person mentioned in the song, but Sam's very own country boy.

Too afraid to turn around in case he spooked her, HW stared fixedly at the Morgantown pastor who was now standing right in front of him. Ry turned and grinned at Sam as she approached the dais on her father's arm. From what HW could tell, she had a white cowboy hat with a little veil and embroidered silver boots. The rest of her was in white.

Sam kissed her father on the cheek and stepped up next to HW. In his dazzled eyes she looked like some kind of angel come down to earth.

"You made it," HW murmured as a wave of thankfulness rolled over him and he took her hand in his.

"Duh." Sam rolled her eyes. "How could you ever have *doubted* me?"

CHAPTER SEVEN

Sam smiled up at her new husband as they took to the floor to celebrate their first dance together. After the wedding lunch and way too many speeches, the hall had been cleared to create a sizable dance floor for the guests.

"Aren't you glad this is over, Hoss William?" Sam inquired.

"Damn glad that no one needs to use my stupid name in public again for a long time." He smiled down at her. "And it *isn't* over."

"What do you mean?" Sam asked.

His smile was a thing of beauty. "Our life together is just *beginning*."

"That's really romantic," Sam breathed. "Who *are* you?"

"Just a man in love." He gently twirled her in a circle. "And by the way, that dress January lent you? It looks fantastic. I didn't even recognize it. You took my breath away when you came down the aisle."

Sam tried not to laugh, but HW wasn't a fool.

"What's so funny?"

"When this dance finishes, go and ask Yvonne about this dress, okay?"

"Not January?"

"Definitely not January." Sam smiled up into

his golden eyes. He'd gone for fancy western wear for his wedding look, which matched hers perfectly and suited him like a dream. "It's a bit of a tale."

"Like our wedding morning." His smile was crooked. "I suppose it's something to tell our kids."

Sam snorted. "Let's not get too far ahead of ourselves here, Hoss. We just got married."

The music ended and HW kissed Sam, making everyone in the room cheer and whistle at them. Sam didn't think she'd ever felt happier in her life. Her family was here—even her baby brother. They'd stuck by her during some of the worst years of her life and helped her regain her strength and independence. She would always be immensely grateful to them for that.

She'd found a whole new tribe of Morgans, who had accepted her into their lives without question, and she was now married to a man of great worth. Working on the ranch with the horses, the kids with special needs, and the vets with PTSD helped her give back something of herself to those who now needed support.

So many blessings, so much love . . .

Sam walked off the dance floor and was immediately claimed by HW's father, Billy, for the next dance. For quite a while she was busy and didn't see much of her bridegroom, who was being swamped by the ladies in his life. She didn't mind sharing him just a little bit, but as the night wore on, she found herself missing him more and more.

Coming back from a trip to the restroom, which had been something of an experience in itself, she bumped into her bridegroom in the reception area of the center. For the first time all day they were actually alone.

"Are you okay, Sam?" HW eyed her flushed face. "You were gone so long I was starting to worry."

"I just had to pee, and let me tell you, HW, getting myself, this dress, *and* all my underthings into that tiny stall was a sight to behold!"

His lips twitched. "Yeah, I can see that." He tilted his head to one side. "Ah, you might want to do something about the skirt at the back before you scandalize our guests."

Sam reached around and encountered a huge wad of fabric sticking out from her butt like a feathered tail. "Oh Lord! It must have gotten stuck in my spandex!"

HW started laughing, grabbed her by the hand, and whisked her into one of the business offices that lined the hall.

He framed her face in his hands and kissed her. "Never change, Sam Kelly Morgan. Promise me that."

She frowned at him. "How about you help me

491

with my dress, and we get to the lovey-dovey stuff in a minute?"

"Okay, turn around."

She presented him with her rear. "I think the top skirt has gotten caught up in the petticoat."

"Yeah." She waited, but nothing else happened. "To be quite honest, Sam. I don't know where to start."

"How about you try and extract the top layer of the dress?" Sam suggested.

"Got it."

She craned her neck to look over her shoulder as he carefully released each delicate panel.

"It really is a beautiful dress, Sam," HW murmured as he worked. "I'm glad Yvonne went and found it for you."

"It was very sweet of her and I'll never forget it," Sam reassured him.

"You could've told me, you know." He looked at her, his amber gaze serious.

"In retrospect, I wish I had." Sam sighed. "But knowing our luck, if you'd gone to get the dress, *you* would've ended up stranded in Vegas or something. How's it going back there?"

"I've released all the top skirt, so you should be able to untangle the petticoat from your underwear now," HW said.

"I've got a better idea. I hate this stuff." Sam grabbed hold of a wedge of spandex. "I'm taking it off. Don't look."

By the time she'd puffed and panted her way out of the clingy undergarment, HW was laughing so hard he was wiping his eyes and sitting on the floor at her feet. She grinned down at him.

"There goes my feminine mystique."

"Like you've ever been shy around me," HW replied. "That was one of the funniest things I've ever seen. Do all women do it like that?"

"Not much choice," Sam muttered. "I'm burning that thing tomorrow."

"Please don't. I haven't watched you put it on yet."

Sam bent down to pick up her lace panties, which had also ended up on the floor, but HW was faster.

"Hey! Give them back!" Sam protested.

"Not a chance." HW stuffed the panties in his pocket.

"But now I've got nothing on under my dress except my socks," Sam complained.

"Exactly." HW came toward her, picked her up, and sat her on the edge of the desk. He pushed her thighs wide, and she held her breath.

"Oh."

He sank down to his knees, and very gently lifted her gossamer skirts.

"Beautiful."

Sam gathered up the panels of her dress and drew them to one side. "Does this help?"

"Oh, yeah." He slid his hands up her inner

thighs making her shudder as he leaned in and kissed her mound. "The most amazing sight in the world."

"Better than my actual face?"

"Just different." He let out his breath. "I've been thinking about tasting you all day."

"Then don't let me stop you," Sam reassured him.

He flicked her bud with his tongue, and she shuddered with longing. With a satisfied sigh, he set to work proving to her yet again the amazing things he could do with his mouth and fingers. She cupped the back of his head as he nuzzled her most sensitive flesh and then grazed her with his teeth.

"HW . . ." she gasped, and climaxed in long waves as he waited her out. "That's just . . ."

She opened her eyes as he stood and stepped away from her.

"Where exactly are you going?" Sam asked.

He studied her. "I've been thinking."

"About *what?*" Sam demanded.

"All the crap you've put me through today." His slow, sexy smile made everything inside her stand to attention. "I think I'll make *you* wait awhile."

"For *what?*"

"Me." He blew her a kiss. "You can last another hour, Sam, can't you?"

"You—"

Before she could finish her sentence, he winked at her and strolled out. It took her a few seconds to realize that he wasn't coming back, and that he still had her panties in his pocket.

Sam scrambled down from the desk, found her abandoned spandex, and dropkicked it into the trash can. Sometimes HW Morgan could be extremely annoying, but she wasn't going to let him get away with it this time.

"There you are, HW."

Sam came toward HW, a smile on her face that immediately made him nervous. Mind you, he'd just walked out on her mid-foreplay, so he probably should be worried. He'd retreated to the bar end of the room, and was sharing a quiet word and a beer with his twin while he waited for his raging hard-on to subside.

With a deliberate thump, Sam sat down on his lap wriggling like a salmon in a net, and he almost came in his pants. He was the only person who knew she was naked under her dress. The mere thought of all her soft flesh so close was making him sweat. Which was exactly why she was sitting on his lap . . .

"You okay, honeybun?" she cooed. "You look a bit hot."

"I'm great." He smiled up at her. "By the way, I think Avery was looking for you."

"Then I'm sure she'll come and find me right

here." She wrapped his arm around her waist. "Where I'm supposed to be."

Jeez . . . if she kept this up their wedding guests might get to see far more of the consummation part of the day than they probably wanted to. Her breasts were now right at his eye level and every time she breathed out they brushed against his cheek.

"Sam . . ." HW murmured.

To his never-ending gratitude, Avery appeared beside him and beamed at them both. "Are you ready to cut the cake? I think some of the older guests won't make it much past nine, so we really should get everything under wraps."

"Sure!" Sam braced one hand on HW's shoulder and made an inordinate amount of fuss getting out of his lap, which made him silently yelp. He might not make it past nine himself. . . .

Eventually, in desperation, he picked Sam up and set her gently on her feet. She reached back for his hand, and he gave it to her.

"Come on, then," Avery said brightly. "Yvonne's already put the cake on the table and we're all set to go."

By the time they reached the front of the room, all the guests were ready for them, and the music had been turned off. Yvonne had created an amazing chocolate and salted caramel cake, which meant both he and Sam were happy.

Yvonne offered them a huge knife and stepped out of the way.

HW grinned at Sam. "You ready?"

She laced her fingers in with his. "Go ahead, cowboy."

The knife slid through the light sponge like butter, releasing the sweet scent of caramel and spun sugar. HW had thought he couldn't eat another thing, but he was suddenly ravenous again. He cut out a few chunks of the bottom layer and then faced Sam, who was already laughing at him.

"On three?" she suggested. HW nodded as she began to count. "One, two—"

He shoved the cake in her face at exactly the same time she did it to him, and everyone cheered. It tasted so divine that he had no wish to waste any of it on a pointless food fight. Luckily, Sam seemed to feel the same. Avery and Billy took over and distributed plates of the cake while Yvonne boxed up other pieces.

For a wedding that had come together in two weeks, his family ranch was doing them proud. He took a piece of cake over to his grandma Ruth, and she patted the seat beside her.

"Sit down, HW. I've barely seen you all day."

"I've been busy getting married," HW joked. "I still can't believe we actually made it."

Ruth chuckled. "From all accounts it was a bit of a miracle. But I always say that if something is meant to be, it will happen." She patted his cheek. "I think you two will be very happy together."

"I hope so." HW hesitated. "We're still going to fight a lot."

"Which is quite okay."

"You sure about that?" HW met her gaze, and she smiled.

"Ask Roy to tell you about me and your grandfather one day. We weren't exactly a model couple, but we were very happy. You remind me of your grandfather very much sometimes."

HW took that as the huge compliment it was.

"Thanks for everything." He kissed her wrinkled cheek. "For bringing me up when Mom and Dad weren't around, for making me go to school, and do my chores . . ." He hesitated. "For helping make me the man I am."

"It was all inside you, HW." Ruth held his gaze. "You just had to realize it. Now get along with you, and take that new wife of yours to bed. She looks worn out."

HW glanced back at Sam, who *was* looking a little weary, and remembered that her day had started at six in the morning, and that she'd ridden out twice. His conscience smote him. If she were tired out, he wouldn't hold her to his dare.

He stood and went to find Avery. January had gone off to settle Chase William down to sleep, and his besotted older brother had gone with them. Everyone else, except Sam's elderly grandparents and Dr. Tio's grandmother, was still present.

"What's up, HW?" Avery asked.

It was interesting to see her in her element, making the wedding function so effortlessly. She was often the quietest member of the Morgan bunch, but she had a strength all her own, and was regaining confidence every day thanks in part to his brother's love.

"I think it's time for Sam and me to head out. If that's okay with you?"

"Sure." Avery nodded. "I'll get Ry."

"Why do we need—?" HW spoke to the back of her head as she was already on the move. "We're just going up to the ranch."

HW made his way over to Sam, who was chatting to Nancy and Cam. She smiled when she saw him, and everything inside him became peaceful. She was the right woman for him. The way they chose to express their love and conduct their relationship was up to them. He had a sense that if either of them *did* end up being polite all the time that would be the end of their marriage.

"Ready to go?" HW asked.

"Yes," Sam sighed. "It's been an amazing day."

He took her hand and brought it to his lips, admiring the solid wedding band on her finger, which was made of rare Morgan gold panned from the creek that ran through their property.

Avery cleared her throat. "The bride and groom are about to leave. Anyone who wishes to throw rice or confetti, please step outside."

There was a stampede of people, leaving HW and Sam alone and staring at each other.

"Rice?" HW asked.

"Avery says it's more organic than paper apparently, although the confetti is biodegradable," Sam said.

"As long as it's not been cooked or is still in the can, I suppose I can live with it," HW muttered. "You ready for this?"

"Ready as you are."

"I'd rather sneak out the back," HW said. "But we can't disappoint our guests, now can we?"

"Nope," Sam agreed.

He offered her his arm, and they walked out into the lobby and then outside to a hail of rice and confetti and the cheers of their friends and family. HW kept his head down and kept going, Sam clinging to his arm and laughing her head off. When they reached the steps up to the porch of the house, he finally slowed down and grinned at Sam.

"We made it."

Even as the words left his mouth a window opened on the second floor; Ry leaned out and dumped a bucketful of confetti and sparkly stuff all over them.

Sam spluttered and charged into the house

leaving a trail behind her, and HW followed. Neither of them bothered to shed their boots in the mudroom as they hoofed it up the stairs and right into HW's room where he locked the door.

HW took off his hat, and twenty million pieces of sparkly confetti cascaded onto the floor.

Sam was laughing so hard she could barely stand up. "We're going to be washing glitter out of our crevices for weeks!"

"Yeah. When Ry finally decides to get married I'm going to think up something far worse to do to him on his wedding night," HW promised her. "Maybe a trip to the pigsty, and an accidental falling in. That'll teach him."

Sam sat down on the side of the bed and tossed her hat onto the chair. "You do realize we'll have to go out there again to use the bathroom?"

HW frowned at her. "It would serve them right if I peed out the window."

"I can't do that," Sam pointed out. "And I have to take all this makeup off my face."

"What makeup? You look fine to me," HW said.

"Which is why I love you." Sam went toward the door, her expression determined. "Wish me luck."

"Don't take off your dress yet, will you?" HW called out to her. "I want to do it."

"Sure."

"Or your boots."

"Perv." Sam shut the door behind herself.

HW started on his own clothing, hanging up his best jacket and removing his boots and belt. He was pleasantly tired, but not too tired to give his new wife everything she desired.

Sam came back in, and he went and washed up fast, keeping one wary eye out for the appearance of his twin. When he returned to the bedroom, Sam was sitting on the window seat that looked out over the pasture where the horses were grazing. She turned to look at him and he paused, his back to the door, to appreciate the sight of her in his room, and soon to be in his bed.

"You okay?" HW asked as he walked toward her.

"Definitely." She smiled into his eyes. "This has been one heck of a day, but it turned out exactly how I wanted it to be."

"How was that?" He took her hands in his and helped her stand up.

"Me, here with you?" She cupped his chin. "Right where I belong."

"Yeah, you do, and I don't want you ever to forget that." He kissed her very slowly and thoroughly until she kissed him back and wrapped her arms around his neck.

"Are you tired?" HW murmured against her lips.

"Actually, I'm exhausted," Sam confessed. "Who knew getting married was so complicated?"

"Then we can just go to sleep." HW ignored his own needs, kissed her throat, and she shivered. "Together, naked between the sheets."

"Okay."

"Let me help you out of this dress."

Sam stood very quietly as he undid the buttons on the bodice and released the concealed zipper on the side of the skirt letting the dress slide down to the floor.

HW picked it up and placed it over the back of the chair. Without Sam in it, the dress looked really insubstantial. He returned to kiss her newly bared skin, pausing only to ease her petticoat down and undo the back of her bra.

"You're so beautiful," HW whispered in her ear and she shuddered against him. "So very, very beautiful."

She started unbuttoning his shirt and pulled it out of his pants, making little humming noises of approval as she uncovered him. He didn't stop her busy hands as he was too busy worshipping her breasts and cupping her mound.

"HW?"

"Mmm?"

"Maybe I'm not that sleepy after all."

He picked her up in one fluid motion, making her squeak, and walked her over to the bed where he placed her right in the center.

"I still have my boots on," Sam objected.

"Give me a sec, and I'll get to that."

HW was busy stripping off the rest of his clothing. He didn't want her to know quite how turned on he was by her being naked except for knee-high socks and cowboy boots or he'd never hear the end of it.

"I can take them off—"

"No, I'll do it," HW hastened to reassure her as he climbed onto the bed and stared down at her, his tongue practically hanging out with lust. "Just give me a moment to . . . appreciate you."

Sam's green eyes narrowed in amusement, and she slowly parted her thighs. "Go on, then."

"Go on what?" HW feigned innocence as his throat closed up with lust.

"I know you want me just like this, boots, and all." Sam met his gaze. "It's all good as long as you don't mind my heels in your perfect ass."

HW wordlessly shook his head and surged forward, forgetting all about the concept of foreplay or anything, really, except the need to be inside Sam as quickly as possible.

She gasped his name as he filled her, and raised her hips, offering him even more, and he just rocked into her and took it all. He started to come almost immediately, and when Sam joined him it was all over, and he was left gasping and stranded like a beached whale.

Sam bit down on HW's shoulder, but he didn't even seem to notice as he breathed in and out like he'd just completed a marathon instead of the sixty-meter dash.

"Sorry," HW mumbled, and rolled off her. "That was . . . inexcusable of me."

Sam turned onto her side and brushed the blond hair out of his eyes. "It's all good, HW. Every woman dreams of one-minute sex on their wedding night."

With a growl, he came up on one elbow and stared down at her.

"It's your fault."

"What did I do?" She blinked up into his hazel eyes.

"Exist?"

"That's one hell of a lame excuse if you don't mind me saying, HW." Sam tried not to laugh.

"Okay, it was the boots."

Sam glanced down at her feet. "They are pretty awesome, aren't they?"

"Yeah, especially when the rest of your bride is completely naked."

"Can you help me take them off now?" Sam asked.

"Sure."

HW moved down the bed and eased her right boot off leaving her long white sock. He visibly swallowed as he looked up at her and she smiled.

"Keep going."

He took off her left boot and dropped them both with a crash over the side of the bed. She'd already noticed that his body had recovered from their one-minute tryst, and that he was more than ready to go again.

She lay still and let him stare at her. He was the first man who never noticed her scars or was frightened off by them. He'd kissed every single one and made sure she knew she was beautiful in his eyes.

"I want you again," HW said hoarsely.

"I'm glad to hear that." Sam nodded solemnly. "That was hardly your best work earlier, was it?"

He smiled. "Maybe this whole being married thing has screwed with my head."

"I hope not because I don't want to get divorced *right* now."

"I think I've gotten my head around it." HW leaned in and planted a kiss on her stomach. "I obviously need more practice."

She tugged on his hair. "But it's my turn now."

"Says who?" HW kissed each of her hip bones, grazing her with his teeth, making her shiver.

"Says me, your lawfully wedded wife." Sam tugged harder. "Give it up."

With a martyred sigh, HW sat back. "Okay, where do you want me?"

Sam pointed at the headboard. "There."

HW crawled past her as she shifted down the bed and sat with his back to the headboard and his legs in front of him, his eyes narrowed with a combination of lust and love that Sam wished she could bottle and keep with her forever.

"Put your hands behind your head," Sam ordered him.

HW raised an eyebrow. "You're not thinking of tying me up, are you?"

"Not tonight." Sam held his gaze. "I'm worried that I'd fall asleep, and you'd be stuck like that."

He obligingly placed both hands behind his head, spreading his elbows wide. Sam studied the effect on his muscled arms and the ridges of muscle in his abdomen. He really was ridiculously hot, and now he was all hers. Sometimes, after all the heartache in her life, she still couldn't believe she'd been lucky enough to find her perfect man.

"What are you smiling at?" HW inquired.

"You, and your gorgeous abs." Sam licked her lips. "Which I am shortly going to taste along with other outstanding parts of your anatomy."

HW glanced down at his groin. "You promise?"

"If you stay still, then yes."

"I'll do my best." HW nodded.

His breath caught as she leaned in and kissed his throat, and then licked, and bit a path down his sternum, pausing to admire his abs up close before homing in on her ultimate target. She took him into her mouth, and he sighed as if he'd died and gone to heaven, his hips rolling forward with the ease of an accomplished horseman taking advantage of the pressure of her lips.

"God, that's good."

HW groaned, barely resisting the urge to lower his hand and thrust his fingers into her hair to keep her right where he needed her. He'd ended up gripping the headboard with both hands as Sam sucked him harder and harder until he just gave in and let the pleasure flow through him.

Eventually, Sam raised her head, giving him one of the most visually satisfying pictures in his life. His very own naked woman, panting as she pleasured him, her nipples hard, and her mouth soft. . . .

"Sam . . ." he whispered.

"What?"

"I love you so much."

She came up on her knees, her breasts resting against his chest, and framed his face with her hands.

"I love you, too, Hoss William."

He wrapped his hands around her waist and helped her ease herself down over his hard jutting flesh. When she was settled over him, he just held her, content to just be one with her.

"I won't leave you," Sam whispered against his mouth. "I want to share every moment with you for the rest of my life."

"That's good." HW could barely form words.

"Mmm." Sam slowly squeezed all her internal muscles, and HW's eyes nearly popped. "Definitely."

He spread his legs wider letting her sink down over him even more, and kissed her slowly, mimicking the pulse of his need buried inside her until he couldn't slow down any more.

With a stifled curse, he rolled them both over and thrust into her until she came all around him and he had to join her.

"Better," she murmured, her face squashed against his shoulder. "Next time let's go for ten."

He lay on his back, and she cuddled up against him, drawing one knee up over his thigh.

"Your foot," he murmured.

"Oh yeah." She sighed and rolled over. "I forgot all about it."

HW pulled down the sheets. "Stay put, I'll sort it out for you."

He rolled down her long socks and discarded them, determinedly ignoring the way his dick twitched with interest, and examined her prosthetic left foot before carefully releasing it. He frowned as he noticed a couple of sore spots on her skin.

"You should've taken this off earlier."

"I know, but I was enjoying myself too much," Sam said sleepily, as she smiled down at him. "I'll make sure to put some salve on it tomorrow, okay?"

HW nodded and drew the bedclothes up again. Sam came back into his arms and he held her close as the old house creaked and settled around them, and the people he loved. For a moment, HW simply appreciated everything he had gained and had once thought lost to him forever. His home, his family, and a new career helping others rather than risking his life on the rodeo circuit.

Life had a way of coming at you fast, and sometimes you thought you'd never find your way back. But HW was living proof that if you really wanted something and were willing to forgive others, and even more importantly, forgive *yourself,* then nothing was impossible.

Sam started to snore, and HW kissed the top of her head. With Sam beside him and his family at his back, the future was looking just fine.

Dear Reader:

If you enjoyed this novella about Sam and HW's wedding, please feel free to check out the rest of the Morgan family romance novels. You can find all things Morgan on my website, including recipes, free reads, and a link to join my newsletter at www.themorgansranch.com.

Happy reading!

Kate Pearce

Center Point Large Print
600 Brooks Road / PO Box 1
Thorndike, ME 04986-0001 USA

(207) 568-3717

US & Canada:
1 800 929-9108
www.centerpointlargeprint.com